ACCLAIM FOR MARY WEBER

"There are few things more exciting to discover than a debut novel packed with powerful storytelling and beautiful language. *Storm Siren* is one of those rarities. I'll read anything Mary Weber writes. More, please!"

—Jay Asher, *New York Times* bestselling author of *Thirteen Reasons Why*

"*Storm Siren* is a riveting tale from start to finish. Between the simmering romance, the rich and inventive fantasy world, and one seriously jaw-dropping finale, readers will clamor for the next book—and I'll be at the front of the line!"

—Marissa Meyer, *New York Times* bestselling author of *Cinder* and The Lunar Chronicles

"Intense and intriguing. Fans of high stakes fantasy won't be able to put it down."

—CJ Redwine, author of *Defiance*, for *Storm Siren*

"A riveting read! Mary Weber's rich world and heartbreaking heroine had me from page one. You're going to fall in love with this love story."

—Josephine Angelini, internationally bestselling author of the Starcrossed trilogy, for *Storm Siren*

"Elegant prose and intricate world-building twist into a breathless cyclone of a story that will constantly keep you guessing. More, please!"

—Shannon Messenger, author of the Sky Fall series, for *Storm Siren*

"Weber's debut novel is a tour de force! A story of guts, angst, bolcranes, sword fights, and storms beyond imagining. Her heroine, a lightning-wielding young woman of immense power and a soft, questioning heart, captures you from word one and holds tight until the final line. Unwilling to let the journey go, I eagerly await Weber's (and Nym's) next adventure."

—Katherine Reay, author of *Dear Mr. Knightley*, for *Storm Siren*

"Mary Weber has created a fascinating, twisted world. *Storm Siren* sucked me in from page one—I couldn't stop reading! This is a definite must-read, the kind of book that kept me up late into the night turning the pages!"

—LINDSAY CUMMINGS, AUTHOR OF *THE MURDER COMPLEX*

"Don't miss this one!"

—SERENA CHASE, USATODAY.COM, FOR *STORM SIREN*

"Readers who enjoyed Marissa Meyer's Cinder series will enjoy this fast-paced fantasy which combines an intriguing storyline with as many twists and turns as a chapter of *Game of Thrones*!"

—DODIE OWENS, EDITOR, *SCHOOL LIBRARY JOURNAL TEEN*, FOR *STORM SIREN*

". . . readers will easily find themselves captivated. The breathtaking surprise ending is nothing short of horrific, promising even more dark and bizarre adventures to come in the *Storm Siren* trilogy."

—*RT BOOK REVIEWS*, 4 STARS

". . . fantasy readers will feel at home in Weber's first novel. . . . detailed backdrop and large cast bring vividness to the story."

—*PUBLISHERS WEEKLY*, FOR *STORM SIREN*

"Weber builds a fascinating and believable fantasy world."

—*KIRKUS REVIEWS*, FOR *STORM SIREN*

". . . this adventure, in the vein of 1980s fantasy films, has readers rooting for the heroes to smite the wicked baddies. Buy where fantasy flies."

—DANIELLE SERRA, *SCHOOL LIBRARY JOURNAL*, FOR *STORM SIREN*

"Mary Weber's debut novel reflects an author sensitive to her audience, a stellar imagination, and a killer ability with smart and savvy prose."

—RELZ REVIEWZ, FOR *STORM SIREN*

"Between the beautiful words used to create this fairy-tale world, to the amazing power of the Elementals, to the aspects of slavery and war, I'd say this book is a must read for any fantasy lover. It's powerful and will keep you turning pages faster than you thought possible. I can't believe this is Mary Weber's debut novel. Congratulations!"

—GOOD CHOICE READING BLOG, FOR *STORM SIREN*

SIREN'S FURY

OTHER BOOKS BY MARY WEBER

Storm Siren
Siren's Fury
Siren's Song

SIREN'S FURY

BOOK TWO IN THE STORM SIREN TRILOGY

MARY WEBER

THOMAS NELSON
Since 1798

Published in Nashville, Tennessee, by Thomas Nelson. Thomas Nelson is a registered trademark of HarperCollins Christian Publishing, Inc.

Author is represented by the literary agency of Alive Communications, Inc., 7680 Goddard Street, Suite 200, Colorado Springs, CO 80920, www.alivecommunications.com.

Map by Tom Gaddis

Thomas Nelson titles may be purchased in bulk for educational, business, fund-raising, or sales promotional use. For information, please e-mail SpecialMarkets@ThomasNelson.com.

Publisher's Note: This novel is a work of fiction. Names, characters, places, and incidents are either products of the author's imagination or used fictitiously. All characters are fictional, and any similarity to people living or dead is purely coincidental.

ISBN: 978-1-4016-9038-0 (trade paper)

Library of Congress Cataloging-in-Publication Data

Weber, Mary.
Siren's fury / Mary Weber, Mary Weber.
pages ; cm. -- (Storm siren trilogy ; 2)
ISBN 978-1-4016-9037-3 (hardcover)
1. Magic--Fiction. 2. Shapeshifting--Fiction. I. Title.
PS3623.E3946S55 2015
813'.6--dc23
2014048037

Printed in the United States of America

16 17 18 19 20 RRD 6 5 4 3 2 1

To Dad & Mom,
for always reaching bigger,
further,
higher.
And yet continually showing me the path home.
You are the heroes in my story.

And to my sister, Kati,
whom Nym is based upon,
for pillaging the mind villages with me
and fashioning them into castles.
And for knowing that some melodies are meant to be sung.

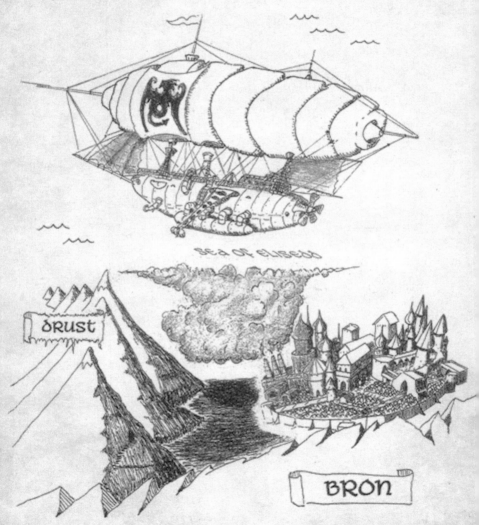

Faelen

Sea of Elibead

ÐRUST

BRON

*"Around me I gather
these forces to save
my soul and my body
from dark powers that assail me:
against false prophesyings,
against pagan devisings,
against heretical lying
and false gods all around me.
Against spells cast."*
—FROM SAINT PATRICK'S BREASTPLATE

CHAPTER 1

FIVE MINUTES EARLIER . . .

T HERE IS A MOMENT, JUST BEFORE EVERY STORM, when the entire world pauses. As if the atmosphere, in unison with the ocean tides, the wind, the sky's watery teardrops, is forced to hold its breath. A bracing against the violence it knows will come—the tempest that perhaps this time, this moment, might actually shred the world's soul.

I am in that moment now.

I *am* that moment.

My Elemental blood is paused in my veins—I can feel it the same way I feel Eogan's hand on my skin as the golden candle orbs float past my window, ascending from the Castle's courtyard celebration below. On their way to the stars, their round glow shines through the glass pane to reflect off the floor, the glossy walls, the bedpost in my room. They illuminate Eogan's beautiful black skin and the jagged bangs covering half his face as his green eyes search mine.

"Are you all right?" His voice is ragged, fresh from the peace-treaty speech he just gave with King Sedric.

I nod and glance over the healing bruises and cuts I can see, and the internal ones I can't because they're hidden behind that unfair tweak of a smile. *You?* I want to ask.

His grin widens as he traces a finger down my cheek to my jawline and leans his tall self in until he is inches away and I am breathing in his familiar scent of honey and pine mixed with something oddly musky. His gaze drops to my mouth.

I swallow.

Never better, his eyes answer. He bends closer so that, for a second, his lips nearly touch mine.

I swear it almost dissolves every piece of me in the in-between as I wait for his kiss. Just as I've waited for this moment, this time, finally alone with him, for the past week since the battle at the Keep.

But the kiss doesn't come.

Instead my breath, my veins, they remain bated as the cheers from the courtyard erupt louder through the shut window—the Faelen people extolling Eogan and King Sedric for the truce the two kingdoms just signed.

"To our own King Sedric!"

"And Eogan of Bron! Lost prince who helped defend Faelen!"

Lost prince who is now king *of Bron.*

I lean back and clear my throat, then tip my head toward the sound. They're calling for him to go back out there. Instead he's here consorting with a slave.

I give him a sly grin. What *will* they think? But abruptly my heart is dithering and thudding because, *yes, what will they think? What will* he *think?* The only man I've cared for is now the most notable person in the Hidden Lands. And I am still Elemental—recently elevated to revered status in Faelen maybe, but I doubt his Bron subjects will feel the same.

He doesn't answer. His grin just ripples and broadens.

Suddenly his whole body is rippling, shaking beneath my fingers.

I frown.

Next thing I know he's raised a scornful brow and uttered a growl and the broadening smile turns toothy.

I pull away. *What in hulls?*

The firelight bounces off of those teeth a moment, making them look long. Shiny. I'd think he was teasing if it didn't look so disturbing, but he's stretching his neck and shoulders, extending them up as if adjusting his spine beneath that undulating skin. When he straightens it's to glare down at me, as if he is still Eogan. And yet not.

Very carefully he sweeps his black bangs from his face and tucks them behind his ear in a sickening, all-too-familiar trait.

It makes my stomach lurch. I swallow and retreat another step in my velvet slippers and white waste-of-someone's-good-fortune dress.

No.

It can't be.

"I warned you at the Keep," he whispers.

Oh, please, no.

Before I can ask or curse or make my mouth work in any way that forms words, he tips his head to reveal the slightly healed gash running down the back of his neck. Not a gash. A clawed incision.

Exactly like Breck had when Draewulf cut her open and crawled inside her skin.

I shake my head. *It has to be a trick of Lord Myles. He must be alive and using his mind powers in retaliation.*

I squint, searching his face, waiting for the mirage to change, but he merely bends closer and tucks a swag of *my* hair behind my ear as a disgusting snarl mars his rich voice. "I told you that you couldn't save both Eogan and your country."

My lungs empty as my heart crashes to the Castle's stone floor.

I blink once, twice, to clear my blasted vision. But there's nothing to clear.

It's not a trick of Myles.

It's the face of the man I love taken over by a 130-year-old shape-shifting murderer.

Draewulf. My breath is reeling and my heart is choking out of my chest. "You didn't. You couldn't—"

"Couldn't?" He lifts a hand to my snowy-white hair.

My veins ripple, and that half smile I've come to care for most in the world goes eerie as his green eyes flicker to reveal black wolf eyes. "You chose Faelen," he murmurs.

One heartpulse . . .

Two heartpulses . . .

"You should've kept a better eye on him, Nym."

No, no, no, no. This is not happening. I curl my hand into a fist and cause the sky to thunder so loud my words shake the walls. *"What. Have you. Done?"*

He bends closer. "Took over Eogan while you were too busy saving the pathetic people who enslaved you."

My breath explodes and I ignite like fire and maelstrom and murder. My body sizzles with the static sweeping through my blood as the siren inside that pushed back the airships, the siren that saved Faelen, flares through my Elemental veins.

I lift my deformed left hand and place it against my trainer's broad chest that now holds a monster. He clamps down on my arm.

I don't even think about it—I just let loose a surge of energy against him, as if to burn the beast from his body before considering the damage that doing so might cause. His skin lights up like brilliant night skies, but instead of melting him out, my energy molds into a shield over him—Eogan's block somehow countering me in the only way it's ever been able.

"Mother of a toothless—" I let loose choice words owner number four's mum taught me and press harder, drawing in a mass of clouds above the Castle courtyard where the atmosphere darkens.

"That erratic temper of yours that he found so appealing does *not* amuse me, girl. You'll stop. Now."

A flick of my wrist and the lightning it elicits rips through the slit in the window seam, blasting the whole pane open in explosive shards across the floor. The lightning narrowly misses the bed as it cracks the air and practically shatters my eardrums. Eogan growls, and the curtains catch fire—the flames of cloth quickly drip to the seat before sliding to the small carpet.

He snatches my crippled hand as if to soothe me, control me. "You *will* stop or—"

"Or what?" I shove into his chest again to shoot a thin layer of ice from my gimpy, curled fingers, spreading it out across his skin and down his body onto the floor, toward the window and up onto the seat and curtains where it smothers the fire. The next instant the ice is crawling up from my hand to enter his mouth, his throat. His breathing turns labored. He begins choking. Gasping.

Dying.

Eogan's body is dying at my hand.

His eyes widen. As if Draewulf in him is surprised. Impressed. "Kill me, and you'll kill his body." His voice crackles in a tone that's suddenly too close to Eogan's. Too intimate. Too perfectly familiar.

My hand falters.

His grip tightens over the memorial tattoos on my left arm and Eogan's ability to soothe rushes my veins, muting the fury, deflating the curse in my blood.

I pull back. How dare he use Eogan's block against me.

But his lips curl as his other hand lashes up to rest right above my screaming heart. And suddenly he's squelching something. Sucking the life-pulse.

My insides are being carved up and cut out.

"What the—?" The siren in my veins begins fluttering and beating, like a bird flailing for escape from the wave of heat barreling through. I try to jerk away, and for a second, I swear a cry breaks out from my rib cage before the hot surge courses in and cools to harden like doused metal underneath my skin, searing my blood to my bones. The siren's scream falls silent and there is nothing but heaviness.

My powers.

My ability . . .

I twitch my wrist at the sky to resummon the storm, but the clouds keep dissipating. *What in hulls?* I wrench harder, twisting my fingers to claim the night air, the wind, the rain.

Except it's not there.

It's gone.

As if my Elemental blood has been drained and I am left a normal, non-Uathúil, Faelen person.

"What did you do?"

He merely pinches harder.

I bat him away as his hands grab for my waist, my shoulders. I shove and squirm from his grip, but his fingers crumple my dress as he draws me firmly in place against his chest and sneers down from the mouth that kissed me exactly one week ago when we stood at the Keep while the world went to hulls around us in bursts of bombs and lightning. "Consider it a gift—a deliverance from your curse," he whispers.

I struggle against him, except even as I do, I'm inhaling Eogan's scent of pine and honey mixed with smoke from the extinguished fire, and I am simultaneously yearning for him and disgusted. My fingers claw at his arms but he doesn't seem to notice.

He just smirks and slides his hand up to my throat.

I stiffen and refuse to let him see in my expression how I'm bleeding at every single one of my heart seams. "Go ahead."

His fingers constrict.

I gasp. Wheeze. And wait for the slow death of him shape-shifting into me even as my fingers try to tear chunks from his flesh.

His hand crushes harder into my neck, cutting off my air. My vision swims until I'm clawing and writhing and a cry has seeped up from my throat. *Oh hulls I can't breathe.* I knee him in the thigh, but he doesn't even flinch. Then I'm gasping, flailing, dying.

Just as my legs give way and my vision starts to blacken, he relents and I drop to the floor.

"Like taming a pet," he snarls. He flips around and strides to the door and opens it to a rush of music from the Great Hall that drowns out the shouts from the partygoers in the Castle courtyard. "Don't be late to the banquet. I'd like to think you'll especially enjoy my toast praising your help in destroying Odion and handing me Bron's throne."

The door shuts without him looking back, sending a parting chill of horror to settle over me.

I stare at the cracked, silver-plated wood as the realization emerges . . .

I have saved the world only to lose the most beautiful pieces of my soul: Colin. Breck.

Eogan.

CHAPTER 2

I GLARE AT THE CLOSED DOOR, SIMULTANEOUSLY holding my throat while cursing that illegitimate bolcrane offspring to come back.

I can't stop shaking. *Exhale. Inhale.* His scent is everywhere, piercing my nostrils, digging down my throat until I'm gagging on smoke and pulling myself up to scramble around the broken glass and ice. *No no no no no!* I lunge for the charred window and push my face out into the night air. The noise below is deafening—as if my erratic weather bursts only encouraged the people's frenzy.

I concentrate on breathing. Another inhale to clear my burning throat.

My body sways heavily and shakes harder, and for a second I swear my veins seize up.

I frown at my arms. *What did he do to me?*

"Focus on the atmosphere, Nym," I can almost hear Eogan whisper. "It's yours to control."

I shut my eyes and lean in, yearning to feel him against my

achy skin and chest cavity where, until a few minutes ago, my world existed. "I can't focus," I whisper. *I don't want to focus.*

"Nym."

No! I can't do this without you.

But the moment slows anyway.

"Focus on the atmosphere."

I grit my teeth and open my eyes.

Fine.

I shove my hand toward the sky.

Not even a breath of wind stirs as the golden candle bulbs rise into the now-perfect, starry heavens.

I try again. And again—this time with both hands. Then with my voice, begging the Elemental inside to waken and rise.

But it's no use.

The curse I've spent my entire life abhorring—the thing I trained so hard to control with Eogan. No. Longer. Exists.

Just as Eogan no longer exists.

"Are you jesting?" A scream rushes my lungs and explodes from my lips, but it's hollow and heartless, with no thunder to back it up. Like the voice of a powerless child, it drowns into the party noise below. "This isn't how it's supposed to be!"

I turn back to my room, pick up the largest glass shards with my good hand, and hurl them at the walls, the fireplace, the door. How this happened I don't know—I scarcely looked away from Eogan as he fought Draewulf at the Keep. Only a matter of moments. And afterward—when he was talking to his generals . . .

Litches.

His skin had looked sallow. Bruised. Bloody. With that incision behind his neck.

My stomach turns. The thought of Draewulf slicing him open

while I stood feet away—of Eogan dying, his essence being absorbed by the monster wearing him like a shell of flesh . . . I fling a thick glass spike into the door. Then another, and another.

The last one thuds so hard it creates a crack across the overlay just as a knock sounds on the other side.

"Miss?" a man's clipped voice calls through.

I pause.

"I've been asked to summon you to the banquet."

What? I look around. *Now?* An awareness of what I'm supposed to be doing sinks in, as does the roomful of dissipating smoke and broken glass and the blood covering my palms that are somehow sliced like ribbons.

Oh kracken. I don't know what to do. I don't know how to do this. I bend over as my head spins, bringing bile up my throat. "Why didn't you just kill me too?" I yell at Draewulf.

"Miss?"

"To hulls with your blasted banquet," I snap loud enough for the man to hear. But I go ahead and dab my hands on my dress and step over to the washbasin to dunk them in case he barges in.

The cold water burns like litches. It scalds and sears the smoke from my head—enough to register the fact that not only am I supposed to be at the banquet, but Draewulf left me functioning enough to attend it. I steady my trembling arms. Bite my lip. Whatever he's planning, he kept me alive to watch.

"Miss." The man's voice comes again with a more insistent knock. "Please. We need to hurry."

Narrowing my eyes, I shove my blasted feelings so deep that the numb rises and spreads over them in a thin, fragile layer. *Just go see what he's got planned.*

I grab the drying cloth and stride to the door. I yank it open to find one of the captain's guards. Tannin, if I recall, with his brown eyes, brown skin, and hair that sticks up like a thatched roof.

His expression is full of admiration as he tips his head politely. "The celebration—" He stalls, and I watch the discreet slide of his eyes down my white waist-length Elemental hair to my blood-smeared dress. He makes a shocked noise in the back of his throat.

"I'll be a few minutes."

I shut the door and, turning back to the water-basin table, pull one of my knives from its sheath. Shakily, I use it to shred the drying cloth into strips and tie the material around my bleeding palms, pressing them hard until the oozing subsides, then walk to the wardrobe King Sedric had someone fill with the lavish-type dresses we both despise. Not because they're not gorgeous—they are—but because they're a disgusting waste of money when the peasant population has spent the last forty years starving.

I pull out a sleeveless black gown with no layers or buttons, which makes it easy to slip into despite my sliced palms and my left hand's fingers that are permanently curled inward almost to a fist. The fingers that never healed right after Brea, owner fourteen, took a mallet to them when my lightning strike took her husband's sight because he couldn't keep his anger to himself.

Once on, the dress shimmers and flows around my frame. A look in the mirror while I carefully drag a brush down my hair shows the dress does more than flow and cling. The color sets off the black trellis of owner- and memorial-tattooed markings circling my bare arms. It darkens them, making them look eerie. Uncomfortable.

Huh. Good.

I pick up my sheath of knives and strap the blades to my calf, then tug my dress over them. I firm my jaw. *Hold it together, Nym. At least until you figure out what the kracken to do.*

Except everything within me whispers that I already know what I need to do.

"Miss?" The man taps on the door again.

I lift my chin and straighten my unsteady shoulders. And harden my blue eyes before forcing the falsest grin I've ever smiled and walking over to open the blood-smeared, glass-impaled door.

Tannin's still standing there. He doesn't offer an arm. The veneration in his gaze is shadowed by a flash of fear. *He's afraid to touch me.*

I almost give a caustic laugh. Up until twenty minutes ago he should've been terrified.

Now? "I'm as impotent as you are," I nearly tell him.

"Glad you could join us." His expression edges back toward that ridiculous awe that the guards and knights and so many in Faelen are newly inclined to place on me. I frown. He looks about to say something further but seems to think better of it and waits until I shut the door before falling in beside me. "King Sedric sent me to persuade you."

I nod stiffly.

"He's requested to see you," he prods. "And I must say what an impression your style will make this evening." His eyes dip to my wrapped palms. "Very . . . stunning."

My attempt at politeness falters. I can't do it. I clench my teeth and let my glare smolder down the corridor in front of us, and after a moment he, smartly, seals his mouth like a tomb.

One minute. Two minutes. Three minutes eke by until we reach the Great Hall. Before he leads me in, Tannin turns to face me. His cheeks are blushing like berries and suddenly he's fumbling a crisp, folded kerchief from beneath his guard doublet and holding it out to me. "Miss, I was wondering if you'd mind giving a token, a kiss perhaps, for me to take home."

I stare at him.

He smiles as if he's serious.

Is he insane? Up until a week ago my kiss would've been considered a curse. "I'm not a lady for knights to request tokens from," I mutter, and go to push past him.

"It's for my daughter."

I stall.

"Please."

I peer at him. Loosen my jaw. "How old is she?"

"Eight. And she's real proud of what you've done for us—for Faelen."

A moment longer and I hold out my hand for the cloth and place it against my lips in what is the most awkward thing I've ever done in my life. "Tell her it's the innocent who died in battle who deserve her respect, not the warriors who lived," I say, returning it to him. "Especially not one who was only there because of accidental powers."

He blushes even darker. "Yes, miss. Thank you, miss."

I go to stride past him but catch the look as he drops his gaze. I hesitate. "Tell her it's people like her father she should respect," I say softer. "The ones who serve because they have faith in justice."

He peers up and his eyes widen, then sparkle, and I try not to feel ill while turning to enter the shiny balcony.

The space is already filled with heavily perfumed people, most of whom are looking down upon the enormous lower room that's stuffed to the walls with prominent individuals fawning over food-heavy tables and a minicarnival.

I shake off the embarrassing cloth-kissing and dart my gaze about for Eogan-turned-Draewulf as acrobats, panther-monkeys, and even a baby oliphant prance around on the stage below. Behind them, giant arched windows and mural-painted walls edge up against the open doors and outside patios, giving the room a depth that brings the frescoed firefly trees and Hythra Crescent Mountains to life.

I search the corners for Eogan, but only find vedic harpies swinging from cages, humming their songs about the sea. Their music is enough to trigger a bizarre homesickness for my previous owner Adora's home and her parties with Eogan and Colin. I purse my lips. Who'd have thought I'd miss anything about that woman?

Turning my eyes, I tune them out even as my stiff shoulders threaten to buckle. Blasted hulls, Eogan, why couldn't you have let me shield you?

Find him and do what you have to, Nym.

"This way, miss." Tannin beckons me to the crowd in the center of the loft where he proceeds to weave me around their warm bodies. The elegant people fall away from us with eager glances and murmurs. Some are already too full of wine to walk decently, but apparently not enough to prevent them from noticing my sea-blue eyes and everything else about me that shouts *Elemental.*

"They say she took down Bron's airships with a single lightning strike," someone excitedly whispers.

"Two," another says. "The first took out the archers."

"No, no, she used her breath. Inhaled the wind and blew them back to Bron."

I raise a brow and can't help the smirk at that one. It fades as soon as my chest tightens with the rawness of not having Colin beside me. He would've laughed and never let me hear the end of it. *My breath?* I straighten. *Keep walking.*

"Either way, do you think it wise having her at the High Court? Look at those bandages on her hands. Are we certain she's safe?"

"No, but it doesn't matter. Rumor is she'll be invited to leave for Bron with King Eogan soon."

"Figures," a man's voice titters too loudly. "Anyone can tell she's vying to be that man's queen. Can you imagine? A week ago she was a slave. As if she'd know the first thing about court life. Now, if it was that visiting Cashlin princess, Rasha . . ."

I keep my head up and don't give them the luxury of knowing that my ears are, in fact, clearly working even if the man's insults are more comforting than any of the praise. I look around. *Where* is *Princess Rasha?* Less than an hour ago she was in my room playing with knives and hinting encouragements about Eogan. *How did she not see this coming with Draewulf?*

Tannin stops and I almost trip over him onto King Sedric, who's speaking with men I recognize as part of the High Council. In their shiny green doublets and pointy-heeled shoes, they remind me of the garish Adora. Especially beside His Royal Highness who's as boyish-looking and underdressed as ever. I curtsy as protocol dictates and nod at his guards nearby. They visibly relax and my hard eyes soften a bit at this man-boy who's two years older than me—nineteen—but seems twenty more, and who fought without flinching at Eogan's and my side.

He stops speaking and turns a kind smile. "Nym."

"Your Highness."

"I'm pleased you could make it down this evening."

"I'm honored to be invited." My throat tightens. *Tell him about Eogan.*

His merry gaze falls on my clothbound palms and narrows with apparent concern. "I hope you know this celebration is as much in praise to you as it is the treaty."

"Thank you, Your Majesty, but the gratitude is rightly placed on your shoulders." My eyes flick behind him, beyond the guards, in search of Eogan. *You have to tell him, Nym.* I clench my fingers and feel the pain from the cuts shoot up my arms.

Tell him you're all in danger.

I open my mouth again.

But my tongue thickens and heat clogs my throat. I don't know how to do it. I can't make the words come out from my lips that will sentence Eogan's body to death by the hands of someone who hardly knows him. Even if Sedric is my king. "You have my respect and gratitude," I whisper instead. "Especially regarding your mercy toward my Elemental race."

King Sedric grins and glances at the councilmen who are sloshing the drinks they've raised in our direction. He leans politely toward me. "I'd relish the chance to speak with you about your heritage as well as the plight of the Faelen citizens, if I may have the honor of a dance later this evening?"

I nod before retreating so he can return to his conversation.

"Good luck, miss," Tannin says, and, with a grateful wink and a half bow, leaves me alone in a sea of people I barely know who're full of blatant gawks and wearing giant, poofed hats that look exactly like the black-and-red Bron airships. Complete with larva-shaped balloons.

I swallow and head to the balcony's ledge and glare over it. Colin and Eogan should be here with me, mocking the ridiculousness of the outfits, of the luxury, listening while I scream that Draewulf is not dead.

Instead I swear I hear their ghosts whispering that he's going to wipe out this entire room and take Faelen. Just like he tried to at the Keep.

I grit my teeth and lean over the gilt railing to peer down below to look for him.

The lights flicker oddly, urging me to hurry my scan of the faces. *Where is he?*

Nervous chuckles break out as the candle lights blink again. I straighten and look up just as the glow flickers a third time and the crowd's laughter ceases.

"What's going on?" someone whispers. "Who's putting out the lights?"

CHAPTER 3

T WAS A HUNDRED YEARS AGO AND THE BLOODIEST night in Faelen history."

The creepy voice is accentuated by dimming candles and a low rumble of drums, and the entire room is instantly focused on the ten-foot-tall speaker in front of the stage.

My relieved sigh slips out. I don't even have to see the man to recognize him as the funny dwarf, wearing stilts, from the Travellers' Carnival who gave me, Colin, and Eogan breakfast the morning after I caused an avalanche. The morning after Eogan first kissed me.

Allen the Fabler, Travelling Baronet. A smile rises at his kindness, at the memory he brings, but I'm fairly certain acknowledging it would dissolve what wisps of sanity I have left.

He looms over the audience, flourishing his short arms to make shadows on the wall. "Three kingdoms—Faelen, Bron, an' Drust were at war." His voice booms through the air. "Except the *real* war was here, near where you're all standin'. And Faelen's streets began runnin' with *blooooood.*"

I recoil and go back to my search just as shivers and whistles reverberate through the crowd, urging on the dwarf's recount of Faelen's most horrific legend—*The Monster and the Sea of Elisedd's Sadness.* As if the story is somehow now of interest to those high courtiers who doubted Draewulf ever existed as anything more than a past rival king. Have they decided to acknowledge him now that he's supposedly dead? Or maybe they're simply celebrating the happier ending tacked on. *What has King Sedric told them?*

"Under a fog-cloaked night," the dwarf continues, "Drust's evil king, Draewulf, snuck through these streets." Behind him a group of wild-looking actors emerge on the low stage.

"Shape-shiftin' into human form to draw in men, women, and youngsters. Then returnin' to his wolf form to slay 'em, *one by one.*"

"Stop," I want to hiss at him. "You're only encouraging whatever Draewulf's got planned." But I keep my mouth shut and the dwarf keeps going as I push my way through the audience. The men and women I bump into give me startled looks followed by comments of "well done" and "Faelen's weapon." I ignore them. *Where is he? He should be close, enjoying the sound of his own disgusting story.*

A loud growl from the dwarf just about yanks me from my skin. My swearing is met by that of the spellbound listeners as the performers do five flips before falling theatrically on the ground—all except for the one dressed as a wolf, who pretends to devour them.

The dwarf laughs. "But when the captain o' the guard caught up with him that evenin', Draewulf was dressed up like one o' the men he'd just killed. Climbed inside his body and slowly absorbed his soul. 'Til there was nothin' left except his wolf self hidin' inside the man's *flesh.*"

I should've plugged my ears. My stomach turns. I begin weaving faster through the balcony crowd. There are too many bodies and giant hats swaying to the dwarf's word rhythm. *C'mon, Eogan, where are you?*

"An' the only reason the captain was able to catch him and bring him in? The shape-shifter *allowed* it. Wanted an audience with Faelen's King Willem."

Someone tumbles against me and I reach out to keep from tripping. "Beg your pardon," I mutter, before recognizing one of the few Bron guards allowed in the Castle this week. Part of Eogan's personal protection unit left here from Bron. He stares coolly, but there's a slight awareness in his gaze that says he knows who I am.

He doesn't move.

I don't either.

"Where is he?" I demand.

"For twenty months he'd been makin' war with Bron and Faelen." The entertainer's voice grows more exuberant by the second. "Now he was lookin' to make a deal! Swore he'd become Faelen's ally. For a *price*. Which was . . ."

The guard in front of me glances at the dwarf and smiles.

My neck twitches. *Ah litches.*

"Our Elementals," someone in the crowd shouts. And just like that the entire room shifts its attention.

I don't have to look beyond the first few faces to know that two hundred more gazes are glued to me.

"So tragic, so horrific," the dwarf says. "The price was the Elementals. Condemned to death by King Willem's and Draewulf's treaty note. An' the Sea of Elisedd, she's churned noisy 'bout it ever since. Cryin' for those Elemental children for the past hundred years. Until . . ."

To the side of me a woman giggles too prettily. When I peer

over, there's a man with jagged black hair beside her, leaning into her, and a host of Faelen soldiers nearby.

The audience abruptly roars, and then the Bron guard steps around me, blocking my path. When I glance up he shrugs. "King Eogan's not available yet. You should watch the show." He points toward the dwarf who has jumped and vaulted himself across a portion of the room to land below the balcony where King Sedric is standing. The little man shoves his hands up to indicate the young king. "Until King Sedric, the Elemental, and King Eogan defeated him!"

The spectators erupt. Even King Sedric applauds and yells over the noise. "Finally someone who'll tell the legend as a banner of victory rather than a warning!" Then, before the entertainer can pick the story up again, the king raises a goblet and beckons for quiet.

"My friends," his voice rings loud. Confident. "I toast the demise of Draewulf and the end to our hundred-year war. Here's to the ushering in of a new era. Of peace. Of sanctuary for all, including our Elementals." He looks past his subjects right to me and grins. Tips his glass. "Beginning with Nym, whom I offer the gift of freedom from slavery and the undying gratitude of our entire Faelen nation!"

Whoever's working the wall mirrors flashes the candle lights onto my face. I step back, half blinded, as the citizens whoop and toss their hats in the air with drink-heavy approval. It takes me a second to remember to curtsy in spite of the fact that everything inside me is tempted to scream at them that we're about to be anything but free.

But the guard moves and the lights leave my face to land on the cluster surrounding the giggling lady and the jagged-haired man, whom the dwarf is now pointing at. The man lifts his head. It's Eogan-who-is-Draewulf.

I open my mouth. To out him. To unleash on him the Faelen soldiers who may believe me, or more likely would just think I'm drunk.

I move toward him. But he merely stands there looking out over the audience, giving a brandishing wave and an enormous smile, followed by a respectful nod toward King Sedric. I scowl— *What's the wretch waiting for?*—and edge to the side while keeping between him and the king. I reach for my ankle knives as the crowd continues cheering.

As soon as the lights flash away, the monster goes back to the woman beside him—one of those who'd giggled when the tittering man had insulted my slave status minutes ago. *What's Draewulf doing? Why is he keeping Sedric alive?*

I work my way closer until I'm only feet away and can see Draewulf shift his gloating attention to the dwarf, then back again to the lady. He bends over her and says something.

I freeze just as his hand reaches up the back of her dress's skirt and grabs her thigh. She laughs but there's a hint of discomfort in it now.

My gut slithers to the floor. If there were any siren left in my blood, he'd be dust.

His hand gropes higher. I choke. Then abruptly, Eogan-who-is-Draewulf moves his wolfish gaze up to connect with mine. He smirks. And something clicks.

He's going to kill us all.

Before I can look away, his other hand slides up the woman's back and casually slips around her neck, like a noose. She chuckles and it sounds like she's hoping he's playing. Too bad she can't see his expression, which is as black as hulls.

The dwarf's voice grows louder as back in front of the stage he's assuring the crowd the shape-shifter will never again enjoy the scent of fresh blood. "And his only survivin' kin isn't a shape-shifter," he yells. "She's a Mortisfaire."

From beneath my dress I slide out one of the knives Eogan made and wait for the dwarf to add something about how Lady Isobel can turn our hearts to stone with one touch. But he doesn't because King Sedric speaks again.

"I can assure all of us that Draewulf's daughter will no longer be a threat. After her betrayal of Faelen, she's not welcome here. If Lady Isobel appears—*when* she appears—she'll be held accountable for her crimes of betraying our Faelen kingdom just like the Lady Adora!"

The crowd cheers as, in front of me, Eogan whips toward the king. His eyes narrow to slits, and I'm close enough to hear his feral growl over the crowd's rabid hollering.

I take the final step behind him and the woman and lean in to inhale Eogan's scent. A rush of horror and heartache finds my stomach, my nostrils, my throat. It burns and trickles and digs into that part of me that knows, without a doubt, that Eogan is already gone and I am saving our people once again.

"I'm so sorry," I whisper anyway.

Four, five, nine seconds I count before I grip the handle tighter and, with a quiet sob, shove my blade in my trainer's back.

CHAPTER 4

N YM!"

I freeze.

Eogan's broad shoulders stiffen, then he turns. His amused expression morphs into a glower aimed at my face as Princess Rasha floats over in her Cashlin-styled, glossy red gown, her dark brown hair twisted in a single spiral down to her delicate elbow.

"Nym," she says again, in that whimsical tone that sounds as if she's on herbs.

I frown and glance over to find her eyes riddled with shock and ringed with the glowing scarlet tint that indicates she's using her Luminescent ability, which, when focused enough, reads people's intentions.

Suddenly the weight of the knife in my hand feels awkward even though it hardly connected with Eogan's skin. I doubt it even drew blood. I pull back and attempt to hide the blade against my thin skirts.

Until I realize her look of alarm is not for me.

Rasha's gaping at Eogan, her gaze glimmering stronger.

Abruptly she clamps herself to my side and wraps her hand around my arm as the audience breaks into applause. The larger candelabras are reigniting and the dwarf's ending his story to louder cheering than I've ever heard the legend met with.

Eogan-who-is-Draewulf scowls at Rasha as if he's quite aware of her ability—as if he knows she can see into him and who he really is—before he turns to resettle his glare full on me. His lips twist. "Pushing your luck, aren't you?" He juts his face near enough that his damp breath fuses to my hair. "Don't make me tire of this, pet. You'd hate to be . . ."—his gaze darts in the direction of King Sedric—"the *cause* of any unfortunate accidents."

My blade is thrusting for his stomach before he can blink, but Rasha's hand stops mine. "Nym, *wait*." Her grip becomes insistent, forcing my retreat. I turn to demand an explanation but she's still staring at Eogan with an expression that's gone beyond horror. Her sunburn-colored skin has drained to pale.

"Nym—"

"He's Draewulf, I know," I whisper. "Now let go."

"But Eogan—"

"I *know*."

Her fingers dig in as she turns to look me full in the face, her eyes willing me to understand. "He's *still Eogan*."

"Yes, now—" I frown. Blink. "What?"

Eogan dips next to me again, so close his suit brushes my bare shoulders and a musky wolf scent fills my lungs. He reaches for a wineglass from the lady who, up until a moment ago, was flirting with him but now appears to be trying to distance herself from the lot of us. He hoists the drink above his head and snorts hot breath in my face.

"Your Majesty!" he says, and turns. "A toast to you!"

"Hear, hear!" The requisite cries swell throughout the Hall as the lights flit off the mirrors to focus first on Eogan, then Sedric. "To the king!"

"King Sedric!"

I spin on Rasha. "I don't understand. He's Draewulf."

"Yes. But Eogan's not fully dead yet." Her voice wafts its high pitch. "Draewulf's still in the process of taking over."

No.

"Like butterflies sharing the same chrysalis."

I step back.

Oh hulls, *no.*

I look around with no idea how to be in this moment. *What* to be in this moment. Because if the discovery of Draewulf shifting into Eogan's body was unbearable, this . . . this is the undoing of my spine.

The grave I've spent the last hour trying to seal up while keeping the final pieces of me from falling apart has just opened to reveal the person inside isn't quite dead. Only half dead. Half consumed. And now I will watch his final remnants fade as the monster who killed Colin, and is now devouring Eogan, gloats.

I brace for my Elemental curse to itch and surge, to exact revenge for what's been done, but it doesn't. And the realization crashes in all over again that I no longer have it. That I am merely a carved-out, angry-as-hulls girl.

I think I'm going to vomit. "Rasha—"

"And to you, King Eogan," King Sedric speaks up. "And your kingdom of Bron, Faelen's new friend and ally."

"Hear, hear!" Eogan joins the audience's cheers, his tone mocking, turning my stomach sick with what he's about to do. I lift my knife again to the low of his back.

Rasha's hand slips down over the bandages on my fingers and grips the blade handle. "I said wait," she whispers.

"And to the kingdom of Cashlin!"

"To Cashlin!"

"And Princess Rasha!"

"Princess Rasha, marry me!" some rabid swooner yells.

Without releasing my hand, she responds to the compliment by sashaying a flamboyant curtsy at the court and yelling back, "Feel free to ask my mum's permission." The crowd laughs and the blinding lights slide away, but Eogan raises his glass once again and they're instantly returned to us.

"If I may go beyond a toast, Your Highness," Eogan says.

I yank away from Rasha. "Oh of all the litches, let's just—"

"Nym, you have to trust me." Her frantic voice fills my ear.

"I am honored by Your Majesty," Eogan-who-is-Draewulf booms. "To carry your extension of friendship home to Bron, both in the form of your word and your delegates when I depart. No one knows better the amount of work required in upcoming days to make this peace treaty a reality among our subjects as we rebuild our hearts and lands." He pauses. Clears his throat. "Thus, if I might be so bold to ask . . . as a continued symbol of goodwill, and in celebration of what is to come . . ."

His tone grows elevated, agitated. Obligating, as it carries over the entire room. "I'm officially requesting that I, and your delegates, move up the departure date for the trip to my homeland. I will leave first thing tomorrow morning."

My gasp joins the audience's. I peek at Rasha. Was this what she wanted me to wait for? To hear Draewulf announce his intention to depart sooner? We won't even make it until then.

King Sedric hesitates a moment, and I catch the flash of

concern. Then he's extending his goblet toward Eogan. "Go with the Creator!" he bellows, and the approval it elicits is overwhelming. Just like Eogan's sneer as he turns, suddenly in my face, consuming my vision.

"Sleep well tonight, pet." There's no attempt to hide the malevolence coating his words. He steps away to join his Bron and Faelen guards and the lights move away for good.

I twirl on Rasha. "What the bolcrane just happened? You wanted me to wait until—*what*—he moved up his time frame for taking you and the delegates to Bron? What blasted difference does that make?" But even as I say it, my voice cracks.

"If you'd killed him, you would be dead right now! And Eogan—"

"Do you think I care? Look at him! You could've let me free him and myself quickly. Because if I don't, we might all end up dead."

She grabs the side of my skirt as I start to follow him. "That's what I'm telling you—I *am* looking, and Eogan's still whole inside his body. Whatever Draewulf's done, he hasn't managed full control." She throws her hands up, glancing around as if trying to find a better way to explain. "Draewulf hasn't been able to even *begin* absorbing Eogan."

The world stops.

My breath stops.

Even as the room keeps going and the crowd's voices keep soaring.

"Eogan's soul, his *essence*, is still intact. Draewulf's not taken it."

I shake my head. That's not possible. Maybe her Luminescent powers don't work as well as she thinks they do—Eogan once told me they're not always clear. Maybe her sight is hazy. "Draewulf indicated he took him over at the Keep a week ago, and I saw the bruising and the incision even then. I just didn't connect it."

"I'm not debating that he invaded his physical form. I'm just telling you what I see. And what I see are two whole men sharing the same shell. Eogan just can't surface."

Hope, joy, heartbursts tear at me. Eogan's still whole? Is that actually possible? I flip around and watch the back of him stride through the crowd toward the balcony door as the party guests press us toward the railing and stairs. My breath is thin. "Rasha, how good is your sight?"

"There's a lot of interference in here, but I'm still better than most Luminescents twice my eighteen years."

"Have you ever heard of anyone surviving a shifting before?"

"Never."

I slip my hand in hers and pull her to follow him. "But somehow *he* did and we need to figure out why."

"I'm working on that, but where are we going?" she says a tad too loud, which garners interest from a few people.

I smile for their benefit and keep walking, pointing a discreet hand toward Eogan. "Just following him," I say in a way I hope makes me sound lovesick and not like a desperate murderer.

"To do what exactly?"

"To keep an eye on him. To figure something out. I don't know—can't you tell what I'm planning?"

"Maybe if your ideas weren't fluctuating all over the place like a band of hyper ferret-cats. Because honestly? I'm not a magician." Except the way her reddish gaze is suddenly narrowing in on me, we both know she might as well be.

I ignore the blossoming frown and duck us around one of those councilmen with the giant airship hats. "Can you see what's keeping him alive?"

She jerks me to a halt. Her eerie stare is boring holes straight into me. "Your ability . . ." She actually sounds incredulous. "I was so focused on . . . I didn't . . ." Abruptly, she takes a step backward and nearly trips as she whispers, "He took it."

My chest, my veins, my nerves ache. I turn and keep walking after Eogan. "He used Eogan's block to cut it out."

"And you're unable to get it back," she says in her airy voice, as the full picture apparently dawns in whatever way it does for Luminescents. She jumps to catch up. "When?"

"After you left my room earlier." I weave us around a servant with two drink trays, and then we're at the door Eogan and his men have just left through. I see them ahead down the candlelit hall, rounding a corner. "Just tell me how much time he has. *Is* there any chance of him surviving long enough until Draewulf moves on to take another host?"

"I don't know. Up until now no one thought it possible to survive *this* long. It's something to do with his blocking ability."

"What about separating Eogan from Draewulf? I mean, if there was a way . . ."

"It's never been done. The host would die."

We round the corner and spot them again up ahead. "But hypothetically?"

"Hypothetically? There are always possibilities."

I may only have known her a matter of days, but even I can tell she doesn't believe it. I ask anyway. "Do you think you could see clear enough to *know*?"

Another two bends in the hall, and we take them in time to see Eogan unlocking a room. There's a brisk exchange between him and his men while the Faelen guards look on before he enters and his door clicks shut. The Bron guards position themselves on each side of it like huge onyx statues, and the Faelen soldiers settle around them.

Rasha looks at me sideways. "I'm not sure. Their intentions are all over the place. Between Eogan and Draewulf and the block—it's like the positive and negative are morphed. Hazy. Same as when someone's not yet decided on a course of action." A pause and then she perks up. "Although . . . it doesn't *appear* that either of them have harmful objectives before he leaves tomorrow. On that they seem aligned."

I didn't realize I was holding my breath until I let it out all in one tremble just as one of the guards turns our way. Rasha and I pull back behind the corner and study each other. Her eyes dim to their normal dark brown coloring, her ability receding with the glow.

"Are you telling me he's not going to destroy the court or King Sedric tonight?"

She shakes her head. "Not from what I can determine."

"Can you promise that?"

"Nearly 95 percent."

I bite my lip. "I need time," I finally whisper. "A couple of hours—maybe a day or two even—to watch for any change. To see if Draewulf absorbs more of Eogan or to research whether it's possible he could survive a shift. After that, we'll do . . . whatever needs to be done."

"I'm all for letting Eogan live a bit longer, and *you* for that matter, which is why I stopped you from getting stabby back there. But a couple of *days*?" Her voice lilts higher than normal. "You're holding the fate of five kingdoms in your hands. This should be taken to King Sedric."

"Right. So he can kill him."

"Or he'll lock him up until they figure something out."

I tilt my head and stare at her. Does she actually believe that?

She peers away.

"He'll kill him and you know it," I say. "Which will only restart the war, and Bron will come down harder on our heads. Except this time . . ."

She bites her lip.

This time my abilities are gone and I won't be able to stop them.

"I'll stay in this spot until he boards the airship," I whisper. "After that . . ."

Her eyes flash toward me and widen with their reddish hue for a half second. "After that?" she says in a tone that says she's just seen exactly what *after that* is going to entail. She snorts. "Are you insane? Bron isn't going to welcome into their kingdom the person who destroyed their armada. You're just as likely to get *yourself* killed."

"Which is why I'll make sure I'm not seen."

She withers me a glare. "This is a bad idea. If they catch you sneaking aboard their king's airship, they *will* kill you. And on top of that, perhaps killing Eogan right now might restart the war, Nym, but so will having King Sedric think Eogan stole you."

"I'll leave a note. If anything, he'll blame my lovesick heart and the rumors of elopement he's heard. In the meantime . . ." I glance around the corner at the guards again. "If he moves an inch I promise you I *will* have my knife at his back."

"A *knife*? If he moves, you should be telling King Sedric and screaming it to every Hidden Lands kingdom! Think about how easily he stole your ability, Nym."

"I wouldn't say *easily*. And I *will* handle him if—when—I have to."

She purses her lips together.

"You said his intentions weren't harmful here, and it's not like he can do much damage while on that airship."

She snorts.

"We'll be there to stop him."

"I said they didn't *appear* to be harmful here. And that speaks nothing as to once he's in Bron, nor does it mean I'm agreeing to this." She rubs her arm. Then sighs. "Look, I have to alert my own guards and send word to my queen mum. I also have to find out what time we're leaving because, oh hulls, I need my wardrobe packed!" Her face takes on a look of panic as she glances down at her evening party dress. She turns to me. "Will you be okay until I return?"

I nod. *Yes.*

Maybe.

Her gaze falls to my bandaged hands before lifting to narrow in on my eyes. After a moment, my internal mess of emotion sealed beneath the numb suddenly shifts and I look away. *Blast her.*

She tips her head once. Because abruptly we both know that probably nothing about me is okay. Because in the course of one daft night, I've lost both my ability and the only man who ever made me feel safe enough to love.

I peek around the bend at the two Bron soldiers pacing in front of Eogan's door. Do they know it's not their king inhabiting his body? I grit my teeth—*Let's just do this*—and turn back and shrug because, even though I'm thinking it, my words won't work.

She sighs. And plants a kiss on my cheek. "Right. I'll hurry. *Forty* minutes. And my guards will be here sooner. I'm still not saying I'll comply with your request. I'm just speaking with my men. If Draewulf moves before then, yell for King Sedric *please*."

Her soft footsteps clip down the hall in the direction of Eogan's room. I hear her voice offer a "Good evening, handsomes" to the guards before her steps fade down the corridor. I lean against the wall to ignore everything except figuring out how to get aboard that ship.

CHAPTER 5

A QUARTER HOUR LATER THE SOUND OF HEAVY footsteps draws my attention to the hallway on my right where three of Rasha's guards are striding toward me. I tighten the grip on my knives tucked between the folds of my dress and stay planted against the inverted corner that simultaneously allows me to face the approaching guards and the corridor where the group of soldiers are still hovering around Eogan's shut door. The surly glares the Bron unit has been shooting my way make it clear my presence is considered not only an insult but a threat.

"Her Highness will be along shortly," the middle Cashlin says quietly when they near me. Reaching into the folds of his red doublet, he pulls out parchment and an ink quill with a tiny pot attached at the tip. "From her."

My hands are steady as I set down my blades and scribble awkwardly with my right hand, since my gimpy one can no longer write, on the parchment as fast as possible.

When finished, I sign my name at the bottom and hand the ink back.

The three of them settle in place a few feet away, heightening the offense and interest of the Bron and Faelen soldiers. They eye us and almost in unison slip their hands to their sword hilts.

"Perhaps the little Elemental is looking for a duel," one of the Bron guards says, prompting the others to snicker.

"As long as it's to the death," another replies.

A Faelen soldier steps between them and my line of sight. "I'll caution you both to watch your words." He waits a moment, then resumes his previous position, and the look the first Bron guard sends me says it's only the Faelen and Cashlin men's presence that is keeping him from descending on me.

I finger my knives and stare at them as the seconds tick by.

Those seconds slip into minutes. Which slide into hours.

Two hours pass in the uncomfortable, tension-filled hallway, and it has gone from absolute silence to the occasional weary shuffle of the guards' leather or metal. The sudden *clip-clip-clipping* of Rasha's shoes and the tromping of two guards with her bring me to a standing position.

"My apologies," she whispers hurriedly, glancing between me and her soldiers. "Sending an immediacy letter to my mum via the High Court runners proved more difficult than expected." She peers down the other corridor to Eogan's room. "Has anything happened?"

I shake my head and catch an eyeful from one of her men, whose frown I gather is disapproving the fact I've not curtsied before Her Cashlin Highness.

"All has been silent, Princess," he says.

"When's the airship scheduled to leave?" I ask.

Rasha turns to me. "In two hours. But—"

A click down the hall echoes loud, and in unison we both freeze.

Eogan's door opens and his guards step back as a swath of Bron soldiers emerge, and in the middle of them, *him*.

"But Eogan is boarding now," Rasha says.

A burst of sour slides up my throat. I slip one of my blades into my ankle sheath before handing her the letter for King Sedric and, keeping the other blade tucked into my dress skirt, nod. "Then let's go."

Before I can move she grabs my arm and lowers her voice. "I still think this is a bad idea."

I narrow my gaze and glance down the hall toward Draewulf. And bite back the remark that I don't care what she thinks right now. We have to go.

She sighs. "But seeing that you're obviously set on it, first make me a promise."

I raise a brow.

"I've decided to agree with you regarding the politics of exposing Draewulf on Faelen soil. And I believe that if we can make it to Bron, it'd be wiser to do it there, in front of his council, especially considering he's just offed their King Odion. However . . ." She stops and waits until I look at her. "You have to promise me that you won't get caught, and the moment anything goes wrong, you won't even hesitate to do what needs to be done."

Is that it? I give her a sharp nod. *Fine.*

"*Nor* will you stop me if I decide to do so." She waits for me to nod again before slipping off the cloak she's wearing. "I've figured out where to hide you on the ship, but we need to disguise you as my maid-in-waiting to—"

"That won't work. They'll investigate and as soon as they see my hair, they'll recognize me."

She curls her lips wryly at me. "Which is why I still think this is a terrible idea. Perhaps—"

"I'm going," I interrupt, watching Eogan and his entourage disappear from the far end of the hallway. "And I have a better idea."

Rasha raises a brow before she nods and looks to her men. "You two guards follow Eogan. You other three come with us."

We've gone down three corridors when I tell her men, "It'd be best if you stay here."

Rasha tips her chin at them just as we reach the door we're to go through. I shove it open when a voice rings out, "May I help you, miss?"

Litches.

I stall. Turn. *Tannin.*

He looks at Rasha's men, at her, and then at the door I'm holding ajar.

"I was heading up to grab a cloak," I say.

His smile falters. He stares at the gilded wood behind my head as if he can see around it and is quite aware that this direction leads nowhere near our rooms, let alone my wardrobe. "Would you like me to get it for you, miss? Afterward I'd be glad to escort you to King Sedric. I believe the waltz is about to be played."

"Thank you, but—"

"I think I'm in need of some fresh air," Rasha says.

"Then allow me to—"

I wave him off. "The princess and I just need a few minutes for . . . *woman* issues."

A blush blooms on his cheeks, and before he can say anything further, I flip around and push through the door to rush with Rasha up a flight of candlelit stairs, vaguely aware that her guards have settled into place to prevent Tannin from following.

It's black as hulls and freezing when she and I step outside the palace door onto the Northern Wing's upper courtyard. The place has been converted into some type of platform for the airship, and the few torches lining the far wall flicker through the fog. Their light glints off the giant metallic ship floating in front of us—or at least the underside of it, which is the only part visible since the makeshift scaffolding rising up in front of us is stretched out to surround the entire top portion. On the ground nearby, a ribbed-looking base for holding the ship has been slid away, allowing the hull to float a good five feet off the ground. Large ropes tether it in place, but even so it lists toward us and the scaffold.

"Your quarters have already been assigned?" I whisper.

"Yes, but—"

"On which side are they?"

"This one," she murmurs. "Four stories up on the deck level. But I don't think—"

"So just above that window there?" I count four perpendicular windows and point at the topmost one that sits just beneath the spiraling planks hiding our view of the ship's upper portion.

"Nym." Her tone sparks uneasy. "I really think we should wait until Eogan's boarded the ship and then try to—"

A man's voice breaks through the fog. "King Eogan and the rest of his men, Captain."

I peer up at the scaffold rising in front of us and listen to the tromping feet cross it. Squinting down, I eye the two beams closest to us with a crossplank at the bottom. They're higher up than I'd counted on. "I'm going to need a boost."

"Are you insane?" Rasha grabs my shoulder and pulls me around. Her brown hair and face loom toward me in the dark. "You're going to *climb*?"

"They won't believe I'm your maid. They'll see my face beneath that cloak, and the minute they do . . ."

There's a clatter above our heads, then another from an alcove in the torch-lit wall opposite the courtyard where we're tucked into the shadow. A whistle from up top and then the soldiers' voices are talking over each other, muffled by boots along the ramps. "Your Majesty, this way," someone shouts.

"Bron guards! A second sweep of the yard below!" another yells in an accent.

Kracken. "Hurry, give me a lift before they search this area!"

"You actually think we can fit through there?" Rasha snorts, pointing up at the round window that is slightly ajar.

"All I need is a lift. I'll meet you inside once you board with your men." Without waiting for a reply, I slide from the door and duck into the shadow of the giant ship's hull. She follows with an expression declaring this is crazy, even as she weaves her hands into a stirrup and hoists me to the first plank.

I begin to climb.

Within moments I'm sweating as I stretch from one board to the next and nearly fall in the first two attempts because my curled fingers can't grasp onto anything this size. *Curses.* I finally settle on a sort of shimmy that effectively punctures my arms with splinters and shreds every last thread of my dress, but I manage to move from one post to the next. My arms and legs and bandaged hands burn with the strain. *C'mon, Nym. Just get up and get in if you want to help Eogan.*

I'm a quarter of the way up when the clang of metal against stone is followed by guards' voices. I glance down only to discover Rasha has somehow jumped and is following me up. *What the—?*

Accented muttering floats up from below her, and abruptly two Bron soldiers appear, swords in hand, in their sweep of the courtyard.

Litches. I plaster myself as close to the slightly tilting ship as I dare and hope to hulls she follows suit.

The scowling men move unbearably slow, looking around at the Castle's doors and into the courtyard shadows as they talk. Rasha's warning from the hall makes my palms ache. *"If they find you sneaking aboard the ship, they will kill you."*

Apparently their conversation is more interesting than doing their actual job though because they continue on around the side without ever glancing up, and I exhale in relief.

Except two seconds later Rasha starts climbing again.

I give her a look and beckon her back, but either it's too dark for her to see it or she's too busy gasping for breath between planks because she gives no indication of a response other than to keep going. *Bleeding hulls.*

The airship lilts toward us, bumping into the scaffolding enough to make the wood moan, and for a moment I envision the whole thing giving way and crumbling on top of us, or else bringing the guards back. I adjust my grip and watch Rasha brace against one of the beams until, after a moment, the airship steadies and there's no reappearance of soldiers. I wait for her to reach me.

"Are you crazy?" I hiss. "Go back. There's no sense for both of us to be killed."

"Which is exactly why I'm here," she whispers. "If the Bron soldiers discover you without a delegate, they'll not act mercifully. Now move."

I open my mouth to argue, but the ship lists again and soldiers begin to shout overhead. I scowl and continue skirting up the rest of the beams.

When we finally reach the window, it's barely ajar. I press into it with the knuckles of my twisted hand while holding on with the other. For the smallest moment the thing is jammed and I'm scared we'll have to climb back down. But the next, the glass gives way and squeaks open wide enough to allow Rasha and me to pull our way through.

The room we fall into is a pantry lit by a single light on the wall. The glass-enclosed flame illuminates the space like a candle but with less movement. I frown at it, then pull Rasha up and point us both to the door. "This way."

We slink up the absolute narrowest set of steps I've ever seen until we reach another door that opens onto a thin hall also lit by those strange lights.

I jump as a crash sounds from the other side of one wall, and the men's voices from earlier heighten. *They're just outside.*

"*Which way?*" I mouth.

Rasha squints as if looking for her bearings. "In there." Her tone is panicked as she indicates a room a few yards from us.

We're just sliding along the hall toward it when the sound of her harried breathing is replaced by a low chuckle. It slips through me with an intimacy that makes every hair on my body bristle.

I flip toward the stairwell we just left, only to see the space undulate in a way that curls my insides. Another wave of floor bending hits and I grab the wall, but the rippling grows stronger and my stomach's suddenly lurching and I'm leaning over again right before a mental image of a bolcrane fills my vision. The beast opens its jaws and raises a shiny black claw as its scaly body barrels toward us. I duck and force my mind to scream *It's not real, it's not real, it's so blasted not real.*

Then the image flickers.

The floor tilts and the ceiling falls.

"Well, well, wellll," a muffled, snakelike voice purrs. "If thisss isn't a quandary."

CHAPTER 6

THE HALLWAY SHIFTS AGAIN, RIGHTING ITSELF. Except this time there's something else with it. A shudder in the thin layer of atmosphere.

I choke and grab Rasha's arm in case she'll screech, just as the wretch pushes a tiny cabin door open in front of us to reveal himself—Myles, Lord Protectorate and Blasted Oaf. Standing three feet away. Sporting a handsome face that's looking a bit nauseous behind a smooth grin.

The odd, enclosed lighting glimmers off that one silver tooth among a row of white, perfectly straight ones. He steps forward, props his arm against the wall, and grins at me. "Rough evening, love? Need a hug?"

I leap at him faster than he can brace himself and clamp my bandaged hand around the cravat at his throat while my gimpy hand reaches for my knife.

"Ah-ah, careful with the clothing."

I tighten my grip on his frilly bow and jerk him toward me, then slip the blade near his gut. "I should kill you."

"Ooh, let's torture him first," Rasha whispers. "But maybe in the room because Eogan's men are right outside the hall."

Myles sneers at her before peeling my hand away even as I continue to hold the blade inches from his stomach. "Seeing as you have just been found sneaking aboard an enemy airship after refusing to report that Eogan has been taken over by Draewulf—not to mention the fact that the little Elemental lost her powers—it seems to me neither of you are in the position for threatsss." He straightens his cravat to match his impeccable suit and smooths his shiny black hair.

I frown. *How does he—?*

"Or did you forget that knowing things is my specialty, dear? Because I can assure you, having spent a portion of thisss week in treaty chambers with Eogan and King Sedric, I'm quite aware Eogan's not the man I know and despise. And the tragic messss in your bedroom tonight gave the rest away—not to mention that if you still had your powers, we'd all be suffering your thunderousss wrath right now." He reaches out to stroke my arm.

I slap him away. "Treaty chambers? What are you talking about?"

"Nym," Rasha murmurs. "Ask him once we're in the room."

The floor beneath us tilts to the side as the airship suddenly lists and bobs and voices rise from beyond the door. Rasha presses her hand to the wall, and I plant my leg against the baseboard. And watch Myles's pasty face turn a nauseous color of green. After a moment of what appears to be him repeatedly swallowing, the airship balances out, and I shove my knife again toward his stomach, forcing him to retreat through the doorway he emerged from.

Rasha follows us into the room, which is little bigger than a water closet and boasts a single cot, a covered window, and a mirror. "This is where you'll stay and my maid will bunk with me," she whispers in my ear.

I nod. And keep my knife pointed at Myles. "What are you doing here? What have you done?"

"I'm here because I'm part of the Bron delegation, of course. Thank you, by the way, for not outing me to King Sedric. Would've been horridly inconvenient for my plansss. And as lord protectorate, I did exactly what needed to be done the last few days. Sssimply ensured we all made it through without *you* causing trouble."

He lifts his shaky hand, as if to study his manicured fingernails, and in doing so reveals the bruising on his knuckles. Combined with the thin, healing scar across his jaw, they appear to be the only signs of injury from our tussle a week ago. "Couldn't have you ruining anything before we made it out of Faelen, could I?"

"*We?*"

"I assumed you'd get aboard somehow, and I was right." He runs his gaze down my tattooed arms.

I glance at Rasha.

"I didn't tell him," she says.

"Let's just say in this case I wasss . . . *amusing* myself to see *if* I was correct as well as ensuring your conscience didn't kick in and send you running tail between those lovely legs to tattle on Draewulf to my pathetic cousin, King Sedric."

Rasha snorts.

"You're despicable," I say.

"Yesss, and your insults were much more attractive when you had actual powers to back them up."

My blade is back at his gut, but my retort is lost as more voices drift beyond the hallway. "Did *you* know Myles was in council chambers this week?" I mutter to Rasha.

"No. I've been kept to the political sidelines as much as you while Faelen worked out its treaty with Bron."

"Not that it would've mattered." Myles steps back and tips my knife blade away before moving over to settle against the wall opposite us. "She wants Draewulf alive as much as I do. Or should I say her dear queen mum will once the message isss delivered."

Rasha shoots him a withering look. "*You* are a sad little roach and you know nothing."

"We should report him," I say.

"If we do, he'll tell King Sedric about Eogan." Rasha's eyes spark red. She sits stiffly on the single cot beside me.

Myles grins. "Good. Ssso it's all worked out then. We all get what we want and King Sedric's none the wiser. Nice to think we had similar interestsss."

Is he jesting? "You're a traitor who tried to kill my friends and betray your own king."

"Tsssk. I only *threatened* to kill them. And for the most part, those threats clearly didn't work on you."

"Threatened? You fed that orange-haired politician to Adora's warhorses."

"Well, that one, yesss. And you might've too if you'd known what he did in his private life." His face twists as the airship lists and we all pitch forward.

"And," he adds in a shaky tone, "your words sound a bit fickle for someone who hunted down every favor house in Faelen in the past week and threatened the owners with injury."

How does he know? I didn't tell any—

"Now"—he saunters a foot forward—"as lord protectorate I can *order* you to turn over those knives you're holding, or I can be civil and tell you that the Bron guards will be bothered enough when I tell them you're on this ship as my *personal* guest. But when they find you have weapons? Even my influence won't prevent their wrath. They'll see it as a threat to their new King Eogan."

I actually laugh. "Not a chance in hulls you're taking these. Especially since you've not answered what you're really doing here."

He spreads his hands out and looks insulted. "Why, achieving safety for all, same as you."

"He's here because he wants to rule the Hidden Lands," Rasha says from the cot.

Ignoring her, Myles holds out a hand for my blades. "I'll stow them away until we reach Bron."

"I don't think so."

A loud *thump* overhead echoes through the room. Myles jumps, and Rasha gets up. "Nym, I'm going to make sure the other rooms along the hall are all empty, but then I should go. Whatever else the little roach intends to say or *do* . . ." She glares at Myles and her eyes are back to blazing illumination. "I can already see. And it's all idiotic. I suggest we push him off the ship once we're over the ocean."

The ceiling bumps again. I nod. "I believe he was just leaving as well."

She reaches out her hand to squeeze mine, but suddenly her gaze is softening and her pupils grow brighter. "Nym . . ." She studies me. "For what it's worth, I'm sorry for the way things are. I'm sorry about Eogan."

I shrug and return her squeeze and say nothing.

"Before I go, is there anything I can do?"

I shake my head. I don't want her pity. I consider jesting, "Hey, I'm no longer a curse or a slave—so it's not all bad, yes?" Only right now, I'd give anything to have both those things back if it meant saving Eogan.

"You've done enough," I murmur. "I just need to hide and think a bit."

From his spot, Myles clears his throat. As if even he knows I'm lying.

"Shut up," I snap at him.

"Just stay in this room, okay?" Rasha says, turning to glare again at Myles. Then with one last compassionate glance at me, she sashays the four feet to the door.

Myles sniffs. "Whichever god decided to curse the world with that woman—"

I lunge for him.

He dodges from the room and, before I reach the door, jerks it shut behind him. Leaving me standing in front of it, shaking and half contemplating going after him or working my way through the entire airship with my knives.

Not that I'd get far.

With one last curse, I click the lock on the door before slipping over to plop down on the tiny metal cot that is little bigger than a coffin.

After a moment I lie back and pull the thin covers over my head like a lid.

CHAPTER 7

I HAVE NO IDEA HOW LONG I STAY IN THAT POSITION curled beneath the blankets. But I can feel it when they begin loading the other passengers onto the ship. Muffled voices and footsteps emerge and fade in the passageway right outside my door. I hold my breath and scoot against the wall as much as possible, but no one ever touches the lock or handle, and soon the sounds are taken over by a low humming that grows into odd vibrations. The tremors are so strong they seep into the walls and cot and every inch of air until my bones are rattling with them. At some point there's a jolt and my stomach flips as the world around me feels like it's lifting.

I ignore it and just lie there. Until eventually my mind drifts to what Eogan is doing right now—what Eogan is thinking right now.

Whether he is aware of Draewulf overtaking him.

With that question comes an emotion I am not prepared to face, so I roll over and simply imagine I am dead. That my heart can't feel, my chest can't move, my mind can't think past anything but the numb, numb, numb until the humming has created its own sort of buzzing silence. Except after a while it's that silence that's screaming the loudest. In my bones. My blood. In the not knowing if Eogan is dying in this second or the next or the next. Not knowing if he's even aware, if he can feel what's going on, or if he's in pain. All I know is I can't do a blasted thing at this moment, and it feels more fragile and vulnerable than I ever imagined.

How ironic considering a week ago I was more powerful than any of us could've imagined.

That realization alone should make me bitter-laugh, but instead my mind won't stop replaying those moments at the Keep when I could've chosen differently. I could've anticipated Colin stepping in front of me. I could've forced Eogan to let me shield him until Draewulf was dead. Or I could've let Faelen get attacked longer and fought Draewulf myself.

And tonight . . .

Tonight I could've caught on quicker and reacted before Draewulf stole the one thing that has always been mine even when I detested it.

I roll over and listen to the ache and sputter of my heart beating the refrain that despite all the "could haves," this world is a pit of hulls.

I scratch at my wrist.

It's not until I scratch it again that I notice the old itch beneath my skin creeping in along my arm.

I scrub my fingernails over it, but no matter how hard I claw, the blasted feeling keeps coming back. Like this slow drip, drip, drip of poisonweed in my bones.

Until soon it won't stop and it's burning, scalding its way into my flesh with its hunger to carve an injury into my skin. *Go away, go away, go away,* I try to tell it, until I'm swearing and then I'm choking, and suddenly it's like this dam inside me erupts through the hate and fury and fear, and brings with it a blasted hurricane of grief.

Abruptly there are tears. And they aren't just clogging up my throat—they're spilling onto my cheeks, dripping onto my arms and hands and down to soak into my blanket. And I've no idea what to do with them or how to stop them.

I just know that eventually, mercifully, I succumb to a measure of sleep.

I'm aware of this because when I wake, the room is considerably brighter and my body's been sobbing long enough to become sore and empty except for that throbbing near my heart.

I sit up and find my way through the dim to my door and out to the hall where two Faelen guards jump to attention. Neither seems surprised at my emergence.

"The water closet?" I mutter.

One opens a door directly across from my room and positions himself in front of it once I've entered.

After I've used the bowl and finished washing my hands, I lean against the water basin and breathe in, and, after a minute, look up to find a tiny mirrored reflection of a girl with sunken eyes and a face so gray I barely recognize it.

Nice. Even my appearance looks lost.

I turn to go, but abruptly that thought hits and nearly splays me out against the wall.

I am lost.

I can't remember anything about me. I can't remember what I'm supposed to be aside from what Draewulf has taken.

I grip the bowl. Shaking. Horrified as the entirety of that realization sets in. *I don't know who I am.*

I reach down and pull out one of my knives from its sheath.

Desperate for some way to feel the burn deep enough to reach my soul and remind me of who I'm supposed to be. To erase that blasted itch that just won't cease.

I rinse it off with soap and water and press it against my left arm, beneath the tattooed bluebird, and begin to create a short, shallow line meant to be a branch for it to land on. To find her feet on.

I wait for the pain. The relief.

But even my old habits betray me as a sick feeling settles in my stomach that there is no rush, no horror. I utter a gargled laugh. There's nothing other than a few drops of blood and a dull sense of a scratched itch too easily appeased. I resheathe the blade and brace against the wall as the airship dips down. The nausea grows worse as the only emotion washing over me is a sense of gut-wrenching shame, that after all my newfound resolution two days ago, I have let myself down. Let Colin down. Eogan.

Litches. I blink hard and shut away the memory of his reaction the first time he saw me with a fresh self-inflicted wound.

When the airship steadies, I shred one of the drying cloths and bandage it around the shallow scratch. Then listen a moment as voices surge outside the room. It's Myles from the sound of it. I disengage the lock and edge it open, then peer out into the hall where the two Faelen guards and Myles are speaking.

Myles looks ill as he turns to me. "Ah, I've jussst come from explaining to the Faelen delegates that I have brought you along as a guest." He holds out a shaky hand. "Your knives, if you don't mind."

"Go to hulls, Myles."

"You certainly could've sent me there if you so desired." He studies my puffy eyes with a look of humored arrogance. "I'd like to think you chose not to because you couldn't bear the thought of never ssseeing me again."

"Maybe I thought I *had* killed you." But even as the words snap harsh, my undertone betrays me. We both know I *could've* killed him at that cave. I only left him alive because I couldn't bear the thought of adding another murder to my name.

With a click of Myles's fingers, both guards head down to the far end of the hall. He follows them with his eyes until they're a good distance, then he shifts his gaze back on me. "Oh my dear, you've a sharp wit but you're quite the wretched liar." He reaches a finger out to trace one of my memorial tattoos without actual touching it. "Perhaps that's why you can see through my abilitiesss."

I snort. "That or your abilities are more pathetic than you think."

His hand is instantly clamped on my arm, crushing my tattoos. My vision fades and then flares and suddenly I'm outside the cave where I left him and there's a bolcrane tearing through the forest into the clearing. The screams of the men it's killing are loud and real and just as haunting as my dreams ever since. The image shifts and Eogan is in front of me. The real Eogan—his eyes holding my gaze a moment before dropping to my lips. And then his mouth is brushing over mine just as another picture takes its place of Eogan's throat being slit. I gasp and push back.

"Pathetic? I think not," Myles says. "Which leaves me pondering why you didn't tell King Sedric of my ulterior allegiances. Fear perhapsss? Affection?"

"It doesn't matter." I blink away my fury as the vision fades and Myles's face and the hall come back into focus. There's not a bleeding chance I'm going to tell him the simple truth—that after a couple days, I really did fear the bolcranes had finished him off. And with everyone being so busy making good with Bron this past week, Rasha and I had been little more than ignored.

Tromping noises clomp from whatever room is above us.

He lifts up his fingers and flexes them into a fist. "Such a shame about your *own* abilitiesss. To no longer feel that power coursing through your blood—tell me, does the loss of it ache? Does it hurt to know you could've taken me up on my offer at the cave?" His fingers flutter over me again, this time brushing the skin on my neck and shoulders, sending an image into my head of what Myles and I could become together. Standing hand in hand over the five kingdoms. Powerful. Beautiful. Perfect. With Draewulf dead at our feet.

He leans close. "Too bad you don't know how to get them back. Especially since they might've allowed you to save lover boy."

I pull out both knives and jab for him, but suddenly the guards are there grabbing my arms.

"Ah, there we are. Now that wasssn't so hard." He takes one blade, then the other, and sticks them in his belt.

I hate him for it.

Next thing I know the airship pitches hard and he looks like he's going to vomit all over the lot of us.

"Excuse me," I say, and cross the four feet to my room and close the door. And wait for Myles's disgusting voice to fade down the corridor until only the airship's humming fills the air. Then pull the covers back over my head while I face the fact that, no matter how much I wish it, I am not dead.

CHAPTER 8

*S*CRITCH-SCRITCH.
  Scritch.
  Scritch.

The annoying sound overhead interrupts my space like every other whirring, clunking noise on this metal ship. Except this one is followed by a thump that's more suggestive of rats in the walls than gears turning. Or maybe I'm just going crazy from being stuck in here for an entire blasted day.

Scritch-scritch-scritch.

I yank the covers from my head and glare through the dim at the ceiling as it tilts slightly to the left with the bobbing of the ship. *They've got to be jesting. Where are the ferret-cats to take care of their vermin?*

I'm just climbing from the bed to pound on the wall and scare the fool things off when a small utterance of, "Busted hulls," slips through the thick, flat bars of a small metal square covering an air vent six feet up the wall in front of me.

I raise a brow and reach for my blades before remembering

Lord Myles, the blasted oaf, took them. Too late—the metal square is moving, pushing out. It wobbles, then drops with a *thunk* to the red-carpeted floor, and a black head pops out from the resulting hole that is too tiny for a normal person to fit through. *What in—?*

Wide, dark eyes blink at me, then frown.

I frown back. "Can I help you?"

Without replying, the head wriggles and stretches and suddenly the body it's attached to comes tumbling out, catching itself with its hands on the hole's rim before sliding swiftly and neatly to the ground.

It's a boy.

A very short one.

I wrinkle my nose. *And quite dirty by the smell of him.* He's wearing a suit that's black and red like the Bron guards and soiled from soot and grease. Even though the clothes look about three sizes too big for his small frame, his dark skin and proud set of his shoulders suggest he's used to wearing those colors.

A Bron stowaway?

"Are you her?"

I cross my arms and stare.

He narrows his gaze and pulls a knife from the back of his over-size pants. "I asked a question. Are you *her*?"

"Depends on who you're referring to."

"The Elemental. And don't lie 'cuz I already know you're her because of the—" He juts the blade toward my hair.

Very observant. I sniff and glare at his knife. "Are you here to stab me then?"

"Maybe." He eyes me. "Maybe not."

"Well, if it's all the same, I'd prefer not. All that blood. And what would your parents think? Or have they lost you?"

"They did no such thing." Fury flashes through his gaze and across his face. He lifts his chin. "I am responsible for myself."

I try not to smirk. Or acknowledge the fact that, despite my weary mood, I might like this small person. "Yes, I can see that."

I pick up the cup of water left by someone beside my bed during the night—probably a guard, *hopefully* a guard—and take off the lid to sip it as the ship shudders and rolls to the right. I take a seat on the cot and continue the bizarre stare-down with this boy who can be no older than eight. "Would you like a seat while you decide what it is you've spent the better quarter of an hour climbing through my air vent to do?"

He scowls. "I know what I came to do."

"Right. Perhaps we can start with our names then before commencing with the knife poking. I'm Nym."

He shifts his feet but says nothing.

I wait.

A moment longer and he utters a sigh. "Kel. And I just wanted to get a look at you."

I take another sip of water. "Now you've seen me—"

"Is it true?"

"Pardon?"

"That you could've done more damage to our army but you stopped?"

I slowly replace the lid and set the cup down. "Who told you that?"

"That's my business." He needles his blade toward me in a smooth gesture that says he actually knows how to use the thing. "Now answer the question. Are you more powerful than you showed everyone at the Keep?"

Who in blazes is he and why does he care? I study him harder as he stands there holding his breath, waiting for my reply, because something about this boy seems familiar. Not in looks or size, but in spirit.

It takes another moment for the awareness to dawn that, oh hulls, he reminds me of Colin.

A simultaneous ache and warmth hits my chest, and I swear my heart nearly splits open over this boy whose expression is still puckered in arrogant demand.

"Yes," I mutter. "And yes, I could've."

"A lot more? Then why didn't you?" His tone is insistent. Desperate.

"Just because you have power doesn't mean you have the right to harm others with it. I did what I had to for defense, not damage."

He nods and it's so serious, so solemn-like, as if this is somehow the answer he was seeking, although I have no idea how that helps anything. "Are you coming to Bron to attack us?"

"Of course not."

"Then why *are* you coming?"

"To be a delegate." I eye the blade still pointed at me. "How long have you been on this ship?"

"Since the battle at the Keep."

"You've been on here for a week? Hiding in the air vents?"

He pushes the toe of his soft boot into the carpet. "Only certain ones. And not all the time. There are a couple pantries and closets they don't use often."

"How'd you get to the battle in the first place?"

A shadow crosses his face. "That's Bron's business and not your concern." Without warning, he sheathes his knife and deepens his scowl. "I have to go now. They'll be flushing one of the cooling vents soon and I don't want to get caught in it. But . . ." He glances to the door behind him, which groans as the airship shudders on a wind current. "I warn you not to tell anyone you've seen me. Or else."

I put my hands up and try not to grin. *Got it.*

"They, uh . . . might not know I'm here." He turns to jump up twice toward the vent, only to discover he isn't tall enough to reach the hole's edge with his fingers. He lunges for it a third time while I watch, arms folded across my chest, impressed at his incredible prowess that is, unfortunately, unmatched by his height.

He growls and I bite back a chuckle.

I'm just debating whether to offer to hoist him when he apparently realizes that if he climbs onto the bed beside me and uses the extra two feet of height it gives, he can easily touch the opening. Before he leans forward to pull himself up, he flips back around to me. I straighten to look as solemn as him.

"I'm not finished with you, Elemental. I'll return when you least expect it."

"I sincerely hope you do."

And I mean it.

Then he's climbing back through from where he came, and I wait until he's disappeared to stand on the bed and put the small metal square back in its place.

And smile in total confusion.

CHAPTER 9

O pen your eyes, Nym."

I do and Eogan's face is the first thing I see. My heart lunges and soars all in one inhale—we're back in the Valley of Origin. I can taste the magic misting the air.

Tiny jeweled water droplets cling to his dark lashes. The drips shiver as he smiles before they release to join the millions of others floating around us in rainbow-lit colors. His brilliant green eyes smolder down at me, his heartpulse alive against my hand, sending my stimulated lungs clamoring for my throat.

I swallow and the storm in his gaze crackles in amusement. "You have no idea how extraordinary you are."

Suddenly I can feel the hunger pouring off of him as thick as it's leaching from me.

My jaw drops. The clouds in the distance roar and the floating droplets ascend to create new clouds of their own as a gale picks up, whipping my hair back.

Eogan raises a brow, and that thing in his eyes blazes. As if the same lightning storm above us is now poised at the edge of his heart, determining whether or not it will engage. I hear his breath shudder as my mind forms a definition for the look in his eyes: Craving. Conflict. Apology. The pulse in his neck quickens as his gaze slides down to my lips. He pushes a hand along the side of my throat and into my hair, then runs a thumb down my jawline as he tilts his face to hover an inch from mine. His finger stops beneath my trembling lower lip.

My world pauses.

His eyes flicker up. An agonized smile, and suddenly he's clearing his throat. But his voice is still husky when he says, "Look up."

"Nym. Look up."

I open my eyes.

"Nym. *Nym.*"

I blink.

And wake up, only to have my heart wrench through my rib cage as Eogan's face evaporates along with the memory of our afternoon spent in the Valley of Origin.

They're replaced by Rasha invading my vision. "Finally!" She's bending over me with an expression of relief and pushing open the small rain-speckled window.

Two seconds later the whole room rolls to the left and she loses her balance and tilts into me before the ship rights itself. The loud, incessant droning sound grows even noisier—like a swarm of bees that invaded an oliphant nest.

"Sorry." She shoves herself off. "The ship flies rougher than I expected. Seems they still have some problems to work out."

I sit up and look back to the window, and then I turn over to press my face through the open pane to the day-lit endless mass of glittering gray.

The familiar saltwater taste pricks my tongue and skin with that Elemental ache the sea invokes. That melodic whisper that strums like the notes of a death toll and solstice waltz all in one. But before I can grasp onto the sound, it's gone, and I can't recall the sensation.

I push the covers down and peek up at the metal square in the wall, half expecting to see the boy's face from last night. But the bars look as unmoved as before. Where did he disappear to? And why did he stow away in the first place?

Suspicion says he couldn't pass up the opportunity for an adventure or a chance to get a look at his, until recently, enemies. I smile. *Good for him.*

Glancing at Rasha, who's busy smoothing down her hair, I stand and promptly cringe at the flaring soreness in my legs. "What time is it?"

"Afternoon. Didn't you hear the men bring your meal this morn—?"

Her gaze lands on my arm. On the makeshift bandage covering it.

"Oh Nym," is all she says.

I force down the guilt that flares just as a knock sounds down the hall. We both jump, and I scramble to cover my arms before a Bron guard appears in the doorway.

"The dining area is now open if you ladies desire to join the other delegates there." He scowls at me.

"About time," Rasha says. "A day and a half's a bit dreadful to coop us up in these rooms, handsome. That is"—she sniffs and her voice goes airy—"if one can call these closets a room. We've been locked in these quarters since we took off—very inconvenient. I mean, look at me!" She swags a hand down her brown silk dress. "All but two outfits are in the storage bay! I made Lord Myles put a bag there for you as well," she says to me. "You're welcome."

The guard's eyebrow twitches. "Keeping everyone in their quarters was necessary for safety. The size and increased speed of the airship combined with the storm require we have as few individuals as possible in the main areas."

And what about in the ventilation pipes? I'm tempted to ask.

"And my men? I've not seen them since boarding."

"As I assured you earlier, they are being attended to with the utmost care."

"Of course they are." Rasha pats his cheek. "You've too friendly a face to treat them otherwise. Right, Nym? But I'd still like to see them."

This time his lips twitch, as if he's trying not to be flattered. "My apologies, but that's not possible at this time. They're rooming on the ship's lower level."

He steps out of my room and she follows. "So you're saying you have no access to the lower levels?"

"The weather and speed combination require us to maintain balance in each section. It would be unwise to allow any of the delegates into other sections while we're out over the sea."

I follow them into the narrow passage and bump into the two Faelen soldiers I saw the other night when Myles took my knives. "You and Myles got to keep *your* bodyguards. Well, at least two of them," Rasha says.

She sniffs. "Although I suggested he assign you an entire brigade."

The two men nod at me. In the light, one looks strikingly like Tannin, so much so that he could be his brother. Did they hear the boy and I talking last night? If so, they don't hint at it.

"Thank you for being here," I tell them before shadowing Rasha to where the Bron soldier is knocking on what I presume is Lord Myles's door. He's met by a loud groan of, "Go away," from within.

"He's been in there for hours. Apparently, airsickness." Rasha grins as the guard turns back to lead us down the short hall and out a metal door into a good-size dining area made up of stark metal walls, thin red carpet, and lanterns hanging from the ceiling. All focused around a long, thin, metal table at which the three Faelen delegates are seated. My stomach coils. I glance around but Eogan's not here.

"By the way," Rasha whispers in my ear, "Myles informed the other delegates that you're here at his request and King Sedric's permission. However, one of them's not, uh . . . too thrilled."

Glancing up, I catch the polite curiosity displayed on the faces of Lord Percival and Lady Gwen. Both of whom I recognize from attending Adora's parties. The third, Lord Wellimton, is openly ignoring me.

"Impressive, yes?" Lord Percival says to Princess Rasha, his eyes wide on mine. "A dining room that actually flies."

I turn in a full circle to take it all in as they stand to greet Princess Rasha. The airship must be the size of a glorified common house. On one side, two windows give a heart-gasping view of the sea, and there's even an outside deck. Clearly this is a royal airship rather than the battle ones we so recently sent running. Not exactly luxurious, but definitely impeccable in its simplicity—formidable even.

I look at the Bron guard and don't have to wonder how he feels about that. About losing the battle. And us.

"Where's Eogan?" I ask.

"King Eogan regrets he will not be joining the group at this time." The guard stiffly indicates the table laid out with mainly fruit and a type of gummy substance.

"It tastes like bread and keeps you chewing until it dissolves," Rasha whispers as the guard moves to stand with my two Faelen soldiers against one of the walls, which is reflecting a sliver of after-noon sun coming through the windows.

I nod at her and then stride over and peer through the thick panes at the stormy sea and gray sky pierced with yellow rays. The expanse of ocean is endless, and we're above it, soaring beneath the interspersed cloud covering. This must be how it feels to break free from the dust and flit away to inhale the sky. Like the bluebird carved into my arm.

The impact of that thought nearly pulls the breath from my lungs.

Abruptly, the cut in my arm warms along with my insides as the emptiness in my veins remembers it can no longer feed off the sky's static.

I join Rasha and the others before the sensation collapses me.

"And what of Lord Myles?" Lady Gwen asks Rasha.

"He's currently admiring the inside of the water closet."

Lord Percival nods. "Ah, seasick. Or airsick I suppose it's called."

"Have you enjoyed your time so far?" Lady Gwen reaches for a larkfruit, which as I recall from Adora's High Court parties is one of her favorite foods. An odd thing to remember except she's one of the few women on the High Council and, like Adora, comes from a long line of politicians. Although, unlike Adora, I'm not convinced she's ever wanted the job.

"Not particularly," Rasha says. "You?"

The three delegates' faces widen with surprise. Lord Percival chuckles awkwardly. As if he's hoping Rasha's joking.

When it's obvious she's not, Lord Wellimton clears his throat. "As guests on this ship, I've found the time alone to be quite restful."

"Well, I don't consider forced confinement restful," Rasha says airily. "Nor, I doubt, do my men. If anything, I find it distrustful."

"I'm sure you'd agree the confinement has been for our safety."

Without peeking up from the tea I'm pouring, I can feel Wellimton's gaze and tone indicating me. As one of King Sedric's top officials, he's the oldest bachelor on the War Council, and he has unfortunately chosen to wear that claim as a badge of honor as well as an excuse for his notorious irritability.

This is a waste. Where in blazes is Eogan? "I'm not the one you should be worried about," I say, handing the tea to Rasha. When she frowns, I quickly add, "Does anyone know when we *will* be graced by Eogan?"

"As I mentioned, he sends his regrets," the Bron guard growls from his spot along the wall.

"Oh, I'm certain this flight hasn't been all that dangerous, or Nym would've used her abilities to soften the storm for us. Right, miss?" Lord Percival dabs his mouth with a napkin and doesn't wait before turning to Rasha. "Princess, are you finding your negotiations with the new king thus far are up to Cashlin's satisfaction?"

"I've not had a chance to meet with King Eogan yet. Hence part of why Cashlin is sending me to Bron."

A pleased look passes over the delegates, as if they're relieved to still have the advantage of already starting the negotiation process back in Faelen.

I look at Rasha and consider telling them the truth—that their political insecurity is meaningless in light of what they're walking into. That there will be no negotiations in Bron because the king is not the king. And that I couldn't control a raindrop if I tried.

Rasha continues eating. I glance away and sip my sea-dragon-colored tea and chew on a giant piece of bread goo, leaving them to their momentary ignorance.

"Is your queen mother planning to send more delegates?"

Wellimton asks. "Or has she sanctioned you to decide what's best for Cashlin without her royal advisement?"

"Oh, I'm quite sanctioned," Rasha says cheerily.

"Not that she'd have any reason to doubt your political talents, of course, Your Highness. But considering the delicacy of the matter, I couldn't help but feel concerned for you when I observe Faelen has seen this venture important enough to send four delegates while Cashlin is only sending one."

I pause midswallow and almost laugh. *What a bolcrane.*

"You're correct she has every confidence in my talents, m'lord. And as I'm certain you're aware, I was the only Cashlin delegate available in Faelen at the time of our departure." Her smile stays just as wide, but I swear there's a falter in her tone. She grabs a plateful of the bread stuff and shoves a piece in her mouth.

I snap a look up at him. "What about *you*? Are you fully sanctioned?"

Wellimton frowns. "Of course we carry the full weight of King Sedric's authority."

"To do what?"

"To handle anything that may occur."

I clear my throat. "I bet. And what will you do if, say, when we arrive the situation's not as you've prepared for?"

Wellimton sniffs. "Young lady, I'm not sure why Lord Protectorate Myles or King Sedric deemed it necessary for you to come, that is, *if* in fact the king *did* allow it, seeing as we were only told about your attendance once in the air. But considering you've not been raised in politics, nor in a High Court home, I don't expect you to understand the process, nor the level of trade by which we'll be negotiating. We're clearly prepared for anything as long as you stay out of the way."

"Anything?" I can't help the smirk.

"I think the better question is, are *you* prepared for anything?" He bats a hand my direction. "Is that storm gift of yours under control?"

"Lord Wellimton," Lord Percival interrupts. "Perhaps we should be more charitable toward the heroine who is the only reason our nation is intact enough to trade with Bron. I'm positive the lady is quite capable of controlling it without Eogan even around!"

"A fact for which I am exceedingly grateful," Wellimton says. "As long as she's able to keep that level of control needed—at least until we get the negotiations wrapped up." He glances over at the Bron guard.

"I can say with certainty that I am the least of the problems you're walking into," I murmur, and ignore Rasha's look that says to quit egging him on.

"Good." Wellimton lowers his voice my direction. "And in regard to any rumored affections you might have toward the Bron king, I trust, if called upon, you'll do well to remember whose side raised you from childhood."

Gwen leans over to pat my hand. "Because, of course, if anything goes wrong, we're now counting on you to do your part, dear."

Do my part? I draw back from them both and stick a piece of fruit in my mouth. And shove down my cough before it gives away the fact that whatever expectations they have of using me are complete litches.

One, two, three moments of silence settle in, during which Rasha flicks me with cautious glances. I, in turn, extend sympathy to her for these ridiculous political games she's stuck in. Is this how the High Council operates? No wonder her Luminescent self gets overwhelmed by too many people in one room. Constantly hearing barely civil words being said while sensing what's left unsaid. It's all laced with suspicion and need.

The quiet is broken by Lady Gwen setting her cup down too loudly. "And what, Princess Rasha, may I inquire is Cashlin hoping for most in terms of negotiation and trade?"

"Our hope is to begin a friendship with Bron and build our way up from there. As far as trade, that will greatly depend on what Bron has that we deem worth trading for."

Lord Wellimton smirks. "A very to-the-point statement, Princess. Some might even say supercilious once you enter the negotiation chamber. Especially considering your kingdom avoided taking sides in the war at all costs."

"Cashlin makes no apology for being a pacifist nation."

"Of course not. But you can see how a good intention such as that could be misinterpreted at the negotiation table. It could appear your interests only lie toward what you can gain rather than in hard-fought-for unity."

Her voice stays steady but her shoulders tense. "Cashlin enjoys its friendships, Lord Wellimton, and we unabashedly support unity. However, we've discovered that taking sides in a war does not always result in desirable unity, nor does it mean we feel obligated to give up our natural resources easily. As I said, our hope is for the start of a relationship between Cashlin and Bron, just as we have done with yours."

Lord Percival tips his head in apparent approval just as the airship dips and rattles. From what Colin once told me, tipping his head is what Lord Percival does best. "It's his most pleasant and worst feature," Colin had whispered one evening while we were spying on him at Adora's. "It's like he can't 'elp but agree with everyone on everythin', includin' the king and the council. Even his wife from what I hear."

"Smart man," I'd mumbled, and Colin had punched me in the arm. But somehow that head tipping makes me now inclined to like him.

"And what about you?" Rasha continues. "What are you most hoping for?"

Wellimton shoots Percival a look. "Ahem. That's currently a matter of private discussion. You unders—"

"Access to your waterways for trade with their metal mines?" Rasha says in her airy tone. Her brown eyes exhibit a slight red glow. "With maybe some airships thrown in?"

The delegates' faces pale.

Before anyone can respond, I stand. "While this has been most interesting, I think I'll take a walk on the deck outside." I look at the Bron and two Faelen guards for permission, but the entire room shudders loudly and tips. With a clatter, the plates and food tumble across the floor and it's all I can do to hold on to the back of my chair, which, mercifully, is bolted down as is the rest of the furniture. I keep my feet beneath me until the ship tilts back. It trembles again and then the Bron soldier is holding his hand out to us. "My apologies, but the storm is picking up. I must return you all to your quarters."

"Why?" Lady Gwen asks.

"For safety. Now you'll all come with me, please."

"Oh Nym, take care of the weather, won't you, dear?" Lady Gwen flutters her hand at me. "That way we can stay and finish our chat!"

Percival nods. "Yes, show us how it works for you. It'd be fascinating to watch an Elemental control a storm. Here, what do you need from us?"

"That would be highly dangerous," the guard interrupts. "The use of her abilities would threaten not only this airship, but the one travelling behind us. Please, I'll see you to your rooms."

I shoot him a grateful eyeful, which he ignores, and step toward him when a shimmer of lightning flashes maybe seventy-five terrameters in the distance. Despite the ache it brings, I stride over to watch the three, four, five lightning bolts follow it. Because something about feeling its effect on the sky creates a fleeting sense of normal. A sense of power, even if from the outside rather than within, if only for a minute.

Lady Gwen's screech is jolting. "But those strikes are going to hit us. She can stop them!"

"No, mum, they won't. But we need to get you someplace secure. Miss?" the guard says in my direction.

I brush past him without replying, and as Lord Percival, Lady Gwen, and Lord Wellimton are led through a door separating their rooms from our corridor, Percival whispers, "You will stop them though if we need you to, right, Nym?"

When we reach the room, Rasha plops down on the cot. I sit beside her and pull my legs up, folding my arms around my knees. "Well, that was rather dramatic. Are you all right?"

"In regard to the fact that we're riding in a metal ship near lightning or those ridiculous politicians?"

"Both."

"I wouldn't be queen someday if either upset me." But she's wringing her hands as if to banish her nerves even as the words tumble out. Her hesitation is followed by, "And why wouldn't I be all right? I've got excellent political acumen."

I bite back a smile. "You were most definitely the smartest, most rational person in that room."

"I was, wasn't I?" She sniffs and a pleased expression replaces her worried features. "Although now I've got a stomachache," she confesses with a grimace. "I tend to eat fast when people get intense. What about you? They were rather needy about your abilities, I'll say."

"I'm wondering if we shouldn't just tell them."

Her look suggests I'm a daft fool. "About Eogan or your abilities?"

"My powers. The delegates seem to have rather high expectations," I admit.

"Who cares? Your ability is none of their business."

"Maybe. Except those expectations are only going to get higher. And when the time comes—" I drop my voice with the sudden awareness that the vent boy could be listening. I peer up at the metal square in the wall.

"You're not their obligated savior, Nym. They were going to Bron before they even knew you were coming."

I've not heard anything in the pipes other than air blowing since we entered, but I keep my tone low enough to be covered by the ship's noise just in case. "True. But even at the party the other night . . ." I scowl. "It's like they think I'm some kind of token that will protect them. It's suffocating."

Her smile turns sly and she pats me on the head. "Of course you're a token. A magical one who's only disappointing in matters of clothing choices."

A chuckle bubbles up in spite of myself. "I'm serious! Look at this." I tighten my deformed fingers into a fist. There's not even the slightest tingle in the air.

"So you're saying the power you always wished you didn't have is gone, but because everyone admires it, now you wish you had it back?"

"Not admires it. Expects it. And I'd rather they'd not do either.

But at the same time . . ." I search for the right words. "Maybe it's that I finally just learned how to use my curse to actually help people, and now . . . now I'm very likely going to let those people down."

She chews her lip and grows sober. "While I might not have known you for long, Nym, I can tell you your strength doesn't lie in your powers or the ability to cause a storm or whatever else the rest of them want to call your gift. It lies in your ability for compassion." She pokes a finger in my chest. "It lies in you."

I nod. *Right.* Except having compassion without the power to change anything is useless. I should know. I tried for years to untwine those two and it couldn't be done. And not just useless, it's dangerous. Because it breeds false hope.

Not only that but . . . being me *is* being Elemental. I feel out the bandage beneath my sleeve and press into it until my skin aches. I don't know how to explain it to her.

"Besides, if Bron and the delegates found out right now, can you even imagine what would happen?"

I roll my eyes and groan.

"And anyhow, the delegates wouldn't believe us. They'd just see it as a political stunt, and I'm not sure how that'd protect Eogan."

"I'm pretty certain I can protect Eogan without giving them false security in me. But I'm beginning to wonder if it's really a good idea to let them find out I've no power while we're in an environment Draewulf controls."

She shrugs, as if it's the question she's been wrestling over every bit of her waking moments with no solution.

"Exactly."

She leans her head against the window and stares out of it. "Draewulf won't completely control everything—he still has to prove himself to the Bron people. If that's even his intention."

"You think Draewulf will keep the façade up in Bron?"

"He's actively trying to eradicate all internal trace of Eogan, so my guess is yes. Especially since even the Bron guard on this ship doesn't know Eogan is Draewulf."

I follow her gaze through the rain lines beginning to drizzle down the pane—to the purple-gray ocean and, in the distance, the sun's muted glimmer. "Or maybe Draewulf's trying to eradicate Eogan because he knows Eogan can survive if the shape-shifter leaves his body too soon."

Her expression softens. As if she knows how much my heart is hanging on that one single hope. She opens her mouth. Closes it. And allows us to simply sit there, staring together at the ocean shimmering a few terrameters beneath us as the ship continues its race toward Bron.

"About your arm." She rouses after a bit. "You want to talk about it?"

"It was a mistake. I'm better now. Do you think Myles knows what Draewulf wants?"

She makes a sound very much like a scoff but doesn't say anything. Just shakes her head.

"What if we ask Draewulf the questions straight to his face— about what he plans to do with us and if there's a way to free Eogan? Could you determine Draewulf's thoughts then?"

She scrunches her cheek and peers back over at me. "I'm not sure. With Eogan's block in the mix, I could probably see if Draewulf's lying but not read his mind. Unless he's clearly planned out his path and Eogan's not confusing it. I'd have to be near him long enough to get a better sense, but even then . . . If the things you're hoping for have never been done, Draewulf himself may not actually know the answers."

"So it's worth a try."

Her smile is gentle. "I think so. But the better question is, can we get him alone for a few minutes *to* try it?"

I look down at my cut arm. At my fingers as I flex them into a fist.

"Let me take care of that."

CHAPTER 10

I HEAR THE BOY A GOOD HALF MINUTE BEFORE HE reaches the metal grate, mainly because he's grunting and cursing up a storm. The wall square squeaks, then pops out to fall and hit the floor again just before Kel drops into my already-darkening room.

He scrambles up and tries his best to look very serious, which ends up with him merely showing those big white teeth.

"You're back."

"Told you I would be."

"Well? What do you want?"

He shrugs. "Just making sure you're not doing anything you shouldn't be."

Because I assume he's doing enough of that for both of us. "Who have you been trying to stab this time?"

"I haven't. I've been sleeping mostly. I was listening in on the delegates for a while, but all they talk about is stuff they want from King Eogan. Well"—his face sours—"except for the cranky one. He talks a lot about his head and his back and his hard bed and the ship's noise."

I grin. "So does that mean you can get anywhere on this ship?"

His little face turns furiously proud. "Just about."

I eye him. "Such as the room where King Eogan is?"

He frowns. "You want me to spy on him?"

"It wouldn't be spying. I just . . . want to know if he's all right."

"You want to spy on him."

"Look, boy—"

"Kel."

"Look, Kel—"

"Is it 'cuz you want to kiss him?"

" 'Cuz I want to—*what*?"

"When a person likes someone and wants to marry them and have babies, they kiss them. And I heard one of the delegates say you like King Eogan. Is that why you're spying on him?" His tone says he finds this not only unnecessary, but wholly repulsive.

I stare at this boy who is the strangest small person I have ever met in my entire seventeen years. And burst into laughter. "No. I most definitely am not spying on him so I can have babies with him. I simply . . . want to ensure he's feeling all right. He's been ill and—"

"Then why's your face turning redder than the carpet?"

"I am not turning red."

He rolls his eyes and walks around the room, poking at the walls and lightly kicking the cot I'm seated on.

"Look, can you or can you not get near King Eogan's room?"

He shakes his head. "The only air vents I can travel are along this and the other delegates' corridor. Also, the kitchen and bathrooms and a few soldier areas. Besides, I wouldn't listen in on the king for you anyway." His face takes on that stoic expression, which is promptly darkened by a flash of fear. "And I don't think you should have babies with him neither."

Good, then we're both agreed. *Except* . . . I frown. "Did you know King Odion?" I ask on a hunch.

He nods and looks out the window into the night.

"Not very nice, eh?"

"He was a great king, brave and strong, the most powerful in all the Hidden Lands."

Right.

His small brow furrows.

"But?"

"He wouldn't have liked you. And he wouldn't have approved of you coming to Bron—not just 'cuz you defeated his army, but because he wouldn't have liked that you tried not to harm my people."

"*Not* to harm them?"

He nods again. "My people believe power is a responsibility to be used for striking down those who'd endanger our community. They'd think what you believe weakens it."

I don't tell him that at the moment I'm tempted to agree with his people and dead King Odion. "And what do *you* believe?"

He shrugs. "I don't know. Maybe power comes in different forms, and maybe we get a choice how we use it." He glances down and his eyes darken. "Maybe not everything that seems weaker is."

Then he looks back up. "But I gotta go now." He climbs onto the bed. "And you're not going to see me again until you're in Bron. But when you do, don't let them know you've met me. My father and family, they . . . they wouldn't like that."

I almost grab his foot to pull him back as he clambers up through the square hole. He can't go. I have more questions!

Too late though.

He's already through and *scritch-scritching* away.

CHAPTER 11

THE BRON GUARD DOESN'T ALLOW ME OUT OF the room again until the following afternoon, and just like before, the two Faelen bodyguards follow as well. Rasha and I are barely in the hall when she stops us all and says, "Can you give us a minute, handsomes?"

Is she going to bring up the boy, Kel? Has she seen him too?

The soldiers wait as she tips toward my ear and lowers her voice. "In case I don't get the chance to say this later, I want you to know I believe Myles is going to offer you something once we reach Bron. And on absolutely no condition should you accept."

Oh.

I glance toward his room. *Offer something? What could he have that'd be remotely desirable versus nauseating?*

"I sensed it the other night when we snuck on board and ran into him."

I wait for her to elaborate. She doesn't. "Okay. And his offer will be . . . ?"

"I don't want to say in case he changes his mind. I simply wanted to make sure I mentioned it before the day was out. Mainly because what he's got in mind is . . . unnatural."

Ha. I bet it is.

"I'm serious, Nym. What Myles *is*—what he does . . . I don't want to see him do that to you. I'm just telling you so you'll believe me and steer clear of whatever he's selling you."

"Oh, I believe you. I just have no idea what you're talking about."

A strange expression slips across her face. She narrows her gaze and seems about to say something but stops. "I apologize for the confusion, but I'd rather caution you against an idea than introduce you to it. And it won't matter as long as you decide now not to consider it. You are enough as you are. You'll figure this crisis out without his help."

An uncomfortable ache edges against my spine. I look ahead toward the door the Bron guard's holding open to the noisy dinner room.

Rasha's voice softens. "Promise me you won't follow him because while some of his desire is to actually help you, his other motives are not."

"What are his other motives—aside from the world-rulership obsession, obviously?"

"To use you."

I snort. *Nothing new there.*

"Fine." I pat her hand and pretend it really is fine. "I wouldn't trust Myles with a ferret-cat, let alone with whatever it is you're worried about."

Her sigh is loud and relieved. The next moment she's grinning and flourishing a hand at the waiting guards. "In that case, onward with the torture, gentlemen."

"Torture is the accurate word," I mutter, when we step through the door to find that, not only are all the delegates seated around the dining table, but so is Eogan.

I choke on the unbidden lump in my throat as everything within me begs to slip over and touch him, to connect with his calm, his closeness, to forget for one moment the monster beneath his skin. The next second I'm rocked by the look of absolute vileness on his face and have to fight the urge to locate the nearest knife to shove in Draewulf's gut in payment for what he's done.

Rasha gives my arm a quick squeeze of caution, and after a moment of glaring at him, I force my legs to move and make my way over to a chair at the end of the table near the windows. I sit and study the beast while Rasha takes her seat and my Faelen bodyguards hover nearby.

Lady Gwen is leaning over her plate. "So what did you say in response?"

Draewulf curls his lips. "I didn't say anything. I simply waited until she fell asleep and then sewed her mouth shut."

The three Faelen delegates burst out laughing, and for a moment their noise drowns out the airship's drone permeating the walls as Draewulf's disgusting comment slips effortlessly from Eogan.

I stare at them. *How can they laugh at that?*

He turns me a sly gaze and tucks a strand of jagged hair behind his ear. I narrow my eyes and debate revealing his horrific identity.

"Aren't you hungry, girl?" Lord Wellimton calls.

"I thought slave girls didn't get hungry," Draewulf says. "After all, the good ones are only useful for one thing."

The group howls with renewed laughter, and a shiver shreds my spine as he continues to leer.

The words the vent boy, Kel, said about his old king despising compassion float into mind. If that was the case, what will he

84

think of this new king? Will Bron applaud this disgusting Draewulf version?

Rasha stands, about to voice a defense from the look of it—but I stand as well and drain my face of all emotion. "It's fine. I was just leaving anyway."

On my way toward the door leading to the deck, I stop long enough to brush up against Draewulf and curl my fingers into a fist, as if my powers have returned. I lean into his ear. "Tell me, how does it feel to know you haven't quite won?"

Without waiting for a response, I straighten my shoulders and proceed to the small deck.

A Bron guard is positioned outside the door. "You have thirty minutes until we—" he says, as my Faelen bodyguards join him.

I nod, straining to hear him above the engine noise. Then stall because whatever he's mouthing suddenly doesn't matter when I look up.

The enormity of the airship is beyond comprehension. Overhead spans a white, larva-shaped balloon easily a quarter the length of King Sedric's castle. It billows slightly at the curved ridges and along the one tip I can see. Whatever's powering the ship is burning and creating heat ripples in the air around a giant metal chimney chute. Steam flows from it into a hole in the base of the balloon that is attached to the airship by metal ropes similar to the ones Eogan used to control our man-eating warhorses.

The ship bumps five times in a row, as if it's a farm cart riding over tills of soil. The vibrations beneath my feet are jarring compared to standing on the floor inside. I edge to the railing and glance down over the bulk of the ship to what I presume is the lower level. A few windows dot here and there, but for the most part, it's a hull of shiny, glistening metal big enough to hold servants, guards, food storage, and probably whatever fuel they use for burning.

Above it sits the level we're on, which appears to simply be the dining and bed quarters. And on top of that sits a smaller section—made up of what, I can't tell. I peer high at the single row of windows. *Is that where Eogan's been hiding?*

"A bit freezing out here, don't you think?"

Flipping around, I discover Myles ten feet away. A superior smile is playing around his pale mouth as he leans over the metal railing, arms spread like a bird with the wind and rain ruffling his black hair.

I frown and walk over to him to find the raindrops are being thrown full force beneath the balloon here as the ship rushes along on the air currents. The water pricks my skin, making it feel alive and nervous as Rasha's warning flares in my head. "Where are my knives?"

"Not hungry, eh?" he says, ignoring my question.

I scowl at him, at his thin face which is pale, but no longer green. "Couldn't stomach the company."

"Ah yes. Whereas me? I couldn't ssstomach the food." He glances out at the ocean. "Impressive though, isn't it?" He stays watching a minute longer before turning back to smooth his hair and tip his head at the dining area. "About that nauseating company . . . Care to speculate what his plansss are?"

"The man who makes it his business to know everything, doesn't know?"

"Ah, but Rasha would've already told you I don't."

"How about a guess? I hear you're good at it."

"I suspect in thisss case, your estimation is as good as mine, my dear."

"Then I'm afraid neither of us is going to get far."

He turns back to staring at the ocean.

I step closer, my tone cautious. "How long do you think before he does something with all of us?"

"I think the better question is, how long do we have before Eogan loses his battle inside his own body? That, I suspect, will be the defining point for the rest of usss."

I make a snide face. Clearly he doesn't seem too traumatized by the prospect.

Except . . .

My chest tightens. I narrow my gaze and study every crease and twitch of his aristocratic profile. "Do you think Draewulf can be separated from Eogan's body without killing him?"

"How would I know?"

"Like I said, you make it your business."

"Alasss, that is not an area I've ever cared to look into. Although . . ." He eyes me. "If anyone could have helped separate them, it would've been an Elemental. Too bad you don't have the ability any longer to find out."

"That's not funny."

"It wasn't intended to be."

"If my abilities could've freed him, I would've done so the other night."

"If you'd been trained correctly, yes. Especially considering Elementals have always been the most powerful Uathúilsss. But, as I said, how would I know?"

"You're suggesting you could've trained me to separate them?"

His gaze moves from my eyes, to my hands, to a quick, aloof sweep down my body. "I may know someone who could've advised me."

He has my attention as well as my suspicion. "Who? Are they still around?"

"Ah." He taps the side of his head. "That, my dear, is, for the time being, my business to know, not yoursss. However . . . it wouldn't make much difference, would it, now that your abilities are gone. Unless . . ."

I clear my throat. "Unless?"

"Unless you got new onesss."

I exhale. "That's not possible. Everyone knows you can't give a Uathúil abilities. You have to be born with them." I turn from him and his vapid game and glare out at the water. If the idea of training me was his offer, it's nothing new. And Rasha had nothing to worry about. She and I can laugh about it later.

"My dear girl, is that what Eogan told you?"

I go still.

He smiles. "How do you think I have powersss?" Abruptly the ship bumps and tilts beneath us and Myles's expression goes the slightest bit nauseous.

I swerve to stare at him. My breath is suddenly clobbering my throat. Maybe I should go inside now. Except I want to hear what he has to say. Besides, Rasha said that *if* he offers anything, he'll do so in Bron. I count to thirty before I give in. "How?"

"*How* what?"

"How's it possible? How do you have them, and how would I?"

"If I told you, that'd take the fun out of it."

"So in other words you don't know, and even if you did, you'd never willingly help Eogan."

He smirks.

Exactly. "Why don't you go back to your water closet?"

"I'd never willingly help unless I've set my sssights on bigger things than Sedric's throne." His gaze slides down my arm, as if bigger things could have anything to do with me. My responding glare could rip his eyes out.

He licks his lips. "I assure you that while you are in fact one of the more fascinating women I've ever met, I wasn't only referencing you. Believe it or not, I may have a mind to save the world when all isss said and done."

"By taking it over? How heroic."

"Oh sssweetheart, we both know I'm not heroic. I'm nearly heartless and completely brilliant and a wonderfully attentive suitor when feeling up to it. But no, no, this has little to do with heroicsss." He leans close and swipes a long, cold finger down the sleeve covering my left arm. "Let's just call it . . . a sssoft spot I have for power, which will benefit all five kingdomsss, and you, if you'll allow me to help."

A sick feeling emerges, like ill-placed hope blossoming at the base of my mind. I shake it off. "It can't be done."

"The new abilities or the separating? Because I promise the first can."

I stare at him.

Coils of twisted hunger slip down my spine and touch my heart. *This is his offer.*

New abilities that could save Eogan.

His finger swirls over the bandage beneath my sleeve. "Such a shame to see your powers so quickly discarded. Especially when they sssimply needed a more effective trainer . . ."

I shake him off. "Even Rasha doesn't believe separating them can be done." But my voice is weaker this time. How could she not have told me? How could she have acted so casual if she really knew what he would offer? If she really knew what this could mean. To me.

Especially when she admitted there are no other options for saving the one person I care for.

"She may be right, on that I won't lie to you. But when you go to sssleep tonight, ask yourself which one of us would be willing to risk and find out—a passive Luminescent or the second most powerful Uathúil you know trained by Eogan himself?"

His words snag at that slithering hope and without my permission billow it out with what we both know to be true—if anyone could know how to do this, it would be him. Suddenly I'm jittering all over. "I can't," I whisper, as behind us a door opens and then closes. "Don't bring it up again."

He looks up and lowers his voice to a mumble. "Your choice. But if you truly want to help him? Ask yourself if Eogan is worth *your* risk." With that, he pushes off the railing and strides past me.

A few seconds later I hear the door to the dining room shut, and I am left with an armful of questions and horror and a desperately inflating hope that's burning more questions into my mind than answers.

Could Myles help me get my power back? Would I actually be able to free Eogan in a way he could survive?

Could I free him in time?

I stare at the span of clouds and the sunset peeking between sky and water on the horizon and try to make some sort of sense out of the possibilities. Because while something tells me Rasha's right—that Myles's idea feels more slimy and more sinister than he let on—the very thought that I could free Eogan, that I could set this right, is enough to make my angry, hateful soul feel like breathing again.

CHAPTER 12

I'VE STOOD THERE A GOOD FIVE MINUTES BEFORE THE new presence emerges in my consciousness. I feel him before I see him. Standing there watching me.

For the split second after I turn to face him, Eogan looks normal, with the clouded sun rays and rain misting on his broad cloaked shoulders and face. My heart surges. The next moment his expression has morphed into a mixture of annoyance and suspicion and he's demanding information with his eyes. As if Draewulf's come to ensure his job of removing my ability has remained intact.

I shove aside my newfound hope and nausea and firm my fists. *Get the answers from him, Nym.*

He's walking toward me. I peer past him toward the dining area, but the door's windows are too small to see through. *Where's Rasha?*

And where are my Faelen guards?

"You may think you're smart sneaking on board this ship, but tell me you didn't truly believe it was luck that no one caught you," Draewulf says when he reaches me. "Or did you think me such a fool? You're playing a bloody game here."

"Where are my guards?"

He snorts. "I asked them to give us a moment of privacy."

"And they obeyed?"

"I didn't really give them a choice." He holds out his hand.

When I don't move, he glares down that attractive nose and grabs my arm. And presses into it hard enough that I can feel the pulsing of my own blood in my veins. I jerk away, but he's already releasing it, seemingly satisfied that I have no power, although how he could tell is beyond me. Perhaps because I didn't erupt and send a lightning bolt through his face.

He tucks a strand of bangs behind his ear and bends low enough that the wind whips my hair against his. "Make no mistake that I will kill every delegate here the next time you pull a stunt like that."

He glares at me for one, two, three seconds longer. Then, without another word, he turns to stalk away.

"You'll kill *them* but not *me*?"

He stops.

My arm begins throbbing where the cut is, and the grief and hatred abruptly blend in with the idea that he honestly believes he can take everything that's mine. I narrow my gaze. "Why not? You could just finish me now. Or is it that you need me for something?"

He snarls. Flips around.

"Or perhaps it's Eogan inside preventing you." I step forward until I'm near enough to see the disgusting wolfish black of his eyes rimmed by Eogan's green. "Tell me how it feels to know he's still in there fighting you. To know he could still destroy you."

Before I can dodge, his hand reaches behind me and yanks my head back, exposing my neck. He shoves me against the railing and about breaks my bones with the impact. He raises a fist, his body rippling in rage as he brings it toward my face.

I don't even flinch. I smile.

I have found his weak spot.

His arm is an inch from my cheek when it stops.

Suddenly the rage shaking his body is growing stronger, more violent, and an odd look erupts in his eyes.

I frown and watch the black recede from the pupil and the green become brighter as his face flickers with confusion. As if waking from a dream and unsure of what's real.

He looks around us, at the ship, at the sky, at his own body and me. He drops his hand. "Nymia?"

My heart stops.

My blood stops.

Everything stops.

Because it's him. It's those green eyes that are pure and brave and slightly arrogant in their own right. The kind of arrogance earned from a once-unfeeling heart that's tasted brokenness.

"Nym." His voice is husky. "Oh kracken—are you all right?" He tips my chin and searches my eyes before sweeping his gaze down as if inspecting every spare inch of me. His tone lowers to anger. "Did he hurt you?"

I have no words. It's all I can do to breathe while my insides become an instant roar of joy and hope crashing against the broken spaces as his hands slip into my hair. I shake my head because, no, he didn't, then nod because yes, he has, and I don't know. I don't care. The question is—"Did he hurt *you*?" I push back to look in his handsome face as his expression clouds and run my fingers up his onyx cheeks. I press his jagged bangs from his eyes. "Are you okay? Is he actually gone? What did you—?"

He shakes his head and leans into my fingertips as his body keeps doing that shivering thing. I watch his eyes close. Suddenly he's pulling me into him, holding me against the warm beating of his chest even as he's trembling in a way I've never seen.

"Nym, you have to kill me before—"

I choke loudly and pull back. *What?*

"He'll destroy you and then everyone else. My people. Your people."

"How do you know? Can you see him? Can you see how to stop him?"

He shudders. "He's still here. I'm blocking him, but it won't last long. And I can sense enough to know whatever he's plotting will end in bloodshed for all of us. I keep trying to do it myself but he's too strong. If you destroy my body before it's too late . . ."

I'd rather cut out my own veins. "You don't know for sure it'll end badly."

His green eyes find mine. *Yes, he does.*

No. I want to cover my mind. *I can't believe this.*

"It's not open for argument. It *will* happen unless you—"

"Not a chance in hulls," I whisper. "You can't ask me to do this—and even if I could, Draewulf took my powers."

"I know. You'll have to use a knife. If you plunge it in at the back of my neck, it'll kill us both."

I don't answer. I can't. My lungs are blocked, my breath is blocked, and *how can he think I could do this? How can he ask me to kill him?* I look around for something—anything—to fix it. To stop this. *Myles.* "Myles thinks there may be a way to save you, and if I can just—"

"*Myles?* He's dangerous—"

"I know what he is, but are you serious, Eogan? What you're asking of me . . . I won't. Not before I have the chance to try. And Myles says—"

"You can't trust anything he says." He takes on his trainer tone—the serious one he'd use when Colin or I would take risks too heavy for us. "I'm telling you . . . I'm asking you—"

"I hear what you're asking! But are you jesting me right now? Your people need you. *I* need you." My voice cracks.

His face softens. He flutters a finger down my face, my hair. "I've already damaged you enough for one lifetime—there's no bleeding way I'm doing it again. Or have you forgotten what I did to your parents?"

What a bolcrane. "Don't you dare use that on me, because honestly? What would you do if I was in your predicament right now?"

He snorts. Then he inhales and pushes a black hand through his black hair, which only succeeds in making it endearingly messy in his all-too-familiar way. "It doesn't matter because it's *not* you. And—"

"Right, it's not. So are we honestly going to stand here arguing about it when we should be figuring out how to free you?"

He runs a hand through his hair again and eyes me. "I've been working on that."

"And?"

A flash of apology crosses his face.

"I don't believe that. I *refuse* to believe that."

"You have to. Otherwise . . ." His voice hardens even as his gaze drops to my lips. "Please believe me that he's going to hurt you, Nym. And while that may not matter to you, it certain as hulls matters to . . . others." I watch him swallow as the expression in those beautiful green eyes turns begging. He traces a finger down my cheek. His thumb stops beneath my chin and nearly crumbles me. Abruptly I am dissolving against his chest like paper flowers in a puddle and he is enclosing himself around me. "Listen. When you get to Bron, I need you to find Sir Gowon and explain what's happened to me. Tell him about Draewulf." He leans into me so close, as if to ensure only my ear will hear. "Tell him Elegy 96. He'll know what it means."

"Will he be able to help you?"

He doesn't answer.

"Eogan, will he be able to help you?"

"Hopefully he won't need to by th—"

I move my mouth to his so fast to shut him up. He startles, but the next moment his lips are pressing down against mine, drinking in as if he's been thirsty for emotion and warmth for far too long. Melting me into a tangle of heartstrings as everything I am, everything I thought I'd lost, rises to the surface. I push my fingers into his hair to pull him closer, tighter, because I cannot leave, I cannot breathe, I cannot let go of this moment.

His teeth catch my lip just as the shaking in his body grows stronger. He pulls away. "Promise me you'll end this."

I shake my head because nothing in me is ready for this. I still need to know—to find out—what will become of us, of him, of our future. I refuse to answer.

His response is one single nod. I can see it in his eyes—he knows I will not do it. Not when hope is standing here in front of me.

The next thing I know he's gently edging me aside and placing his hands on the airship railing. His fingers grip down, and when I look up he gives me one last look of apology.

What is he—?

He lunges. I grab for his arm but it doesn't matter—whatever control he has isn't enough to throw himself over. His knuckles turn white and his muscles are rippling with the effort. He's straining forward, but his body won't move, as if pinned by another force.

His expression collapses in pain just before his body flaps like the air around us.

I grab his shoulders and shake, but his eyes are already altering. "No, don't—" The black seeps over the green and that glimmer of Eogan fades, and Draewulf tips his head at me. As if unsure of where we were in our conversation.

He looks around, then smirks. "Rest assured Eogan will be gone soon enough once Isobel joins us. And then? Every time you look at me, you'll know what real control is."

He spins around and takes two steps before halting. I glance around him and see the Bron guard standing there. How much he's heard I'm not sure, but his face has paled to match the color of ocean foam.

Draewulf utters a deep, guttural growl and strides toward him and, faster than should be possible, yanks the guard off his feet.

No! I gasp, but my grabbing for him is too late. The monster's already lifted him by the Bron jacket and shoved him toward the railing. He flips him over it and the guard cries out, but the wind carries the sound away, a lone voice fading as his body flutters and floats to the water.

We're up high enough that I don't hear the splash when his body hits, but it's big enough that I know he's instantly dead.

The next second I'm reaching for my blades, which aren't there, then I'm throwing myself at Draewulf, pounding his chest. I shove his arms, his shoulders.

His response is a backhand across my cheek.

I teeter at the force but don't fall—I've been struck enough times to know how to take a hit. But my eyes burn all the same. I grit my teeth and watch the guard's head sink below the waves.

Draewulf grips my gimpy arm and a flash of disgust ignites in his gaze. Followed by a hardening that makes my veins burn. My hand curls beneath his as I will it to scald him with a slew of ice from my fingertips. Nothing happens but I'm clenching his shirt anyway, because I don't know how to let go as a stream of curses lashes out of my mouth and whips down to share its saltiness with those same waves that consumed the guard.

"I hate you," I murmur. But my voice is the the broken chirp of a bird.

He laughs without mirth and pushes me off like some girl from a favor house. "You've lost already. Don't debase yourself more than you already have."

He smooths his shirt just as an enormous horn sounds out above us, causing me to cover my ears and him to jump. He spins around and I follow suit to see land in the distance, just where the sun is peeking out along the purple-ribboned edge of storm clouds and horizon. Below it sits a city gleaming with red, orange, and pink reflections from the sun.

"Welcome to the beginning of your end," Draewulf snarls behind me.

CHAPTER 13

THE HORN BLASTS AGAIN AND BY THE TIME I TURN back, Eogan is disappearing round the corner and all five delegates are tumbling onto the deck followed by the two Faelen bodyguards. I'm still reeling as the delegates' delight carries above the ship's droning. Murmurs of, "Will you look at that? It's fantastic!" and "Look at those warboats!"

They're pointing at the stretch of coastline between us and the city. I wipe the rain and fury from my face and realize they're ogling the same boats I pushed back from Faelen. Large. Maneuverable. Painted in red and black with an aura that screams "death" to anyone approaching. Here and there undamaged Bron airships loom above them like giant flags strapped to the boats' bows and sterns, sporting those painted-on dragons.

"Are you all right?" Rasha slips in beside me. "I mean, I see you're still alive."

"Where were you?" I hiss. "I had Draewulf alone!"

"I was stuck arguing with Lord Wellimton." She frowns. "I saw your guards come in but they looked confused."

"Never mind that." I shake my head, my lungs feeling like

they're shriveling. I stare at her until I've got her full attention and I'm not sure whether to laugh or whimper. "I saw Eogan."

Her eyes widen.

"He forced aside Draewulf so he could speak to me. It was fully him, but . . . then it was Draewulf and he killed the guard so fast I couldn't stop him. He said he'd do the same to the delegates if I interfered again."

Her eyes have grown to the size of hornets' eggs. "He did what?" She moves her stare from me to behind us where Draewulf disappeared. "How did Eogan find that much control? And how could . . . how . . . ? Did he say anything that could *help* us?"

I glance around. At the delegates. At the guards. I'm fairly certain the Elegy 96 message was meant for my ears alone. "He asked me to kill him," I say softly.

"*Pardon?*" Her shocked tone draws the attention of the entire group. "Was that all he said?" she whispers.

"I asked if he knew Draewulf's plans but he didn't. Although he could sense enough to say it's not good and killing them both is the only option."

"*How* not good?"

"Something along the lines of 'we're all going to die.' "

Behind us, Myles chuckles. "Tell me something we didn't know. Next time how about asking a few more specificsss."

I glare. "He was pretty specific about you. And I'll take my knives back now, seeing as you've nothing better to do."

"You'll have to check your luggage bag, which is—"

"Nym." Rasha snaps her finger twice in front of me. "Did Eogan say *how* you could kill him?"

I swerve my gaze back to the shoreline and purse my lips before muttering, "A knife to the back of the neck."

She falls silent, but I feel her nod beside me as a few feet away, the delegates' anticipatory chatter grows deafening.

Myles bumps me, and when I glance up, his expression is a mixture of what surprisingly appears to be legitimate sympathy and that slimy, persuasive offer. I blink and refuse to acknowledge it—and instead go back to staring at the coast as the drizzle lessens into a fine mist.

The rain stops altogether as soon as we're flying above the warboats and the host of downed airships behind them. Which, mercifully, don't look as mangled as I'd expected. A few appear battered and waterlogged, but most show signs of having been purposefully landed in their current, if random, positions.

Lord Percival gives a quiet whistle. "Nicely done, Nym."

I don't respond. Nice isn't the word I'd use. *Necessary* maybe. Although something in my raw heart lightens a bit. *I didn't kill as many men as I feared.*

We pass over them, and soon the beaches turn into tan dirt that stretches out into a bland-looking landscape just as the clouds ahead part to reveal the last death throes of a late-afternoon sunset.

"Look at that place." Lady Gwen points at the silver city spreading out in front of us.

It shines like an engraved metallic button on a brown coat of earth. The nearer we get, the more intricate it becomes, with everything about it looking intentional, efficient, like one of the round gears on a horse cart, with a river running through the middle. Even the buildings resemble miniature axles crammed together alongside clusters of towers, which are topped with pointed copper domes. Near those, giant pipes rise up from the underbelly, pumping out smoke or steam as if the city's whole foundation is on fire.

Myles shoves between me and Rasha to stretch over the railing and look down. A moment later the whole line of us has followed his example to take in the city's surrounding wall. It's enormous, with holes where the tributary is pouring forth on the far side into a river that sparkles like the city beneath the cloud-cloaked sky. Aside from rust-brush dotting here and there around the banks, the landscape looks devoid of plant life—of any life for that matter beyond the smattering of strange houses with flat roofs and few windows.

My heart winces for Eogan. What a depressing place to grow up in. The look on Rasha's face says she's thinking the same.

A metallic scraping sound is followed by the entire ship suddenly shuddering around us. Then we're coming in fast and the city is looming, big and metal with streets jutting out from the center like spokes on a spindle wheel.

Lady Gwen shrieks that the airship's going to scrape the highest building when it makes another loud shifting noise and tilts and lunges toward the side, forcing us to keep our grips on the railing. We descend toward the long, wide streets filled with people. Thousands upon thousands of them, all the beautiful black color of Eogan's skin, and Kel, and the Bron guards around us, all dressed in red, all moving and waving together like some rich carpet, covering the walkways and blending in with the red-and-black Bron flags hanging from the sides of the metal buildings.

The sight of them curdles my stomach. *Draewulf's going to destroy everything. My people. Your people.* Oh hulls—what have I done? How do I choose him over them?

"It's a party." Myles promptly smooths his hair back and adjusts his oversized cravat.

The ship drops into the shadowed straightaway of the first street, so fast and low it's a wonder we don't squash the crowds or scrape the buildings rising up beside us. A fine red dust begins filling the air in front of us, breezing into us. People are sprinkling it down from the highest windows. It smells sweet—like flowers and fruit—and clings to our skin before slipping down to the ship floor and then off onto the masses clamoring in the street below.

"If only my grandfather were alive to see me here," Lady Gwen whispers. "It's beautiful."

"It's a parade for their new king," Lord Percival says.

A new king who isn't a king at all but a monster who will murder this city with abandon.

Welcome to the beginning of your end.

Lady Gwen is fluttering one hand while keeping a death grip on the railing with the other. "A positive show of support for us despite the fact Nym almost destroyed their entire armada."

"Let's hope what they remember is the fact that she *didn't* destroy it," Myles says.

I tug my white braided hair back and tuck it beneath my shirt so it's mostly out of sight as Lord Wellimton looks over. "Let's hope her being here doesn't cost us these negotiations. So I'll remind you that this is the part where we wave and make them love us. So smile, everyone."

They smile.

And wave.

Although the more spindled streets we turn onto and the more people the delegates smile for, I'm sure I'm not the only one noticing the inflating tension in the place. A sense of wariness.

The crowds are putting on a show too.

Is Kel watching from one of his ventilation pipes?

"Do you think they were forced to give thisss greeting?" Myles says to Rasha through his teeth.

"There's too much noise for me to tell, but I suspect it's a test of strength."

Myles snorts. "Ours?"

"Of Eogan's as their new king."

Sixteen, seventeen, eighteen streets we've travelled down when Myles leans over again. "You sssee that? The houses and buildings are almost identical. It's their way of keeping order. They've made everything uniform so there'sss no competition. Very smart when you think about it."

Rasha recoils. "But how do they distinguish themselves creatively? How could they feel unique and that they can succeed to something better?"

"They're warriors, not philosophers, Princess. A sense of duty and unity keeps them a well-oiled machine. Quite literally, from the looksss of this city."

She sniffs. "You sound as if you admire it."

"Oh, I do," he purrs. "Why do you think I wanted to come? Imagine the way I can use my gift on them."

I turn him a look of disgust, at which he scoffs. "Don't look so repulsed. If it makesss you feel better, it's their purity of motivation I find refreshing."

"And how often did you visit here when you were betraying *your* country?"

He bends so near a rush of chills scampers down my skin. "Careful there. My experience here could save lover boy and everyone else's livesss."

I clench my jaw and glance at a preoccupied Rasha. He returns to smiling and waving.

We've finished the thirty-sixth street when the airship crosses over one of the outer circular ones and turns onto a thin road that looks as if it will take us in one final curve around the entire city. Here, the buildings are neat and ordered, but their style is different, more intricate in their windows and archways. They're older.

"Must be where the wealthy live," Lord Wellimton murmurs.

"We don't have castes here," a Bron guard behind him says. He's flanked by three others as well as the two Faelen soldiers. I wince with the sudden reminder that there should be another Bron guard with them. Do they know yet that Draewulf tossed him overboard?

Wellimton makes a sound of interest, so the man continues. "In our city, no one is wealthy or poor. Our citizens are simply seg-regated into jobs. This section is for the elderly and our teachers."

"What about that out there?" I point to a large patch of land in the distance, terrameters beyond the circular city wall. It looks black, smoky in the late-afternoon light, like a carpet of crawling darkness.

The guard shrugs as if it's of no consequence and turns his gaze. But not before I catch the flash of fear in it.

I look at Rasha who's leaning over the edge, fluttering her hand at some children below. When I peer up, I see Myles, too, appears to have missed the guard's reaction.

The airship follows the rim of the spindle all the way round the city's edge until we're abruptly facing the palace. *Eogan's home and place of his birth.* Even with the sun down, the copper that covers every inch of the outdoor staircases and walls all the way up to the spires at the top is shining. As the ship moves into position over it, I can peer down into a giant, flat courtyard garden atop the main roof—the first real bit of green we've seen since entering Bron.

I frown. "Are the farms farther outside the city?" But no one seems inclined to give an answer, least of all the guards.

The ship shivers as it slows, groaning when we come to a stop over a giant stone-paved pad.

No crowds congregate here. Only guards, forty by my count, a few of which are the size of ten-year-olds, standing at attention on the platform, while five more hold the ropes for the lowering ship. Aside from the droning noise and the excited chatter of the delegates, there's little other sound.

Just as I think the ship's captain means to actually set the hull on the ground, the order is given and a plank is lowered into a slanted position. I turn to watch as two of the soldiers walk up it and stand aside, and Eogan appears from the cabin beside the dining room. The men slap their right fists over their chests in salute.

My eyes narrow but the monster inside Eogan ignores me and proceeds to descend the ramp.

At the bottom, an elderly man is waiting. He holds out his hand, which Eogan-who-is-Draewulf takes and places over his own heart, and the air deflates from my lungs at the reminder that he has been here before. With Isobel, when Eogan was a child, for a few years by my recollection of Eogan's story.

He'll already know their habits. And their weaknesses.

I look back at Myles and Rasha with a mouth tasting of ash. Rasha's watching the old man intensely, but Myles's mouth presses into a thin line as he stares back at me. Challenging me with the quiet question of what risk I'd be willing to take to fix it. To fix all of this.

"This way," someone says, and our flanking guards lead us to the plank.

"How does a balloon of air hold up such a thing?" Rasha murmurs.

I shake my head, but as soon as we've reached the bottom, I pull her away from it as fast as they're leading, lest it tilt and accidentally crush us. The thing looks three times as intimidating as it did in the dark back in Faelen.

The waiting Bron soldiers surround us, and I realize the shorter ones aren't just the size of children—they are children, perhaps between eight and thirteen years old, leading us across the courtyard toward one of the copper doors of the palace. I search for Kel among their faces even though I know he's still on the ship. *Is this what he does too? Act as a child soldier?*

My legs feel like jelly and Myles's must as well because he's limping funny.

"For admiring the warrior spirit, you don't walk like one," Rasha tells him. She peers back at me and giggles. "He's certainly a wobbly baby, no?"

Myles sniffs and looks like he'd like to make her face wobbly. Which only makes her laugh more as we enter the building and the long hallway lined with more soldiers.

One hundred, two hundred, three hundred paces, the floor is gradually tilting upward so that by the time we emerge into a wider corridor with windows, we're looking out over the city again. But I'm hardly paying attention—I'm watching Draewulf edge along outside our group, with his shifting eyes and that same expression he had when he killed the poor airship guard.

He's eyeing every Bron here with it.

I slow. The delegates keep walking as the elderly man who met Draewulf at the base of the airship moves ahead and announces, "His Majesty has matters to attend to. Come, I will show you to your rooms."

I dig my fingers into my bandaged palms and look to the side for Draewulf.

"Don't look so nervous, pet." His growl in my ear makes me jump. "They'll think you don't trust me."

When I turn, that disgusting wolfish curl of his lip is two inches away. I lift my fist.

"Ah-ah. Watch yourself or else their blood will be on your head." He smirks. "At least, sooner than the timing I have planned."

"Leave me alive and I *will* kill you," I say quietly.

"If you still had your Elemental power, I'd believe you. Sadly, that's why I had to eliminate your kind." He reaches out and pats my face. I flinch.

I grab my stinging cheek only to find that when I pull my hand away, it's tinted with blood. "You blasted—"

He raises his hand to give me a good look at his fingers, which are beginning to curl and his nails are growing longer. Like claws. He leans in. "Don't worry, pet—not much longer and he'll be free. Forever. Because even you can't stop me now." With that he turns and nods to the Bron escorts who instantly enfold him before hurrying him away.

Leaving me with the terrible assurance blooming that he is beginning to absorb Eogan's body.

I swallow and watch him, that horror in me growing, suffocating, as my hands are still clenched into fists. As if holding my fingers gripped like that will keep some part of him in existence— will keep some part of me breathing despite the knowledge that I am so close to losing the one person I care for in this world.

Knowing that when I let go, the rest of me will shatter.

Ten steps.

Fifteen steps.

Twenty steps.

The steady sound of Eogan walking away clips out a rhythm. *Kill me, kill me, kill me.* Thirty steps. *Kill me. Kill me.* Like a mantra burrowing its moldy fingers into my bones. Until I can't bear the noise of it anymore, and I crush my hand bandages beneath my fingers just to feel the shock and pain jar through me. To shut out the internal voice yelling that he and everyone else are going to die if I am weak and unable to do what needs to be done.

I can't do this. I can't stop Draewulf like this.

Draewulf turns the corner. Just as the last of him disappears and the guards surrounding me prod me forward, I swear a whisper floats back. Eogan's breath breezing across my soul, *"Don't let him take who you are."*

They were Colin's last words.

Except Draewulf's already taken who I am. *What* I am. *Along with the people I love.*

I pick up following the delegates who've stopped to wait for me and glance down at my bandaged hands, my fingers, my gimpy wrist, as the words stir something in my soul awake.

I won't let him take any more.

I glance ahead at Rasha who's in conversation with the old man. Then at Myles who's watching me.

And I give him a sickened nod.

CHAPTER 14

THE BANQUET WILL BEGIN IN LESS THAN AN HOUR," the elderly man says, leading us to a series of rooms assembled in a row down one hallway near the place Eogan left us. "Until then, we hope you find refreshment in your quarters."

From what I can see through the open doors, they each look exactly the same in size and beautiful furnishings. Mine is third down, after the two Rasha's been assigned. I stand and watch the guards sort the other delegates into theirs. Lady Gwen, Lord Percival, and Lord Wellimton—they promptly disappear through doors before the soldiers click their feet and step back to pose one on either side.

"Be ready as soon as the banquet's done," Myles mutters when he strides past me.

My nerves rise. "We can't wait. He's already—"

He cuts me off with a wave and strides on toward his quarters, leaving me to twelve guards, six from Faelen and six from Bron.

I inhale and eye them, trying to recall how Draewulf took over Breck—did he ever emerge through her skin early on? Through her hands? I can't remember anything other than her shift in personality. Maybe Draewulf's bluffing. I clench my jaw. Or maybe not.

Either way, you can't do anything about it right now. So smile and start out on a good foot with the guards.

I force a brazen grin and nod to them. "You gentlemen look worried like I'll strip down to my Elemental abilities and run ruinous through the Castle."

The Bron men may have Eogan's onyx skin and hard expression and broad chests that are thicker than three versions of Lord Myles, but they're clearly missing his humor. There's not even a smirk. I sniff and turn for my room, but before I can step forward, the largest guard reaches out and slides his hands through my hair and down my neck.

My palm is against his chest faster than a bolcrane claw, except without an Elemental surge the result is nothing more than a shove of annoyance. Two Bron soldiers grab me and pin my arms to my side as my Faelen guards offer no help, and the first man continues his search of my body.

I shudder and fight to ignore his rough touch down my skin and the slave memories it evokes.

"Just checking for weapons, miss."

As soon as he finishes, I push him off and step into my quarters, then slam the door to the sound of tromping footfalls. A moment later, I hear an entourage enter Rasha's room—the level of her squeal and the murmured fawning voices suggest it's her bodyguards and lady-in-waiting.

Shaking off the sensation of the man's hands, I turn to my room. *Get familiar with the environment.*

It's elegant, with walls covered in white paper flecked with giant black paisleys and set off by a black rug and a smooth-edged iron bed. Nearby sits a couch, and a desk stands against a white-curtained window. I stroll over to peek out and find a full view of the airship pad we just left, with the ship now settled on giant metal ribbing while the balloon above deflates.

A knock on the door is followed by a man's voice. "Your bag, miss."

I open it up to one of Rasha's bodyguards holding a case that has Faelen's crest on the side. He tips his head. "From the princess."

There's no armoire in my room, so I unload the bag onto a set of five empty iron shelves stacked against one wall like the wood ones in Adora's library. I'm halfway through tugging out my blue leathers before it occurs to me that the clothes have already been rifled through. Which means the Bron guards sifted over every inch of this bag, and they didn't bother to hide the fact.

My knives.

Yanking out the rest of the clothes, most of which look suspiciously like Rasha's Cashlin style, I feel around down at the bottom of the case for my weapons. Not there. I slide my fingers along the sides until I come across a small slip of material that, when pulled on, reveals a false front. Not there either.

Litched cranes.

I glare around the room and, chewing my lip, try to squelch the feeling of helplessness. *What was Myles thinking? No powers, no knives, not even the blasted sheath with the straps . . .*

I freeze.

And turn back to the bag. What *was* Myles thinking? Because knowing him, he most *definitely* was.

I feel over the two stiff straps attached to the case and, sure enough, at the base of each is a section that's hard and unbending. I tug the material open along one of the seams and there, wedged in, is the tip of one of my knife handles with its blade jutting into the side lining of the bag. It takes a bit of work to slide the blades out, but when I've got them in hand, my breathing eases.

I tear up an undergarment and use it to strap the knives to my ankles before putting the rest of the clothes away. After that I turn to find the water basin for washing. Only there isn't one. It takes me a half minute of searching the room before I think to try a thin door in the wall near the bed.

It's a water closet of some sort. Similar to the one on the airship with its fixtures made of iron rather than wood, and the basin for hand washing fused to the table. This one's larger though. I poke at the weird spigot arched above the bowl and abruptly jump back as a stream of clear liquid shoots out at me. *What the—?* I prod it again and the stream pours out into the basin. *It's like an indoor well pump.* But the water is warm.

My gaze falls on a bigger version set into the floor. *For washing the entire body?* And beside it sits something akin to a waste bucket, but it too has a spigot of water over it. Considering there's not much of a smell, it appears to be for rinsing the bowl when one's lavatories are finished. *Huh.* I poke it to confirm my assumptions and am rewarded with a splash of water to the face.

"Teeth of a motherless pig!" Cursing the inventor of such an obtuse item, I use the coarse cloth on the table to wash down my body with the hand basin spigot. Once finished, I take my hair down from its thick braid and find the brush Rasha packed to run through my tangles before peering at the clothes she sent. I hold them up and wrinkle my nose. Most of them seem to be missing sections where the stomach and shoulders should be. "How on earth—?" I flip them sideways. I drop them and opt to change into my nicest pair of leathers.

I've just pulled my last bootie on when a commotion in the outside hall suggests it's time to go.

I slide over to the door and press my ear against it to hear the elderly man's voice announcing an invitation to the king's banquet. It's followed by a procession of taps on metal, including the door I'm leaning against.

I straighten my shirt and shoulders and, firming my jaw, open it to discover the old man is standing a few feet in front of me. He nods stiffly, and as his eyes catch mine, there's a coldness in their brown depths. It's so unfeeling, so unwelcoming. I glare back at him before his gaze moves on to the other delegates emerging into the hall. I shoot a quick peek around for the boy, Kel, although, of course, he's not here. I hope he made it off the ship without getting caught.

"Good evening," the old man says as soon as we're all assembled. His cheeks crinkle in thick lines belying the stiffness in his tone. He reminds me of owner number two's grandfather.

I sneak a peek at Rasha and am relieved to discover she's preoccupied with her Cashlin guards. I inch toward Lord Myles, who smells like he fell into a barrel of cologne.

"I am Sir Gowon and I extend to you Bron's highest welcome." The old man raises his fist to his chest and thumps it over his heart, and my ears prick at his name. I look at him closer. He's the man Eogan said to speak with.

"We're honored you've come. And even more honored you have returned us our king, Ezeoha—or as he is known to you, Eogan—Bron's prince long thought dead. For this you have our people's gratitude and my personal thanks." For a moment I swear there's a hint of warmth in his voice.

I wonder what Eogan means to him.

Or what he meant *to him.* I flinch as Eogan's comment slips into mind that by the time I told Gowon, it would be too late for him.

I turn to Myles. "We need to go do it now."

"And assume he'd not notice your absence at the banquet? You're jesting."

"Eogan doesn't have time left." My words come out a shrill whisper.

"Patience is a skill, my dear. One best used to your advantage."

Sir Gowon extends a hand. "Now if you'll follow me. Tonight we celebrate the new king's return with a banquet."

I look back at Myles, who flicks a glance toward Rasha. She's still busy with her Cashlin entourage. "Are you wanting Her Royal Princess to know your planssss?" he asks casually. "I'm merely wondering how long you think it'll take her to home in on them with you acting like a skittish bolcrane cub."

I purse my lips and inhale because he has a point. *Fine.* "But we go as soon as it's done."

Flanked by a squadron of Bron soldiers and most of our Faelen guards, we head down a series of metal corridors, each one lit by lanterns with a tiny flame contained in some type of thick glass that give off a surprising amount of light and no smoke. Like the lanterns on the airship.

I'm just contemplating how to pull Sir Gowon aside to give him Eogan's message—*What was it? Elegy 96?*—and ask for his help, when Rasha says behind me, "Does this mean you weren't in love with my dresses I picked out for you?" She sidles up with a pouty smile.

I try not to even think anything of Myles or Eogan in case that's the way her Luminescent ability might work. Clearing my throat, I eye the traditional Cashlin silk skirt and midstomach blouse cutting nicely on her voluptuous frame. She's even wearing the wraparound shawl I've seen her in on official occasions. "They were missing some of their parts. But I think they're lovely. Especially on you."

"Funny. But flattery won't get you off the hook next time. Fair warning."

I grin despite my nervousness.

Distract her. Keep her talking. "Did you see their water closets?"

Her eyes grow as large as wasp's eggs and she nods. "The water's even warm!"

"I know. So are the walls."

"One of my men said they built the palace with pipes in the walls so they can pump heated water through them."

I lift a brow. *That's brilliant actually.* If Eogan were himself, I'd . . .

I swallow and shift my thoughts to the floor in front of us.

Myles brushes against me as he leans over. "Allow me to commend you ladies for the fact that, of all things right now, you're talking about the water closetsss. Seems to me your time would be better spent discussing what this evening might hold for your necksss—"

His voice breaks off as Rasha and I both snicker, and Sir Gowon stops at a giant copper door. Rasha jabs Myles in the stomach. "Perhaps. But I would've thought you, of all people, would've been most impressed with those closets."

"Ah, here we are, ladies and gentlemen," Sir Gowon says.

In unison, the Bron soldiers retreat two paces, and the large one who searched me earlier steps forward. Slowly, he opens the door.

CHAPTER 15

THE ROOM IS EMPTY.

Which makes the squeak of the metal that much louder as it's pulled shut behind us. It echoes in the enormous space that's lined with row upon row of tables leading up to a platform on which sits the king's table at the far end. Hanging from the ceiling along the center aisle droop more of those enclosed lanterns, blanketing the entire place in light and exaggerating the walls we're all staring at. They're covered from top to bottom in maps showing all five kingdoms of the Hidden Lands. And they're uncomfortably detailed.

If my nerves were on edge before, they're close to unraveling now.

"Such curious decor," Lady Gwen says in a small voice.

"A tad thick on the world domination side if you ask me," I mutter.

Myles chuckles and Lord Wellimton utters something akin to a gasp. "Young lady, I'll ask you to keep hold of your manners—what few you have—so as not to ruin the greatest negotiation opportunity between the two nations."

I shut my mouth as Rasha asks Sir Gowon, "Where is everyone?"

He doesn't answer. Just smiles tightly and walks us down the center aisle between the rows of stark, smooth-lined metal tables and handcrafted silver seats to those nearest the head table.

With his hand, he indicates chair assignments for each of us. "Please sit."

Lord Wellimton slides into a seat closest to the king's table while Rasha stares hard at our host. The other delegates stand awkwardly with expressions probably mimicking my own. *Be seated for what?* My nerves go from taut to churning knots. I should say something to Sir Gowon. I should tell him now what Eogan said. But my feet are rooted to the cool floor.

"Sir Gowon, will others be joining us soon?" Lady Gwen's tone wavers.

"They'll be along shortly."

Rasha releases her stare on the old man and tips her head at us. "From what I can tell it's fine."

It doesn't ease the tension, but I follow her example and take my assigned spot next to her, all the while studying Sir Gowon and attempting to find the right words to say. Because somehow "Oh, by the way, Eogan has become Draewulf" doesn't have quite the air of authority it needs.

After a moment, Lady Gwen sits next to me, then Lord Percival, with Myles stealing the end closest the door. Our Faelen and Cashlin bodyguards take up watch against the wall with a heightened air among them.

"I'm sure this is normal," Lady Gwen murmurs in my direction. "I mean, I'm sure seating their guests before anyone else is merely part of their culture."

I force a smile. "I'm sure it is."

Her responding grin is grateful. "That's what I thought. I doubt they'd invite us here just to, well, I'm certain this is the decor they were stuck with on such short notice of us coming here."

"I'm sure it was."

She nods, but after a second she says, "Although, would you mind asking Princess Rasha if her Luminescent abilities are picking up on anything?"

Rasha bends in front of me to pat Gwen's hand. "You have nothing to fear, Lady Gwen. It will all be fine."

"Of course, I knew that. But still, it's good to know. However . . ." She looks back to me. "If anything was to go wrong . . ." She smiles and peers up at my white hair and at my blue eyes, as if comforting herself with the fact that she and the other delegates have brought security with them.

"Lord Percival," I say, to distract her. "What would your wife say to all this?"

He frowns. "My wife? She'd be thrilled with the warm water and demand we hire their decorator." His forehead creases in a manner that makes me think he's rather glad she's *not* here. I smirk.

He turns to Lady Gwen. "Of course if anything went wrong, Nym would take care of things. But nothing's going to happen. We'll be fine."

My shoulders harden. I glance away, fidgeting under the weight of their gazes that feels like an ill-fitting coat. I slide my hand beneath the table to feel out both knives on my ankles. *How long is this banquet going to last?*

"Please just tell me this isn't going to be a trial and execution." Lady Gwen is praying.

Princess Rasha's brown locks catch the light when she tips her head as if to reply but stops as her gaze stalls on me. As if trying to assess something. I promptly dip my head away. *Kracken.*

I'm saved by a set of double doors bursting open at the far end of the room, and men and women and children come filing in, their voices low. My fingers slip from my knives as a gasp escapes Rasha's lips.

They're dressed beautifully, if not austerely, in black, silver, or red suits that wrap around their bodies like second skin and appear to be made of stretching material. The clothing hugs the men's broad shoulders and etched waistlines and the women's curved hips and chests. Each outfit is decorated differently, with metal loops and symbols here, and silver fabric plumes woven there. Nothing extravagant like Adora's wardrobe, but elegant in their total simplicity.

"How lovely," Rasha breathes, pointing discreetly to the ladies' hair, which is pulled back from their foreheads and twisted into various knots that curve and swirl in intricate patterns.

I nod. The designs are stunning and regal, especially set off by the men's short-cropped hair. I wonder if Eogan's longer hair and jagged bangs were a sign of independence during his four years away or simply his effort to keep from being recognized as Odion's twin. Not that anyone in Faelen had ever seen Odion. I recall Eogan telling me once that his brother preferred hiding behind Bron's generals and war rooms rather than showing up on the battlefield or negotiation chamber.

Until the battle at the Keep apparently.

Lord Percival makes a sound in his throat, drawing my gaze up to discover that the people are openly staring at us, taking their seats at the rows of tables. I look for intention in their expressions but am met by stony reserve.

"Anyone got a splash of hard ale?" Myles says.

"Will you please shut up?" Lord Wellimton snarls.

The doors near our end of the map-covered room open and my chest first leaps, then crashes as Draewulf-posing-as-Eogan steps in, flanked by guards on each side and an assortment of other eminent-looking people. Generals by the looks of their red surcoats. As they get closer, I recognize two of them as among the Bron generals who spoke to Eogan at the Keep. After he'd been taken over already by Draewulf . . . I narrow my eyes and switch my focus to searching him for any sign that he's absorbed more of his host's body.

Not that I can tell.

Draewulf's gaze flicks around the room with something akin to boredom as he steps into position at his table and the crowd falls silent. "Ladies and gentlemen of the Assembly, thank you for joining us this evening." His voice rings out clear and rich and so normal that, for a second, my hopes rise.

Sir Gowon hobbles over to whisper at him. Draewulf nods and replies before turning to bestow the biggest, falsest smile on us. My wish flails.

"May the festivities commence," he declares.

A ripple of cheering goes through the room, but it's dull, muted. I peek around to find most of the adult Assembly watching him as Draewulf takes a seat and his entourage follows suit.

The citizens pick up their talking and hardly glance back when the double doors open again and a host of young boys stride in carrying silver trays covered in various foods that make my mouth water and my anxious stomach twist at the savory smell.

The large platters are placed two to a table beginning with Eogan's, followed by ours, and then on down the rows. I watch Sir Gowon for a minute before turning to eye the people across from us dipping the chewy bread substance into bowls of black porridge. I force myself to follow suit if only not to draw the attention of Rasha, whose red-lit gaze hasn't stopped darting around the room since the Assembly walked in. How hard must it be to single out individual intentions amid a sea of noise and moods and heartpulses.

Next come trays of drinks, most of which are foaming and smell fermented. I stick with a simple tin cup of water and try an assortment of thin food ribbons that taste like rabbit cheese.

"It's good," Lord Wellimton grunts, and suddenly the other delegates are agreeing and the tension among them easing. Soon they're chatting with each other while furtively sizing up the Bron citizens.

"How young some of the boys are," Lady Gwen says.

Lord Wellimton leans over and nods as if approving. "Sir Gowon said they train them starting at age five. Smart and economical."

If any of the Bron people overhear us, they give no evidence of caring. Although I notice with the continued partaking of the food and drink, the Assembly's reserved expressions begin to slip a bit, revealing what appears to be a genuine affection for each other and an enhanced coolness toward us. A few times I even catch some of them looking my direction with what I swear is outright resentment. And when a group of younger boys takes up pointing at me, it's with traces of malice in their gazes.

I keep my expression clear and sift quickly through them for Kel, but he's not there. Then go back to my food. *How can I blame them?*

Another ten, fifteen, twenty minutes slide by before Rasha tips toward my ear. "I believe I've focused in on a few members who might hold information we can use, if I can get them in a quieter room. Those generals surrounding Eogan have been here for years, and if he dies they will send this land into a civil war in their fight to succeed him. One of them being Sir Gowon."

My hand pauses holding a spoonful of food halfway between my plate and mouth. "Sir Gowon wants Eogan's throne?"

"No, but from what I saw in him when we first arrived, his commitment is even stronger to Bron than who sits on its throne. If Eogan dies, he's willing to do what needs to be done to keep order. However, seeing as he's known Eogan and served this kingdom since Eogan's childhood, I believe he can be valuable to us."

I don't look at her. Instead I flutter a glance at Eogan, who's immersed in conversation with the generals at his table, and hesitate before asking, "Valuable regarding saving Eogan?"

She frowns in confusion. "No. Helpful regarding knowledge of Draewulf's plans in the past as well as any old agreements Bron made with him," she says slowly, staring at me. Abruptly her eyes flare faintly, but we're interrupted by two Cashlin guards slipping up behind us. One bends down to whisper in Rasha's ear. I can't hear what he's saying, but her countenance falls. She pushes back from the table with a hurried, "Excuse me, I have to go," tossed in Wellimton's direction. She turns me a worried glare, which she extends over to Myles, before being hustled from the room by her men.

I rise to go after her, but the expressions of both the Bron and Faelen guards make it clear I'm to stay. "It's a private matter, miss," one of them says.

Private. Yet he looks worried too.

I purse my lips and turn back, only to notice a number of the boys openly glaring at me. I smile at them, which seems to rattle their gazes until suddenly they're looking to the king's table where Eogan-who-is-Draewulf is standing and clanking his metal goblet against his plate.

"My Bron family and Faelen friends, I trust you have enjoyed your feast as richly as I have."

There's that muted cheer again.

"I'd like to believe that the flavors and generosity with which our feast was prepared tonight will be a foretaste of the conversations that lie ahead. During the past week I've spent in Faelen, King Sedric and I developed and signed a peace treaty. At tomorrow's meetings we will talk in greater detail about the specific policies and requirements surrounding that treaty. However, for now, let us continue to celebrate by way of traditional Bron entertainment!"

A little more approval for Eogan is shown this time in the voices and clapping.

I look at Sir Gowon. *Does he notice any difference in the man before him?* I glance behind me for Rasha, who's not returned yet, and note the host of guards still blocking the door. My spine squeezes. What happened to make her leave like that?

I look at Gwen and my guard. "I'm going to sit by Myles."

He nods and allows me to take the seat on the other side of the lord protectorate.

"How much longer is this?" I growl.

"What's the commotion with Rasha?"

"I've no idea, but considering she left, we can too."

"*She* will have a believable explanation, and *she* is not Eogan's favorite Elemental at the moment. So no, we can't. Now tell me what Rasha's guardsss said to her."

"I couldn't hear, but whatever it was she looked worried." I peer around for a time gauge on the wall. "And I think she might have caught on to our plans."

He utters a curse word. "Remind me never to rely on you for information."

"Information? Eogan is *dying* right now."

Myles's expression turns sickly humored. "Yes, and I have to admit I'm rather enjoying watching you squirm. Almost as much as seeing how much that group of boys seems to hate you."

"And you wonder why people aren't more enamored with your charming personali—"

A commotion of doors creaking open cuts me off. Two men dressed in thin, full-bodied pantsuits enter and stride down the center aisle to the middle of the room. One is lithe and carrying a sword, the other is of a monstrous size and holding an ax. By the look of their muscles and hardened faces, they're soldiers. Good ones.

If the cheering of the crowd before was feeble, it's now loud and authentic sounding and apparently serves to commence the start of the two men engaging in hand-to-hand combat.

The first ax thrusts by the larger man swing wide.

I bite my tongue when the third connects with the smaller man's shoulder. He falls back with a grunt, and the man brings his ax down again.

It crashes into the floor as the small man rolls out of the way before twisting to bring his sword up under the larger opponent's arm.

This is entertainment? A blood sport?

Blood is already spilling on the floor when he pulls it back. He turns and, with another thrust of the sword, swipes at the giant's neck.

My gut leaps into my chest and my mouth turns sour. If the large man hadn't spun away in time, he'd be dead. I look around. This is what the vent boy was talking about—a community earned through power rather than differences.

Eogan, the real Eogan, would never have allowed something like this. At least not in recent weeks. But no one other than myself and Gwen appears to find it disturbing.

On and on the soldiers fight while my discomfort builds and I try to look away.

Parrying. Sparring. Until blood is coating every inch of their bodies and the floor in a circular pattern as they move. It's even spattered on some of the onlookers.

The cutting and blood continue until the smaller, faster of the two men lands a jab near the other's heart and drops him to his knees. I hold my breath. The victor stands over him, sword raised, and looks to Eogan.

I start to rise but Myles stops me. "Oh my dear, please keep your seat if not your head. This is their culture, not ours. You'll only cause trouble for usss."

"He's going to kill him," I hiss. I look down the table at the other delegates. They look odd sitting there, backs straight, faces stiff. *Is this part of their job—not to react in political settings, or do they just assume it will be fine?* Myles catches my eye and with his gaze indicates I should look up at Eogan. When I do, my chest unclenches. Eogan waves a hand and the fighter lowers his weapon. He bows to the king, then to the Assembly, and stays standing there as his defeated foe is escorted from the room.

I ease back in my seat but set my hand on my knives. It's only when I peer up again at Draewulf that I realize he caught my reaction.

He tips his head at me and sneers in that hideous, wolfish style and, without looking away, twitches his hand to beckon one of the guards. He says something to the man before he moves his gaze from me back to the room.

A moment later, the doors open again. And what looks like a mound of furs is standing there. My tapping leg stops moving.

The woman beneath them begins peeling each one off, like the rind of rich fruit, and dropping them to the floor as she strides in. Almost exactly like she did two weeks ago when she was at Adora's party.

And just like then, her entrance is met with an audible gasp across the room.

"What's she doing here?" someone in the Assembly murmurs.

"How long has it been—six months—since Odion last summoned her?"

"I thought she betrayed us to Faelen!"

"It was a ruse to get her father, Draewulf, close to their king and ours. She betrayed us both!"

"Is Isobel still betrothed to King Ezeoha?"

The comments float through the room making the smile on Isobel's face that much wider as she strolls down the center aisle toward her father, who inhabits the body of the man she's the same age as and was once engaged to.

"Ladies and gentlemen," Draewulf announces, staring right at me. "May I present to you Lady Isobel."

CHAPTER 16

B Y THE TIME DRAEWULF'S DAUGHTER IS DOWN THE aisle and standing in the bloodied makeshift arena next to the victor in front of us, she's stripped down to nothing more than a tight, glistening pantsuit made to hug every curve of her seductive, tall frame. A quarter of the Assembly is standing, and another third is grumbling. I'm silently cursing. She tosses a smile in my direction and that old jealousy flares along with the recollection of our last meeting when she tried to wrap her body around Eogan's neck.

Myles slicks the sides of his hair and lets out a low whistle of enjoyment.

I slide one of my knives out beneath the table and prick his leg.

He jerks and says something uncouth, but I'm already looking past him to Draewulf, whose mocking, proud, fatherlike expression contorts the slightest bit. I freeze. The black in his eyes retracts into what appears to be pain and I swear his body jerks.

The next second, he's smiling and nodding to Isobel.

I turn on Myles. "Did you see that?"

"If you're referring to anything besides Lady Isobel's superior curvesss flexing in front of me, then no, I didn't."

It's an impressive feat of self-control that I refrain from jab-
bing Myles in his family heirlooms just as Draewulf tips his hand
in Isobel's direction. She grins and strides the last two feet to the
victor of the blood sport and, in one swift movement, presses her
hand over the man's chest and mutters a chant. His face sags. His
black skin yellows. He stiffens and falls in a heap on the floor.

Every member at our table gasps, and Gwen, Lord Percival, and
I are all immediately standing. *What the hulls?*

"Is he dead?" Gwen asks.

"Fascinating," Myles murmurs.

The footsteps of soldiers sound behind us. I flip around to find
them lined up, their cautioning stares bearing down—Bron's men
indicating we should sit back down and Faelen's guards hinting
they'd rather not get in a fight here. Beside me, Myles gives a soft
cluck of his tongue, although something in it hints that he's wary too.

Ignoring them all, I lean forward to study the fallen soldier,
scrutinizing his chest for signs of breathing just as Eogan claps
heartily. The rest of the Assembly joins in. Gwen and Percival
reclaim their seats as Isobel bows, and the doors are flung open
again by a soldier who ushers in a boy of maybe seven. He's dressed
to match the victor in that shiny silver suit, but his face . . .

His face is that of the boy, Kel.

Isobel moves back, and as she does, the victor I'd thought dead
moans, sits, then quickly pulls himself into a fighting stance once
again. A stream of blood drips from his nose, and from the way he
staggers, I'm sure whatever Isobel did will kill him sooner than later.

Myles yanks my elbow. "For hulls' sakesss, sit down."

Kel steps forward and raises a blade curved in the shape of
a crescent. He doesn't look at me, even though I've no doubt he
knows I'm here. The bleeding victor lifts his sword.

The air in the room pauses as they wait. The Assembly waits. I wait. For . . . what? I don't know. But I want to lunge for the boy—to help him—to stop him—because this is so wrong.

I feel Draewulf's eyes on me. "Are you an imp, boy, or a man?" His shout makes me jump. "Show us how they've trained you here."

Kel moves forward even as I catch the twitch in his pale face. Something shifts there and for a second I see a flash and recognize the fear. Not of what might be done to him, but of what he'll do to the bigger man.

It almost kicks in my chest.

I rise as he uses his foot to toss the beaten fighter's ax over to the bloodied victor. Offering him another weapon. He's trying to making it a fair fight.

Even though everyone in here knows it won't be.

"Faster, boy!" Draewulf yells, and abruptly the entire room is goading the child on.

"Do it!" another calls.

"Take him down!"

Is this a jest? What's wrong with these people?

I peer around and notice the horror blossoming on Gwen's face before I continue on to look at the old man, Sir Gowon. He appears only slightly less uncomfortable, but the focus of his gaze tells me it's nothing to do with the fight and everything to do with Lady Isobel, who's moved to Eogan's side. She's staring at Draewulf with a mixture of pride and disgust.

And Draewulf's staring at me. Leering. Waiting.

Next thing I know Isobel's turned her gaze my way as well. Her face clears of everything but arrogance before she looks back toward the young boy, who's suddenly dropped the blade to the ground and stepped away from the injured man.

The gasp that rocked the room when she walked in is equaled in strength by the level of silence now.

Kel's eyes focus on me. I stand there staring right back at him. *What's he doing?*

But I know exactly what he's doing. His words from the airship surface. *"Maybe power comes in different forms. And maybe we get a choice how we use it."*

He blinks, then turns expertly toward Eogan as the guests seem to hold their breath in unison. Even Myles is devoid of smart remarks.

Kel tips his head forward. "Your Majesty, please forgive my decision not to complete this task. I don't think this man guilty of an offense and therefore can't find justice in killing him. I'm willing to perform another task instead to prove I'm your humble servant."

An angered intake of breath erupts among multiple council members and guards, and even audibly from Sir Gowon. Their stares of disapproval all move from Kel's face to mine.

I somehow find the chair beneath me and sit, and wait as Eogan's expression turns darker than I can ever recall seeing it. His hand shakes and even his shoulders appear to quiver. "Someone bring another who has more respect for Bron's tradition and its king's wishes. And see that this one is—"

Sir Gowon steps in. "I'll see to it, Your Majesty." He beckons for two guards and Kel, who doesn't look back as he strides, neck stiff, eyes straight forward, out of the room after Gowon.

Another boy enters as he leaves. He's a head taller than Kel and his features are harder, fiercer.

He's one of the group who've been glowering at me.

Without waiting for the guests to recover from their shock or for the injured man to prepare, he pulls out a straight, twelve-inch-long blade and lunges at the man's leg.

The soldier utters a cry as the strike lands, and he drops to one knee. The boy's gaze goes hard.

I push my chair back.

Myles's hand is on my arm again faster than I can blink, pulling my wrist down to hide the blade. "Don't be a fool. Make a scene now and you'll embarrass the Assembly and endanger all of us."

"I refuse to sit here and watch a child be used for blood sport. Even the other boy saw the idiocy in this."

"At their ages, they're considered soldiers. They're showing off technique. It's a rite of passage."

"And the injured man?"

"Welcome to politics, sweetheart. This is where we pull our panties up and pretend to approve of another world's customsss. Now put the blasted blade away and let the poor man die with dignity before you get usss all killed."

I wrinkle my brow and look toward the door Kel was led through. "What are they going to do to him, you think?"

"Shh."

I glare at him. *I can't watch this.* I turn toward Eogan's table. "Your Highness," I say in a voice that carries farther than intended.

The room stops. The cheering stops. All movement stalls.

The edge in Draewulf's eyes is sharper than anything that's drawn blood tonight.

I nod to the warrior and the boy standing with his blade held up for the death blow. "I applaud your plan for demonstrating the same compassion you're known for in Faelen. By showing the use of killing as a last resort rather than sport. Just as the previous boy was displaying."

His calculated smile falters. "Ah, you speak kindly of my

reputation, m'lady. But here in our home culture, would you have me rob this boy's honor? Where would the compassion be in that?"

"Is it not King Eogan's sense of honor that showed mercy on Bron and Faelen that saved both our lands? And thus would it not be more honoring to these warriors who have shown such skill in fighting, to show control through mercy?"

His face goes blank and flickers confused before it softens. A flare of green widens around his black wolf pupils, and abruptly there emerges something majestic in his face. Noble. I inhale. Because I swear it's the Eogan I know. He begins shivering, and it's so hard that he clenches the table with his hands as he looks from me to the boy and frowns. He starts to rise just as Isobel slides her hand over his chest and leans down to whisper in his ear. The green fades and his grin returns, more twisted this time, changing into the same smirk his daughter is wearing.

He releases the table.

"Interesting words spoken from the woman who chose not to withhold her Elemental mercy from many loved ones missing from this room. Alas, I promise you're soon to discover mercy and death are often the same." He waves at the injured man, now spitting up blood, and commands the boy, "Finish it." He twitches his fingers at the guards behind me.

The straight blade comes down with a repulsive thud.

I look away only to realize the soldiers' blades are poking into my back. "You'll join us in the corridor," one snarls. "Alone," he adds when Myles begins to rise.

I clamp my gaze on the lord protectorate oaf and slide my knife back into its makeshift sheath. Myles's glare is asking what the hulls I've just done because not only did I fail to save anyone, I may have doomed the rest of them. I don't blame him. Of all people, I should know that compassion without the power to change anything is futile. Is dangerous.

Stumbling to the door amid the angry guards and daggers, I glance back to see Draewulf's expression. Instead of gloating, he's wincing. And when I trail my gaze to the hand resting on his chest, I see it belongs to Isobel.

She grins and blows me a kiss right as the door opens and I'm pushed through.

"No!" I cry out, but the metal shuts in place behind me.

"You've been invited to Bron by special request of Lord Myles," one of my Faelen bodyguards says in my face. "Do you realize what those people think of you? What they could do to you?"

"Her being here is already an offense," growls a Bron soldier. "She's lucky we didn't just cut her down then and there."

Their irritable words—they keep tumbling out, swirling around reproachful faces that are all glaring and yelling at me.

I snap. "Look, King Eogan obviously allowed me to come, so I will take it up with him. Now let me back in there."

"Believe me, *we* took it up with him," Sir Gowon's elderly voice says, slipping out from a door nearby us.

He steps forward and the soldiers fall silent. I'm surprised there's not smoke wisping from his nose for how obviously he's fuming. He looks at the Faelen guard closest me. "Your girl here needs to understand that most of the Assembly in there see her as a threat and an affront. Yes, our king has allowed her to be here, but if she wants to stay alive, she'll need to behave like the rest of your delegates. What she did in there is not acceptable, and if she repeats it again I will personally see her punished."

My guard frowns. "We understand perfectly, sir. It won't happen again."

"But the delegates are in danger. I have to—"

"The delegates are safe, and I suggest you do your part to see they stay that way," Sir Gowon snarls at me. "Which, right now, means refraining from flouting our tradition or aggravating our Assembly further while you're here."

I try to jerk free. "And perhaps your guards should refrain from aggravating me."

The large Bron soldier who searched me earlier leans down until he's level with my face. He looks angrier than seems warranted, as if I've provoked him personally.

Sir Gowon slides his hand between us. "That's enough. The king wants her left unharmed." He looks at me fully now with those cold eyes. "But that doesn't mean you'll be spared watching the harm you've caused."

He snaps his fingers and two other soldiers grab my arms as he turns to my Faelen guards. "She'll watch the boy's punishment. You're welcome to attend with her, which I'm certain you'll insist on anyway."

Without waiting for their reply, he steps toward the room he emerged from and through which the sound of lashing is suddenly emitting. My stomach plunges.

Sir Gowon pushes it open, enters, and is followed by my Faelen soldiers. The large guard shoves my back and I stumble into a small, brightly lit barren room where Kel is kneeling in the center of the stark floor with his shirt off.

The edge of a thick metal whip is sliding off his shoulders, wielded by a tall, callous-looking Bron. And even with Kel's head down and eyes shut, I can see tears dripping off his cheeks. There's no blood or broken skin but the bruises and welts appearing suggest the damage underneath might be worse than if there were.

"Stop!" I spring forward but the large guard stalls me with a hand to my chest.

"You want to make it worse?" he growls, but his furious expression is shaded with shame. All of their expressions are, in fact—aside from Sir Gowon's.

The whip comes down again, bringing unbidden tears from my eyes. *No!* The lashing pulls no sound from him, and he sags forward even farther.

And I suddenly realize why he's not screaming.

CHAPTER 17

THE BOY'S PASSED OUT.

Sir Gowon wipes his sweaty brow with a kerchief. "That's enough. Any more and he won't survive." He turns from the soldier inflicting Kel's punishment and I swear his face has gone a bit gray.

"But sir—"

"I said that's enough," Sir Gowon barks.

"You've nearly killed him!" I curl my hand into a fist to call down the whole of a storm upon all of their blasted heads. When nothing happens I reach for one of my knives.

The large guard grabs my hand before I can yank the blade free.

"I think you mean *you've* nearly killed him," Sir Gowon spits out. "Just by your being here. Clearly your influence has infected his reasoning." He wipes his brow again and steps closer, his gaze narrowing. "I've no idea why you've come here, but seeing as King Ezeoha is the only reason you were allowed into Bron in the first place, let alone alive, I will respect that. Likewise I'll ask you to respect our people and customs from now on or stay confined to your room and risk punishment. Is that clear?"

The big guard snorts. "If she so much as pulls out another dagger or rumbles the clouds above us, she won't need a punishment. I will personally take her head off."

Sir Gowon is glaring at me, but his words seem addressed to us both. "His Majesty has given an order, and the fact that he's assigned the guards here to keep you alive means they will follow it. And the fact that he swears to me personally you are in no way a threat, means we are responsible to honor that trust even if we do not hold it ourselves."

Gowon nods at the rest of the surrounding soldiers. "See her to her room."

"But the boy." I press toward Kel, who's still passed out on the floor.

"That boy is not your concern. You should merely be grateful I am overseeing his punishment rather than another. The penalty for what he did back there is death. At least I have allowed him to live."

I think I might throw up. I wipe my eyes.

"Guards."

Stiffening, I push forward again, but this time toward Sir Gowon—and stare him straight in the face. "Before they take me, I have a message for you."

He snorts and peers around.

"From Eogan."

His brow goes up and I bend close enough that I can smell the old powder scent of Sir Gowon's suit even as three swords aim at my neck in an instant. I lift both hands from my cloak and raise them in a nonthreatening stance. Sir Gowon stares at me with a look of intolerance.

"Eogan said to tell you Elegy 96 was his favorite," I whisper.

"He also said to tell you he's been taken over by Draewulf, and because of his block, they are sharing the same physical body."

I've never seen a grown man grow so still that even his breathing ceases. To the point I'm hoping I may have caused a jolt to hit his brain and he's just died standing there staring at me.

Ten heartpulses go by before the old man blinks, and I swear I can see the words trying to jumble into some form of making sense behind those repulsed, suspicious eyes that are asking if I'm mentally unhinged.

"He was taken over at the Keep," I murmur. "You are aware Draewulf appeared there?"

The next moment he's waving the guards to move in on me.

My voice rises. "Did you not just hear me say he's dying? If you won't believe me, then take me to him. I demand to speak to Eogan."

"That's not your choice to request."

"I'm not requesting."

"Do not mistake his protection of you as anything more, no matter what rumors have circulated regarding your status with him." His tone is beyond biting as he tips his head and my guards grab my arms.

A Bron soldier stoops to take my knives, but Gowon stops him. "Let her keep them. Just because the king's given orders doesn't mean some won't try to off her. No doubt she'll need them before her stay here is over."

The big guard scoffs too harsh. Too loud. "I'm surprised the assassins haven't picked her off already."

The old man nods and, turning to leave, tosses out at my men, "On that note, I'd strongly advise against her taking off or attempting to wander alone while you're with us. There's a black-market price on your girl's head that's worth more than all of Faelen."

He exits the room and the door snaps shut behind him. The big man grabs my arm as I try to see past him to Kel as everything within me aches for him. "This way."

Except before any of us can move, the door creaks open again and a voice hisses, "Excuse me, gentlemen. Perhapsss I can be of assistance in getting her there."

CHAPTER 18

"GOOD EVENING." MYLES SALUTES THE LONE SOLdier in front of us. "I've asked the captain here to attend me on the eleventh-hour roundsss."

The man frowns and lifts the hilt of his sword from its sheath as I shoot a nervous glance at Myles, only to watch the air around him fluctuate again. Abruptly his dark-haired, pasty-skinned self has transformed into a Bron general. I shake my head. Blink. And look down as my own black cloak and female form are replaced by captain's clothes and a boy's physique.

The soldier releases his sword and straightens. Despite the perplexity crossing his features, he snaps his heels together. "Of course, sir. My apologies for not recognizing you."

Myles nods and keeps his grip on my elbow as he steers me past the man and through the metal door to a spiraling case of stairs that descend.

As soon as the door shuts behind us, I peek down at myself again, focusing in until I see the edge of my cloak beneath the visual blur. And try not to allow the panic to seep up my throat.

"You'd be wise to quit ogling yourself and watch the stepsss." Myles releases my arm to lead the way. "I didn't pull you from a host of guards merely to watch you break your neck."

"You keep turning me into a fourteen-year-old boy with sweaty hands."

"Not nearly as fetching, I'll admit. But less likely to invite questionsss."

"What about that boy back there—the one Sir Gowon had punished? Do you think he'll be okay?" Even thinking about it makes my heart hurt.

"Eventually. I suggest you concern yourself with minding your own business from now on."

I shiver. What kind of society trains its children to kill and then punishes them when they don't? Even for as broken as the laws are in Faelen and for as poorly as slaves are treated, they don't *teach* violence. They don't *require* it. "What about the delegates? Are they safe or—?"

"I doubt Draewulf's foolish enough to do anything toward the delegatesss while the Bron Assembly is in turmoil over whether to trust him. At least not yet. Now would you please keep that despicable conscience of yours reined in while I try to remember the way?"

I bite my tongue and follow.

After a moment he peers back, as if surprised I've obeyed. He blinks. "Here, by the way." The atmosphere around us both shimmers just before our façade of being a captain and general falls away, revealing our black hooded cloaks and Faelen clothes. He turns and descends faster.

I take the steps two at a time to keep up and try to refocus before my anger at the Bron soldiers and Gowon boils over for what they've just done to Kel. "So that's how you do it—create a mirage out of air."

He shrugs. "A mental mirage perhaps. It's merely a matter of using words to manipulate the untrained mind."

"But it worked on *me*."

"Because you heard me suggest something as true to the guard. Thus, for a bit, you saw it as such."

"Except I could see through it."

His voice lowers. "Hmm. Yesss. Better than most. Still haven't figured out how."

"Can Rasha see through your mirages?"

His answer is simply a face contorted in irritation as he stops and waits for me at the staircase base. He opens another door, this one unguarded, and leads us into a hall lit by those same curious hanging lanterns.

"What do you think Rasha's guards needed her for?" I whisper.

He snorts. "No idea, but let's hope her royal wretchedness is putting those Luminescent curvesss to something sensually useful."

I glare at him. "Don't talk about her that way." And walk faster to shove down my guilt that I'm doing the very thing she asked me not to. Not to mention I've no idea where she even is.

"Hmm. You're in a rather testy mood tonight."

"I just think that rather than being a pig about her, perhaps you could've used your abilities to help her. Or to help the man killed in that blood sport, or the boy Sir Gowon just had beaten, for that matter."

"You and I both know that man was already dying—his opponent merely ended it quickly. And having spent your life as a Faelen slave, you should know better than most that people worship their own lawsss and tradition—and flouting them will always inflict a penalty."

"Which is exactly why if I'd had my abilities, I would've stopped them both."

"And started another war. As for *my* abilities, I prefer to keep them hidden as long as possssible, if you can manage that for the time being."

"Nice justification."

"Saysss the girl still keeping Draewulf alive."

He halts in front of a door and waits for me to catch up before we're slipping outside into a small moonlit alcove where two palace watchmen are standing. Even though I nudge the metal shut without a sound, they turn and peer in our direction, hands on their swords. I press against the wall in the overhang's shadow, instinctively thinking to squat and feel around for a rock to toss in distraction. But Myles takes my elbow again and steps into the light.

"Merely making the roundsss, gentlemen."

"Ah, very good, sir."

Without another glance, they wave us through the alcove before returning to their discussion. Ducking around them, we step out into one of those wide streets that make up the spindle city.

I gasp.

It's foggy and serene and cast in a dreamlike glow, lit with torches mounted in perfectly distanced rows along the walkways.

Myles's cold fingers press over my cloaked arm, his chill creeping through my skin as he pushes me to the left walkway and begins hurrying from one street to the next through the organized maze of matching buildings.

It's not until we've gone down four of the streets that I notice the quiet. A shiver runs across my shoulders, because even though we're doing our best to hide in the shadows as we go, there seems no need for it. The place is empty. Not just empty, it's silent even inside the houses.

"Where is everyone?"

He glances down an alley. "It's past curfew. Those who are not part of the banquet are asleep."

I raise a brow. "And that's not eerie at—"

A small movement catches my eye, bringing me up short. At the end of the alley ahead of us something's huddled under a cloak. *A child? A man?* I crinkle my brow and step hesitantly toward it but stop after five paces. The smell. It's gagging and vaguely familiar in a way that reminds me of that one section in Litchfell Forest with Colin. The bodies. Even the bolcranes had left them alone. It smells like the plague. "Something's wrong," I whisper.

"For bleeding's sakesss, girl—do you ever stop talking? I can't imagine even Eogan finding it endearing." But he's looking down the alley too as I glare ice picks up his thin nostrils.

"Probably someone whose lover threw them out for talking too much." But he flips around and backtracks us up one of the side streets we just walked. I'm tempted to argue, to go see if they need help, but . . . that smell.

"So this woman we're going to see—what kind of abilities will she give me?"

"That, my dear, is something to ask her."

"But will they be like yours?"

"No one's are like mine." He gives a sniff.

"When did you get yours?"

"None of your businesss."

I stop. "I'm walking with a man I trust less than half of my previous owners, on my way to consume powers in an act that for all I know is illegal and dangerous. So I'll thank you to answer my blasted question."

"Sixteen," he growls.

"By the woman we're going to now?"

He nods.

Right. "And how old are you?"

His tone falls as he slows. "Why do you want to know?"

"Just wondering how you can know she's still here."

He steps in front of me and stops. And leans in. "There are no guarantees of anything except I'm risking my neck to help you. So if you're interested in having second thoughtsss, please say so now and let's be done with thisss rather than when we're standing on her bleeding doorstep. Are you in or not?"

I chew my lip. Stare at him. "I'm in." I tip my head. "But let me make one thing clear. You are helping me, so I thank you for that. However, I'm not doing this for you or to help you accomplish whatever alternative reason you have for assisting me. I'm doing this for Eogan. So perhaps the better question is, are *you* in or not?"

His reply is simply to smirk and turn down the street toward wherever it is we're headed.

I hurry to catch up and try to shove down the sick feeling brought on by his smile as Eogan's and Rasha's voices fill my head with their invasive warnings not to trust Myles.

I'm not trusting him. I'm simply . . . doing what needs to be done.

For whatever reason though, I lower my voice. "What if Eogan's block can work against these abilities too? Won't Draewulf just use it to cut them out like my Elemental ones?"

"Not if he doesn't know you have them until it's too late."

Good point. But the nausea stays.

We're nearing the outer edges of the city. I can tell not only because of the general direction we've been moving in under the cloud-covered sky, but also because of the buildings. This is the older, more embellished area. *Curious.* Is this mystery woman one of their elders?

He points toward a house. It's got an old wooden door and no windows, and it's sandwiched between two larger, fancier buildings. How he remembered this was here, I can't imagine, but my legs suddenly feel like the chewy bread we've been eating. "What's she like?" I almost ask but don't.

He raises his fist to the door, but just before knocking, he turns and looks me up and down. "You can still change your—"

I shove in front of him and bang on the door myself.

He grins and follows up by tapping five times in some kind of rhythmic signal.

The door is opened to reveal a well-lit interior behind an unbelievably old woman nearly as short as Allen the tallish dwarf. Gray hair, gray robes, everything about her looks aged and clean and impeccably neat and, more than that, especially beautiful. A whoosh of incense puffs past her into our faces—it smells of embalming powder and fish.

My lungs gag up my throat.

"You are here for my services?"

CHAPTER 19

I PEER AT MYLES.

As if reading my mind, the old woman says, "No one wanders the streets past curfew unless they're looking for a fight or a cure. I assume you'll want the latter."

For as aged as she looks, her voice is impeccably smooth. Like an evening tide sifting onto a sandy shore. She waves us in and clicks the door behind us. "It'll be 650 denalla."

Payment. How much is a denalla, and how does she know what we're paying *for*?

Myles pulls out a leather purse and places it in her hands. "Eight hundred for your discretion."

Despite my lack of fond feelings, I shoot him a grateful, "Thanks," as she grabs it and licks her lips.

"I'm always discreet, but suit yourself." She bestows a full grin on him beneath glittery eyes that look like ghoulishly beautiful pits. She peers closer and, quick as a blink, stretches a hand out to grab his chin. "I remember you. The half-breed."

A half-breed? My eyes widen. *Of what?*

He sneers at me a clear warning—if I open my mouth or breathe a word of what I've just heard, he will likely kill me and Eogan himself.

Releasing his face, the old woman beckons us into a low-ceilinged room cluttered with too many shelves arranged haphazardly against the walls. Bottles and dried weeds appear shoved at random along them, crowding every inch of their spaces. In fact, every surface in the room is covered besides the table standing in the center. On that sits a short stack of books and a single elegant bowl.

I sniff and suddenly Myles and I are both shrinking back.

I scan the room for dead bodies—bolcranes, ferret-cats—anything to explain that embalming scent. I've been around it enough times, with enough owners, to know what it's used for. The Faelen poor don't share the frivolous mindset of having stewards prepare their family members for burial. Their slaves do it.

Rasha may be right about this being a bad idea.

Come on, Nym. Just get your abilities and go.

The woman crosses her arms and stands in front of the table. Waiting. I firm up my shoulders and step forward as Myles shuffles behind me. I clear my throat. "I'm looking to regain abilities. Are you able to do so?"

"Depends on what you want them for."

"I need to help someone."

"She's specifically looking to use them on another's powers," Myles adds.

The woman appears more interested. "Anyone I know?"

"Doubtful." My scalp tightens.

"We'd prefer to keep it anonymous," Myles says.

She shrugs and presses her wide face closer so her gray hair is brushing my cheek. I stiffen and try not to pull back from her black eyes. For a split second something about her looks familiar. I look at Myles before staring back at her.

But no, I've never seen this woman before.

"How is it done? How do you give them?"

"Oh, I don't give them, child. I simply . . ."—she flourishes an arm around the room—"enhance what you already have."

"Which might be a problem seeing as mine are gone." I glance at Myles. Did he lead me here for nothing? My nerves are crawling through my skin.

"Are they, now? Interesting." She walks around the table to a tea-cup set on the mantel. She picks it up and takes a loud slurp. "Well, no matter. The Uathúil blood within you still exists. What I can give you will attach and turn it into a . . . better variation." She turns to leer at me, and everything in me swears she meant to say "darker variation."

I point at Myles. "Did he already have Uathúil blood when he came to you?"

"Only a slight trace—otherwise it wouldn't have worked. No use trying to enhance what you don't got. It'd bind to your blood and simply kill you."

This time I can't help the quake down my spine. "Will what I get be similar to my Elemental abilities?"

Her eyes flash so sharp I stumble beneath her intensity. With three steps and a slosh of her tea, she grabs the hood of my cloak and pulls it back. She's faster than she looks for her age.

"A female Elemental. They let you live?"

I pull away. "Just answer the question."

"They'll be better," she says slowly. "Interesting . . ." She turns to Myles. "Do you know why they let her live?"

He shrugs. "A female Elemental's never been possible. I presume by the time they realized what she was, they were afraid she'd curse them if they harmed her." He glances at me. "Our people are . . . suspicious."

"Do *you* know how I was born Elemental?" I ask the old woman, studying her expression.

"The blood of Uathúils is passed down from either the males or females of their type. In your case, it's always passed through the men."

"My father wasn't one."

She nods and bends close again, breathing on my skin, my neck, assessing me. A moment longer and she smiles odd and understanding-like. "I see."

"See what?"

"Nature decided it was time. You need him and he needs you." She leans back as if this is of great amusement to her. "Oh, what I wouldn't give to watch that take place."

"*What* take place? Who needs me?"

"Draewulf, of course."

What? I open my mouth but my words are lost. I shake my head. "I don't know what you're talking about. I just want to separate him from someone's body—will these powers enable that?"

"Perhaps. Depends on which of you breaks first."

Good hulls, this woman's not making a lick of sense. "Depends on *who* breaks first? And *what* does Draewulf need me for?"

Her curious gaze is steady on me. "To achieve it, of course. I've been wondering how long until he figured it out."

I might, in fact, bash my head against her face. Slowly, patiently, I ask, "To achieve what? What. Does. He need me for? He already took my powers."

"Oh, you may not have your powers, dear, but *he* hasn't taken them. He has to absorb into a person to do that. As I said, Uathúil powers are tied to their blood. And as for what he needs you for, I can't be telling you. I will give you a bit of advice though. Interrupt the blood of kings before it's too late. And whatever you do, don't let him take the final one."

Is she jesting? Is that honestly supposed to mean something? The blood of kings? "You must—"

"That's all I can offer," she snaps.

"But—"

"Ask me more and I'll throw you out. Now, did you know how to control your Elemental abilities before they were taken?"

I calm my voice. "I was getting better at it."

"Then these should be a dose of candy. Although, if you ever . . ." Her voice fades along with her cautioning gaze. She doesn't finish.

I look at Myles. He shrugs. "If I ever what?"

"If ever nothing. Come. Sit." She pokes me into a wood chair beside the table in the dim, smelly room and places my hands on the armrests. "Hold still." The old lady smiles that eerie smile and walks over to a row of dusty wooden chests covering the wall of shelves. They look warped. As if at one time something damp leaked through and bent them.

She picks three of the chests up and sets them on the table. Their hinges look rusty but they open smoothly. From the first one she takes a pair of thin metal ropes and brings them over to my wrists.

Oh litches. I rise. "This isn't—"

"It's for your safety," Myles soothes.

"It's for *all* our safety," the woman says.

I don't care what it's for. My flesh is crawling like an oliphant's nest. "Do it without them or I'm leaving."

"Suit yourself and leave." She shrugs. "Just know that the young man's blood you hope to save, as well as his kingdom, will be on your head."

My gaze flares at her. I sit back into the chair and glare at Myles, but he lifts his palms as if to swear it wasn't him who fed her everything she seems to know.

"No, no. Don't blame your friend for a witch's second sight."

A witch?

Of course she's a witch.

I grit my teeth. How much else can she see with that "second sight"?

It's a half minute before I acquiesce to her tying me with those cold ropes, and only then on the condition she leaves my ankles bound loosely. I want to be able to pull my feet through and shove my knees up so my hand can grab my knives if necessary.

She merely nods and begins lashing my wrists to the armrests. The metal bites into my skin, starting up an internal shiver.

I conjure up images of Eogan. Of the bloodied man tonight. Of the flash of fear in that young boy's face, and the hope on the faces in Faelen a few days ago. I focus on Isobel and Eogan and on what Draewulf will do if no one can stop him. The metal keeps biting in harder.

Then the old witch is pulling out a pot from the second chest and placing it on the coals in the fireplace. Back and forth she walks, from the fire to the table, adding powdery-looking things from collections of jars and bottles and weeds crammed into more chests. She tugs a stool closer to the hearth and sits. And stirs. And hums an unearthly tune that sounds like it's from the time of ancients.

Stir, stir, stir. Hum, hum, hum.

The smell is slow, drifting, dragging itself through the air in a green wisp to settle around Myles and me in a disgusting scent of more fish. I crinkle my nose and stare straight ahead. At her. At the pot.

Stir, stir, stir.

Is this what Myles had to go through when he came years ago? Drink fish-smelling stew? I look at him and smirk. I wonder if he threw it up.

Stir, stir, stir. More humming. More stirring.

I swear hours go by with Myles and me just sitting there, waiting and watching as she stirs.

Myles yawns and polishes his hair until, eventually, he's apparently satisfied with his appearance and nearly passes out on the table.

A short while longer and suddenly the woman hops up from her seat with an exclamation. She shoves the pot in my face. "Here. Sniff."

I careen away with a gag. "Is that what I need to drink?"

She jerks it back and huffs. "You? Of course not. It's my tea. But don't it smell good?" She settles the pot on the table and spoons out some of its liquid into her teacup. Takes a sip and smacks her lips. "Mmm. That's the thing right there."

I raise a brow at Myles. He shrugs, looking more frumpy and frazzled than I think I've ever seen him, with a patch of his dark hair actually out of place and his sly eyes sagging heavily.

I turn back to the witch. "Are we . . . going to be here much longer? Just curious," I rush to add.

She slurps her tea, louder this time, and eyes me. "This ability you're wanting . . ." She juts her chin toward Myles. "Is half-breed boy going to help you practice using it?"

I nod.

"Good, good," she says more to herself. "Like I said—piece of cream using your new abilities. But just in case, you'll need someone to keep an eye on you for a bit so you don't accidentally kill everyone."

Lovely. "Is there anything else I should know?"

The woman sets her cup on the table and stands on her tiptoes to open the third chest. It creaks as she pries the lid. "Only that if you're hoping to use the ability on that boy . . ." She turns to me as if to ensure I'm staring right at her, listening. Her smooth voice grows rough, firm. "Don't wait much longer." She flips back to the chest and pulls out a clear bottle with a cork stopped into it and then walks to one of the shelves to fetch another mug.

And I'm sitting here staring with my mouth open. "Is there any hope for saving him?" I blurt out.

She doesn't answer. Just places the mug and bottle on the table before taking another slurp of tea. After a moment she uncorks the bottle and leans down to peer inside it with one eye. "Uh-huh. Just like I left it."

I watch her tip it over and a sledge of black liquid flows from it down into the cup. I frown. The bottle she's holding is see-through and empty, but the ick keeps dripping out as if the thing is full. She recorks the bottle and swirls the mug to mix it.

She carries the cup over and thrusts it in front of my face. "Drink."

That's it? That's what we've sat here waiting for? I sniff. *Ugh. What in the name of—?* It smells worse than the tea and when I peer over the mug's rim, the liquid is bubbling. *Boiling.*

She tips it near my lips and I lean back because maybe we should take a second to be certain this is the right stuff and also to let it cool. "Wait—"

My words are cut off as she crams the cup to my mouth and

jerks my hair back so my jaw opens. I gasp and choke as suddenly the sledge is slipping between my teeth and down my throat.

Dear hulls, what kind of plague is this stuff?

But it's not burning. In fact, it's cold and bubbly and it tastes of honey. Even if it smells like death warmed over. I swallow it down until it's gone, and once she pulls the mug away I'm thinking the chances are fairly good I might vomit. My stomach feels swollen and the honey is sticking oddly to the back of my tongue. The woman doesn't seem to care—she just sets the cup on the table and pulls her stool over to sit and wait. And hum.

I'm not sure what it's supposed to do or how it's supposed to work, but I suspect she mixed something wrong. Abruptly my stomach is on fire and my bones are icing over—as if all the heat from my body and blood is being pulled into a whirlpool made of the potion.

My head starts vibrating first. The rest of me follows quickly—shaking, shivering, flailing, my wrists and ankles chafing at their restraints as my muscles lose control of themselves. The old woman's got me by the back of the head and she's stuffing a dusty cloth in my mouth.

That's when I begin screaming.

Because my entire body is being frozen alive and my veins are turning to powder as the cold sears through my bones and skin. Then I'm screaming because the woman is morphing, changing into a hideous black beast, a spider the size of a ferret-cat. It's coming closer and Myles is merely standing there watching, staring at it. What's he waiting for? What's he doing?

The spider-lady shuffles forward.

Clack, clack, clack.

Her legs tap on the floorboards as she scuttles for me, humming her song that now sounds like a chanting death knell. I squirm and gag on the dirty cloth. I try to lift my hands, my legs, but the straps are too tight—they're cutting my skin.

The spider talons dig into me as she latches first onto my leg, then jumps to my stomach. She begins crawling, clawing, scratching her way up my bones, my flesh, onto my chest until suddenly I can't breathe. She's suffocating my lungs.

"Help me!" I try to yell, but no sound emits through the rag.

Clack, clack, clack. The legs move along my chest up onto my neck, my throat. The spider's hundreds of eyes twinkle down at me as her hideous coarse-haired body leans into my chin. She puts two legs on my lips. I shiver, but she yanks out the rag and is clawing, forcing my mouth to stay open.

I shake my head and writhe, trying to throw her off, but the talons cut deeper and suddenly she's crawling inside my mouth and forcing her way down my throat. Her bristly legs scratch up every inch of it as they scuttle down into my chest, my heart, my blood.

Next thing I know someone's pulling the rag from my mouth just as I begin vomiting into a pot placed in my lap. And when I look up, the spider's sitting in front of me but she's re-formed back into the old witch.

CHAPTER 20

Crisscross, back and forth, the spider spins her web, while the carved-in bird on my arm flutters and whimpers and chirps out a song that sounds very much like one I used to know. There's something beautiful about it really—the way the spider weaves to the music, strumming my veins onto her loom, like an intricate dance of sinew and flesh. Leaning down every so often to bite and push her venom further into my blood.

Clack, clack, clack, her legs scratch. Transforming the thrum in my veins into pockets of cold, swirling energy.

Until she looks up with those glittering eyes, and I swear she scowls. Her scratching legs pause, then suddenly she's skittering for the carved-in bluebird on my arm. I try to brush her off, but my fingers are heavy and cumbersome and by the time they twitch she's pounced. A horrid chirp is followed by a broken note, and the last of the melody is replaced by the crunch of bones and chewing.

Vomit bubbles up. What has she done?

I try to move but the venom hits my spine and my veins begin to freeze. Then sting.

Suddenly my bones are seizing, writhing, as the poison rips out every last bit of Elemental so that all I can hear is a voice screaming to make it stop. Please make it stop.

The spider keeps devouring my arm.

I wake up screaming and clawing at my arm, but it's too dark to see what in kracken is going on. I slap and hit at the beast before finally fumbling for the light along the bedside, twisting the gear to illuminate the scratching legs attacking my skin.

Nothing is on my skin.

Other than a crisscross of scuff marks made by my own nails along the puffy bluebird's face.

I lean back and shut my eyes, aware that my sweat-drenched body is shaking like one of the earthquakes Colin used to make, and I can't hold still because everything's so wet and cold, and my bones are seizing. *What in—?* With a jerk, my chest curls down around my knees, and suddenly every frozen muscle I own makes a cracking sound. Like ice under too much pressure.

Oh litches.

My body is going to break wide open.

I force myself up into a sitting position and clench my arms around my legs to make it stop, to make them still. A movement in front of me catches in the corner of my eye, and it's not until I glance up that I finally notice someone's seated near my desk, rubbing her eyes, staring at me.

I frown. *Rasha?*

The red glow of her gaze is there. Growing. It's lighting the dark between us with an intensity that says she's scared, or concerned. Or furious.

"Nym, what in hulls have you done?" Her voice sounds like a ghost. An angry one.

I blink stupidly and continue shaking.

"I told you—I *warned* you not to trust him."

I glance around the dim room before swerving my eyes back to meet her face. "What are you doing in here? What time is it?"

"Half past four." She stands and draws near. "But do you even have *any* idea what you've done?"

I grip my knees harder so she won't see how badly my legs are quaking. "Yes, I know exactly. How long have you been here?"

"For the past three hours and, no, you have *no idea.*"

"Where's Myles?"

"Why didn't you ask me? Why didn't you *come* to me instead of lying about it?"

"*Me?* I asked you when you brought up his offer and you refused to tell me anything. Did you know this might allow me to save Eogan? That it's the *only* way to save him?" I glance around again, my bones clacking around. "And *where is Myles?*"

"If he has any bleeding sense at all, he's shaking in his nightmares for fear of me. And I'll thank you not to lay it at my feet as if it's my fault. Once he offered, you could've asked anytime."

"Maybe if you'd stayed at the banquet I would have. If you'd seen what they did—"

"You'd already made your decision at the banquet. But if you'd stayed and heeded my warning instead of tromping off to absorb a power you know nothing about—"

"Your warning made no sense!" I choke out. "Look, it's half past four in the morning and you standing here lecturing me in my room before my head can even think is not helping anything. I'm not going to apologize for trying to give us a chance. This can help all of us—Eogan, you, me, the delegates."

"You don't know it'll give them a chance! If anything, it's just as likely you'll end up like Draewulf!"

I peer sharply at her. "What's that supposed to mean?"

She clamps her mouth shut.

My throat is jittering so hard I'm having a hard time getting the words out. "What do you mean?"

"I mean that that's exactly my point. You have no idea what you're dealing with or what it will do to you."

"But apparently you do and you decided to withhold it from me. Lovely. I think I'd like to go back to bed now if you don't mind." I jerk my head toward the door.

Her eyes flash and by the time she's crossed the five paces and opened it, her gaze has lit up her hair so she looks like an angel of death. She walks out and the whole room shakes as she slams the door shut behind her.

Bleeding hulls.

I sit there a moment, cursing her out in my head, then cursing myself out even more. After a moment I get up, and, quaking like a blasted avalanche, peel off my sweat-soaked leathers and slip on the only normal-looking dress I can find in the dim light. I wrap my warm cloak around me before yanking open the door.

Six guards snap to attention from a game of stones they'd been leaning over. Rasha is already gone.

"Can we help you?" one mutters.

I clench my teeth. "Take me to see Lord Myles."

Every guard turns toward me and I swear their eyes all harden at once. It takes me an annoying minute before the awareness dawns of how such a request must appear. The girl from Faelen, rumored to be Eogan's love interest, embarking on a tryst with Faelen's lord protectorate.

"Miss, are you—?"

"Now."

With an uncomfortable *tsk*, the Faelen man turns and leads me down two doors to Myles's chambers.

He taps.

Taps again.

I reach out my shaking, deformed hand and bang on the blasted thing just like at the old woman's house.

There's a mumbling followed by a crash inside just before the door's yanked open. Myles is standing there in a pair of pants displaying the whitest bare chest I've ever seen on a man who prides himself so highly on looks.

"There'd better be a bleeding fire or a woman with very good legsss standing here because . . ." He stalls, seeing me for the first time. His face pinches. "Oh."

"I'd prefer not to be seen as either of those," I say, jaw chattering. I slip by him into his room, which, from all appearances, is identical to mine. I pick up a pair of what appear to be his silk pantaloons tossed onto his desk and drop them on the floor, then slide up to shakily perch myself in their place and tug my cloak around me.

He flips around. "What do you want?"

"Help." I lower my voice and glance toward the door. "Whatever that woman gave me is poisoning my body. Something's wrong."

"And thisss is cause for getting me up before the Creator himself is awake?"

"How do I fix it?"

"You're a woman—how in hulls should I know?"

"I had a dream—"

"I would be too if you weren't ruining my sleep."

"Of spiders."

"How nice for you. We can talk about it tomorrow, now would you—"

I narrow my gaze. "I'm not leaving until you help me."

"Help you what?"

I glare at him and lift my gimpy hand from my robe, holding it out to him as it violently tremors.

He shuts the door. "Tell me about your dream."

I tell him about the spider and the glittery gaze and the poison in my veins and arm. He closes his eyes as if imagining them, except now he's moving his lips, repeating my words, and the air around us has rippled until I'm watching the very same spider crawl across the carpet toward me.

I yelp and yank my legs up onto the desk, and the creature dissipates.

Myles opens his eyes. "Interesting. Other than the cold and shaking, how doesss it feel?"

"Like there's a blasted vortex inside tugging my bones apart."

He smiles and rubs his face with the base of his palms, then turns to pull a shirt off the foot of his bed to slip on. *Thank hulls.*

By the time I glance back, he's walking toward me—stopping three feet away to roll up his sleeves and smirk. The moonlight glints off his silver tooth, making my spine rigid a moment.

"As to your question if this is normal, I'm no expert, but I'd say the potion'sss working through your system and attaching itself to your blood. The chill and tremorsss will ease once you've managed some control. You recall your training with Eogan?"

I ignore the hunger such a simple comment brings. Of course I remember. That's part of the reason I'm standing here—because I don't want to simply remember. I want it back.

I swallow and nod, which feels more like a jiggle since even my head is convulsing with cold.

"He taught you to tap into the idea of protecting others as a way to control your Elemental abilitiesss, did he not?"

"Among other things. What's your point?"

"Were you ever able to gain complete control of them?"

"Not without his help, but only because he hadn't finished training me." I swear my chest bones crack a little wider as the words tumble out.

"Exxxactly. Lucky for you I'm going to finish his training—just the other side of the coin, so to ssspeak. The side he wouldn't show you for fear you'd become too powerful for even him to control."

"Because he knew I'd keep hurting people if he didn't help me."

"And so can I. The difference isss . . ." He steps closer and lifts his hand, touching one finger to a strand of my white hair. "I don't think you need to be controlled. I think you need to be ssset free."

Eogan would be horrified. My teeth begin clacking again as a shudder lurches through me. The bluebird marking on my arm begins aching, flaring, flittering her crushed wings against my pulsing vein. But when I look down, it's nothing.

I grind my jaw. "So get on with it. Show me."

"As I said, Eogan used the technique of tapping into your, shall we call it, merciful side. My way is similar. Except I'm going to teach you to reach for your jussstice side." He dips his face near mine and whispers, "The part of you that hates Draewulf for what he's done—that hates the injustice done to you by years of being enslaved to perverse owners. I'll teach you to fight against that."

My stomach turns. How many times did Eogan and I argue

about this—about my fear of becoming a weapon? "I want to do justice, not strike out in vengeance."

"Oh my dear," he breathes. "When I'm finished with you, you'll be able to use thisss power for whatever you want."

I swallow and force my head to believe him even if my heart doesn't. "Because I'll be able to control it."

"More than control it, you'll be able to control *others* with it. Like Draewulf."

"That witch said Draewulf needs me to achieve something. Will this stop it?"

"It'll do more than stop it. It'll kill him if you want."

Something in the way he says it curls my spine. "By interrupting the blood of kings," I whisper.

His answer is to slide his hand from my hair he's been toying with down to the fifteen owner circles on my right arm. And squeeze.

The old familiar energy comes, but instantly it's not familiar. This one is slicker, cooler, oozing into my veins where my Elemental strength would've surged. With it comes an utter sense of hopelessness, of emptiness, as if everything in me is being poured into that vortex in my chest and is flowing, fading inside it, draining everything that is me into an entity that is pure energy.

I begin to yank away but pause.

There's a quickening in my veins even as the shaking slows and the teeth chattering ceases. The rush is sick and nauseating and thrilling, and for the first time in days I feel a fleeting sense of normal.

Because I feel physical.

Powerful.

Myles's words are quick, stirring the atmosphere and confusing my vision as he conjures up the scene of the little redheaded girl at the auction stand. The one I accidentally killed trying to defend her from her new owner just before Adora purchased me.

I start to pull back, to yell at him, but his voice is swift. "Don't resist the power this time. Follow it. What is *the ability* wanting to do?"

It wants to destroy the man all over again.

"Do you feel it?"

I nod.

"Good. Now act on it."

I can't.

I won't.

I flatten my good palm against my curled fingers and hold them stiff.

He lessens his grip on my owner circles. "What you're seeing— the little girl, her owner—they're not real, but in order to release this new energy, you have to act on what it wantsss. Act and watch what happensss."

I reach one hand toward the mirage of the man and, crumpling my gimpy fingers into a fist, allow the energy to increase. Instead of bringing down lightning on him, the energy in me is seeking to deplete his. I can't curb it. It lets loose and I immediately see a darkening mass accumulating in his chest. I hear his heartpulse slow. It doesn't stop though.

Even when he slumps over and his skin has gone gray, it keeps thumping, but something tells me his ability to torment others has been drained from him forever. The bloodlust has faded, and the little girl is left. Unharmed.

The vision dissipates until it's just Myles and me standing in his room. Surprisingly, confusingly, the cold in my bones has lessened.

I smile. Because as terrified as that scenario was, it also felt safe. And I haven't felt safe since the last time Eogan held me.

"Again," I mutter.

The air ripples like before and this time Draewulf's standing before us in Eogan's body. He reaches for me like he did yesterday on the airship, going for my throat, black eyes burning. His claws sink into my skin, but instead of evoking fear, it unleashes a vortex of hunger, a craving to draw out his power and destroy it. Destroy him. I lift a hand to his and feel the cold in my lungs start to surface.

It erupts and fades in one clench of my fist as Draewulf clamps down on my owner circles. I tug away but he's too strong. He keeps pressing down, until what felt so powerful a moment ago now settles limp and small in my veins.

His ability is too great.

I sag and the vision fades. Myles is standing there with his arms crossed and an eerily pleased smile.

I cough and wheeze. I nod, and we run through the scene again.

And again.

The fourth time my shoulders and chest grow feeble as Draewulf leans in closer, smelling of wolf and metal and sundrop skies on Eogan's skin. His gaze flickers and abruptly it *is* Eogan, his touch, his warmth, his hand on my neck that is taking over, accessing the ability in me and bringing it to the surface. I gasp. My chest cracks and crumbles until it's disintegrating and falling, falling, falling into nothingness. A faint cry pushes up my throat, and I fear my aching heart might burst open to bleed all over this room.

The vortex inside me begins tugging, lashing up from my chest and out through my arms and fingertips. I reach for him, pressing my palms against him as my lips spill forth mutterings that make no sense. The gaping black inside me grows wider as does the hunger, and suddenly my hands are drawing the breath and life and energy from Eogan's body. His eyes flicker between wolf black and emerald green until all at once they're gray. His entire face is gray and he's slumping, falling, as his life energy becomes mine.

I gasp and pull away.

The air ripples and Myles is standing two feet away. His pale complexion has turned the color of ash, but he's grinning.

I slap at him. "What was that? What just happened?"

His smile broadens and my skin tightens. "The images feed on fear."

A knock on the door interrupts. He steps back. "Enter."

It's the Faelen guard from earlier. He's hesitant, peering around the door before pushing it farther open. He exhales when he sees us, relief softening his features. "Pardon, miss, but . . ." He indicates the hall with his eyes. "I thought you might want to be informed the other delegates will emerge from their rooms shortly. In case you preferred to be there instead of . . ." His gaze flashes to Myles and the hint is clear.

"Thank you." Flexing my gimpy hand, I slide off the desk and head for the hallway, looking back at Myles. "Let's resume later."

His response is a nod, but I barely catch it because just as I reach the hall, I notice the chill shored up inside me is no longer consuming me.

And my spine has stopped shaking.

CHAPTER 21

T HE BRON AND FAELEN SOLDIERS ARE STILL IN THE hall, stones gone. They eye me as I walk by the row of them. One, three, five of them purse their lips and I'm acutely aware of something rippling beneath all their stiffness. I peer closer. One of the Faelen guards shifts his gaze toward Myles's door.

I frown. "Is Princess Rasha in her room?"

"She and Lord Wellimton are already in the Negotiation Hall. The rest of you will be taken there momentarily," a Bron guard says as, simultaneously, Lord Percival's and Myles's doors open.

"Good morning," the lord protectorate oaf says a bit too loud and cheery for this time of day. He shoots me a broad, suggestive grin that is clearly meant to entertain the guards.

I pull my cloak tighter around my warming face and mentally stab him to a thousand deaths. I'm just begging Lady Gwen to hurry up, when a moment later she steps out to join us.

The Faelen and Bron guards, including the angry-looking large one who wanted to rip my head off last night, proceed to escort us to the Hall. I refuse to look at Myles as we walk, but he sidles up to me anyway.

"What did you tell them?" I growl, indicating the soldiers. My face is still hot.

"Funny thing there . . ." He tilts his mouth so only I can hear. "The truth is you dropped out cold once we returned to the base level of the Castle last night. I had to carry you back, which was not an easy accomplishment while trying to fool the nightwatch, if you know what I mean." He rubs his arms as if they're sore. "Ssso when we reached your room, well . . ." He chuckles. "I dumped you outside your room to a host of ogling bodyguardsss. I should warn you, they were absolutely taken aback at your recklessss behavior." He sniffs. "They thanked me quite profusely for rescuing you and promptly dropped you in bed. At least I assume they did."

I go back to refusing to look at him and feel the chill itch at my insides again. "What'd you tell them I'd been doing?"

"Merely that you'd managed to slip out and find a batch of unseemly friendsss and Bron ale. By the time I came across the poor Elemental girl, she was drunker than a common-house owner." He shakes his head. "Ssso unbecoming of a delegate."

"So you *didn't* lead them to believe you and I were . . ." I clear my throat. It's so repulsive I can't even bring myself to say it.

"Oh, don't flatter yourself," he purrs. "Although, believe me, I was tempted to hint at it, if only to see how infuriated you'd be."

He's saved from having his tongue sliced out by the fact that we've stopped in front of the doors leading into the same hall we were in last night. The only difference this time is that it's already full of people when we walk in. Some of the faces I recognize from the banquet. Others are part of the general blur. I sift through them for Kel's, although just as before, I know he won't be there.

"Have you heard how the young boy's doing? The one from last night?" I whisper to Myles.

He shakes his head as my gaze homes in on the room's center, to the blood spatters I expect there, but all traces of violence—and food—have been washed away and the space is back to looking sterile and foreboding with its war maps.

"I heard he would be all right. Apparently they have decent healers here." Lady Gwen points to Rasha, who's over at the same table we sat at during the banquet. Beside her, Lord Wellimton beckons us to join them as they stand talking with two of the men who were seated with Draewulf last night. The rest, including the shape-shifter, are noticeably absent.

"Good morning," Rasha says in a tight voice when we reach her. She swipes a look at me with red, puffy eyes and narrows in on my dress. "I see you're wearing my nightgown."

"I assumed it was your knitting clothes," I admit.

"So of course you chose to wear it." She attempts a smirk but it doesn't match the panic and exhaustion in her expression.

"Are you all right?" I whisper.

Without replying, she turns her back to me and faces Lord Wellimton and the other delegates. "Lord Wellimton and I have just been discussing the discovery of three of Nym's Faelen bodyguards murdered last night."

I freeze. *What?*

"Oh my!" Lady Gwen says.

"When? How?" Lord Percival asks.

"While we were at the banquet," Lord Wellimton says. "Which is why Princess Rasha was called away."

"Some Bron soldiers stumbled across them." Rasha's voice shudders in spite of her stiff stance. "One of my Cashlin guards insisted they come get me."

Bile rises into my mouth. "Why didn't they come get *me*?"

"Perhaps because by the time my men spoke with me and I'd sent them looking for you, they couldn't find you," she says coolly.

My gut turns.

"Where were they found?" Lord Percival asks. "Are you certain they were only Nym's guards?"

"Yes, and they were found in a private section of the palace. We're not sure how they got there other than it appears they were dragged part of the way."

That cold is seeping around my bones again. "How?" I ask. Sir Gowon's warning from last night slips through my mind. *"There's a black-market price on your girl's head worth more than Faelen."*

What have I done?

"Their throats were slit and their bodies . . . torn."

"In pieces?" Lady Gwen squeaks.

Lord Wellimton nods.

"Who did it?" Myles is staring hard at Rasha but tips his head toward Eogan's empty seat.

The disgust for him in her expression is as clear as the slight shake of her head, *no*. "We're not sure. But . . ." She pauses and shifts to glance around the room in clear indication that it's why she came here early today. *To study the faces of people as they walked in.*

I peek back at the host of guards. There are more of them than yesterday.

"We've been assured, though, that the Bron military are doing everything in their power to look into it," Rasha says.

Something in her tone doesn't ring right. I grab her arm and turn her toward me, lowering my voice. "Rasha, what—?"

She winces and pulls away. "Nym, your fingers are ice!"

"Sorry." I step back before reclaiming my hands to the warmth of my cloak. "I just . . . what can I do to help?"

She rubs her wrist. "I think you've already done enough."

Lord Wellimton's voice grows loud. "Lord Myles, in light of these circumstances, I'd appreciate you allowing me to do most of the negotiating. Since I'm certain we can agree it's for the best. I know you're the king's cousin, but as a senior member of Faelen's High Council, I must insist that I'm better prepared for this discussion. In whatever direction it takes us."

Myles gives a soft snort, but Wellimton simply nods at the two Bron generals and takes a seat before they move off to the king's table. Rasha slips in next to him, in the same order we were last night. The set of double doors we're facing down the long aisle abruptly opens and the other three Bron members who ate at Draewulf's table last night file in. Following them is Sir Gowon.

My mouth goes stale. I wonder if he's thought any more about the Elegy, or the Draewulf accusation I made last night. If he's even considered it.

Before I can think on it further, Draewulf's Mortisfaire daughter, Lady Isobel, enters, head high, black hair swept behind her, wearing a skin-suit with porcupine quills woven to feather out over her chest and shoulders. I may not be into fashion, but even I would wear a suit like that. She looks compelling. Powerful.

Potent.

The already noisy room grows even louder as Assembly members talk over each other and some stand to get a better view of her.

Eogan-who-is-Draewulf strides in last and the whole group proceeds down the aisle in what feels like an awkward parade because half the crowd is frowning and arguing and the other half is nodding and yelling support. Draewulf looks amused.

He stops in front of the table we're sitting at, and I'm tempted to try out my new ability right here, right now. To punish him. To try to release Eogan while there's still time. "What is the blood of kings, Draewulf?" I want to whisper.

But I don't. I don't even move. Because something tells me this new ability's not ready, and if Draewulf finds out too soon . . .

He's two feet away and lifting his hand. He murmurs some type of foreign word as he casts a glance at the noisy Assembly. Abruptly they fall silent.

He drops his hand and walks up to the king's table to take his chair.

That's what will happen.

I look around, but if anyone other than Rasha at our table notices, I can't tell. Perhaps they thought the Assembly simply obeyed his raised hand for silence. Except those in the crowd look confused.

Sir Gowon shuffles behind and waits until Draewulf is settled in the king's center chair before leaning down to place a set of documents in front of him.

Draewulf twitches an idle hand to cue Gowon to get on with it, and in a loud voice the old man introduces each guest at our table to the larger Assembly.

"Cashlin's esteemed princess, Her Royal Highness Rasha. Faelen's Lord Myles, who is both lord protectorate and King Sedric's cousin. Faelen's Lord Wellimton, Lord Percival, Lady Gwen, and the delegate Nymia. Bron officially recognizes and welcomes each of you to our kingdom and our Assembly. We pray these upcoming negotiations will find favor and benefit the entire Hidden Lands realm."

I'm watching the room as he's speaking, and it's a small relief to realize not everyone here seems as put off by us as it appeared last night. Out of the hundred or so faces, I count a good twenty that are smiling in what might be approval.

"Well, that's something," Gwen whispers.

I nod my agreement and catch the snarls of some of the boys who are dressed sharp in black suits with silver material sewn around the neck to look like sea-dragon teeth. Something about it is unnerving and I go back to listening as the elderly Sir Gowon opens the floor for negotiations.

"First issue on the agenda," he states, "is the treaty that King Eogan signed with Faelen's King Sedric on behalf of Bron. You all were presented with a written copy upon leaving this Hall last evening."

He nods to Eogan who looks over the room and displays the slightest hint of teeth, which, if I didn't know better, I'd say was a show. Because his underlying expression is humored, as if something is a jest and he's merely biding his time. "Begin," he says.

A general at his table stands. The stitched color rank on the shoulder of his black suit suggests one of the highest positions. He looks Eogan's age of twenty-two years but with a long nose and hair dyed silver. "Forgive me, but I can't help pointing out that according to our statutes, the entire treaty should be considered void since the Assembly was not part of its signing in Faelen."

A much older, more wrinkled counterpart beside him nods. "How can we negotiate under the terms of something we had no part of—let alone trust the country King Eogan signed it with?"

"A better question is how we can negotiate while Faelen's Elemental weapon is sitting in the same room as us?" A gentleman from the Assembly stands and waves a hand my direction. "Why is she here? To insult us? Are we to discuss a treaty when the cause of Bron's loss hovers in our very midst?"

The Assembly members turn their gazes on me.

I keep my head up and stare back at them. And ignore the shiver in my blood as the vortex and ice push further into my bones, boring into me. Even as I tell myself I did what I had to for Faelen.

I will always do what I have to.

"Lord Myles, King Sedric's cousin, brought her as an act of goodwill," Lord Wellimton says, even as he flicks me a dramatic glance of suspicious disapproval.

"Or perhaps to force us into accepting the treaty as valid," another Assembly member argues. "Because she's certainly not here to be used as a weapon on *our* behalf—especially as I noticed no mention in the treaty for the recompense of funds by Faelen to Bron. Most of which, I'll remind us, was lost due to *her*."

There are uncomfortable seat adjustments among the Faelen delegates as Lady Gwen and Lord Percival seem to distance themselves from my chair.

"Recompense of funds?" Wellimton sputters and his face turns red. "Your Majesty, may I ask for a more thorough explanation of such an accus—?"

"I think the greater question is whether we can even trust His Majesty to have signed such a treaty," the silver-haired general interrupts. "King Ezeoha, you left us four years ago in the hands of your brother. Then you allowed your own people to believe you dead until you appeared and killed Odion on Faelen's behalf."

Eogan-who-is-Draewulf smiles. "On *Faelen's* behalf? Is it not your governing belief to let the strongest survive and claim what's theirs? The circumstances surrounding how I chose to survive or gain rulership are not for you to question. Or do you challenge my wisdom and loyalty, General Cronin?"

The silver-haired general ignores him and looks around the room. "King Odion led us into battle just like his father, but he . . ." Cronin points accusingly toward Eogan. "He fought against us at

Faelen's Keep. He has sold us out to the very country we should now own."

That dull, drumming cold in my bones is spreading up my spine. I shift in my seat toward Rasha. "Why are they discussing this in front of us? Wouldn't it be better handled privately?"

Rasha turns me her reddish gaze. "In this room I believe they are required to do so, especially in regard to political matters."

"You speak as one still stuck in the old days," a white-toothed, rough-faced Bron general near Draewulf is saying. "What Eogan has done for us is innovative at the very least; at best it's saved us manpower and multiple deaths. While all of us here grew up accustomed to the war, not all of us saw the need for it."

I see eight, maybe nine people agreeing.

"A nice sentiment, but how many here would back you?" General Cronin's voice grows louder. "We are a people of war! And we, as Bron's leaders, have a country that after one hundred years of war has been promised a victory! Submitting to anything less than that will be viewed as a defeat, and all of us will lose the respect of our citizens."

Heads are nodding.

"We want repayment," several voices mutter.

"We want victory!" others say.

Oh.

Oh litches.

"They still want a war," I murmur, awareness dawning.

"They do?" Lord Percival whispers. "With who?"

Apparently my voice carried louder than intended because the old, wrinkly general looks me square in the face, then breezes his gaze across the other delegates. "It's not even that we want a war—it's that we're in danger of our own. The plagues from Drust have reached the plains and rumor has it Lady Isobel's Dark Army is shortly behind them. Yet here Lady Isobel sits. Sire, perhaps it's not our place to ask where you've been the past four years, nor to speculate on your current relationship with Faelen. However, we cannot negotiate and find stability in a peace treaty while Drust is breathing down our neck. There are dark dealings over there, ones your brother chose to ignore in his hunger to launch against Faelen."

I look at Lady Isobel's flawless face and note the strain of her flexing muscles. I wonder how much self-control she's exercising right now.

"And I argue," the rough-faced general says, "that we've got citizens tired of war and wondering if this peace treaty—as well as an attention to things closer to home—might not be wiser."

"Except we're a nation of war," General Cronin groans. "You can't merely change who we are."

"Maybe once. But I think you'll find a few of the newer Assembly, as well as some of the people we represent, are weary of it. Why not save our resources and pursue what we want through diplomacy rather than force?"

"Which is why we're all here, is it not?" Eogan says, spreading his hands.

The silver-haired general guffaws. "I would agree with you, Your Majesty, except one cannot help notice a representative from Tulla is not part of this delegation. And Cashlin?" His mouth curls. "No offense, Princess Rasha, but you are all your country saw fit to send? It leads one to doubt the seriousness with which your country takes these negotiations."

"As you well know, my people lacked the ability to get here from Cashlin as quickly as needed," Rasha says. A ratlike, sly smile comes out in full play on her face. "However, I assure you that, merely because a task has befallen you in recent days which you are ill-equipped to handle, sir, does not mean that I am impotent for mine."

The man's cheeks pale as fast as her grin disappears, and I've no idea which pantaloons of his she just aired, but from his panicky expression it's clear they're quite awkward.

"Let's move on," he mutters.

Except His Majesty's not listening. He's leaning back speaking with a soldier wearing the eerie black mask and garb of the Mortisfaire. *Isobel's guard? How did one of them get in here?*

Ten seconds later he's twitched his hand again and murmured whatever incantation brings that unnatural silence over the room. "Perhaps now is a good time to take a three-minute refreshment pause."

CHAPTER 22

B ESIDE ME, LADY GWEN RISES AND MOVES DOWN
to question Myles. I lean into Rasha and shake off the few
stares I sense from the Assembly as they get up to talk
amongst themselves. "About the guards killed," I ask her. "Do you
think it was specific toward them because they were *my* guards?"

She eyes me stiffly. "We believe so, seeing as the Bron people
are clearly not pleased by your presence here." She purses her lips.
"Little did they know they needn't have bothered killing off half
your protection unit considering you've managed to endanger
yourself much worse through Myles."

"You can't be serious. I wasn't endangering *anyone*. I'm trying
to help."

"Maybe so, but at some point the lust for power requires a
price."

"Price? Are you saying *I caused* their deaths?" I peer around at
the generals and delegates before lowering my voice. "I went with
Myles as a responsibility to my people. And even to *these* people."

"Just because you won Faelen's war doesn't mean you have to
do it again."

I scoff. "I wish it were that simple, but you didn't see how scared Eogan was for everyone. How he looked at me and begged me to *kill* him yesterday."

"If you were that concerned, maybe you should've done what he asked."

The cold warping my bones flares. Is she jesting? How could she say that? "Is that what you think? That I should've let everything go without even trying?" I wrap my hands around my arms. "You've lived in luxury with friends who've trained and honored your ability your whole life, but I haven't. And that . . . *animal*"—I jerk my head toward Draewulf—"just stole what few things I call mine, not to mention he's about to steal a lot more lives. So before you judge me, consider the fact that in my situation, you would've done the same."

She snorts. "No, I wouldn't. And if you think that, then you don't know the Luminescent race very well."

"I know them well enough to know that while for the past hundred years Faelen's been fighting a war they didn't start and my Elemental people have been slaughtered, the Luminescents stood by caring about little else but themselves."

The second it exits my mouth I wish I could take it back.

Oh hulls—that came out wrong. "Rasha, I didn't mean . . ."

"Yes, you did." She looks around at the delegates reseating themselves. "We'll discuss this later. The meeting's starting."

I look at her and watch her expression turn stony, as if I don't exist.

You're blasted right we will.

Because I can't leave it like this. I can't lose her too.

When I look up, I find Eogan watching me again, but it's with black wolf eyes rather than the emerald ones I'd give anything to see again. I sharpen my glare at him and will him to read my mind:

I've no idea what you need to achieve through me, or what the hulls that even means . . . but I will stop you.

I will not break first.

Sir Gowon wastes no time in calling the meeting back to order, and it occurs to me that in the three-minute intermission, there's been a shift in the air. Not merely between Rasha and me, but between the hundred Assembly members facing the table of Faelen delegates and Bron generals. Although, as far as I can tell, the only physical difference is that Lady Isobel has seated herself right next to Eogan this time.

If she feels me staring, she doesn't let on. Her condescending interest is on the generals as Sir Gowon waves the water servers from the room. When the last doors have shut, the old man folds his hands behind his back and steps up behind Draewulf.

"His Majesty has the floor."

"Delegates and Assembly," Draewulf announces smoothly. "I see no point in drawing this meeting out with endless negotiations. We have made a treaty and will therefore stand by it and will not replenish our storehouses through Faelen. I expect you to support this decision as subordinates who are to obey. Especially as, I believe, you'll find what comes next will silence further arguments from here on out."

When he takes his seat, Lord Wellimton's sigh of relief is so heavy I can almost feel his wet breath slather across the table just as unease twists in my stomach. I glance at Princess Rasha, but she's studying Lady Isobel. The part of her face I can see is narrowing and there's a small red glimmer.

The silver-haired General Cronin rises and gives a long, slow clap of his hands. "Bold speech, my lord, but will the majority here support you? Especially those who feel they are owed more by a man *seeking* to establish himself as king? You would deny them replenishment of their very livelihoods?"

The wolfish black in Draewulf's glare thickens until the whites of his eyes are nearly hidden. He stands enough to lean down the table toward the general. "I never said I wouldn't reclaim what is owed Bron. I simply said we won't do it through Faelen."

He looks at the whole Assembly. "I will give you the war you've been thwarted from—a war that will supply your storehouses with food and minerals and natural resources deprived you far too long." He rocks back on his heels and suddenly smiles, and it's more unnerving than his threatening gaze when he lifts a hand and lets his voice boom.

"I set forth the motion that we prepare for war against Tulla, the land we have easier access to thanks to my treaty with Faelen."

I freeze as a visceral gasp rocks the room.

He wants to go after Tulla?

That's Colin and Breck's homeland.

The delegates shift in their seats, making them squeak, the sound only diluted by Myles's mutter of, "You've got to be bleeding jesting."

The words sink past the chill in my skin and pull the cold back down to the marrow of my bones as I watch Sir Gowon's expression turn as stunned as the rest of ours. His gaze focuses in on Eogan's face.

Between Lord Wellimton, Percival, and Gwen whispering to each other, I can barely hear the silver-haired general stuttering. Like a little boy trying to cover his embarrassment for a game he's losing. He looks over at me for a second. I don't know if he reads my horror or my flinch as the iced poison bleeds deeper into my veins.

I clench my teeth and will it to recede, but it doesn't. It just settles like a low vibration in my blood.

General Cronin is back to glaring at the king. "A positive step, King Eogan." Except his tone is as challenging as the sneer on his face. "But may I ask when and how you propose we do so?"

Draewulf slides a paper in front of him. "Your report stated thirty-five airships are still battle sure. It also states you have enough men to operate them."

"Enough engineers, yes," the old, wrinkled general chimes in. "But many of our soldiers are still out of commission. Practically speaking, we can be ready in six months, but—"

"Good, General Naran," Draewulf cuts him off. "Then we won't need to wait." He stands again and splays his palms to the room. "I plan to move on Tulla immediately. To give—"

"Forgive me, Your Majesty, but I don't see how that's possible," General Naran interrupts. "Our warboats—"

Draewulf's expression turns lethal. As quick as a lightning crack, he lifts a hand and touches it to the older man's arm. The general doesn't wince, but his voice cuts off even while his mouth continues forming words. It takes him a second to notice and fumble to a silent halt as confusion forms around his wrinkled eyes.

Sir Gowon looks sharply from Draewulf to me. I look at Princess Rasha.

She's still studying Lady Isobel, who peers up and says in a tone so low that I swear it rattles the floor beneath my feet, "We only need the airships and a few waterboats."

The silver-haired general stirs from staring at the silenced man. He scoffs. "*Only?* And what, may I ask, do you know of this? How do you propose we provide the soldier-power?"

Draewulf holds out his hand to Lady Isobel in an invitation to stand. She rises beside him and stares at the Assembly with disgust.

That chill in my bones shifts. Until it's rattling, spiking, warning that something is off.

Draewulf's teeth poke out through Eogan's lips as he announces, "Lady Isobel's Dark Army will provide the soldier-power."

CHAPTER 23

AS IF IN UNISON, EVERY SINGLE MEMBER IS YELLING.
"Your Majesty, the Dark Army doesn't exist!"
"Are you insane? Lady Isobel hasn't even answered for her attempt to betray us to Faelen!"

The old, wrinkly-eyed man, General Naran, who'd been silenced, speaks up. "Going to war is one thing. But this is inviting war to our very doorstep! These things—these monsters—have no sense of morality! Rumor has it they've already laid waste to the western border."

"Not just laid waste!" someone in the crowd yells. "They've invoked a bleeding plague! First on the livestock, then on our nomads! It's the same thing that wiped out our forces on Faelen's island cairns—it wasn't the Faelen army, but the plagues and monsters!"

The anger, the fear in here—it's humming around me, and my nerves are soaking it up.

Feeding off of it.

This is what Draewulf had planned?

The king raises his hand for silence, and I peer up at Sir Gowon. *Now does he believe me about Eogan?*

"I assure you the Dark Army does in fact exist," Draewulf says. "Is it dangerous? Yes. But a dangerous army is exactly what's needed, and if one has already been developed by a country under our subjugation, I see no reason not to utilize it to the full extent of our purposes."

General Cronin stands, his silver hair glinting beneath the lights. "You knew about them and yet kept that fact from us once you arrived yesterday?"

Draewulf flips around. "Treasonous words considering every top general here heard news of such an army months ago—and a week ago you received evidence confirming it."

"We kept it quiet until the rumors were verified," General Naran says. "We saw no need to worry our people until we sent soldiers to investigate."

"And what did they find?"

"Half . . . half of them didn't come back."

"Because of the plagues," someone calls out from the crowd.

General Cronin pounds the table. "Because the Dark Army is a menace which *she*"—he points at Lady Isobel—"is controlling!"

I glance at Lady Isobel who sits watching, then my gaze falls to Rasha. Her expression is complete horror. This is what she was seeing on Lady Isobel's face a moment ago. The army. The plagues. I recall my ride through Litchfell Forest where the plagues had struck just before Bron attacked. The treetop houses reeked of death and disease. Even the bolcranes had left the bodies alone.

She peers over at me. *What have we done by keeping him alive?*

"Your Highness," one of the generals protests. "Odion never

would've approved this decision. Isobel approached him months ago offering her services, and he turned the Dark Army down out of understanding of what it would cost Bron." He hesitates. The flash in his eye says there's more—there's something else he's not saying.

General Naran puts his hand out as if to calm his colleague. "Your Highness, allowing Lady Isobel here for questioning is one thing. But allowing *this* may likely start a civil war. Yes, we want to pursue what we need from Tulla, but allow us to do it with our own people in a time of better choosing. Not with a rabid army we know nothing about who is a threat to our very existence."

"You disagree with my tactics?" Draewulf snarls and his tone feels like a stone being sharpened.

"I think you unintentionally have conveyed disregard for our people, our generals, and our way of li—"

His voice cuts off so smooth that General Cronin picks up speaking for him, unaware of Draewulf's hand stretched out. "What is it—four years you've been gone? Perhaps it's time for new leadership the Bron people can trust to hold their best interest."

Rasha rises.

Isobel's hand flashes out and slips between the man's shoulder blades so fast, General Cronin doesn't even have time to wince. Nor to notice the cracking of his colleague's neck beneath Draewulf's fingers.

The silver-haired general's face has already paled and suddenly the only sound emerging from his lips is a gasp for air followed by a gurgle before he slumps chin-first onto the table, dead like his wrinkly cohort, blood oozing from both their mouths.

Lady Isobel steps back, and every face in the room is riveted on her and Eogan-who-is-Draewulf.

I pull out both knives and am preparing to toss them low when Eogan's hand flicks and an unseen force flips my blades down, impaling the knives into the ground at my feet. Without batting an eye, he twitches his hand again, and this time, that invisible force is pressing me against my seat.

I try to lift a fist as the darkness slides along my veins like a raw hunger stirring. Why the members here aren't alarmed at Eogan using powers his real self isn't capable of is beyond me. Or perhaps he's been away so many years, they no longer know what exactly he *is* capable of anymore.

Abruptly that cold in me is coiling with this whole scene. My skin is cooling rapidly and my heartpulse is speeding up, but when I try to focus on it, to see if I can funnel it toward Draewulf or his daughter, nothing happens beyond the chill fusing deeper to my bones.

A vision of the spider biting, numbing, working her poison through my blood materializes, and the thought erupts again that the abilities are not expanded enough to work here, not now, on real people.

On the people I want to kill.

And I *do* want to kill them.

For the first time since I can ever remember, instead of guilt following a murderous craving like that, my hatred just grows stronger.

"Anyone else want to question my judgment?" Draewulf challenges. "Excellent," he says without waiting for a response. "Then allow me to introduce you to your new war general—the Lady Isobel." He smiles. "If you have any concerns as to her assignment, I'm sure she'd be pleased to persuade you."

He turns in a semicircle, as if to make eye contact with

everyone in the room, and the way Isobel leans in, it's like she's hoping someone will.

"Now, let's see, where were we? Ah yes, preparing to take over Tulla." He tips his head to his daughter.

She snaps her fingers and signals her personal Mortisfaire guards—three of them along the wall on either side of us, their faces masked and hair flowing out. They walk to the end of the room and throw the doors open.

I smell them before I see them. The scent of moist earth and bone-dust and decay, swirling its fingers, stirring the room with rank suffocation just like in the alleyway last night. It's the scent of bodies long dead.

It's the breath of plague that is not of this world.

The smell saturates until some of the Assembly and delegates are coughing as the Mortisfaire step back to expose two thin, eerily tall forms draped from head to foot in ratty gray robes. Silent. Gray. Like something from the grave, except they're walking.

As they get closer I realize they're hissing, and it's only when they stop ten paces from the table to stare at us beneath those icy gray cloaks that I get a full look at their faces.

Princess Rasha and Lady Gwen's uttered cries match Lord Wellimton's, as do those of much of the Assembly.

They are animals morphed with long-dead humans. And they reek of unnatural magic.

I will my face straight, will my eyes not to give any reaction as the horror dawns, slow and nauseating. This is what Draewulf can do. It's what he's been doing for years.

But where did he get the dead bodies?

A sickening feeling creeps into my gut.

A noise from beyond the doors overpowers the outcry from the Assembly.

"What in litches' name?" Lord Wellimton mutters just as I careen my head to see behind them. And then they're jostling, writhing, spilling into the room—an entire hissing horde of them.

The wraiths cover the space in a horrific wave until they're surrounding the Assembly and filling up the center aisle behind the first two who entered. Around me, the delegates' faces mimic the revulsion plastered on those of the Assembly's, and Lord Percival seems to be making some type of gagging noise with his throat. Lord Wellimton's red face is swelling up so heatedly, he looks in danger of popping.

Eogan-who-is-Draewulf extends a hand. "My friends, my countrymen. Just as Odion brought Bron into the future with technological advancements, so I carry us even further. This Dark Army is the key to your future. Cooperate with me, and together we will take what we need from Tulla. Choose not to cooperate with me and . . ." He nods toward the two wraith-things facing us, who immediately let out a hiss. "We will advance without you."

The way he says it, I've no doubt we all know what he's just implied. He spells it out anyway. "The Dark Army is currently moving through Bron toward us. Even now, many are camped outside the city, ready to . . . lend assistance as we prepare."

"What about the rest of our negotiations?" Lord Wellimton's face is five shades of insulted. "Surely Your Highness doesn't think we delegates, nor Faelen's treaty—"

"From here on out you will continue to consider yourselves my guests. It is not your country we are going to war against. However—"

Lord Wellimton actually stomps his foot. "I demand—"

"You'll demand nothing. Interfere with our plans and you and your kingdom will be considered enemies of this Assembly, Bron, and the Dark Army itself."

With that, Draewulf waves his hand and our Bron guards, accompanied by three of the terrifying wraiths, appear to escort us and the Faelen bodyguards to our quarters.

CHAPTER 24

I CAN'T BELIEVE HE WOULD THREATEN US WITH THE very weapon that defeated Bron seated in front of them!" Lord Wellimton's voice clips off the walls of his room we're stuffed into. He points his frown at me, as if to indicate I should've done something. Said something.

The expectation in his gaze makes my chest bones ache with the expanding weight of that vortex inside. I'm shivering again. I turn toward the door to where our Faelen and Cashlin guards are standing, having been taken semi-hostage along with us. I need to leave. I need to focus—to continue training before the shuddering and poison in my bones set in to the point I'm cowed over.

"Perhaps it's the best solution," Lord Percival says. "After all, he's in a delicate situation trying to hold on to his throne."

Every one of us rotates to stare at him. He ducks his head. "Or perhaps not."

"War is never the best solution," Princess Rasha says.

Lady Gwen looks scared. "Most of the Assembly seemed confused or furious. How could King Eogan keep his throne by murdering their generals? Why don't they fight back? Were this Faelen's council, my father and grandfather would've never allowed this when they were alive."

Rasha's perched on the couch. She smiles tight. "The Assembly just lost a war and aren't prepared to fight another of this magnitude. Especially one that snuck up within their own territory."

I recall Eogan saying something similar a few weeks ago to Colin and me: *"If anything, Bron's arrogance has blinded them to the real danger in recent years. Their focus on Faelen will be their undoing."*

I nod. "Eogan said Draewulf's been developing the army for years under Bron's nose. They just refused to acknowledge it until now." I eye Rasha but she's still declining to look at me.

"*Eogan* told you?" Lord Wellimton's face thins. "Meaning the same man who just murdered his generals and informed us he plans to destroy Tulla?" He snorts. "Seems a bit convenient, don't you think? He hides out in Faelen a few years, scouts out our weaknesses until opportunity strikes, and then happens to kill the shape-shifter to take over his army? Not to mention he spent weeks courting the only person who could probably put a stop to it." He leans near me. "The person who, if rumors be true, is vying to be his queen. Tell me, did you know about this?"

I don't dignify him with a response. Just turn to the others. "We need to send word to King Sedric and Cashlin's queen as well as Tulla."

Myles scowls. "You think Eogan'sss merely going to allow that, do you?"

"Maybe one of his dissenting Assembly will."

"On what? A guarded airship?"

"Excuse me!" Wellimton bursts out. "Is no one else concerned by the fact that Nym did nothing back there to stop that, nor will she answer a fair question? Because I think it's time we discuss where her allegiances lie—"

His voice is grating my head. I crush my fingers into a fist to lift in his direction as that icy ache flares, craving to shut him up. I feel the sensation press out toward him, like a wave, and mid-sentence his face turns a strange shade of gray. The tension in my veins pulls harder, as if wanting to drink the idiotic air from his lungs.

Then he gasps and begins to gag, and the cold flare inside me dims. I drop my hand and look down as if it's just caught fire. *What in hulls?*

When I peek back up, only Wellimton and Rasha seem to have noticed my action as anything more than a gesture of annoyance. The princess gives a sharp frown, and Wellimton's face alters from gray to pale as he coughs.

I fight to steady my frightened breathing and temper. "I assure you, Lord Wellimton, that the king in that Hall is not the same man he was in Faelen. And I will do everything I can to stop this, in the right time, in the best way." I keep my gaze averted from Rasha.

He nods once, quick, then peers away—to recover his composure, I suspect.

"Might I ask when you think that will be?" Lord Percival says hesitantly.

"I think the questions we should be asking are, why is Bron pursuing this now?" I say. "Why against Tulla?"

"You heard him—the resources." Lady Gwen looks back and forth between the delegates, and her voice goes shrill. "Except now they'll bypass Faelen with that treaty, and even if King Sedric finds out, we'll be used as hostages."

"It's not only about the resources. And they won't stop with Tulla," Rasha says.

"What do you mean?" Lord Wellimton dabs his forehead with a handkerchief and eyes my hand. "What else could it possibly be?"

She glances at Myles and me. "I'm not at liberty to say."

"Now look here, Your Majesty. If you know something—"

"I know a lot of things," she says coolly.

"That doesn't answer the question as to why he would dare chance this when we've got Nym." Lord Percival peers at me.

Gwen nods. "I agree. How could they actually try it while she's alive sitting in their Castle?"

"Maybe they're not planning on having her alive much longer," Myles says, smoothing over his fingernails. "Maybe that's why the guardsss were killed. Maybe they're whittling usss down."

I peer back at the guards. "But who is doing the whittling?"

Two of them shrug at me just as Rasha steps over to them. She rubs her temple and beckons her soldiers. "If you'll all excuse me, I'm going to lie down where I can think without all the noise. It's been a long few days."

I push off the warm wall I'm leaning against even though her expression says she's not ready to talk. Myles joins me as her guards knock on the door, which is promptly opened by the Bron soldiers who, after a moment's conversation, proceed to let us out to the hall. At the end of which stand three wraiths. They hiss when they see me and that vortex in my chest lurches.

Rasha pushes ahead toward her room as her guards step in front of me and Myles, slowing us down.

"Forgetting something, Princessss?" Myles snarls.

"I can't imagine what."

"Perhaps our fate? Maybe when you're done being mad, the three of us could move on with discussing what's next."

"Our fate?" Rasha gives a sharp laugh at her open door. Then dips her tone bitterly. "You'll be lucky if you both haven't already single-handedly sealed it yourselves."

"You know that high horse you're riding is—"

I grab Myles's arm. "Just leave it. She needs more time."

"I hate to point it out, sssweetheart"—he juts his chin toward the wraiths—"but I'm afraid time's something we're running short on."

"Just give her a couple of hours, then I'll—"

A scream pierces the air.

Bron's guards spin back toward the princess's room. In an instant Myles and I are running.

The soldiers don't stop us. They're too busy throwing the door open, and we press through to find Rasha bent down on the floor, holding her maid-in-waiting's head in her lap. Beside her lies one of Rasha's Cashlin guards and one from Faelen. I recognize him from the airship. Or what's left of him. Both of them seem to be missing a limb or two.

I choke and push toward him, but Rasha's men force me back against Myles just as a chill enters the room. Spinning around, I see two of the Dark Army wraiths enter. Their black eyes glitter in the shadows of their dirty hoods and their stretched mouths move in that wordless, off-rhythm hissing.

"Everyone but the Cashlin guards out," the large Bron soldier says.

Rasha looks up through tear-flushed eyes. "Not until I've questioned every person here."

"I want to go over the bodies," I say, but the Faelen and Bron guards are already pulling Myles and me away, dragging us out the door as the hissing surrounding us gets louder. Rasha sets the maid's head tenderly on the carpet and stands, and then her men are closing the door behind us.

"My apologies, Lord Myles, but we need to get you both to your rooms," mutters a Faelen soldier who is clearly as much under guard as we are.

The Bron leader behind us yells at the men stationed in front of Lord Wellimton's room. "Lady Rasha's maid and two guards have been murdered. Lock down the other delegates."

"I'll join Lord Myles in his room," I say.

"Miss, this is not the time to—"

"Do it," Myles snarls.

The Faelen guard acquiesces only after he and two Bron men have thoroughly searched Myles's quarters.

"M'lord," he says after they've finished, "I think it wise if I stay—"

"Leave us. Go check on Lady Gwen and the others."

"Yes, m'lord."

The door shuts and I look at Myles. "We train."

CHAPTER 25

GAIN," I GROWL.

I allow Myles's hand to clamp onto my owner circles and resist the urge to shudder at his touch, which is clammy and cold compared to Eogan's. As is his breath.

An immediate image of Isobel rises from the floor to stroll toward me. Her dark eyes laugh, taunting me to engage in a duel with her. For a second I expect the familiar storm static across my skin, but instead there's a void, as if my Elemental heat has been replaced by cold. The aching hunger flares in my chest and travels up to my mouth. And for a second I swear I can taste it—the beauty, the power, the potential of her Mortisfaire blood.

I find myself gagging before Myles's distant voice says, "Quit testing and make the first move."

The first move.

Eogan would be furious. I should be furious. But I'm not, because that strange hunger is consuming everything but a growing hatred for Isobel and what she's done. For what she's perhaps already done to Eogan.

She steps toward me and suddenly Eogan is beside her. She smiles and giggles and places her hand over his chest like I watched her do that night at Adora's. He grimaces.

My hands lash out to shove her off, to press against her skin and use my anger to diminish whoever she thinks she is. She claws my cheek in her grab for my heart. She thrusts against my chest, but my ability is already working, draining, taking. I can feel it—my fingers absorbing the dark magic she owns. Until she utters a cry and her eyes go wide and she pulls away to disappear in a black cloud from the vision.

Next I turn to Eogan to let the power tug and steal her magic out of his chest, until I can only feel the healthy *thump* of his beating heart.

Except it's not healthy. There's a greater sorcery there.

Draewulf smiles at me through Eogan's lips.

I shove harder and twist as if to grip the very essence of him, the soul he's devouring Eogan with, and try to yank it out—fighting every last bit of him as if I can separate them by sheer force of my hateful will. Except next thing I know my vision's gone hazy and my lungs are seizing up. I can't find my breath. *What in—?*

My legs begin shaking, followed by the floor, and suddenly the lamps and shelves along the walls are vibrating so strong I know they will fall and shatter.

I ease back and shut my eyes to block out the image of Eogan as the wraiths hiss out in the hall. *How strange that I can hear them.* Or maybe the sound is in my head because it suddenly feels light and my thoughts aren't making sense. I open my eyes and turn to Myles. And discover him bent over choking for air.

Abruptly I am too.

It's a full minute before my lungs draw in enough atmosphere for my breathing to steady. And another before Myles puts his hands on his knees and looks up at me.

"What in hulls happened?" I gasp.

"You just magnified your abilities, my dear."

"But it wasn't enough." I shake my head. I can feel it in my skin—that hunger, that need. It strums empty behind my lungs and makes the growing vortex feel wider. *Train faster, Nym.*

"You're aware you nearly drained the air from this room, yesss?"

"Because I can't focus it enough. I need to narrow it in. We try again."

He puts his hands up. "No offensse, but I'm not sure I want to chance being suffocated in my own bleeding room. Perhaps a jaunt—"

A knock on the door sounds just before one of the Bron guards bursts in. He looks around. At the floor, the walls. At me.

"May I help you?"

The soldier's face narrows. "Pardon, but it seemed there was an earthquake of some sort."

"And you thought to look for it in here?" Myles says.

The guard frowns. "We just . . . I was simply ensuring you were all right. Very good, sir."

The door closes.

"Well, your ability was strong enough to grab their attention." Myles glares at the space where the guard was just standing. He stretches the kinks from his neck. "Might I suggest a short break in which you adjourn to your room and I stay in mine? I'd like a final nap before heading to whatever death's being brought on by Draewulf'sss army."

"Did you see those bodies in Rasha's room? We don't have time—"

"I'm simply pointing out we've been at it eight hoursss, and it's now nightfall, and I, for one, have not eaten yet from that plate of less-than-mouthwatering mush sitting on the desk. Nor have I enjoyed the peace and silence that comes when a woman'sss doing whatever she does *elsewhere*."

Eight hours?

I look down at my sweat-soaked shirt and stringy hair. Does the vortex inside of me absorb time as well as power?

"Might I beg food at leassst? After that we can resume up on the roof if you promise to refrain from speaking. Perhaps tossss things over the side at the Dark Army while we're at it."

I nod but I'm hardly listening because something's caught my eye. I frown. My deformed hand. My wrist is straighter. As if the broken bones in my gimpy fingers have almost smoothed back into place.

I lift it to him.

His expression doesn't show the surprise I expect. Instead he almost seems pleased.

As if he was expecting it.

I stare at him but he just shrugs. "I've spent the past two monthsss trying to show you what you can become. You wouldn't listen."

"And what am I becoming?" I ask cautiously.

"Perfection." The way he rolls it out, as if savoring the word on his tongue . . . It evokes that image of him and me standing over Draewulf's dead body and the entire Hidden Lands together. "At least in body and ability. Because I'm fairly certain your personality's hopelessss."

CHAPTER 26

AN HOUR LATER, OUR STOMACHS SATED ON FRUIT and chewy bread, Myles and I slip up the staircase toward the roof. Hissing fills my head even from five corridors away. I try to shake the noise off but it just seeps in, like angry ocean foam spitting at the back of my neck. It makes my skull ache. I shiver. "Don't they blasted ever stop?"

"Who?"

"Those *things* with their ghost language."

He tips his head and gives me a curious sweep with his eye. "What?"

He clears his expression and peers ahead. "An effective method of communication that's undetectable to people for the most part."

"Can *you* understand them?"

"No, but the fact that my mirages work on them means they understand usss."

I halt on one of the steps. "If that's the case, then why not use your ability to stop all of them? You could stop the war! Why the litches are we wasting time sneaking around here when—?"

"As flattering as your confidence is, my abilities do have

limitsss. One of them being their lessened impact the more wide-spread a space they're used on. Sneaking us up here is easy, but deceiving an entire army is a bit much even for me." He continues climbing.

I frown. "Why not use it on a few at a time then? Get the wraiths to turn against Draewulf or Isobel, or each other even. What if they're gathering information or they're the ones that killed those guards and maid?"

"Oh, I'm quite certain they're gathering information. And I think any number of people or *things* could've killed those guardsss. But as I've told you, some gifts are best left unannounced until they're needed. Much like yoursss." He pushes a door open and enters first. It leads us to another stairwell, which, if the cold air is any indication, is close to the roof. How he's so adept at maneuvering us through the Castle, I can only imagine. *How much time did he spend here selling out King Sedric and Faelen?*

Another door, this one heavier, thicker, looms from the dim, and when he clicks the handle and shoves the metal open, we're suddenly outside.

On the roof.

In the middle of a lush garden.

The hissing clobbers my head. It's a million times louder up here and requires a minute to get my bearings amid the noise. After days of only seeing copper walls, everything looks alive and green in the dim—the white brittle trees and tiny flowers and the trickle of a brook. And the sky. Deep, midnight blue, lit up by freckles of stars winking through the leaves. Was this Eogan's mother's garden?

A private oasis in the middle of madness.

I slip my way through the flower bushes and forest and follow the trickling brook, half wary that there's someone else up here and half enamored at the size of the enchanted space. The creek leads us a good many paces toward a waterfall that is taller than three of me put together.

Myles's footsteps might be silent on the soft grass, but his whisper sounds loud. "This way." He leads me through the small forest to the side of the roof nearest the door through which we came. We stop at a low wall that overlooks the main portion of the city, and when I look down on it, the spindle streets are lit up, making the place a giant glowing button.

"Mother of a bolcrane."

"Hmm. Rather nice at night, isn't it?"

But I don't mean the city. I mean what's caught my eye beyond the city. I point over the great wall encircling the capital to where the incessant hissing is coming from. To the soot hovering in the air in a gray dust cloud over that mass of black, crawling darkness. It's interspersed with fires flickering in sparks like a thousand separate stars on a tar canvas. They are surrounding the city as far as my eyes can see.

That sickening feeling that invaded my gut when the wraiths entered the War Room earlier tears through me now full force. I stare at the army. No wonder Myles's ability couldn't work on the entirety. How can there be that many? The guilt slips up my chest again. *Perhaps Rasha and I should've killed Draewulf when we had the chance.*

"Where did he get them all?" I whisper.

Myles doesn't answer. He doesn't have to. Something niggles in my memory, suggesting I already know. The voice of that terrified soldier who'd had too much to drink at the common house I visited with Colin and Breck. *"Draewulf's plagues turned men unearthly. Into monsters."*

"Did you know about them when you came here years ago?" I can taste the bitterness in my tone.

"Only through rumorsss. The difference between Bron and Faelen's views on it at the time was that Bron actually knew Draewulf still existed. After Eogan'sss father and Draewulf had a falling out, it was thought he'd gone into hiding and let Lady Isobel take leadership over their dying land. Now, it seemsss, we know why they were dying."

"He was using them for experiments." I shudder and recall Eogan telling Colin and me as much a few weeks ago. "He made his own monsters."

I let the horror of that settle into my bones, and with it comes a deep, soul-wrenching sorrow. "Why now?"

Myles frowns.

"Why is he doing this now? Why'd he come to Faelen at all when he could've just taken Bron with this army at any time?"

He shrugs. "Maybe he needed something from Faelen. Or someone," he adds, staring at me meaningfully. Then turns away. "Or maybe he simply needed more men to turn into wraith soldiersss."

"So he took some of our Faelen army for this? That doesn't make sense. Why not just take them from Bron?"

"You forget Bron's forces were incredibly powerful until you demolished half of them. I'm surprised Draewulf hasn't thanked you for that yet. And as far as his beasts . . ."

Something in his tone drags my gaze up to his face.

What I see there makes my stomach turn. He actually looks like he admires them.

"Considering he couldn't force allegiance on a large scale, and he couldn't reproduce naturally, beyond bequeathing the world with Lady Isobel, of course . . . Really it's an ingenious idea when you think about it."

My gut twists. "You're despicable."

I turn toward the forest only to pause as something hatches in my mind. Something he said. Something I've never thought of before. I frown and flip around. "How *is* Isobel his daughter? He's a wolf and she's human."

He waves a hand. "He wasn't always a wolf. Nor *is* he always, seeing as he does in fact have his own body. Rumor is, up until ten or so years ago, he could still switch into his own human form. And believe it or not, despicable men can and frequently do tend to marry." His smile appears, but I swear there's a hint of sadness underneath. "Never to normal women, mind you."

I study him. Study that sadness.

Until he covers it up with a smooth smirk. "The story goesss Draewulf was smitten and tried to change his ways for a Mortisfaire who bore him Isobel. But like all men who have vision for the bigger things in life, he couldn't be swayed from his purpose. He returned to his wolf form and pursued it."

"And what *was* his purpose?"

"Ah, that's the silver question, isn't it? With the new developmentsss . . ." He waves a hand at the surrounding army. "I think we can safely assume it's still of the world-dominion sort. How he planss to do that though is what I suggest we figure out before it's too late."

Before it's too late.

"You mean how he plans to use us to make that happen." I stare out at the crawling mass. "Do you think he's going to make us all . . . like *them*?"

"Hulls, let's hope not. Those rags . . ." He adjusts his limp cravat at his neck. "Ssso unbecoming."

"Can't you stop *any* of it? I mean, no offense, but if your abilities are only good enough to sneak around the Castle, I'm beginning to doubt their usefulness."

"My ability will be used effectively when the time isss needed," he snaps.

"What are you holding out for?"

"Nothing. I simply see no sense in wasting it. Nor should you. Now here." He puts his hand on my arm and shuts his eyes. The next second they flutter open and he stares at me as if I've turned into a bolcrane. "Can you feel that?"

"Feel what?"

"The energy you're drawing. From them." He flicks a hand toward the black crawling mass and murmurs, and the next second he's forcing an image. From the ground rises a wraith from the Dark Army. Rags seeped in a putrid-smelling oily substance drag as he walks toward me. His hands are made of bolcrane claws and his face is that of a dead man's. "Take him down," Myles whispers.

I inhale, and to my surprise, he's right. I am drawing energy. Out here in the night air and span of atmosphere, it's as if my body remembers how to do this. How to come alive with power. Just like with my old Elemental abilities, my reactions and control are the same, even if what's feeding this surge feels colder. Stickier. Darker.

I lift my hand and it flattens, the bones not so bent as I press it against the wraith's chest, and it's so real I feel his clammy skin and taste his defiling breath as he lunges for me. I duck and shove my palm harder against him, and abruptly I can sense the energy drain inside him, fueling the hunger inside me. His eyes go blank and his body falls, dissipating into a gray fog.

CHAPTER 27

MYLES AND I HAVE RUN THROUGH THE SCENARIO twice when, just as the last of it fades, the hissing filling the night air spikes louder and I swear I hear actual voices. Myles must hear them too because he tugs my sleeve and steps away from the low metal wall and into a shadow thrown by the white trees. It takes a minute before I locate the voices as coming from the far side of the roof. The speakers don't seem to be moving this way.

My body tingles with the energy in the air, the energy I've been drawing on. I glance at Myles and promptly mutter a curse at him when he whispers up a new façade for both of us, which turns me into a short, balding Bron soldier. I spin on my heel and creep into the forest toward them.

As we draw closer, the gurgling water muffles the voices, but from what I can tell, three speakers are arguing on the other side of the waterfall. Slipping next to the noisy brook and then round the giant rock outcrop, I wedge behind a thick spurt of trees. Sinking my feet into the grass, I peer through the branches.

My lungs arrest.

Draewulf, Isobel, and a wraith.

Myles's slimy hand finds my shoulder and squeezes, whether in reminder to be silent or because he's a nervous bolcrane baby I'm not sure, but I shake him off and, sliding out a knife, hunch down to watch the three carrying on about something.

"Why not crush the Bron soldiers?" Isobel's voice rings out. "We can take full control instead of this farce of working with them!"

"Because, my shortsighted daughter," Draewulf snarls, "we don't expend resources for the sake of a control we already have." His hood is thrown back, revealing jagged hair smeared back in a distinctly unlike-Eogan style. He looks at her with a twisted expression that is at once hateful and weary. The effect only makes him loom more dangerous, like it's requiring effort not to snap.

"Yes, and morphing that many would require more energy than either you or I should spare at the moment. But if we're still in Bron when the Assembly realizes this is a coup—"

"They already know it's a coup and they will believe what they need to in order to stay alive. Just like draining an animal's blood— do it too fast and you'll waste the experience. Drain them slow and you'll get the rush of seeing them whimper and succumb, my dear."

His tone is so cold my spine ripples.

He turns to the wraith. "How much longer until your underlings are ready?"

"The ones assembled to keep hold of this city are near ready. The rest come with us to Tulla." The tall dead thing slurs his gravelly words into the breeze, which carries them low and whips them around. "The timing now depends on you, m'lord. And whether your vessel is prepared?"

"She performed as I said she would. We'll know soon if it took in the way I require. If not, I'll ensure she returns for more. Either way, it won't be long."

"And in the meantime?" Lady Isobel glares at her father. "Are *you* ready? Because you look like hulls, and I'll not have us embark before I know you've managed control over your host."

"He grows weaker as we speak," the wraith interjects, flourishing a long, bone finger through the air at Eogan. A hint of mist follows it before the ghostly thing inhales and pulls the fog toward its hooded face.

I can just make out the shriveled skin and skeletal cheekbones beneath eyes that are glowing a faint yellow. Before I know it the spider serum in my veins has lurched and begun vibrating with that low thirst.

Draewulf shifts and the starlight catches the scowl in his eye. "If your Mortisfaire powers worked the way—"

"It's not my fault something's changed his Medien ability." It's Isobel's turn to snarl. "He's never been able to block me before, and I assure you I will finish it. Perhaps it's time I pay a visit to—"

"Out of the question," Draewulf's voice barks.

"May I remind you that with your own energy being spent maintaining your hold, you are—"

"We knew this would be the most critical. Even now I can sense it breaking," he growls. "Prepare your guards. Leave me to focus. And you . . ." He glares at the wraith. "Alert me as soon as the army is fully in place."

"Yes, m'lord," the wraith breathes.

Isobel purses her mouth and glares. Until Draewulf turns his back on her. She flips around, then heads toward the rock waterfall with the wraith following and disappears opposite our hiding spot.

Draewulf watches them stride away until there's the distinct sound of a door shutting somewhere. I swear his shoulders sag the slightest bit before he turns and spreads his hands toward the black masses in the distance. He becomes still.

Too still.

After one, two, five minutes my calves are aching and begging to change position. I'm just wondering how softly I can shift when he's muttering loud enough for me to hear even if his words are incoherent.

Soon they're so inharmonious and complex, it's giving the effect of multiple voices. Beside me, Myles rocks forward enough that I can feel the tension rolling off him as Eogan-who-is-Draewulf lifts his robed arms to hold up an object out in front of him, as if performing a type of ritual.

Oh litches.

Myles's hand is poking my shoulder, compressing hard. Apparently he's caught on too and worried I might move. He should be.

Draewulf's fingers are clasped around a large leather pouch, which looks very much like the bag the neighbor of owner number seven used for spells. I asked her about it once, and she told me she kept it full of enchanted bones. I never asked whose bones or what kind of enchantment, but the one time she tried to use them to rid me of my Elemental curse . . .

It didn't go well.

I summon every nerve of strength I own to keep me rooted to this spot as Draewulf's voice grows louder. He puts a hand in his robe pocket, pulls out a fistful of powder to sprinkle over the bag, then dumps the pouch's contents onto the ground. There's a clatter and a spark and then it looks like the whole thing catches fire. The smoke from it rises straight, eerily stiff, as it funnels up to the sky. The muttering stops as he watches it. After a moment, he steps into the thick smoke spire and inhales once, deeply.

The faint sound of a leaf being crushed underfoot is my first indication that I've moved. I bump into Myles who's frozen except for his fingers curling into my skin, keeping me still and from giving us away.

"Use your mirage."

I feel him shake his head just as Draewulf's gaze darts over.

"He's weakened. *Use your mirage*, Myles. I'm going to use my ability."

An elongated pause. Then, "My power doesn't work against Eogan's block," Myles admits in my ear.

It doesn't? I glance back at him and almost laugh. So that's why he hates Eogan so much.

There's a low snarl, and I turn back in time to catch Draewulf looking over again. Searching our direction with those green-rimmed black eyes.

There's no way he could've heard us, yet he steps out of the bone-incense spire and his eyes are seeking, glowering, and then they're riveted on me.

Myles fumbles against my foot, and when I slip a hand back to make him stay still, the oaf isn't there. *What the—? Bleeding fool.*

I'm just rising from my haunches when Draewulf growls and, faster than possible, bursts through the low branches. He stops in front of me, inches away, looking furious but also haggard. Beyond haggard. He looks ill.

He studies me, then suddenly smiles and tweaks his head to the side. His expression removes any question in my mind whether he can see through Myles's mirage. "Little impotent girls shouldn't eavesdrop." He lifts a hand. "Unless they want their mouths sewn shut." He scrapes Eogan's short nails against my neck.

I utter a cry at the sting and aim my knee for his stomach at the same moment my hand lunges with my knife. He steps aside and swipes it away onto the grass, as if he can't be bothered with such silliness, before reaching for my chin.

I shove both hands against his chest and attempt to pull nonexistent lightning from the sky. Instead I'm met with darkness. From inside him.

There's a flash and one, two, three of the garden lanterns snap out, dimming the space around us as his hand slides to the back of my neck, as if to crack it. He swears in some language I've never heard, and that poisoned hunger jolts in my veins, burning my skin beneath his touch as the cold in my bones reacts. Suddenly it's climbing, clawing, begging to get out of my fingertips to attack him.

He starts murmuring beneath his breath and boring his black eyes into me. I shut mine and push against him and focus on the energy I'm reacting to. On the sensation of power flowing through him. I begin to dig into it, draw from it, imagining I can feel it siphoning off in shallow waves as it whirlpools more and more into the vortex inside me.

I tug harder and the waves grow stronger, until abruptly his murmuring stops and I open my eyes to see Eogan's body go transparent over Draewulf's dark shape that's glued to my hand. And it's like I'm seeing double. Eogan's eyes begin to clear.

His hand grips my neck tighter.

Air.

I need air.

The trees around me begin to blur and the shapes of three

214

wraiths appear, but Draewulf doesn't even glance over—doesn't even notice Myles's mental creations dragging their decaying bodies toward us.

My breath is blurring, my head is blurring, and my ears are rushing as the *thump, thump, thump* of my blood is flailing through my veins to kill him. I scratch at his chest, drawing off his power, but he just squeezes stronger and chuckles until I'm certain my neck is going to break. I hear Myles draw a knife from his spot five paces away, only to see Draewulf swipe his other arm in Myles's direction, and the lord protectorate goes flying against the rock wall.

"Eogan, please," I hear my own voice utter, and I narrow my energy's focus right above his heart. And push.

Draewulf drops his hand and slumps into me.

What in—? I grab my other ankle knives at the same time I'm choking and gulping and trying to shove him off, to knee him in the gut, but a tremble rips through his body, wavering up his backbone, and this time, when his fingers find my arms, it's for support, not injury.

Eogan?

He lifts his head and there are those green eyes shining through a face that looks old and weary. "For hulls' sakes, Nym, can you please stop trying to infuriate the blasted fool. You're going to get yourself killed."

I raise a brow and draw in another lungful of air. Clearly his personality hasn't suffered. "Well, forgive me for trying to save us all," I choke out.

He stands straighter and eyes me, this time with more lucidity, and breaks into that daft smile that makes my idiot self want to drown in his arms.

I return the grin and for whatever reason feel suddenly shy, which is why it takes an entire two seconds more for the realization to dawn on me. "Oh kracken, you're still alive. Did it work? Did I . . . ?" My words fumble over each other as I glance at my hands. The shock and excitement numbing my tongue. *Did I separate them?*

"Did *what* work?"

"I brought you to the surface!" I clutch my palms that are still shaking with Draewulf's energy, then swerve my gaze back up at him, my eyes widening along with my smile.

Only to be met by the flash of wolfish black encircling his emerald green.

Oh.

Not quite.

He squints. "What do you mean?"

"I mean it almost worked! I brought you out!" And even if it didn't work all the way, I can't help the relief—the exhilaration— the *sheer joy* this knowledge brings.

My powers are nearly strong enough.

His lips curl oddly and he coughs. "So it seems." I can hear it in his undertone—the exhaustion. The wheezing.

I frown. Eogan's body gives the slightest shudder and his jaw tightens. He droops and I go to catch him. "Oh hulls," I whisper, because the look on his face says he may not be dead but something's more than definitely wrong.

A crack of a stick and Myles steps forward, rubbing the back of his head. His expression as he stares at Eogan says he's fascinated. More than fascinated.

He looks greedy. Even as Eogan suddenly looks like he's dying.

I will my abilities to hurry. "It's Lady Isobel, she's—"

"I know." Eogan puts his hand on my shoulder to steady himself. "She's trying her best to finish it." He brushes his gaze down my face until it reaches my lips, where it lingers as he gives a faint smirk. "Thankfully her powers aren't quite as effective on me as she remembers."

I put my hand on his chest and begin to press to absorb whatever it is she's done to him. "I can almost fix it. Let me—"

Eogan's face caves with pain. He jerks back and pushes my hand away. "What in—?" He slips his gaze down the rest of me until it lands on my other hand—on my gimpy fingers that are no longer curled but straight. Nearly perfect.

His voice wanes. "Nym, what did you do?"

Behind him, I catch the flash of Myles's silver-toothed grin.

Eogan follows my gaze, and the next second he's turned and wrapped a fist around Myles's shirt. "What have you done to her?"

The lord protectorate's arms go up in defense even as his voice raises an octave. "Only what she asked for, and it was nothing she couldn't handle."

"That's not what I asked. *What did you do?*"

"You know exactly what I did. I reactivated her. Gave her something to actually fight with, to protect herself with."

Eogan snorts. "Protect herself? Is that what you call it? You bleeding little—"

"Ah ah ah!" Myles tries to shove Eogan's hand away, and when that doesn't work, he attempts to straighten his shirt anyway. "I think you'd be thanking me."

"For what? Giving her a *death sentence*?"

"Perhapsss you're merely insulted that I was able to give her something you're not."

"This has nothing to do with you *giving* her anything," Eogan snarls. "So you'd better undo it, or I will—"

"You know I can't."

Eogan bares his teeth. *"Try."*

Myles wrinkles his lips. "You honestly think *she'll* go for that? She's the one who asked for them."

Without taking his eyes off Myles, Eogan releases him and says in a softening tone, "Nym, please go back to the person who gave them to you. Ask her to undo it. Tell her it was a mistake."

I shake my head. *He can't be serious.* "I can't." *I won't.*

"Yes, you can. Gowon will give you the money for it if you tell him I commanded it."

What is he talking about? "It's not the money. It's the abilities. I can help you! I already did—it's why you're here now!"

He spins around and stares at me in horror and . . . something else. Fear. "Don't you see what those abilities will do to you? Don't you see what they've done to him?" He points at Myles, then at himself. "Worse, what they've done to Draewulf?"

I freeze. "What do you mean?"

His expression darkens from anger to outright fury, and before Myles can dodge, Eogan's grabbed him again. "You litched bolcrane—you didn't even tell her?"

My legs are shaking. "Tell me what?"

He flips toward me and practically chokes out the words. "Nym, what you've done by consuming new abilities . . . *darker* abilities . . . It's how Draewulf came to be who he is. It's how he changed from being a wizard."

My breath dies.

Suddenly the roof, the garden, the starry night sky are falling, and my head is spinning as Eogan's glare turns caustic at Myles. "I will kill you for this."

"Oh, give it a rest. We both know she needs power if—"

"No, we don't know—and certainly not the kind given by a

witch! What I *do know* is that this had *nothing* to do with her and *everything* to do with you, and if it is the last thing I do, I will—"

He keeps threatening but I stop listening. *Draewulf changed by absorbing a power like I did?*

I swerve my gaze to Myles.

He is gasping and yet rolling his eyes at both of us. "Draewulf went through the procedure multiple timesss—who knows how many over the yearsss, and who knows what kind of experiments he performed to get to what he isss now. It's not the same thing. It's not even on the same level."

"Then why didn't you tell her?"

"Because it wouldn't have made a difference," Myles says, looking at me.

I don't reply.

Because standing here so close to Eogan I can feel his heart, his realness, even as he's igniting the air around us with the angered heat pouring off his skin . . . I know it wouldn't have. I would've chosen the same and chanced it.

Eogan suddenly sags. Turning from Myles, he presses against my arm. His tone falls from furious to soft, urgent. "Nym, I don't have much time. Have you spoken with Sir Gowon yet?"

I prop him up with my hands, willing him my strength, my energy whether it's of a darker variety or not. "He didn't believe me. And I'm not certain it would make a difference now anyway because Draewulf's Dark Army has taken over."

"Did you give Gowon the message?"

"I told him about the Elegy, but it didn't matter."

He runs a hand through his hair, and everything about that simple gesture, that familiar act, makes my shoulders ache and my heart whisper its determination that I want things how they were. I want what existed two weeks ago. "You can take care of it all right now." He dips his gaze to my hand still holding a blade.

I glance away. We both know I can't do that.

He sighs. "Listen, I'm sorry for all of this. But I need you to find a way to speak with Gowon again and make him understand."

"He won't listen. He either can't tell you're not acting like yourself or he doesn't care. Either way, he doesn't trust me."

His lashes flutter, and for a moment a glint of shame slips through along with his frustration. He rubs a hand along his stubbly jawline. "Gowon was brought on as my father's advisor when I was young, and I'm sorry to say that any coldness displayed on Draewulf's part is more familiar to Gowon than anything I've become in the four years since he's seen me." His eyes level with mine even as his chest shudders and his body sags again. "But I need you to try again. Tell him to look again at the Elegy. Tell him it's begun."

I swallow. "What's begun?"

His expression ices over as he pulls away. I watch it. One second it's soft and tired and concerned, and the next it's sterile. Something behind it flutters.

"Blast it all, Eogan, what's going on? *What's* begun? Why is Draewulf keeping us alive? And how do I use this . . . *thing* to free you?" I shove my fingers toward him and let a jolt snake out of them, latching onto his shoulder. He immediately lurches back again and thrusts my palm away.

"Nym, you can't use that on me. I am trying my best to survive long enough to . . ." The stiff expression softens even as his voice is gravely cautious.

"Long enough until what? *Until Draewulf leaves you?*"

220

"Unlike Myles, Gowon's a good man, Nym. He'll look out for you and do what needs to be done for the Bron people."

"That's not what I asked," I snap. "Can you survive long enough until Draewulf leaves you?"

A sigh. Finally, "No."

And he doesn't have to explain. Because he is dying too soon. Too fast.

And no one can fix it but me.

Eogan's face yellows for a heartbeat and he looks even more ill. Aged. He runs a finger over a lock of my hair. His breath is coming thick, tangling against my skin and landing on my tears that appeared from who knows where and are dripping off my cheeks and chin. His finger brushes my lips. "Let me go," he whispers. "End this for all of us."

Not a bleeding chance. "Don't you see what I've just done? That I've brought you to the surface? Do you know what this means? We're so close. I can help you!"

"You can't save me, Nym. Especially not with that ability."

My voice cracks. "You don't mean that."

His body's doing that shivering thing again, and it's quaking so hard my body's trembling too. "Get rid of this ability Myles gave you and get away from him. Get away from *me*." He grips my arm but it's not to steady himself; it's to force me back, to force me to listen. "You have to survive, do you understand? For you, for me, for the Hidden Lands . . ." His quivering is becoming violent. His fingers cup my face. "Tell Gowon we were wrong. Tell him he's taking the blood in order. He needed me first."

I'm shaking my head. "First for what?" *What is he talking about?*

"Just as our Uathúil powers are bound to our land, so are they

221

bound to our blood. He needed mine first for the block. To protect him." His head tips strangely. I squint. And suddenly I'm losing him. "I will stay alive as long as I can because I will not let you die at his hands. But you have to kill me or run, Nym."

And then he's leaning in, brushing his lips against mine in a kiss. "If you don't, I swear I *will* come back to haunt the very breath in your lungs and blood in your bones—I will *make* you survive." His chest is heaving, his lungs shoving the words up his throat. And suddenly I'm watching him fade, fade, fade through my fingertips, clamoring for every single breath of consciousness as the black seeps its way back in to muddy those green eyes I could've swam in forever.

"No! I won't let you go. I won't let him take you!" Can't he see that? Can't he see he's the only person who's ever existed that I could feel safe with? That I could be better with?

That I can save?

His lips part into a bemused, ghoulish smile.

And suddenly that vortex in me is growing, craving, calling out for air. I press my palm back onto his chest and feel Draewulf's essence fighting against Eogan.

I squeeze. I *will* free him.

"Nym, don't. I won't be able . . ." His voice cuts off as if he's choking. And it sounds like death in my ears.

"I will *not* let you take him," I say to the monster reappearing. But it's too late because that smile's already turning, twisting, even as I go from cleaving my hand against his chest to beating it and swearing that *I will become strong enough to free him.* "Just give me another day," I whisper to Eogan's fading emerald eyes.

Draewulf raises a fist to smack me.

Then stops. And scoffs, as if I'm not even worth his repulsion, as if seeing me suffer was torture enough to satisfy his sick bloodlust.

He tucks a strand of hair behind his ear and purposefully, casually, turns and walks away. Flicking his fingers to hurl an unprepared Myles once again at the wall.

I lunge after him but there's a rustle and a swirling of thick black fog wisps that fill the air and block my vision, and by the time I've weaved my way through them, Draewulf is gone.

Abruptly I'm bending over and coughing from that chasm in my chest that has absorbed too much energy and yet not enough. Never enough. My bones are rattling so hard it feels like I'm having a seizure and my head won't stop pounding.

Myles's face swims bizarrely in front of me when I walk over to him, and he grabs my arm to pull himself up. For a moment, my skin prickles beneath his fingers.

"Looks like you'll be needing to hurry the training, my dear."

CHAPTER 28

WHEN WE REACH THE HALLWAY TO OUR quarters, five wraiths swarm us with their sunken-in, death-masked faces spouting hisses and glaring at us with their chilling yellow gazes. Their bony hands reach for our arms. "Ussss. Ussss," it almost sounds like they're saying amid the bustling Bron boots and shouted questions as to how we got out and where we've been.

I recoil from the wraiths and lurch for the Bron soldiers. "I need to speak with Rasha," I tell the largest guard, the one who tried to take my knives after the banquet two nights ago.

"You're in no position to ask anything." He grabs my shoulder and hustles me through the wraiths and toward my room, but as we're passing Rasha's, I reach a foot out and kick her door.

There's an immediate click and the giant guard stalls—perhaps to see if she'll allow me entrance or simply because I go limp in his arms and he doesn't feel like dragging me. Either way, the door creaks open and through the partial space I see Rasha slumped on the bed, her brown face pale. She frowns.

"My apologies," the Bron guard says, and drags me toward my room. I could count to five before she calls after us to let me enter.

"But only Nym." She peers coolly past me to Myles, who's being jostled by his own angry set of guards. Behind us, the Dark Army soldiers hiss louder, a low, nerve-clenching sound.

The Bron guard shoves me in and the Cashlin men slam the door behind me, then proceed to make a quick weapons search of me, confiscating my knives before situating themselves, two near the windows and three by the door.

"Well?"

I take a deep breath. "I need your help."

Rasha lifts a brow.

"To speak with Sir Gowon. As much as I hate to admit it, I believe he can help us. And Eogan," I add softly.

She nods as if she already knew this.

I move closer to her bed. "Look, I'm sorry I was a bolcrane and I'm sorry about what I said earlier." I look over at her guards. "For insulting your people regarding the war."

"Me too."

I wait. Because I'm hoping that's not all she has to say.

She sighs. "However . . ." She takes a deep breath. "There may be some accuracy to it." Her intense gaze eases, almost to the point it glimmers with a fleck of shame. "It's true we didn't help your Elemental people," she whispers. "We did more than you know, but not enough. I'll not make excuses because we have our reasons for staying uninvolved, but still, some of the decisions our matriarchs have made have not always been right. Nor favored by everyone."

I nod.

She flutters her hand as if it's no big deal and her voice takes on its airy tone. "Apologies exchanged and accepted then. However, that doesn't let you off from explaining to me what in hulls you were thinking in taking on . . . *whatever* it is you took on."

I peer at her guards again who are watching us in silence. Then turn and stride to the open window overlooking the airship pad. "How much can you see?"

"Enough to know that you went with Myles and took on an ability that's not your own." The bed creaks beneath her weight. "I can't see it clearly, but it looks dark. Oh Nym, what were you thinking? Why didn't you come to me first? I warned you and everything!"

I flip around. "And what would you have told me? That it wasn't a good idea? I knew that but I had to do something. And so far it's been fine." I curl my nearly perfect hands to show her. "Better than fine actually." I look up with a grin. "I almost freed him tonight. Another day and I should be—"

"I would've told you it was more dangerous than you imagine." Her face has grown serious. She slips her feet onto the floor and stands to stare at me with both hands on her hips.

Did she not hear me? *I almost freed him.* "You think I didn't weigh the cost? My Elemental power was dangerous too—the *most* dangerous Eogan once said—and I learned to control it. I can do so with this one too."

"A nice sentiment, but—"

I start toward her. "But what? You would've wanted me to give up? How could I? And now—now it's almost worked, Rasha. We're going to do this!"

She pauses and, after a moment, nods in resignation. "Perhaps you would've chosen differently if I'd trusted you with more information on the airship." She reseats herself on the bed. "And I understand why you made your decision, Nym. I just don't know that in this case the end result will justify the means of getting there."

"Then we should've just killed him when we both had the chance." I look away, at the door. At the ceiling. At anything but her concerned frown as a stab of discomfort pricks my spine. Why do she and Eogan not see what this can do?

A moment longer and I sigh. "Eogan agrees with you if that makes you feel better."

"Agrees how?"

"That this power I've taken is dangerous. He says it's what created Draewulf." I dig my foot into the carpet and swallow hard to shore up my suddenly quaking throat.

She gives a single, sad dip of her head. Another half-minute and she lifts her gaze to one of her Cashlin guards. "Ask them to tell Sir Gowon that the Elemental and I demand to speak with him. If he refuses, tell him I'm aware of a defining choice he made eighteen years ago." She hesitates. "And if the Bron guard outside refuses, tell him I'm aware of what he did last evening."

The guard clicks his heels and unlocks the door to speak with the Bron soldiers out in the hall.

I furrow my brow.

She looks at me and bites her lip. And admits with a subdued smirk, "I have no idea what he did last night, but it's worth a shot."

I grin. "And Sir Gowon?"

Sadness flashes through her expression and into her tone. "You are aware of Bron's rite of passage for their boy soldiers?"

When she doesn't continue, I nod. Mainly because I suddenly don't trust my voice. All I can picture is Kel.

"When Gowon's own son was ready to take it, Eogan's father used it as a test of loyalty, giving Gowon a choice—have the boy prove his and his father's fealty to the crown or be demoted. When it came time . . . The young man the boy was made to kill in combat was his best friend. A child barely a year younger than himself."

My chest hardens. "You read that?"

She nods. "Although it's now in the far past, I'm certain it's still an area of shame for him."

An area of shame yet he inflicts punishment on those who would disobey? Or perhaps that's why he allowed Kel to live the other night.

She clears her throat and drops her gaze to my wrist. "So who gave it to you?"

I glance down as she fluffs a pillow and leans back.

"The ability."

Oh. "Myles took me to a woman."

"*How* did she do it?"

"Through a drink."

"Can you go back and get rid of it?"

I don't answer that. I won't answer. I merely walk over until I'm facing her spot on the bed again. "Like I said, it's been fine. I don't need you to worry about it. I think we should be concentrating instead on what we're going to ask Sir Gowon and how to stop the Dark Army."

She eyes me. "In that case, that's all I'm going to say on the subject aside from warning you that the moment you get scary with this ability, I will not hesitate to do everything I can to take you out myself. And the next time I see Myles, I will most likely rip his head from his neck."

I nod. *Fair enough.*

"Now about Sir Gowon and the wraiths . . ." She casts her gaze over the bloodstain on the carpet, and for a second I'm certain her eyes go misty. As does her voice. An odd ripple of guilt goes through me—not for her grief over her loss, but that it didn't occur to me to even wonder how it would affect her. More than that, that I never even wondered about those killed. What were their names? Did they have kids? The thought digs into me that normally I'd be moved by something like that.

Instead? I feel nothing.

"I'll get you some water." I grab a cup from the morning's food tray to take to the water closet. I rinse it before filling it with water from their pipes in case someone poisoned the pitcher on the table. Not likely with her men standing there, but still . . .

Her faint smile quivers along with her chin when I return. She sniffs. "She was my maid for the past six years."

I put my hand over hers and squeeze.

"Our kingdom is full of life but our palace . . . can be a bit lonely." She clasps back. "With the Luminescents living in it, there's not much need for conversation. Everyone can read everyone else." She twists her mouth wryly and glances back over to the bloodstained carpet. "But Fara wasn't one. She couldn't read my intentions. She was my friend."

"Oh, Rasha." I sit on the bed beside her.

She scoots over and closes her eyes as if in a daze. "At first I thought maybe the murders were to get at you but . . . I'm beginning to think they're targeting everyone."

"Who?"

"I don't know—either a Bron Assembly member or the wraiths. But those monsters are too hard for me to read." She shudders. "It's like they don't have souls to decide things on their own. And the way those murders were done . . ."

I nod. "Do you think . . . ?" But I stall at the grief plaguing her face. Unable to bring myself to ask if perhaps the wraiths were in need of more body parts . . . "What about Draewulf or Isobel?" I say instead.

"Possibly. Although I didn't see it in Isobel, nor do I see how it would suit their needs."

"Except that we don't actually know what their needs are. On the roof with Myles, Draewulf, Isobel, and a commanding wraith said they were waiting for Draewulf's vessel to be prepared. And Eogan kept saying that he and Sir Gowon were wrong—that Draewulf is taking the blood of kings in order. That he needed Eogan's blood and block to protect Draewulf. He keeps talking about Elegy 96. Do you know of it?"

No answer.

When I look down, she's curled up, eyes shut, as if attempting to block out all thought.

I slide up to sit beside her and tug the blanket higher on her shoulder. Patting her arm, I listen to her breathing slow.

After our silence has melted in with the room's atmosphere, her gentle snoring picks up, and her bodyguards quietly begin discussing the murders. I listen in for a bit but they're no further in understanding them than Rasha is.

Soon the men switch to discussing the larger predicament we're all in. Their accented words all seem to boil down to the same question:

Will we make it out of here alive?

Slowly, eventually, Rasha's snoring settles into a deep rhythm, like the patter of rain lessening into a steady, comforting drip.

I pull my arm from around her shoulder and rest my head against the wall.

And eventually doze off too.

230

CHAPTER 29

Enormous paisley designs stare back at me from the wallpaper. Black with thousands of tiny glittery eyes. Moist eyes.

One shifts. Then another. I watch their legs pop up from the white wall, followed by their bodies, and they're no longer decorative paisleys but spiders. Hundreds of them. Covering the room, watching, waiting.

For what?

I twitch my hand into a fist. Maybe I can create a wind tunnel to destroy them, to make them leave—but my body freezes in place. I glance down at my chest and at the vortex swirling there. It's dark, powerful. It's sealing me down, anchoring me into a whirling pool of grief and anger and hope.

The spiders' sound picks up and blends into the hissing outside. *Clack, clack, clack.* They're coming for me. Oozing down the walls like mugplant to land in blobs on the floor. They pop up again and scramble toward the bed, the blankets, clawing beneath them, crawling for my skin, and I can't move, oh hulls I can't move as their teeth find me.

They chew into my flesh and force the last of their venom into the very roots of my veins, until my blood is pooling around me in red circles, spreading to join that stain in the carpet as the hissing from the hall grows louder. The hissing that for whatever reason sounds eerily like words. "Come closer, closer, closerrr," they're whispering.

Closer to what? I look down at my body that is being eaten alive by spiders. Except it's not me anymore. It's Draewulf.

Morning sunbeams flutter against the wall, dousing the crisp black-and-white paper in yellow light, dissolving all dreams of spiders. I squint. I'm huddled, shivering at the foot of Rasha's bed, and she's sprawled out across the rest like a giant moth with silken-robed wings.

Jolting up, I flex my hands, my toes. And exhale relief to discover they are my own skin, pale and real. I am not a wraith. I am not Draewulf.

In fact, aside from the dull throb in my head and the chill clamped like an iron sheet to my bones, the rest of me feels normal.

I shudder. *Please let everything be normal.*

Sitting up, I scoot over and lean against the warm wall to absorb some of its heat into my bones. When that doesn't work, I wrap my thick cloak around my shaky body and get up just as one of the guards nods to a pot of tea and a platter of food on the desk.

"It's safe."

I nod and walk over to pour the tea and poke at the tiny fruit and purple-fleshed meat. I sniff them. No subtle scent of almond or rind.

A quick bite tells me it tastes fine as well, and abruptly my stomach is reacting to the awareness that I've not eaten in far too long. I'm shoving food in my mouth when Rasha stirs and looks over at me. She raises a brow, only to utter a real, true, Rasha-style giggle.

I resist mentioning that she looks even more like a moth the way her hair is standing on end, and by the time she's up and taming it, I've finished my food and am giving her an account of last night's roof encounter.

A knock sounds on the door. One of Rasha's guards unbolts it and a Bron soldier steps in.

"Sir Gowon has agreed to see Princess Rasha." The man's gaze falls on me. "And the Elemental."

I watch Rasha from the corner of my eye as she and I and all five of her Cashlin guards follow the Bron soldier down a maze of hallways. Behind us trail wisps of muffled hissing from two of the Dark Army wraiths. I refuse to look back or acknowledge them, or the alarming sense that just like in my dream, I can almost decipher what they're saying.

As if the words are trapped on the edge of my tongue, but for the life of me I can't recall them.

It makes my skin itch. I glance up at the Bron soldiers leading us far from the Main Hall, then look around for any of the Faelen bodyguards. It's a full moment before I realize they're all still locked away with the delegates.

I look down at my hands. Did any of the murdered guards have families?

I don't want to think about it.

The jittering cold now moves to my jaw, making my teeth

chatter. I clench them and try to focus on the fact that Sir Gowon didn't believe me about Eogan and the Elegy. Will he this time? And if not, how do we make him?

"Did Eogan give you any other clues on what the Elegy refers to?" Rasha says.

A flare of irritation surfaces. Is she jesting? Wasn't she just listening to me recount in her room last night's scene with Eogan? *If he'd said more I would've told her.* "Nothing else," I say tightly, and keep my gaze on the hall in front of us until the guards stop at a door.

Three of Rasha's men go in with the Bron soldiers to search the place, and suddenly the wraiths are hovering too close, suffocating the air with their sounds and scent of decay. I'm tempted to plug my nose and ears so maybe my veins will stop trying to echo them, but instead I force myself to turn around and study what I can see of them beneath their cloaks. To see what they really are and how they were brought into existence.

What I find is as sickening as what I saw the other night at the banquet. Physical conglomerations of humans and beasts somehow pieced together and brought alive. Human torsos and heads emaciated to skulls, blended with animal parts and bolcrane claws.

Did they bring the plague with them, or is the plague a form of magic that turns people *into* them? Either way, the monsters hissing in front of me with sunken-in faces are as bloodless and cold as Rasha's maid lying somewhere in this Castle.

As soon as the guards are done, I stride past them into the room only to find we've arrived before Sir Gowon. The space is dim inside with hall lanterns illuminating it just enough to reveal it's some sort of chapel. My gaze scans the simple floor rugs and a beautiful, intricate table facing what appears to be a landscape mural before I stop at the painting hanging over it. It's an artist's rendering of a man who looks very much like Eogan. Only older and more calloused.

His dead father, I assume.

I give a low scoff. Apparently arrogance runs in the family.

The Bron guards nearby say nothing, but their faces sour as I walk over to it. Even with that awful portrait, this room has more personality than anything else I've seen in this metal castle. It has a sense of history. I run my fingers across the intricate altar and imagine Eogan sneaking into here as a child.

On the wall beside it is a smaller portrait of a woman holding two identical children. The woman has a gentle face but the small boys aren't smiling. The next moment I'm peeking back up to his father's overbearing painting, then lift it to peer behind it to the landscape scene of a valley.

A Faelen valley.

Inhale. Exhale . . .

It's a mural of the Valley of Origin Eogan and I visited.

The brushstrokes and coloring make it clear even to me that this painting is far older than anything else in the room. And not merely older—more delicate. There's a distinct sense of reverence in the edges and lines that suggest this was more than a mural. It was regarded as a place of honor.

I frown. *Is that how Eogan knew to go to the Valley when he was in Faelen? Did his ancient ancestors once worship the Creator there too?*

I'm just reaching out to finger a dust-covered edge of it, when a Bron guard says, "Sir Gowon for you," and the old man is standing outside the door, his bushy brows furrowed in suspicion.

"I trust this is important, Your Majesty, seeing as it's a highly inconvenient time."

Rasha smiles at him. "I assure you it's of the utmost consequence."

"In that case, I caution the both of you not to test my patience. You have ten minutes."

He glances my direction before stepping into the room. Rasha nods to her guards who, albeit reluctantly, leave with the Bron men and close the door until there's merely one sliver of light.

Sir Gowon walks over to twist a knob on a lantern set into the wall, and the room springs alive with golden beams. "Well?"

Rasha tips her head to me. The floor is mine.

My hands are beginning to shake harder. I wrap my fingers around the insides of my cloak and eye him. "I asked you the other night about Elegy 96. Now I'm asking again."

"Is this what you summoned me for?" He snorts and waves a hand as if he doesn't have time for this, then turns on his heel for the door.

"Eogan trusted me enough to have me ask you about it."

"Which only begs the question, why didn't he tell you himself?" he throws out. "And since he didn't, I can only assume you tricked him for the Elegy name."

"You consider his character so weak? Or perhaps you find me so dangerous a threat."

He stops. Flips around. The muscles in his soft throat clench.

My smile goes cold. "Draewulf *has* taken over Eogan, whether you trust me or not, and Draewulf *is* about to destroy you all. The last moment of clarity I had with Eogan, he said to tell you to take a closer look at the Elegy because it's begun. He said Draewulf took him first but is going in order of blood. Something to do with his block and the land."

Surprise surfaces in his eyes.

It's followed by fear.

Before I can press him though, his face hardens and that protective expression I saw the other night flares. "And yet, if your claim was true, he'd have just as easily appeared to solicit help from me himself rather than send a message through you." He glances back and forth between Rasha and me. "And for one supposedly having intentions on him, you insult his honor most easily while he's done nothing but protect you."

I give a caustic chuckle. "Like he protected his generals? Or perhaps like Draewulf's daughter, Lady Isobel. Did you know she's decided she wants to turn your entire Bron army into wraiths? I'm curious, how do you think she'll go about doing—?"

"I swear to you it's his honor we're trying to save," Rasha interrupts. "As well as Bron's. Because Draewulf *did* take your king. You saw him in the meeting yesterday. Is that the man you knew—willing to use Draewulf's army? Even Odion wouldn't have done so."

He gives a humorless laugh. "I've advised Eogan's father since shortly after his and Odion's birth, and I've spent the past twenty-two years watching them grow to take his place. If you knew any of them the way I have, you'd realize how foolish a statement that is. You say Eogan would have me help you, but all you've done is corrupt Bron tradition here." He's almost spitting the words at me.

I clench my hands. The cold in my bones is igniting my veins, and with them my anger. *I don't have time for this.* "Look, Eogan's block is failing, and when it does he'll be dead and Draewulf will have complete control. We need to know what that Elegy says. *What exactly has begun?*"

He doesn't answer. Just firms his stance and crosses his arms.

I snap my chin toward the wall mural. "That's the Valley of Origin, isn't it?"

His eyes flinch. "How do you know that?"

"I've been there with him."

He shifts to the side—out of the dim lantern light so it falls on me—and shuffles closer to scan my face. *He's searching my eyes.*

Ten seconds.

Fifty seconds.

Enough. This is a waste. The ice in my veins is turning into fury, to need, to bitterness that will lash out and claim the information from him if he won't offer it. I'm just reaching out to force the only hope of surviving we have from his throat, when—

"Perhaps don't tell us about the Elegy then," Rasha says in her high-pitched, hazy tone. "Tell us about Draewulf." She strolls over and smiles. "Having lived so close all these years, you must know quite a bit about his origins. Humor us."

It's an elongated minute before the tension has eased enough so that Sir Gowon uncrosses his arms and graces Rasha with an expression of tolerance. "King Eogan killed him. What else do you want to know?"

"Was he always able to shape-shift?"

The sound of his sigh says he's weighing how much to give us. After a moment, he nods. "I will tell you what most people in Bron could already tell you. I'm sure you've heard he was born from a Mortisfaire mother and wizard father. Since Mortisfaire powers can only exist in the female line, he naturally turned to wizarding and managed to do a lot of good until an unfortunate accident. His ability to shape-shift came as a consequence of his experiments at the age of nineteen."

"Experiments?" Rasha's eyes blossom red as she focuses thicker on him. Searching for his answer, and for Draewulf's weakness if she's smart.

"We are all aware there are darker things in this world, yes?"

he asks. "Varying shades of good and evil? Sometimes people play with things that aren't theirs to alter. In one of Draewulf's experiments, he discovered a way to *absorb* things. Powers and spirits, life energy from others, for lack of a better explanation. The ability to do so granted him incredible abilities, but it also came with a price. His attempt to cheat that price has been to live shifted in wolf form. Sometimes the consequences of altering things are mild, but sometimes they're disastrous."

I swallow and shift uncomfortably at the sudden itching beneath my skin. It feels like the spider's crawling through my veins. *I am not Draewulf.*

"Now if you both are quite done . . ."

Rasha gives me a side glance. "What was the price?"

Why is she looking at me? What I did was my only option and it's going to bring us victory.

"Tell us and we'll leave you be," Rasha coaxes Sir Gowon.

He stares at her as if he'd desperately like to believe that. "My apologies, but we are done here. The guards will see you—"

I flick him my glare. "What does the Elegy say?" When he ignores me, I reach a hand for his waist-shirt and twist.

He grips a hand over mine. "You'll kindly unhand me."

I step closer. Squeeze harder. The hissing from outside the room grows louder in my head. "What does it say?" I demand. "*What* does Eogan think has begun?" Suddenly my arms are crawling and my veins, my chest . . .

"Nym, stop!" Rasha says.

"Read his intentions. What do you see?"

Her hand tugs at me. "You're going to kill him!"

"He has the information we need."

"We'll find it another way. We'll ask Isobel! You can't do—"

Can't I? I stare at her as the heat from my fury floods the ice in my blood. I am beyond finished with this man's uncaring for the world going to the pit of hulls all around him while he stays in his comfortable fool ignorance. Then the dark from my chest is climbing up until I'm pressing against him, draining the words, the knowledge we need as the wraiths' hissing in the hall becomes thunderous.

He whimpers.

I pull, yanking the energy from his chest bones. Like marrow I can taste.

Sir Gowon wheezes and stumbles forward. He opens his mouth and I sense it—the words on the tip of his confused, tormented mind.

"Nym!"

I barely feel Rasha's hands because I swear I will make him speak or else—

"When shadows are sown to sinew and bone, and darkness rules the land," he gasps.

"Let storms collide and Elisedd's hope arise,
Before the beast forces fate's hand.

Just as from one it came and to five was entrusted, to only one it can go, to rule or to seek justice.

If his demise is to be Elemental,
Interrupt the blood of kings in each land."

I stare.

"Elegy 96 is a prophecy," he slurs. "Handed down for generations of Bron kings. It's a foretelling of what is to come."

Twenty seconds go by as every vein in my body is curling up like roots around my chest. *Interrupt the blood of kings.*

He's taking the blood in order. He needed Eogan first.

"Nym, let him go," Rasha whispers next to my ear.

One heartpulse. I can feel his thudding beneath my hand.

Two heartpulses.

Three . . . I shake my head. "Not until he tells us more. What does it mean interrupt the blood of kings? What exactly will Eogan's block protect him from? And who exactly is he taking in order?" *Did the witch know of this? Is it supposed to be a caution? A teaching?* I press against him harder, but his head wrenches backward at a bizarre angle.

My gaze darkens. I peer down at my hand, which was deformed but is now near straight and perfect, and for the first time notice how fascinating it is.

How powerful.

He's choking on deep guttural breaths as his lungs shiver beneath my hand. His heartpulse flailing, flailing, flailing as his life seeps away, dissolving into thin black wisps that tickle my skin.

Rasha's hands are around my waist and she's yanking me back. Next thing I know the power is gone along with the connection.

And I'm shuddering so hard.

I look up at both of them. Her expression is horrified. His just looks odd. Gray. As if he's dying. I blink and feel the cold and hunger fade.

Suddenly I'm seeing him standing there so feeble and weak and oh litches what have I done? I jerk back and stare in dread at them, at my fingers, my palms. He begins to slump forward and I go to steady him but he pushes me away.

"Guards!" he gasps. "Take them! Lock them in their rooms!" He peers at me. "Your power is like . . . like . . ." He shakes his head and stumbles again.

I did this to him.

I hurt him.

I look at Rasha and everything in me turns ill. I glance back at him, but he's already walking away while the guards grab my arms and shove us from the room and into the hall toward our quarters.

CHAPTER 30

TING.
Thump.
Ting.

I lie on my bed with the shades closed and lights out, hurling my knives into the metal ceiling above me, then waiting to catch them when they drop. Focusing my senses to know when they'll fall and my reflexes to grab their handles midair once they do. It's a game Colin and I played sometimes in the corner of Adora's barn in between our training sessions. Except I could only do it one-handed then.

With my gimpy fingers now straightened, I play it with thin stockings wrapped around both palms.

Ting. The blade sticks.

Thump, it drops toward me as hard and sharp as the look on Rasha's face before the guards confined us to our rooms. "I didn't mean to hurt him," I murmur again to the ceiling.

Why couldn't Sir Gowon have simply told me on his own?

I grab the knife handle and quietly, methodically, toss it up again. *Ting.*

Thump.

As if what he said made sense anyway. It's been six hours since I met with him and got confined in here, and I've spent every minute of it trying to sort through Sir Gowon's words. *"When shadows are sown to sinew and bone, let storms collide, Elisedd's hope arise, before the beast forces fate's hand."*

I assume it's speaking of Draewulf, but what did Eogan mean by saying it's begun?

What's begun? The beast forcing fate's hand? To do *what* exactly?

That seems to be the question it all comes back to. *What are you up to, Draewulf? What do you want?*

And somehow, destroying the world seems too simple an answer.

"From one it came and to five was entrusted, to only one it can go, to rule or to seek justice. If his demise is to be Elemental, interrupt the blood of kings in each land."

If Draewulf's demise is to be Elemental—does that mean an Elemental will kill him? I wonder if that's why he eliminated the Elementals in the first place. Isn't that what he said in the hallway when we first arrived?

But then why is the beast keeping me alive?

"What in litches is it all supposed to mean?" I yell at the air for the hundredth time.

The muttering voices of the Faelen delegates beyond the wall beside me merely continue without a lull. About an hour ago, they all converged in Lady Gwen's room. I can hear them talking but not enough to dissect what they're saying. I didn't have the heart to go argue with the guards to let me in on it too.

More accurately, I haven't the slightest interest in whatever it is the delegates have been discussing, especially since it'd require walking by those wraiths in the hall. Their noise is a dull thrum through my head, like words blending into hollow humming. "Come to us, come to usss, come with ussssss," I swear they're saying.

"Go to hulls, go to hulls, go to hullsssss," I mutter back, in case they can hear me. I flex my wrist and dig my nails into my bandaged flesh, but the dark hunger beneath my skin only makes their hideous thrumming louder.

Ting.

Thump.

Ting. Thump.

Five more minutes of me ignoring them, and then there's a new commotion of voices outside. The delegates perhaps? No. They're still murmuring on the other side of my wall. *Myles?* I sit up in the dim just as something heavy hits my bedroom door, followed by a scuffle and deep cursing.

Silence falls.

I lift a knife.

A thin filter of light slices the gloomy room as the door softly opens and footsteps pad toward me. A black mask looms from the shadows. I thrust my blade out only to hear a small sound to my left just before a pillow is shoved over my face, slamming me down into the bed.

I slash with both knives and am rewarded with one connecting into muscle. It's met with a cry before both blades are wrenched from my wrists by reflexes better trained than mine.

I kick. I scream, but no noise escapes beyond a muffled gagging as the air empties from my lungs until I can no longer breathe.

I stop moving.

"You've been requested," a panting voice says so close to my ear that my neck tingles.

The hands pinning the pillow over my face ease off, letting it slip aside, and pull me to my feet at the same time they're slipping my blades back into my makeshift ankle sheath.

I blink to focus but the intruder is already pushing me to the door. When I step out into the light, it's into the arms of two more masked soldiers, part of Lady Isobel's personal Mortisfaire guard. The Bron soldiers are sprawled out on the ground. They look stunned, not dead, and behind them five or six wraiths are lurking in those gray rags that barely cover their body parts sewn together with bolcrane pieces or panther-monkeys. I shudder. *What in litches?*

Before I can pull back, the masked soldiers grab my arms.

"You'll come quietly," the woman behind me says.

"Like hulls." I twist and jerk my wrists and begin to pull away, but their hands flail out and become iron beneath their black gloves. I try to peer at their faces, but the thin material stretches over their features enough to hide everything but their sharp eyes. The four of them drag me down two corridors into a thin hallway away from the wraiths. When they stop and release my arms, it's not just Lady Isobel standing in front of us.

It's Eogan. Or, more accurately, Draewulf.

I pull away and smooth my shirtsleeves.

"Leave us." Draewulf bats a hand in the air and waits for Isobel's soldiers to exit the hall before stepping closer.

Bending down, I yank out a knife, but before I can lift it to his stomach, he wrenches both arms behind me and draws his body against mine in a move that, like most of his others, is faster than should be possible. He laughs an ugly sound. "So the Elemental girl can fight off an army but can't handle a few Mortisfaire maids."

Lady Isobel steps forward with that smile that's like a plague on her lips and brushes a graceful hand down my hair. "Or perhaps it's that she has no fight left in *her*. I wonder—has watching her beloved trainer live out his final days left her . . . impotent?" Her hand moves from me to her father and presses down on his shoulder. He makes a bizarre choking sound.

I twist my head around to see his countenance alter as the black of his irises grows wider and his teeth longer. I writhe beneath his grip to stop her, to help him, but Draewulf presses harder on my wrists as any last bits that make up Eogan seem to fade before my eyes.

"Of all the—" I shove my knee up toward Isobel.

She dodges and retreats with a giggle, then releases her father in the process, allowing him to return to Eogan's form. "Oh come now," she says in a pouty voice. "Watching your pretty face flinch is *just* so lovely."

"Let's see if yours stays lovely when *I* make it flinch."

She lets out a tinkle of laughter and glances up at her father. "I think our impotent Elemental forgets who she's speaking to."

"I'm speaking to the woman whose father now inhabits her onetime lover's body."

The same expression I noted back at the banquet when she stood looking down on Eogan in irritation and disgust flashes behind her eyes.

I smirk. "Must be awkward, no?"

Her hand goes up, but Draewulf releases my arms and slides around to block her from slamming it against my chest. "Isobel, quit fooling and tell me. Does she have what we need?"

She narrows her gaze. "Father, I—"

"*Now.*"

Her look is murderous as she slides close to me. "Don't worry. That heart of his you only wished belonged to you is about to cease existing altogether." She pauses to lean into my ear. "Say good-bye knowing he won't suffer. Much."

I wrench a hand free and slap her across the jaw so hard, I think I hear her bone crack.

Her fingers are on my throat, but Draewulf's quicker. He pulls her wrist away and crunches it loud enough with his own that she actually whimpers and I wince. His smile turns disgusted. "I said assess her, not kill her."

Isobel's glare could pierce ice through my skull. She clenches her jaw but stays put, then slips her hand onto my arm covered with memorial scars. She squeezes down as he murmurs against my neck, "Just think, Eogan's gone all because of me. Because you weren't strong enough. And now," he whispers, "no one but you and I and your two Uathúil friends will ever know."

I bring my foot toward Draewulf's family heirlooms. It only lightly connects because he dodges, then jerks my elbow toward my shoulder, but we both cry out.

"There it is," he pants.

"I will kill you—"

"Careful with threats you can't follow through on."

Lady Isobel's hand begins shaking over my arm. It's warming. I cringe and twist my wrist beneath Draewulf's fingers enough to hover it over his chest. Forcing down, I yank as much energy as I can from his venomous, twisted soul.

Draewulf utters a pained curse word.

But it's not enough. I can't focus it adequately as Isobel's hand latches onto something in me, and it's as if I can feel the veins stiffening in my arm and solidifying all the way up my shoulder and down to my heart, freezing it into place. Into stone. My palm immediately drops from Draewulf, my whole being going sluggish, as if I've been weighted beneath metal.

"Enough," Draewulf murmurs as he sags back. He pushes Lady Isobel's hand off me. "Is she ready?"

Her only reply is to nod.

"For what?" I hiss.

She smiles. "The question is, Father, are you?"

Perhaps it's my imagination, but I swear I see the slightest wince in his eyes. "Only a day, maybe less."

"Then the airships depart before dawn."

CHAPTER 31

I N THE HOUR FOLLOWING MY FORCED RETURN TO
my room, I lie splayed out in a near-paralyzed state on the floor
where the Mortisfaire tossed me. My attempts to yell through
the wall to Rasha get me nowhere. Either she's ignoring me or the
water pipes are flowing too loud because there is no reply, and after
a while I give up and focus on breathing through the heaviness in
my lungs. And the awareness that even if I could move enough to
get around the wraiths to reach Rasha and Myles, we'd still have to
find Lady Isobel and Draewulf.

And then what?

I close my eyes and curse myself for not focusing my ability
more when I had Isobel in hand.

Eventually the breathing eases, bringing relief that whatever
injury she did to my heart and veins is waning. The aching following it keeps me near doubled up the rest of the night though. As
does the utter fury that I have no idea how to prevent what's about
to come.

It's almost dawn when another shuffle outside my door alerts
me just before Bron soldiers bust it down. They drag me out to join

Myles and Rasha, who've obviously been freshly pulled from their quarters as well, and proceed to confiscate our knives before shoving us down the hallway.

Sir Gowon leads the way with a stony expression and refuses to answer any of Rasha's questions or Myles's demands, while I glare straight ahead and feel my hatred pound through my chest. It's like a drumbeat from one of the refrains the Faelen minstrels used to sing. Slow. Steady. Hammering in the thought that as much as I try to figure out what anything means anymore, the chill in my veins might as well be screaming that I don't know.

Or maybe I don't want to know.

"Are they bleeding jesting?" Myles grumbles as they force us through the doors leading to the giant loading area we landed on four days ago. It's holding the same airship we flew in on. The balloon's been reinflated. "Couldn't they have waited until a less hellish hour? Especially since, from the looks of it, the wraiths have barely got their blasted army assembled."

The guard closest to us doesn't answer.

Rasha wraps her arm through mine. "How are you?"

"Fine."

"Liar."

Myles peers over at us. Clearly anything to do with one of us lying is of interest to him.

Five, six, seven steps I wait before dipping away from their stares. "Draewulf and Lady Isobel had the Mortisfaire bring me to them a few hours ago. They know about the power I consumed."

They stop to look at me.

"He wanted Isobel to 'assess' me to see if I was ready."

The Bron soldiers ram into us, shoving us forward—accidentally at first, then purposefully. "Keep moving," the large one barks.

His dark eyes flicker menacingly against his smooth black cheeks and short hair that's trimmed clean. He lifts an arm cloaked in its red-and-black soldier's sleeve, and for the first time I notice the number of medals sewn into the material. He points to the ship as Sir Gowon strides up beside him.

"You are not coming with us?" the large guard says to Gowon.

"My duty is here to protect our people, just as yours is to protect our king. We will meet again, my son."

My brow goes up as the two men lock forearms briefly. *Son?* Then we're moving forward.

"Are you certain?" Rasha is asking, and her voice has its airy tone.

"Lady Isobel was assessing to see if you were ready for what?" Myles says.

I peer away from Gowon and the guard and up at the lantern-lit airship as we stop at the loading plank. I can still feel Lady Isobel's hand on my heart. Chilling it. Beginning to harden it. I rub over my chest where the ache is so raw.

"I've no idea, but it felt like a test." My mind flicks back to Draewulf and the wraith's conversation on the roof. *"Is your vessel prepared?"* the wraith had asked. *"She performed as I said she would . . . Either way, it won't be long."*

That word *vessel* keeps crawling beneath my skin, making me shiver. "I think he was assessing my abilities because he's going to use me for something," I whisper. "He said 'she performed as expected.' As if *he* was expecting it to . . . mature."

Rasha flips around. "What?"

"That assumes they were talking about *you*." Myles keeps his tone low and his gaze cool, but something in both tells me he's suddenly worried too. It makes me want to argue with him. But I don't say anything because the very thought that Draewulf could've known, could've been waiting for this thing in me to alter somehow, makes my blood curdle. Because it begs a new harrowing question:

What if "ready" meant I'd reached a point where he knew I could no longer stop him?

"It's not just that." I study Myles. "You heard him on the roof. They asked if his vessel was ready."

"But how could he have known you'd go after the new abilities?" Rasha says.

"That's a good question." I look at Myles as half the guards shuffle past us to the ship's boarding plank.

"If either of you are implying I had anything to do with it, you're sorely mistaken. Or have you forgotten Draewulf'sss a wizard? A very smart one. If he wanted you to have them, he could've influenced any sort of circumstances to ensure that happened."

"Circumstances involving you?" I say bitingly.

We're next in front of the loading plank now. Rasha's half looking around when she abruptly dips her voice. "Where are the other delegates?"

"Mossst likely being left behind." Myles smooths his glossy hair down, as if anyone here cares what his hair looks like at four in the morning.

"Did the guards tell you that?"

"No, but it's what I'd do if I were them. A few hostages left in the homeland are excellent security. In fact, I'm very much surprised he'sss even taking you, Your Highnessss."

Rasha sniffs and watches her Cashlin guards ascend into the airship with an expression that says she fears Myles's repulsiveness will rub off on her.

I look at the large Bron soldier standing in front of us. Gowon's son. "Will they be killed?" I ask him.

His features stay stiff as he waves first Myles, then Princess Rasha onto the plank. "It is my understanding they'll be left unharmed."

I scoff. "By your Assembly perhaps, but what about the wraiths? Or will you just let them take care of that for you?"

"I've been assured they'll be fine." He beckons me to follow Myles and Rasha. "Except for . . ." His eyes flick up almost imperceptibly to the front of the silver airship, which is glowing from lantern light like the rest.

I track his gaze.

Squint through the dim.

What in—?

There's an object tied to the forward-most staff—like a fish tied to a skewer—and it looks very much like Lord Wellimton.

"We'll be taking him along," the guard says. "By King Eogan's request."

"Is he—?"

"He's alive." The guard breaks into a smirk.

Very much alive in fact, if my ears are correct in tuning in to Wellimton's yelled choice of Faelen swear words. My mouth goes dry. I glance back at the guard. "Are King Eogan and Lady Isobel on *this* ship?"

Suddenly everything within me is frantic, panicky. Oh hulls, I need them to be on this ship. The sensation is short-lived thanks to the pursing of his mouth. His gaze shifting toward the room above the airship's dining area is a clear indication, whether he intended it to be or not. I smile smug-like as he gives me a shove onto the plank. Then the other guards are closing in behind, herding us up.

The closer we get to the airship's deck, the thicker my skin bristles and the more I can feel the hissing. Even without seeing the wraiths, their presence hangs like the cloak over my spine, clinging and clammy in the light wind. Their whispers grow louder. Just like the guards who, as soon as I've stepped on deck, are yelling to pull the plank up and telling the captain to take off before I've even had a chance to grab hold of something stable amid the bustling bodies.

I count to ten before the ship shudders and makes a groaning sound, and suddenly we're floating up, up, upward into the air above the Castle and the city. It's another ten, fifteen seconds before my stomach catches up with us, and by that time the glow of the morning sky is bubbling out on the horizon.

We're rising faster now to meet two other ships in the air. The atmosphere surrounding them flutters and bursts into ribboned lines of periwinkle and gold as the metallic fleet reflects the morning sun stretching her rays out to greet us.

It's beautiful. And breathtaking. And terrible all in one. Like these mirrors of glorious light hovering above the heavy shroud of land and city beneath us that is surrounded by half-emptied wraith encampments. The camps look like leeches spotting the area, like a plague on the skin of this kingdom.

"Looks like you should've done more damage with your Elemental powersss," Myles mutters beside me. I follow his gaze to the forty or so airships hovering over an eighth as many warboats out in the ocean. If I thought the brackish army below was a pestilence on the earth, this, this is a pockmarked horror on the face of the Elisedd Sea.

They're dangerous looking. And far too familiar.

"What do they need the warboats for if they have all these airships?" Rasha asks.

"I believe they carry fuel."

Behind us, there's a snap of fingers and we're promptly sur-rounded by a horde of soldiers. "King Eogan would have us see you to your quarters now," the large Bron guard says. He doesn't give us time to question or argue but merely turns, and we're pushed to obey.

They take the group of us through the same dining room to the same door leading to the same quarters we stayed in days ago. I look around the hall, at the lanterns, at the red carpet and metal walls. It also looks exactly the same, except this time, Rasha and I are given my tiny room to share, and Myles and the Cashlin guards are crammed into the other two.

"At least you get to keep your men this time."

She nods and I don't speak again until the soldiers exit, the hall door is locked, and their footsteps are fading. "We need to speak with Lady Isobel. I need to know what the rest of that Elegy means and . . ." I swallow. "Then I need to get Draewulf alone."

Her expression turns cautious. "I agree—only, not the way you spoke with Sir Gowon."

"I'll be more careful, but at the end of it all, we need that in-formation."

"*Can* you be more careful, is the question."

"Of course I can."

"*Will* you?"

Is she jesting? "Okay, first off, he was an oaf. And second? You manipulate people every moment to gain access to their thoughts, so I'm not sure what I did was actually any different."

"He was innocent. And I don't hurt people."

Right. I doubt some of them see it that way. I don't say it though because I don't want to fight. Whether I see the difference or not, I've no desire to go back to not communicating. Not when every moment now hangs on a thread, dangling back and forth like a pendulum.

I bite my lip. "What's done is done. I'll be more in control next time, and you do your best to read every litched intention."

Her expression changes from caution to concern, and for a second she seems to be debating something. Finally, "Be careful not to confuse ability for your true nature, Nym. You are not your powers. If anything, the fact that you think you need them makes you a slave to them, and in doing so, weakens your true capabilities."

This time I actually snort a laugh. Her words are clearly spoken by someone who's never been a slave.

She frowns.

"Fine." I lift my hands because I've already agreed to this and what more does she want? "I won't rely on them too much with Lady Isobel, but if they are the only way to stop this, then I don't understand what your offense is. Or have you forgotten you are willing to kill Eogan in order to stop Draewulf?"

"Yes, Eogan. Not everyone else. And my concern isn't simply for harming others. It's what I see you gain from it. Back there with Sir Gowon, you looked different. You looked like . . ."

She stops but I can almost hear her say it anyway. "Like Draewulf." Or maybe, "Like Lady Isobel."

After a moment she continues. "I can use my ability to see how best to pull the information from Lady Isobel. However, as much as I hate to admit it, we're going to need Myles's help influencing her mind. Even if that man is a disgrace to all things Uathúil."

CHAPTER 32

B REATHE SLOWER IN THROUGH YOUR NOSE AND out through your mouth." Myles gives an example while I look at the open door behind us, through which Rasha and her guards' voices float in from our room. *How much longer are they going to be meeting in there?*

Myles snaps his fingers in front of my nose. "Are you listening? That'll help keep you calm, which will keep the vortex stable. If that'sss in fact what you want."

"Of course I need it stable," I growl. "That's not the issue. I need to wield it *faster* on Draewulf before he or Lady Isobel can interfere. But if we don't get to either of them soon instead of sitting around here pretending—"

"I said breathe slower," Myles growls back. He stalls a second to swallow as his face turns an off shade of yellow, then twitches the air around us and murmurs something. Abruptly the floor falls away and my stomach lurches at the sensation. I shut my mouth and move impatiently to anchor my feet on the carpet and settle my mind on his whispered suggestion that I'm standing on a high ledge overlooking the entire Hidden Lands. I hate this part. Or maybe it's that part of me is beginning to like this part, to feed off this part.

Myles stirs up an image of Eogan holding his hands up in the form of claws, poised to rip his own chest open. The black wisps emerge from around his legs. "Breathe in and let it control you."

"I'm trying but you're just having me repeat the same scenario over and over when we have no idea how Draewulf will actually respond. I'm not sure this is going to get us to Isobel any quick—"

"Just do it."

"*Just do it*," I mutter. But I go ahead and press my hand toward the pretend Draewulf just as he brings down a claw. I press through it without even dodging and force the image to play out quickly, ignoring his moves and keeping my hand to his heart.

If Myles is bothered at my manipulating it, he's too busy trying to keep his stomach bile down to say so.

Eogan's body begins to seize, and then there are two of him. Of them. He slumps over and Draewulf rises out of him, furious and lashing out even as he weakens. I lean and tug harder. And yank Draewulf from his very skin in the same manner as I've done a hundred other times lately.

"Finish him."

"You don't have to say it every time," I snap. I step forward to slip the knife from Eogan's boot and bring it up to slit Draewulf's throat. The mirage begins to dissipate.

I turn. "Happy now? Because I strongly suggest that if we're not going to question Lady Isobel soon—"

Something catches my eye.

Something's off with the still-fading scene.

Both Eogan and Draewulf are lying beside each other, but Eogan has his throat slit too.

The room shudders and tilts and the image vanishes quickly, and Myles is standing in front of me.

"What in litches?" I stare at him. "*What* in hulls was that?"

His hands go up. "Like I've said before—a scenario based on your fears."

"That wasn't my fears. That was your suggestion. I heard you muttering."

He shrugs. "If he'sss not separated from Draewulf in time, you may have to kill him at some point. Are you able to do so?"

"I asked you to train me, not prepare me for what scenario you *want* to happen." I pierce my glare through his face and only lightly notice how strong I'm shaking. "So I'll ask again—what was that?"

"Manipulation. Preparation. Call it what you want, but peace will alwaysss require a steep price. If you're prepared, you stand a much better chance of succeeding at this game."

"The cost of peace took my Elemental race. I think I'm quite aware of what this game requires, thank you very much, but that—"

He gulps twice. "Good, then don't lose sight of the goal because this anger you feel—that'sss what we want. Focus it on him when the time comes. It's what will fuel your abilitiesss."

"Or it's what will turn her into you," Rasha says.

We both glance over to see her standing in the doorway, disgust and concern coating her features.

"I believe you said you wanted to stay out of the training sessions," Myles snarls. "In which case, I'll kindly ask you to mind your—"

"I want to go over our plan regarding Lady Isobel."

"And I'm merely doing my part to help Nym save the world."

"We both know that's a lie, so you can go ahead and drop it. Her training is for your benefit more than charity."

He glares down his nose at her and brushes an invisible speck from his shirtsleeve. "I'm doing more for her and this war than you or anyone else isss. So while you stand there—"

They can't be serious. We don't have time for their bickering any more than we have time to train. I look at them both. "Will you both just shut it for one minor minute so we can move on? So Myles wants to rule the world—it doesn't mean he's got a lick of a chance to actually do so."

"He doesn't just want to. He *thinks* he can." Rasha walks around Myles and faces us. She sniffs and trails a frown down his entire thin frame. "And he needs you to help him do it."

"Of course he does, but I'm not going to. Now let's talk about Lady Isobel."

"And why'd *you* come to Faelen a month ago, Princess?" Myles snaps. "Especially just when the war was coming to a head?"

"To show our support."

I give up and glare at them.

"Oh really?" Myles says. "You were considering sending troops to our aid?"

"We may have."

He sneers. "Or you knew Draewulf would be in Faelen. Or at least suspected it."

Her fake smile falters. "We . . . may have heard a rumor he would attempt to enter Faelen. I personally told King Sedric. Even more, the moment I realized he was in Faelen, I rushed to the Keep, as you'll recall."

"What do you want him for?" Myles asks. "Or more precisely, what does your queen mum want him for?"

"Look," I say over their voices. "We all want Draewulf dead, and while I'm very aware Myles has some ridiculous desire to see himself king, none of that matters if we can't figure out that Elegy and what it means as far as saving Eogan and killing Draewulf."

He turns to me. "The only thing the Elegy's clear on regarding killing Draewulf is that only an Elemental can do so. You'll forgive me for being obvious, but I think you should safely assume that means you."

I ignore the shiver that brings. "I think I'd gathered that, except . . ." I stop. And stare at him.

Suddenly the thing I didn't even realize had been nagging at me since last night bubbles up and bursts forth. *I no longer have those specific powers.*

I open my mouth. Shut it. Finally say, "I'm no longer an Elemental." *Even Isobel referred to me as impotent.*

"That's exactly why you needed new powersss, my dear. You heard the witch—even she believed you could do it."

"But they *knew* I had those powers, and it's like they weren't even concerned."

Rasha's small gasp drags my gaze over. Her mouth has dropped open and her eyes are flaring like fire.

"Nym, he . . ."

I peer back at Myles as his lips promptly clamp closed.

It takes me a minute to latch onto what she's just deciphered before suddenly it's somehow floating in my mind too. *"The only thing the Elegy's clear on regarding killing Draewulf is that only an Elemental can do so . . ."*

Myles already knew about the Elegy.

I'm at his throat so fast he doesn't have time to duck away. "You knew. This whole time you knew what the Elegy said and you didn't say a word. You heard Eogan tell me on that roof that it had begun— that the Elegy was the key—and you didn't tell me what it *was*?"

He gurgles and thrashes his hands at me. He even tosses up an image of Eogan beneath my hands.

I squeeze tighter and lower my voice to ice. "How long have you known about the Elegy?"

He glances at Rasha—whether for help or because he knows she'll see if he's lying, I can't tell. "Since visiting Bron three years ago."

"You blasted— What else do you know about it?"

"Nothing," he chokes.

His tone is off. His lisp is off.

He's lying. How could I not have heard it before? In his voice—in his hesitations?

"You're fibbing," Rasha says.

I grind my teeth. "What *else*?"

"Only that Draewulf's sewing of sinew and bone had begun with the Dark Army. And that only an Elemental can kill him." He wrenches free of me, panting. "I swear."

I look at Rasha. Her gaze is narrowed tighter than I've ever seen it. As if she's filleting his insides one piece at a time in pursuit of honesty. After a moment she nods. "He's telling the truth."

He glares at both of us and adjusts his cuffs before smoothing his long, thin hands over his pant legs. His attitude calms quickly. Too quickly in fact, as his face takes on that hungry expression again I saw on the roof with Eogan.

"The image you showed me—I was killing Draewulf for you, and then . . . I was killing Eogan too." I sharpen my tone. "Perhaps it's time you tell exactly why you've been helping me?"

"I assumed that was quite obvious. I need you to kill Draewulf for me. But pardon if I'm also preparing you—"

"What else do you want?"

He stops. Stares hard at my face. And grows more serious than

I've ever seen him, even as airsickness tugs at his lips. "If Eogan survives the separation—and Draewulf is killed—Eogan will be weak and someone will need to be there to step in. Someone with an immense amount of power to take control of the Dark Army before Isobel can use them. That person will have to do what needs to be done in order to keep the rest of the world from going to hullsss."

"How compassionate you make your motives sound." I snort. "Especially considering your and Draewulf's interests in having me take on another ability." I lean in. "Are you working with him?"

His expression turns five shades of insulted.

"How did he know?" I push. "How did Draewulf know you'd suggest it? How did he know I'd take it on? He said I'd go back even. Perhaps because you'd make sure—"

"Nym, he's not working with him," Rasha whispers. "Draewulf's been around a long time. He's excellent at guessing human nature, and he knows how you and Myles both work. My guess is he knew you'd do anything to help Eogan. But with Myles . . ."

I glance past him to her. Her eyes are a terrifying shade of red illuminated by the level of sickly pale her skin has gone. A look of realization dawns. "What?"

"Myles wants Draewulf's powers," she says, and her hazy tone is more than horror. It's shock.

"For what?"

"So he can become like him. To rule in place of Draewulf."

This? This is his bigger plan he spoke about the last time we were on this ship?

"You want to become Draewulf?" If I wasn't so disgusted, I'd laugh at the stupidity of it.

"Not become him," Myles snarls. "Just utilize his abilities to ensure no one like him ever gains control again."

Does he hear himself? "You do know you sound ludicrous, yes? Not that it matters, because if I can kill Draewulf like you're so convinced I can, then what's to stop me from taking you out as well? I don't care what your ulterior motives are, Myles. I refuse to be part of your endgame. I'll not help—"

"Except you already have." Rasha's eyes are still doing that flaring business, and her smile is sad. "When you absorbed the power. Whatever that witch did—it not only unleashed an ability in you, it attached Myles along with it somehow. Giving him some measure of control over it. Over you." She continues to study him. "He drank a bit of the potion because he's just as irresponsible as his parents."

His tone freezes. "I'll thank you to leave my parents out of this."

I swallow and glare back and forth between them. "How much control?"

He flicks a hand.

"How much?"

"Only enough to ensure you didn't bleeding kill me while I trained you."

My hand reaches out to press beneath his chin. "You tricked me."

"I did no such thing. But thisss"—he glances toward my fingers clamping down—"this reaction has to stop. You're becoming downright unbearable." He shoots a glare at Rasha as if to blame her for egging me on.

I don't care. I don't release his narrow face. Just tilt my head at him. "Rasha, tell me about his parents. How were they irresponsible?"

"Myles is the illegitimate son of a Cashlin lord and King Sedric's aunt."

"And?"

She stays quiet long enough that I finally let go of Myles to glance at her, only to discover her staring at me. She finally tips her head forward, as if willing me to understand.

I frown. A *Cashlin* lord? Wait . . . "Are you saying his powers are Luminescent?" I almost laugh at the strangeness, and for a moment, the wretched mood in here is broken. "Is that why you hate him so much?"

"I *hate* him because of his despicable personality. The fact that he's an abomination to the Luminescent race is a side point."

I look at Myles and, without ever in a million years wanting to, feel the oddest twinge of something very much like compassion for him. Before I know it I've stepped back and muttered something Colin would've said: "Just because this world is on the verge of fear and death doesn't mean those have to overrun who you are in the midst of it, Myles."

He actually laughs. "Funny sentiment coming from you, and much easier said than done, methinksss you'll find."

CHAPTER 33

I T'S A LONG REST OF THE DAY.

And an even longer night.

One in which I can barely contain my impatience with the amount of time we're wasting detailing what to ask Lady Isobel, whether it'd be wiser to attempt going for Draewulf while we're still over the ocean or to wait until we've landed, and how exactly to use our abilities not only to get at Draewulf, but to stop the Dark Army.

The discussion flip-flops round and round, like a busted pinwheel, until my head is near busted as well. "I'm not waiting to free Eogan until we reach Tulla. We can make plans forever, but it's not going to matter if we don't actually *do* something."

Myles peers at me. "You think those guardsss or wraithsss will let us within an inch of Draewulf or Lady Isobel if we don't plan for every possible scenario? You may as well seal lover boy'sss death sentence yourself."

I snort. "Draewulf and Isobel are contained with us on a flying *metal box*. We can't arrange for every possible scenario, but I'd say we have a fairly good idea. Beyond that, your mirages will get us to Lady Isobel and then Draewulf. If your training has worked in the way you're so convinced, we should be able to end this quickly and go home."

"And what happens when Isobel or Draewulf or even you, my dear, decide to let loose powers we've not prepared to deal with? Handle it wrong and we'll bring down this whole airship with usss in it."

"If we don't do this right, you'll never get another chance," Rasha says in a soft voice.

I bite my lip and stare at both of them. After a second I nod and rise, then walk out of the room because I don't need their blasted lectures. The airship's droning is pelting my head. *Yes, we have a plan, but what part of "Eogan's dying" do they not understand?* I meander down the tiny hall to the metal door standing between us and the dining room. Will the spider in my bones be able to open it?

I try eighteen.

Nineteen.

Twenty-one times.

But apparently my vortex abilities don't work on metal.

My night is spent lying on the floor listening to Rasha breathing and the wraiths hissing while my head is swearing that Eogan is dying while we bide our time. It's the following morning when the large guard shows up to let us out of our quarters. He brings a squadron of two soldiers and two wraiths along—I hear the latter before they even enter the hall, with their monotonous, unending murmurings.

I avoid looking at them or replying to their hissed words that reach out to me like bony talons reaching for a fly, and instead focus in on their stench, which is so bad I half expect Myles to vomit. When I glance over, I catch Rasha smirking at him.

He withers his gaze just as the wraiths step in front of Rasha's Cashlin soldiers. "Only these threeeeee," they hiss, while the big guard informs the men that only Rasha, Myles, and I are being allowed into the dining area and deck.

"The airship's delicate balance," he claims, and it's only Rasha's Luminescent assurances of her own safety that keep her guards from causing a scene.

The sterile dining area is clear of all but two Bron men I could almost mistake for furnishings the way their red-and-black skin-suits match the carpet and metal walls. Behind them the sea spans out beyond those giant windows, glittery and foamy and bluer than anything believable. They stare at us as we're quickly led through to the deck with its abundance of fresh salt air. And more half-human, half-animal wraiths.

They're lined up in rows, all stiff, all staring our direction. Their glimmering eyes and bone-dry faces look eerily empty, especially since they're not moving. Not even tapping a clawed foot or twitching a gray hand—it's only that spine-chilling hissing that gives any indication they're alive. If you can call their existence *living*.

I swallow and try not to wonder what kind of men they were before this. Did they die first, or were they converted while still alive? Two of them are standing by the door to the side of us, the door I saw Draewulf disappear through our last time on this ship. The one I assume leads up to the captain's quarters, which rise a story above the dining area and deck and nearly touch the enormous overhead balloon.

The large guard clears his throat and yells over the airship's hum, "You have ten minutes! After that I escort you back to your rooms."

I walk over to the railing and ignore Rasha and Myles who're wandering off as planned—Myles to influence the other guards' intentions and Rasha to read them and find out where Lady Isobel's staying.

The large guard follows me.

The sun's warm rays pull the moisture up from the ocean's surface, filling the air with a sparkling mist that hits my shoulders and back, distracting my straining ears and hopes and heartpulse that are listening for anything that will speak of Eogan.

For the first time in days I don't tighten my cloak around me but let it slide back and flutter away from the red dress borrowed from Rasha. And feel the airy spray on my skin.

"It's lovely," I say to the guard, in my best soothing voice.

He doesn't even look at me.

I shrug and look down because it really is lovely. I wait for the ache that comes with the song in my bones that responds to the salt in the sea. But it doesn't emerge.

Despite the new abilities and training and freezing in my veins, the melody's still gone.

Something purple glints off the corner of my eye and I catch the splash of a tail. A moment later, the purple fish flips out of the water again, followed by another, and then a third, and then there's a whole school of them leaping toward the ship. Suddenly the water's churning and roiling and the beautiful flutter-fish are amassing in a dance ten feet off the surface of the sparkling ocean.

The deck beneath my feet tilts forward and it's as if we're dipping down toward the sea to join them. The silver hull of the ship reflects off the water as we drop down until we're less than a half terrameter above.

I look up at the second-story quarters before back at the guard. "Can Eogan and the captain see them?"

He gives a stiff nod.

"Is that where they direct the ship from?" I ask, casually, and point to the quarters.

His face curls into a snarl. Nice try.

I smirk and gaze out at the other airships now above us, flying in perfectly formed rows. Straight and shiny and droning, like silver bees heading for a banquet. "You shouldn't look so litched, you know. One might think you're worried I'm going to take us all down with my storm powers."

"Why do you think I'm standing here?"

Ha. "With a knife hidden on you, no doubt." I grin wider and lean closer. "What if I just took down a couple?" I twitch a hand up toward the horde of airships. "Ever seen them explode?"

His fingers flash to his side, beneath his armpit, and stall when I drop my hand and smirk. So that's where they keep their blades.

His expression is deadly. "Do that again and I'll pitch you overboard."

"And I'll take every airship in this fleet with me."

"Says the girl who couldn't bear a boy killing another man for honor the other night."

I raise a brow. *Is he jesting?* "Using children for blood sport and destroying an army bent on murder aren't even on the same spectrum."

"And what about the children flying these ships?"

Children?

He eyes me. Calculating. His expression saying he's not lying. And that he knows the hesitation it'll give me.

My stomach twists. If anything goes wrong—if all other resorts fail—in order to destroy this army we'll also have to destroy children. I may not care much about the rest of the people on these ships, but . . . I look at the fleet of them as a lace of discomfort filters in at the base of my skull. When I blew up those airships over Bron . . .

"Who?" I whisper, pushing the words out between my teeth. "Whose idea was it to use them so young?" Was it Eogan's father's? Odion's?

When he refuses to answer, there's something akin to relief in me. I don't want to know. And I'm not sure it matters anyway.

I swallow. "How was the boy before we left? The one Sir Gowon had beaten."

The guard's gaze hardens. "He's fine."

I nod and don't push further because Myles suddenly catches my eye from across the deck where he and Rasha have been coercing one of the Bron men from the looks of it.

He tips his head. They're ready.

CHAPTER 34

I PUSH OFF FROM THE RAIL AND STROLL TOWARD THE dining area, and the guard and two wraiths follow just as I join Rasha and Myles at the door. They both keep their faces straight ahead, but I catch Rasha peering at me. She gives a slight nod. By the time the door's shut and we've strode across the room to our quarters, Myles is murmuring and abruptly the entire wall facing us shimmers and shudders. The two doors in front of us switch places—one leading to the rooms the other delegates used on our last trip, and the other to ours.

The guard beside me blinks. Slow, unsure. Behind him the wraiths do the same, looking even more desiccated with their eyes bulging oily and opaque above the skin hanging off their bony cheeks. They hiss but there are no words in it—just confusion. I shiver. And note the other Bron soldiers in the room rise, clearly confused as well.

Rasha reaches for the far door, which from Myles's manipulation appears to be ours, and opens it to reveal a thin, dark hallway. She flips around and flutters her hand at the men and beasts. "You may leave us."

The large guard hesitates, shakes his head, then mutters some curse word and pulls the door shut behind us. I hear the lock click.

And Myles is still murmuring.

"This way." Rasha indicates the first door on our left. But before she opens it she nods to Myles and says, "Nym, only the questions we discussed. Nothing more."

"Fine. Myles."

I needn't have even prompted him because we're already changing size and bodies. Rasha becomes a Bron guard, and I become the lead wraith we saw on the palace roof. And Myles . . . He takes the shape of Eogan.

I try not to think about it and reach out to knock on Lady Isobel's door.

"We're resting," a feminine voice snaps from within.

"It's me," Myles says, lowering his voice automatically. It's eerie, hearing both Eogan and Draewulf come out his slimy mouth.

The door opens and Isobel's standing there, hand on her hip. There's a flash of Mortisfaire guards behind her lounging on a couch. My gaze stalls on them. Without their masks they look young. *Incredibly* young, and pretty, and normal. And they lounge. Somehow that's not something it ever occurred to me they'd know how to do. One lazily picks up a knife and rises to join Isobel, but is waved back before she gets two feet. She returns to the couch and Isobel steps out. And shuts the door behind her.

"What is it?"

Myles lifts his hand, Eogan's hand, which is noticeably shaking, and tucks a strand of hair behind his own ear. "How soon until the Elemental is ready?" he demands.

"I've told you, the ability in her will only grow from here on out. It's you we're waiting on. I can end it right now," she says, and reaches out for his shoulder.

I jerk him away and hiss, "He is weak. It will not be much longer. But how will we know when to use the girl?"

"Whenever he decides," she says coldly.

"And what of Eogan?"

She frowns and Princess Rasha, as a Bron guard, glares at me.

For the smallest second I swear there's a twitch of Lady Isobel's lip. Of love. Of despising.

I grin. She's conflicted.

The next moment she smiles and seems to soften, but it's sterile, as if something in it is forced. "He will be dead."

"And you care nothing for that?" I growl.

She frowns. "My father's approval is all I've ever needed. I have assured you both of that."

"And the Luminescent and half-breed?" Myles-who-is-Eogan-who-is-Draewulf mutters.

"Once we arrive the Elemental will no longer need to be controlled by the half-breed. Which means I can get rid of Lord Myles or you can—whichever you prefer." She turns to me. "However, the Luminescent and the Elemental will need to be contained while we do so. They seem to have taken an odd affinity for that man."

There's a ripple in the atmosphere and I peer at Myles. Just beneath the surface of his mirage I see his own face, his own dark eyes that flicker in slight surprise and, for a moment I think, soften even as his skin turns sallow and his hands begin to shake.

Rasha nods toward Myles's trembling hands. "Why is his body reacting like this?" Her voice so perfectly matches the Bron guard that it makes me wonder how much more powerful Myles's ability actually is. Clearly I should be more impressed with him.

"You would too if you were 130," Lady Isobel snaps. As if a soldier should not be questioning such things. "Soon he will have his life back and I will remove the thing that pains him." She tips her head and speaks to the man she believes to be her father. "I will make it so you won't feel her betrayal anymore."

I frown. *Betrayal? Whose?*

My question is answered before I can ask by Princess Rasha. She mouths to me, *"His wife's."* Then aloud, "My apologies, m'lady, I was merely wondering how best to help him in this . . . state."

Lady Isobel sneers down her nose at him. "He does not need your help, nor is doing so your concern. Keeping your men in line and preparing them for battle should be your focus."

"Yes, m'lady."

"How might *I* best keep him comfortable?" I say. "And how will I know when he is ready?"

She narrows her brow. "My father is perfectly capable of answering such fool questions himself."

I look irritably at Rasha. *She's not giving us anything to work with.*

"Humor the wretch," Draewulf-who-is-Myles growls.

Isobel snorts and purses her lips before, after a split second, turning back to me. "The green around his eyes will be gone. Now why don't you go finish looking over the battle strategy I submit—"

"What if the Elemental kills Draewulf first?" Rasha asks.

Lady Isobel's gaze contorts in confusion followed by suspicion. "The Elemental is impotent. We've saved her for another purpose." She starts to turn.

"But her new ability," I murmur. "Rumor has it she'll use it to try to free her trainer from your father before we land."

She stops. "What did you say?"

I swallow. I'm sure she's already aware of this part of our plan because Draewulf has to be, but it still feels awkward. Like maybe we're showing too much.

Rasha retreats and dips her shoulders to make herself look smaller, humbler. "Forgive me, m'lady, but it's something I heard them whispering of. That perhaps she could use the ability for this purpose."

In the twitch of an eye Isobel swishes forward and wraps long fingers over Rasha's guard tunic. "You know nothing of how our powers work, nor of why we had her take the new ability on. And you will learn to stay silent around me from now on if you wish to stay breathing. Is that understood?"

The guard-who-is-Rasha nods and is released by Lady Isobel.

I stand in shock as the lady dusts her hands together and Rasha gives us the slightest tip of her head. She's read Lady Isobel as much as she can. It's time to go.

But I can't.

"How did you know the Elemental would take on the ability?"

Lady Isobel stops. "Pardon?"

"*How?*"

"My father's quite good at guessing Uathúil nature." She peers at Draewulf. Then closer at me. "Why are you asking?"

"What did you need it for?"

Lady Isobel frowns and backs up. I reach my wraith hand out and press it to her collarbone. She jerks back against the wall beside the closed door, but I don't let her slide away. "What does the Elegy mean?"

"What—?"

"The Elegy," I hiss.

"Stop," Rasha says beside me.

"Let her ask," Myles murmurs.

Lady Isobel lifts one single brow and crushes her lips in a mocking expression before lifting a hand and placing it over my heart. "You'd be wise to let me go."

I lift a hand and place it over hers. And begin to pull the energy from her very bones.

She utters a cry and tries to pull away.

"Why is he taking the blood of kingsss? And why was Eogan first—why did your father need his block?"

No answer.

I pull harder along with the air from her lungs until she's gasping and gaping, but I won't stop until she tells me.

She looks at Draewulf again and her gaze flutters. She's figuring us out. I tug harder until her face turns the color of ash.

"Stop." Rasha grabs my arm. I shove it off.

"Read her," I snarl.

Lady Isobel utters a cry. "He needed it to protect him when bonding with the other kings' blood."

A scuffling noise emits behind the door beside us. Before I can tell Myles to grab it, he's wrapped his fingers around the knob and murmured up a mirage for the Mortisfaire inside. Of what I can't tell—I'm too focused on Isobel—but it's enough to stop them from coming out.

"Why does he need their blood?"

Lady Isobel's hand over my heart is weakening, and if it's done anything to me I can't tell. I can only feel the hunger and anger and the need to know what else she's not saying. I need her answers before I finish her off. Releasing her hand, I force my palm firmly against her chest. Just as I do, Myles's fingers come up to grip my memorial scars. I start to pull away from him because *what in litches is he doing* while I'm trying to get answers? But then I feel it.

It's like a flood. Like he's just tapped the edge of the vortex in me and somehow brought it into center. Why he didn't do this in any of our training I don't know, but there's a spark in her energy and it's as if a dam just broke. Surging. Roaring. Roiling around inside her, slowly gathering in her veins to become mine. A drip of blood oozes from her nose.

"Tell her," Myles growls.

Lady Isobel begins to blink, then sags into the wall.

"He needs the Uathúil kings' life forces—" She emits another cry, this time of anguish more than fury, as her breath becomes ragged. "He can't become human again until he gains them."

"Human?"

"He's stuck in his Draewulf form."

"Draewulf's living on borrowed time," Rasha says, her airy voice now laced with horror. I'm not sure whether her tone is because of me or Lady Isobel's admission, but she's staring at Isobel now, her eyes reddening. "He morphed into wolf form during that experiment when he was nineteen and found it protected him from aging. It also enabled him to absorb others' energy. However . . . each time he's changed back to his normal body, the years and magic have caught up with him, until now." She looks at me. "He can't become human anymore. He's surviving off others."

There it is.

His weakness. No wonder he inhabits others' bodies.

I press harder. "How will the blood of kings help?" And for a moment I swear her power flows from her mouth to swirl around us in a black mist before it touches down on my skin to float into my veins.

Rasha looks at me. "The blood of the kings is tied to their land and their abilities—making it powerful enough to give him back

his life. But it's also more powerful than he can handle without Eogan's block." Rasha's gaze widens. Her voice falls to a whisper. "Nym, he has to kill them. He's going to take the rest of the Hidden Lands' monarchs."

Lady Isobel is glaring at me alone now—as if she can't even hear our conversation. She's just trying to get my hand away from her, but her energy is failing. "I need . . . I need—"

Her words stop. Her face pales. And she tips backward with a sigh, sliding down the door to the carpet.

"Nym!"

I don't move as Rasha bends to check Lady Isobel's heartpulse. I simply stare at her in amusement for how weak she is and at what I've done. At what my ability's done. "Wisdom would suggest we kill her right now."

Rasha whips a shocked expression up at me. "Are you jesting? Do you—?"

"I'm not saying I like it, but this is our chance." Except even as I say it, something within me wonders if I do like it. If the part of me that hates her *does* want it. My chest curls and for a second it's as if the ice in my veins surges over the space in me that has always detested becoming a weapon. That has always feared hurting others.

"You think we should murder an incapacitated woman? Nym—"

I glance at Myles for help. "Isn't this what we've been talking about? Stopping Lady Isobel and Draewulf?" How hard can it be to connect the lines?

He's studying Lady Isobel. "If we kill her off now, we'll not only show our hand to Draewulf and her army, but we'll bring down their wrath on usss as well. And it's too soon for that. Until we land, they have the upper hand on these shipsss. I hate to say it, but we need to keep her alive a little longer."

Rasha removes her fingers from Lady Isobel's neck. "Still alive, but—" She looks up at me. "Barely."

"And when she wakes? She'll have *us* killed for what we've just done." I look at both of them like they're insane.

"Not if we keep her bound and hidden. No one else knowsss we have her—they'll busy themselves with searching for her but won't be able to directly accuse usss."

I stare at Myles and Rasha, a feeling of digust for both of them building. "Mark my words, if we don't kill her now, she's going to do a lot worse to others. She's already done worse."

"So have you."

It's hardly a whisper, Rasha's statement. But it lifts in the air to land like a slap on my face.

I bat it away as if it were a hornet just as the door to the dining area bursts open, and one of the guards is standing there, looking confused.

Without thinking I press my hand out and imagine his lungs, his soul, his blood, and just as with Lady Isobel, I draw the breath inside him toward me. I can feel it enter my hand from five paces away. His fingers go to the door frame as his eyes find Lady Isobel slumped on the floor. He rips his gaze up to Myles-who-is-still-Draewulf, then to me, as if unsure whether to step away, or charge us, or run. The next moment he's holding on to the wall for support.

It's not enough support. His body slips to the floor as I draw energy from him.

I drop my hand at the same moment Myles drops our façade.

The mirage ripples and fades, and Rasha cries out and brushes past me to the soldier's side, but suddenly she's coughing and so is Myles.

I follow and push the door open wider and stride into the dining room. And now I'm coughing and gasping too.

What in—? Everyone's laid out on the floor, faces contorted. The atmosphere feels thin as Rasha and Myles rush over to guards and wraiths to touch their faces, their necks, feeling for their heartpulses.

"This one's still alive."

"So is this one," Rasha says. "It's as if they all fainted."

I look at my hand. At their limp bodies. Still breathing. Just knocked out. As if I stole the wind from their lungs. I disabled a mass of them at one time without touching them or killing them, and it makes me smile because I can do this. I can use this. And as nervous as that makes me, it also feels safe. And I haven't felt safe in a very long while.

Rasha turns to me from her place hunched over one of the men. Her face looks more frightened than I can ever recall seeing it. "You could've killed them."

"I could have but I didn't." My smirk grows and I glance at Myles. "Which means the vortex has grown stable."

"Then we are near ready," he says with a blank expression. "Come." He opens the door to our quarters.

Myles stops as an acrid scent pours out of the hall. I peer past him and my stomach lurches. Even with their faces turned away, it's easy to recognize the Cashlin guards with their throats slit open and chests torn apart.

A pool of blood has leached out over the red carpet, staining it darker crimson. I stride over and bend down to feel the first man's pulse although it's clear he's beyond help. Beyond any of our abilities. Beyond dead.

Rasha emits a low moan. "No, no, no, no! Who did this? Why?!"

Myles reaches up to a lamp attached to the wall and twists its knob to brighten the entire area. The glow sends eerie rays onto the carpet where the blood is slashed in as I continue a search of the body. Until I realize that what at first looks like gray creases around the neck and cuts are actually strands of gray rags.

I pull back. And what seems like the slice of knife across the poor man's chest is too rough, too harsh. They're the claw markings from a bolcrane.

CHAPTER 35

TAKE ME TO HIM." I STAND AND THEY BOTH GLANCE at me.

"Who are we speaking of?"

"Draewulf. Get me up to see him."

"Nym, this isn't the time. We need to stick with our plan—"

I spin on Rasha. "When is the time? When we're all dead? When the bleeding world's been blown up?" I look at Myles. "Take me to him or I will get up there myself."

The grim set of his mouth says he knows exactly what I'm implying. He peeks at Rasha but his words are for me. "While it pains me to agree with Her Cashlin Majesty, that idea's not any wiser than destroying Lady Isobel right now. Our plan is set, and your powers—"

"Were strong enough to knock out Isobel and half the guards. They're ready." I step back into the dining room and move from guard to guard grabbing their knives. I sheathe one in my boot and toss the rest to Myles and Rasha.

"And what happens if, say, you accidentally take this entire ship down?" Myles says. "Not that I'd mind, dear, except for the fact that, you know, I'm on it." He sniffs. "We need to stay with our agreement, and once we're over land—"

I begin walking. "You helped me with Lady Isobel; you can help with Eogan. And once Isobel wakes up or her Mortisfaire discover us, I doubt we'll get another chance. Eogan doesn't have time for us to make any more blasted plans."

"Nym, just wai—"

I ignore Rasha and stride to the dining room door. Without looking back I jerk my head at the wraiths still laid out cold. "If you're smart, you'll kill them and Lady Isobel before they wake."

I'm just pushing open the door to the airship's deck when Myles curls the atmosphere around us, turning himself into a wraith and me into Lady Isobel. I smile like I've seen her do and something about it feels oddly natural. Relieving.

I'm going to finish this.

The guards on deck hardly glance our way as we slip to the right and around the corner to the door leading up to Eogan's quarters. "Move," I say to the two undead beasts standing there.

I don't even wait for them to obey before pressing my way through. Their hissing grows louder, but they make no attempt to stop us. "M'ladyyyy," they say, and it almost sounds worshipful. Something about it makes me shiver as I yank open the door.

With Myles behind me, I march up the two, five, fifteen red-carpeted stairs to a room almost completely made of windows except for a wall and door on my right. Three wraiths stare at us, and the two young boys seated at a bench of what appear to be knobs and wheels for steering this blasted ship turn to look at me.

One of them is Kel.

"Lady Isobel," he says.

I don't answer. I'm too busy staring back. *He's alive. And here.*

As a ship captain? Is that how he stowed away on the airship at Faelen's Keep?

I peer at his face, his hands, his shoulders. He's hunched over and near broken looking, but his expression is hard and hateful as he glares at me. For a second I cringe until I realize his loathing is not actually directed at me, but for Lady Isobel, and it's all I can do not to step forward and hug him. *They've forced him to fly this.*

One of the wraiths glides forward. "How may we helllllp you, Eminencccce?" he hisses.

I blink and turn from Kel. "My father. Where is he?"

The wraith angles his cloaked face until it's tilted all the way to the side and studies me—like a pythanese snake. It occurs to me that his hood-shadowed face is covered in wide, flat, mottled-green scales that make the hair on my neck prickle. A second later he raises a crooked finger and points to the only door on my right.

Before I can move for it though, the handle turns and it opens and Eogan is standing there. His face widens a split second before narrowing in anger. He glances at Myles and back at me before emitting a low growl and springing for both of our throats.

The airship swerves and the wraiths' hissing soars as Draewulf's hands clamp onto us. "What do you think you're doing?" he snarls.

"Your wraiths killed our men," I snarl back. I place my hand over the one that's gripping my throat, and rather than push his off, I press it tighter to my neck. It's burning my skin—cutting into the ice in my bones like a torch. I sense the *beat-beat-beat* of his pulse through his fingers.

They're bleeding into the fury of my own heartpulse.

The wraiths behind us are hissing their confusion at seeing

their master attack his own daughter. They don't move though. Just stay standing in my peripheral as do Kel and the other captain who've half risen from their positions at the steering bench.

The beating in Draewulf's fingers grows stronger and his hand grips tighter.

"Now would be a good time," Myles half mutters, half gasps beside me.

The mirage around us shudders but stays in place. Suddenly one of Myles's hands has clasped onto my owner-circled wrist. He begins squeezing as my lungs begin failing.

I swerve my attention to Draewulf's eyes. Eogan's eyes. Rimmed with barely a hint of green. Or is there? My gaze is blurring, and the hunger for power that has been scratching up my veins since Lady Isobel erupts to the surface.

I slide my fingers from his hand on my neck all the way up his arm, onto his shoulder, then to his chest. To warn the trainer inside to brace for what I'm about to do. What I now know how to do. What Myles and I can do.

Except . . .

I glance at Myles. *What is* he *doing?*

The look on his face has gone dark, and there's a struggle clearly etched across it. A temptation. A hunger like that which is opening up the vortex in my chest.

My gut twists and my hand falters.

He wants to kill both Draewulf and Eogan.

Draewulf looks startled for a second. He snarls but I swear there's an amused undertone to it. As if this is, on some bizarre level, a delightful turn of events to entertain him. He turns toward Myles and sinks his fingers all the way around the man's neck.

Myles's grip on my wrist weakens.

The vortex inside me wobbles.

His neck looks like a twig. It is a twig. He must know it, too, because the expression in Myles's eyes goes from hunger to pure terror. He chokes as the mirage covering the two of us dissipates, and then Myles screams like I've never heard him, even when I hurt him back at the cave. This time . . . this time he is in agony.

It's the scream that can only come from Draewulf using Eogan's block to cut out Myles's ability just like he did my Elemental power.

I shove both hands against Draewulf's shirt and press into his skin beneath. I feel his muscles wince and weaken, but if he notices he doesn't care because he waits, seemingly unperturbed, until Myles's scream stops and his neck goes limp.

Draewulf tosses him to the wraith. "Take him below," he roars. "Keep him and the princess locked up until I slit both their throats. And check on my daughter!"

Next thing I know he's dragging me into his quarters. The last glance I get of the room is of the boys—their eyes are big as orange-fruit. Kel's mouth wide open.

The door slams behind us and Draewulf drags me toward the room's far window, still holding my throat, muttering something about the powers having to be in order. About needing me to understand that it will only be a little longer.

The first thought that enters my head is that he's insane.

"The powers from the kings?" I whisper.

He stops and nods as if that's what he's been explaining and don't I see that this is the only way. He's talking like a mad person in a tone that's trying to convince me. Of what, I have no idea. I'm hardly listening now. Something is wrong in my veins. As if the spider I swallowed is reacting to Draewulf, or Eogan, I can't tell which. It's clawing its way out of my chest to attack him while the vortex in my chest responds to the insanity in him.

The spider begins shaking beneath my skin, as if thrumming her web, drawing on all the fury and anger and scared-as-hulls confusion. "What do you want me for? What am I a vessel for—are you going to destroy me too?" I yank his arm and pull myself next to his face. "Because if you are, then just bleeding do it."

His hand is still on my neck and I'm glad because it means he's not noticing my palms on his chest. Working to pull his very soul from his host as the spider crawls through me to claim her victory. I can see it now, Draewulf's eyes flickering before mine, even if there's no green anymore.

I squeeze both hands against his shirt and command the hunger in me to take over. To take it all. To rip Draewulf from the very seams of Eogan's sinew and skin.

Draewulf lets out another roar but doesn't pull away. As if he enjoys the pain. Except the next instance he's weakening. His shoulders slump away from me even as his essence begins to struggle for freedom from the host containing him.

His power attaches to my hands and slips up my wrists. I watch it creep up, a blackening in my skin, seeping up to look like cracked glass as it seeks to break loose. I can feel the energy inside him. Burning. Alive. Full of the lives he's taken. Along with their fear.

That fear is all I need. The chasm in me surfaces, shooting ice through my arm and my once-gimpy fingers that are now perfect, the tips of them drawing every last breath from Draewulf's lungs.

I smile and reach farther, harsher, pressing in stronger, turning my head to watch his eyes for flecks of green, his smile, his face for separation from this demonic spirit. Suddenly I sense it. The tearing inside. The ripping of power and energy and breath.

Black wisps like I saw at the Keep erupt around Eogan's body. They swirl and hiss, and for a moment I can see the animal's wolf face inside Eogan's.

He lunges for my hand, crunching it with his. I cry out but don't release him even as the thought erupts that I can't take him down. He will win this.

I pull harder anyway.

"Eogan," my soul calls to his. I wait for him to appear because I swear I perceive him slipping from the surface. There's no answer.

Suddenly the energy I'm drawing is too fluid, too dark and dank, and too strong to be contained by a block anymore. As if Eogan's block has broken. I press in harder and the coiling within him is unlike any I've felt. This is power and freedom and strength that is on a level my ability could not hold in a thousand lifetimes. Somehow I know this.

"Eogan, please!" I say aloud, but my voice sounds dull. Empty.

Draewulf's energy begins receding from mine. I can feel it just as clearly as I can feel Draewulf's chest shaking in laughter beneath my fingers and the fight draining out of me at the soul-level realization. There is no Eogan any longer. They are one being.

Draewulf glimmers those ghoulish eyes at me, which are not Eogan's but black to match the beautiful black skin that once belonged to him. He pulls back and there's not even a tug against my hands this time.

No.

No no no no no. Abruptly I'm screaming at him that "I will not allow this because I did not come this far and train this hard to let this be how he ends." I scratch for his face, trying to rip it from Eogan's, trying to tear his heart out even as my lungs compress.

Suddenly the airship dips down and slopes toward the water, suggesting I've drained the air from more than just this room.

Good. Then we'll all die.

Draewulf yelps and grabs my wrist. He bends it back until my screams turn to pain, and all the while he's murmuring those blasted foreign words. Then the ship rights itself and he looks down at me and smirks.

I spit at him. "It's not going to end like this," I hiss. Doesn't he know death is too long, too thick a curtain to try to cross alone? I swear at Eogan because doesn't he remember that I told him to hold on? Because everything I've worked for, everything I've fought for, has just ended—disappeared into the sea of black that is Draewulf's eyes.

My body shakes as the realization settles in:

Draewulf has won.

He tucks a strand of Eogan's jagged hair behind his ear and smirks. "It's just you and me now, pet."

CHAPTER 36

DRAEWULF STANDS THERE WATCHING ME, WEARing Eogan's body like a shroud.

It's all I can do to fumble forward and grab the wall to my left and hold on, hold still, and pretend that the grief washing over me is any less painful than that a week ago in Faelen's castle when I believed Eogan was dead.

I scoot as far from him as possible, to the large window in front of us that overlooks the ocean, and press my cold spine against the glass. Keeping my face toward the beast. "Why?" I whisper, and it comes out all jagged.

"Why did I kill him? I think you know the answer to that. Or are you asking why I've not killed you too? I think it'd better behoove you to wonder why I *shouldn't*," he muses. "Except perhaps the simple fact is, keeping you alive is far easier than offing you at the moment." He slinks backward to a chair, which aside from a small table is the only piece of furniture in the black-carpeted, wood-paneled room.

My gaze follows him as he drops into the cushioned seat and rests his chin on his fingers. I refuse my tone to shake with the anguish near-cowing me. "You seem to have found it easy to kill my kind in the past," I say bitterly. "So I'll ask again—why? What am I a vessel for?"

"I can assure you, your kind were hard to kill as well, especially early on in the war when they were more numerous. Although a pact with your kingdom definitely eased the burden of eliminating them myself over the last hundred years. Placing them in your 'safety' camps was brilliant, really."

He sniffs and looks back at me. "You've never met one other than yourself, have you?" When I don't reply he adds, "Curious. I always suspected they'd saved a few in reserve. Funny though how things work out. If I'd known sooner what your kind were useful for . . ."

"They didn't even know I existed."

"How lucky for me. In that case, I shall tell you the male Storm Sirens used the elements very effectively, but not as effectively as you. You can call them forth on a plane unparalleled." He levels a leer at me. "Or, should I say, you used to be able to call them forth."

I settle a glare right back at him, but his gaze takes on a distant expression and drifts to the window behind me. I shiver even as the emptiness in my blood flares in my chest. The irony doesn't escape me that this is more about Elementals, about myself and my race, than I have ever heard, ever been allowed to talk about in my life. And here he is, the animal I hate, explaining myself to me.

From the corner of my vision I see him twitch his hand and suddenly my eyelids drift heavy.

Keep your eyes open, something whispers from the depths of me.

But I can't. My lids are suddenly too heavy and my head too sleepy.

I feel my body slump to the carpet.

My eyes flutter open. Morning sunlight spills across a room of white curtains and windows, with a wooden ceiling much higher than my head. I peer down at the bed I'm curled up on and trail my hands over the cool sheets before wandering them up to touch the sun particles the breeze is lifting through the air. I take a deep breath. The air tastes delicious. Like homemade bread and citrus.

Eogan moves from his spot against a window frame where he's watching me. The honeyed light slips down his messed-up bangs before shimmering along his black shoulders. "I thought I might have to shake you awake."

I rustle my hair and smile.

"Good dreams?" he asks.

"The best one yet."

His smile broadens suggestively, and my face warms before his expression turns stiff. He walks over as I slide my feet from the bed, but before I can stand he's bending over, taking my cheek in hand and willing my gaze to center on his. "Don't get up."

But I want to. I want to be with him. This is the future I want with him.

"I have to go alone this morning," he whispers into my hair.

Go? What is he talking about? Go where?

As if reading my mind, he tips his head toward the open window where the sunlight's pouring through. I squint to see beyond it, to the valley that looks familiar and foreign all at once. There's sweet air coming from it—that honey-blossomed scent—and entwined in that scent is music—an ancient melodic refrain wrapping its notes into the breeze and ruffling around Eogan's beautiful black hands and face and gaze.

The Valley of Origin.

My heart nearly jumps through the roof of my mouth.

"No," I tell him. "You can't leave. Not like this." I will not allow it. I will not lose him this way.

He brushes my fingers against his lips and inhales. I try to yank away, but his hand grasps mine to hold it in place as he raises a brow and smiles. "There are worse ways to leave, trust me."

He leans down and draws his lips across mine, his mouth caressing my own in a kiss.

It tastes of life. And death.

It tastes of good-bye.

Abruptly his face blurs. "Get away from Draewulf. Or I swear I will haunt you with every last breath in me." His words begin to shudder, then slur. "It's time to let go, Nym. Open your eyes.

"Open them now."

I'm blasted awake into a darkened airship room and a cold presence hangs over me. It's so opposite the warmth and color of my dream it takes a minute to recall where I am. When I do, I freeze only to have my soul shatter all over again.

He's gone.

I look around for Draewulf. To hunt him, to hurt him for what he's done. *Where is he?*

The room is lit only by the stars out the windows and the lamplights along the rim of the airship's deck below. Just like the other airships farther out lighting up the night. They twinkle like yellow fireflies—reminding me of the forest back home. My heart pitches.

I wince and grit my teeth and, stretching my muscles, feel around the room until I reach the door.

Locked.

I twist, kick, shove against it, but it's stuck tight. I slump against the wall and beg the darkness to either release or reclaim me, I don't know. At least until we get there, when I will end all of this.

Because I will end all of this.

"Nym?"

Kel.

"Are you all right?" His small voice carries beneath the door.

"Kel, let me out. Unlock the door."

A hesitation. "I can't."

"What do you mean you can't? Just open it! Eogan is dangerous and—"

"I know but I can't. He won't—he'll just—" His voice drops so low I can barely hear it. "Do you need anything?"

Oh buddy. "Kel, you need to stay away from Eogan." My throat tightens even as I say his name. *Eogan.* I force myself to ignore it. "He's not safe for you."

"I know. Are you sad at him, Nym?"

I don't answer that. I can't. Unless I want my chest to bleed out.

A scuffle against the door. He curses. "I gotta go. I—"

"Wait, Kel!" But his footsteps are already padding away.

Bleeding litches.

I lean against the door and try to listen through but can't hear anything further. I turn my head and stare at the dark.

Keep your eyes open, something whispers from the depths of me.

I glance around.

"For what?" I mutter back.

Assess your surroundings and finish the plan.

Or what? I'm not sure it matters anymore.

Assess your surroundings and finish the plan, Nym.

Fine. I go to rise. Except that strange heaviness sets in again along with the scent of magic and I pitch over.

And fall back asleep.

Something is ticking and clacking, disturbing my sleep. The spider is beneath my skin, scratching and tapping its claws like fingers on a wall, as blazing daylight strikes my face.

I open my eyes to find Draewulf leaning against the window exactly like Eogan was in my dream. He's tapping *his* fingers against the wall, still wearing my trainer's handsome body like a rumpled suit of victory.

I stand and curl both hands into fists. And bite back the nausea.

He smirks.

Where's Kel?

Assess your surroundings and finish the plan, Nym.

I gulp. "Where are Rasha and Myles?"

"Under guard with my wraiths."

"Under *guard* with your wraiths? Or being turned *into wraiths*?"

He utters a sound between a chuckle and a sneer. "Does it matter?"

"To the people you've made wraiths I imagine it does," I growl, inching my way toward the tiny window that overlooks the main deck on the opposite side of the room. Through it I can see the airships surrounding us and the area where the soldiers stand side by side with a group of gray-shrouded wraiths that look more ghoul-like than ever. "Tell me, how is it that you do it? Turn them, I mean?"

He smirks. "I kill them and chop up their bones, then fuse them with stronger beasts. They don't question or challenge, they simply obey. Rather ingenious, don't you think?"

I hold back the urge to claw his throat out.

Focus, Nym. "Can they feel?" I eye how many ships are around us and try to calculate how many children like Kel are flying them. "The wraiths. Do they know what you've done to them?" *Did Eogan know in his last dying moments?*

He shrugs. "People ultimately embrace being controlled for the sake of safety. It's a trade-off."

"A trade-off for death?" I snort and peer at the soldiers on our ship's deck. Will he turn them too? Has it already begun and they just don't know it? Perhaps we're all already being turned and just don't know it. "Is that what the plague is for—to make them beg for it?"

"The plague is an unfortunate by-product. Experiments in magic can be so . . . unpredictable."

A movement catches at the edge of my vision. The biggest Bron guard is hoisting something from the forward rim. Lord Wellimton. They're giving him food and water, and he looks rather frozen, but beyond that—his mouth is moving so fast and his face so red that his temper's clearly none the worse for wear.

Draewulf steeples his fingers beneath his chin. "It repulses you, yet given the chance you'd embrace whatever it took to live longer too." His piercing words feel aimed at my skull. "In fact, you have. I suspect even now you can feel it. The power you took on—the way it flows in your veins—scratching and begging to make you more. To live longer. Stronger."

Keeping my eye on the soldiers I narrow my gaze. "The power I took on was to save Eogan."

"Careful, Nym, or your arrogance will deceive you. Because if you truly believed that, you'd have tried to die in this room two days ago when you realized Eogan was truly gone." He unfurls from the windowpane and pads over to me, his movements much like the dog owner number ten used to own. I hated that dog.

If he notices my tightening jawline, he doesn't acknowledge it. "When I took on this spirit, I believed it was with the intention of delivering my people from oppressive rule. It's what I told myself for years every time I morphed. Until the day I realized what it was costing me. In that way you and I aren't much different, you know. Except what I've sacrificed is more than you can imagine."

"How pathetic then that you've failed. You can use the kings' blood to become human again, but in the end it won't save you from dying."

He snarls and starts to reach for me but stops. He retreats and folds his arms. "True, there's always a price. But who wouldn't give anything for what I have—for what I am? My abilities allow me to dissolve like a spirit and invade a person's body." He leans in. "And what I've learned since then . . . well . . ." His mouth twists into a cruel smile as his gaze drops to my owner circles.

I lift a hand toward him. *It won't help you if I kill you now . . .*

A challenge glints in his eye just as there's a shout from the other room. "They've seen us," the boy captain who is not Kel yells, making me hesitate at the youthfulness in his voice.

Draewulf jerks his head toward the window where the clouds have parted to reveal Faelen's mountains to the right of us.

What's left of Faelen's warboat armada is on the side of the pass we're travelling through. We're too high to see in detail beyond movement on the decks, but with this many ships in the air, I doubt the boat captains have to guess our intention. And from the straight aim we're flying, they'll get it soon enough. My chest tightens for my home.

Our airships don't even dip or shudder toward Faelen. We simply keep on course for Tulla's cliffs looming up from the white froth waves like flat polished tombstones in front of us.

"So you will destroy everyone," I mutter bitterly. "Is that your plan? The Tullan people? They have loved ones and children just like Bron and Faelen. And you'll end them for what?"

"At some point you learn that the love of another is iffy at best. At worst, it will destroy what you thought you were. You should be thanking me for sparing you that discovery firsthand."

His voice is cruel, but it's the look on his face that grabs me. I don't know why but it strikes something in me. Isobel's words come back. *I will remove the thing that pains you, Father. I will make it so you won't feel her betrayal anymore.*

I stare at the tall, snow-frosted mountain tips of the Fendres. Then glance away as a wave of confusion lashes against my ache and my anger, with the words Draewulf said earlier—that he'd originally only been trying to save his people too.

I press one palm flat against my legs as if I can force away that thought. This is different. He's different. He's a monster whom I'm fated to destroy.

"You could choose differently," I say through tight teeth.

"And why would I want to do that?"

"It's not like being evil has seemed to go well for you."

He smirks even though his eyes are still staring out over the ships. "Evil is in the eye of the judger. What you judge as evil, I see as progress."

"Progressive for whom?"

He waves a hand. "There's an entire army out there—"

"Half of whom are following Eogan, not you."

His expression darkens and he turns his face to stare directly into mine. There's the barest hint of a shaky undercurrent as he growls, "They're following my guidance, my planning, and my army."

I smile. I've angered him. *Perfect.*

"But if they knew who you were?" I allow a hint of mockery in my tone. "You had to take on another man's persona just to get others to follow, and now you're dependent on a power you needed *me* to absorb. And why? Why couldn't you get it yourself?"

"You would do well to watch your step." His voice is shaking harder now.

"Until what? You kill me?" I snort. "No wonder your wife left you."

He whips toward me so fast, I press against the window frame preparing for him to slap me, but he seems to have frozen in the moment. Staring at me as if terrified of what else I might know. Of what I might say. Even through the hatred and aching bones and muscles and energy cracking inside me, I can't help but feel the smallest flicker of suspicion. It stirs that hint of compassion blossoming without consent in my soul, swearing that the root of who he is still exists. Is that the betrayal that pains him? That he made himself different—better, in his mind—but in the end his wife couldn't accept him?

I open my mouth. The realization abruptly pounds through my soul—*she couldn't accept who he'd become.* My eyes connect with his and stumble across something there I don't want to see. The smug awareness of how easily that could be me—not accepting the curse I was, always hoping for better. And didn't I take the "better" when it was offered—by Eogan and then Myles? What if Colin or Eogan had suddenly decided they couldn't tolerate me? I swallow and feel my expression soften.

The window frame behind me begins shaking. I look down and the quaking is from Draewulf's hand shoved against the wall beside me as his body's shivering, as if building into a rage. I stiffen and start to scoot away just as a beam of sunlight glances off his face. He doesn't look angry, he looks in pain. *What in—?*

I reach toward him, but he utters a bark and bends over just as a black wisp uncoils around his feet and winds itself up his legs and around his chest. As if protecting him.

From what?

I look at my no-longer-gimpy hand. It's pulsing, pumping with the blood hounding beneath my skin and bleeding black into my veins. I inhale and his wisps start to curl around me. And then my spine begins to shudder, then burn, and my head screams that now is the time. Now is my chance.

I could kill him before it's too late.

I reach for him.

The horn overhead blares.

I shove my hand against the side of his neck.

"We're nearly there," Kel's voice rings out beyond the door. It sounds strong and angry.

Draewulf spins and slams me into the wall. He snaps his fingers and the door flies open before he barks at the wraith waiting beyond. "Get her downstairs," he growls. "Tie her up along with the princess, and if she even lifts an eyebrow, slit the half-breed's throat."

CHAPTER 37

LAPPED BY THE ELISEDD'S BLUE WATERS, TULLA'S CLIFFS
shoot straight up on the horizon. The ship lurches and soars
higher in the same way I'm lurching against the cords the
wraith used to lash my wrists to the deck railing beside
Rasha. It takes a second for my stomach to catch up.

"Where's Myles?" I yell above the wind and airship's drone.

Rasha squints and tips her head at the dining area as strands
of her brown hair thrash about. "Still alive. So is Draewulf I'm
assuming?"

I nod and don't tell her that I tried to kill him. That I hesitated
because I couldn't do it just yet. "Eogan was already gone," I choke
out.

Her gaze whips around to meet mine as the sadness and fury
pull at my gut. I can feel it spreading to my lungs. *"Oh love,"* she
mouths.

I blink and look away. I'll weep later.

The peaks we are approaching are covered in snow, but without
any forest or greenery beneath. Just layers and layers of ice-dusted
rock.

The few men and wraiths on deck are growing restless, and I can feel the dark whispers in my blood, in my ears. "Come to ussss," the undead say. "Come to ussss. Come—"

I turn around. "Shut the kracken up!" I yell at them. But they don't stop, and the only ones who seem to notice anything are the Bron soldiers who frown at me. The large one looks at me with an unreadable expression. I hope they haven't gotten to him too. But no, his skin is still black as night, not gray, and his eyes are clear as day. Not that it will make much difference soon anyway.

The entire fleet of airships is flying twenty terrameters above the first peak when a spark flashes and a swell of smoke rises into the air. It's followed by another, two mountains over, and then another, like a chain.

"They're sending off warning pyres," one of the soldiers calls out. *Good.*

"Too bad there's not enough warning time," Rasha murmurs.

I frown and glance down. We're flying over the peaks and pyres too fast, too soon. The snow-tipped mountains fall away beneath us, sloping into colorful canyons sun-spotted and mineral-painted in pinks and lavenders and bluish-greens. The airships around us shudder and dive down, too, approaching a series of jagged rock formations that dot the landscape in giant twisted spires and arches, hovering over dirt that is as red as the sun on a summer day and freckled with clay-looking houses. I wince. It reminds me of the hue of Colin and Breck's skin.

Something softens in my chest at the thought of my friends.

As I watch, people emerge like ants from those houses to stand and point up. I twist my hands against the straps holding my wrists to the railing. "*Run!*" I think to scream at them, but they seem too confused. I've snapped at the straps another five times trying to break free before a few people begin rushing to assemble in strategic patterns. A minute more and it's clear they're preparing to fight even as parents scurry about, scrambling for children playing among the boulders.

My stomach lunges.

"Oh hulls," Rasha murmurs.

Exactly.

I peer up at Draewulf's quarters again and allow the grieving and anger burning my insides to churn, pressing it up toward him, as if I could reach claws up there and tear him from his safety.

He won't be safe for long.

The black hunger in me gives a tiny ripple with the abrupt sense that he's watching me. *Are you thinking the same thing, Draewulf? That only one of us can win?* Vengeance. Justice. I'm not sure what it is boiling in my blood, but I narrow my gaze as if to challenge him. *Come down and let's find out.*

He doesn't. Just stays up in his room while I stay down here watching the land splay out in front of us. Waiting for it.

Rasha shivers and I glance over. Can she sense it too? The air of heightened anticipation. It's feeding the resource lust of the Bron warriors and the bloodlust of Lady Isobel's army that will annihilate this place.

Unless we destroy both Draewulf and Lady Isobel for good.

Rasha points a finger to indicate mounds of squiggled lines forming shapes farther ahead. Beautiful designs of raised earth. As we get closer I see one is made to look like a snake, another a bolcrane, and still another, one of the beautiful Elisedd sea-dragons. Alongside them lie even deeper divots that appear to be carved out of the earth in purposeful strokes.

"They're mineral mines," Rasha says.

Peeking up from a few of them are treetops. Underground forests? My fist stiffens. Colin's people created these. If his home life had been different, if his father hadn't been a drunk or his mother had survived longer, or perhaps if his gift had been discovered earlier, he would've been one of their miners. He would've stayed here rather than restart his life in Faelen.

He'd still be alive.

I tense my hand and hold it against the airship's metal railing. And feel the slightest shiver in response as the metal seems inclined to bend toward me. Toward the vortex. *What the—?* I swallow and will this thing in me to grow stronger.

The people below are scrambling to gather their forces and wits. I see pile after pile of rock beginning to shift, shoving up into walls and caves—to cover homes and land. Only . . . I don't see any weapons. The rock formations they're creating all appear to be for defensive purposes.

Horror dawns at the base of my chest.

These people are unused to fighting. I doubt they've even been trained for warfare seeing as there was no need. For the past one hundred years, the war never touched their shores. But now, for as secure as their defenses would be against any foot soldiers, the bombs on these ships will break through them like pebbles on water.

My mouth turns sour. We're going to annihilate them.

The ship begins rattling and jolting so hard I have to grab the rail again to hold my balance and keep my wrists from being sprained as we soar over a cliff.

Does Kel see the people too? Is he struggling with having to fly the ship here to destroy them? Or is he, like me, hoping to help them?

We're suddenly coming in fast over a city where all the airships seem intent on converging. The capital of Tulla, I assume. Beautiful rich brown staircases and covered tunnels built into the side of the sheer rock wall. The stones have been swirled in such a way that it's impossible to tell where the cliff ends and the city begins. As if the Terrenes carved each tunnel and portcullis from the mountain itself.

No wonder Colin spoke with such pride about his homeland and of the reclusive people who live here and raise their Terrenes to be heroes here.

A horn overhead blares through my eardrums and is followed by a commotion from the dining room. I whip my head around in time to see Bron soldiers and wraiths pouring out the door and filling the deck.

Rasha's eyes widen as she looks at me. We're being squished on all sides by the big guard and a horde of frozen half-dead wraiths with flesh-eaten faces and the claws of bolcranes.

CHAPTER 38

THE AIRSHIP SHAKES AND DROPS BEFORE PITCHING forward to an abrupt stop. Rasha slams into me.

Abruptly the horde of wraiths are crawling over us for the plank.

"Watch it, wretches," she yells at them as we press against the railing. But they've already moved on—a few of the beasts use the plank to disembark, the rest hurl themselves over the airship's side to drop the fifteen feet to the rock wall surrounding the inner city.

By the time the ship's emptied, only Bron soldiers are left with Rasha and me.

"So you're going to let them do the dirty work, then follow when they're done?" I sneer at the large Bron guard.

"I'm going to lead my men as I see fit, when I see fit," he says without looking at me.

I follow his gaze to where the other airships are unloading. Their wraiths are slipping down around roofs and archways, busting through houses made of stone and clay, crawling over each other to breach the thickest part of the fortress. It's like a host of diseased, flesh-eating birds poured out in a mass on the land. And the people living in it are at its mercy.

Except something tells me there will be no mercy. Every person they find will be torn apart by these aberrations, just like Rasha's guards.

I yank against the wrist straps again, but the cords must have metal woven in because they won't give and my hands are bleeding from trying. I look around for Lady Isobel who should be leading her pestilent army. Is she still on the ship, or did she disembark in the chaos of wraiths?

And where's Draewulf?

"We have to do something." Rasha's face has gone pale. She nods to the cliff face, where standing against it is a line of Terrenes ripping up slab after slab of stone from the surrounding rock and sending them at the Dark Army. They're managing to crush two or three with each strike as well as some of their own buildings, but it's not enough. The half-dead beasts keep coming in a swarm.

I keep my tone steady but it's laced with a chill. "I believe I suggested we dispose of Lady Isobel yesterday."

She acts like she doesn't hear me. "We need to stick to the plan. If we can get access to Myles, he can confuse Lady Isobel's powers, as well as some of the ships' capt—"

"Myles could have if Draewulf hadn't taken his powers. And we don't even know where Lady Isobel is."

"You could've killed Draewulf."

"I tried. Twice," I whisper.

There's a loud yell of, "Find the king!" and when I glance up, Lady Isobel is standing with the wraith general a quarter terrameter away on a rampart attached to the Castle's main spire.

She's shouting orders at her troops, sending them like waves ravaging a coastline as they move up from the center streets toward the cliff. When they reach it, they use their bodies to batter against the walls of rock where the Tullan people have sealed themselves in.

The icy poison slips down my spine.

Muffled shrieks break out directly below us where wraiths are pulling a group of men from a broken wall. Two of them are Terrenes based on the fact they're splitting the ground open and using it to swallow the wraiths. But a fresh group of the half-dead steps in, and before I can look away, they slice the men limb from limb. Lady Isobel's expression as she watches is sickening. As if she's enjoying it.

I close my eyes and focus on the energy coming from her, on the energy around me emanating from the wraiths. I allow it—*will it*—to connect with my blood and rip up my spine as, beside me, I hear Princess Rasha begin to vomit.

A sound across the deck says a door is opening, and suddenly Draewulf is ten feet away, walking to the ship's edge where he leans over. His face is gloating and proud. Like a father. Except in this case he's watching his creations demolish an entire civilization with the abilities he birthed in them.

"Have they located King Mael yet?" he growls to the large Bron soldier guarding Rasha and me.

"Lady Isobel is working on it, Your Majesty. It should only be a short time more." His voice is cold and lifeless, but I swear something in his gaze stares uneasily at Eogan-who-is-Draewulf. A second later he turns his eyes to me, then up at the captains' quarters before looking away to the cliff wall where a few of the Tulla men seem to have rallied to create stone weapons. They're using them as spears and knives.

My skin ripples, reacting to the hunger. I focus in on it and call up the power in my blood, willing it to expand quicker, to extend the vortex in Draewulf's direction. Maybe if I can begin to seep more of his energy from here, I can give us a fighting chance.

One of the Terrenes hurls a spear made of marble up at our ship. It skims the railing and lands at Draewulf's feet.

With a swish of his wrist and a curse, Draewulf takes the man out from fifty feet away by hurling him against the side of the cliff. Two seconds later, Draewulf sweeps his arm again and takes down another three Terrenes.

Cold anger swells into my mouth.

"This is taking too long," he snarls. He begins muttering in that foreign language, and there's a rumbling beneath us as the sealed face of the rock fortress starts to shake. Dust rises and chunks from it crumble and fall, crushing the wraiths battering against it. More rush over them into the slowly growing openings until, from inside, there emerges the sound of fresh, throat-slicing screams.

They've breached it.

"No!" Rasha yanks against her straps.

I force all my energy to focus on Draewulf, on weakening his abilities, as he flips around and growls.

The icy swell in me latches onto the ability in him. Slowly, steadily, I reel his darkness in, imagining I'm unspooling it toward me like a thread even as I raise my voice to speak to Eogan inside him. The Eogan who no longer exists, but maybe some part of his soul, his goodness, does. "These people have done nothing to you." I lift a hand, willing him to come closer.

He moves toward me even as his eyes dance in mockery. "Nor did they do anything to help your people, Nym. Don't waste your compassion on those who would care little for those not their kind."

I lift my other hand and sense it as he steps even nearer—the strength in him is burning wild and thick. I pull it and expand the vortex now until it's roiling like a bleeding whirlpool inside my chest, drawing in the bloodlust atmosphere, feeding off it and begging for more. His power may be stronger than mine, but I can certainly weaken him enough to take us both over the railing. And if I have to—take down the ship beneath our feet.

There's a nudge behind me and out of nowhere, I feel the large guard. He slips something metal and cold into my hand—a knife? Then he strides away toward the dining area without looking back.

"At least Nym's 'kind' are actual people," Rasha suddenly yells.

I peer over.

She's trying to distract Draewulf. She felt the knife too. "At least they're not stuck inside a wolf's body, whose only followers are created from the carcasses of dead men!"

The monster snarls through Eogan's mouth, and before I can cut the cords, he's cleared the last three steps and grabs Rasha. "Plucky words coming from a woman," he rumbles. He rips through the ropes that tie her down and drags her toward the railing's opening beside the boarding plank. And holds her there, twenty feet above a wall of rock.

I gasp. She claws and scratches and kicks, and I twist the blade in my hands and slice against the ropes, managing to cut up my fingers, which become slick with blood.

"Do you really want the Cashlin queen's daughter's death on your head?" I yell, working faster. "You'll call down a hailstorm of vengeance on your *own* daughter."

The rope snaps and falls away. I wipe my hands against the back of my skirt and, gripping the knife tighter, edge toward him.

Draewulf smirks at my sudden forward movement, and slips his hand down Rasha's arm until he's only holding her by one wrist.

"No!" I lunge for him. He slaps me backward, sending me sliding across the deck, and lets her sag farther over the side.

She carves her fingernails across his face and shoves her foot into his groin.

He doesn't even flinch. Just smacks her with his free fist and Rasha's head careens back, her body going limp like the yarn doll I was once allowed to play with during my stay at owner number three's. Rasha's eyes have nearly rolled back, but I can still see the edges of them focused on Draewulf holding her. They're beginning to glow red.

I grip my knife just as, from the dining room behind Draewulf, Myles emerges holding a sword and strides through the crowd of staring Bron soldiers. Beside him is the large guard. *Did the soldier free him too?* The guard begins speaking to his men.

Then the soldiers are surrounded by a group of five wraiths descending from the captain's quarters. The men draw their blades. I frown.

"So it's immortality you're after, eh?" Rasha's airy voice floats over, and the heightened way she says it, the loudness—she's offering it as much for my knowledge as to keep him occupied.

"Nym!" Myles points his sword toward Draewulf.

The beast whips his face toward her. "What did you say?" he snarls.

Rasha's eyes are bright red. "You want to live forever."

His expression goes black.

"You don't just need their blood to regain your body, you need it for immortality. You need it because it's tied to their land."

Myles inches closer.

Rasha's voice lowers. "You think you can rule forever."

The vortex in me, which faltered when Draewulf lashed out,

picks up like a low buzzing in the back of my head. I push it out toward him again and say loudly, "Immortality? Seems a bit wasteful considering you've destroyed everyone you'd want to be immortal *with*. Aside from your daughter, of course. Although I have a feeling she's not going to survive much longer." I smirk.

His expression turns enraged but I don't care. As long as it's directed at me. I keep my hand with the blade at my side and flatten my other palm against the air, lightly tugging at his powers again. Taking one step, two steps, three steps closer until I'm almost near enough to touch him. "You'll spend eternity alone."

He releases Rasha over the edge just as I lurch for her, but I'm too late. She slides from Draewulf's grip and I scream. I swipe after her. The moment slows—and I am vividly aware that even as she's falling, the airship is pitching as if to catch her.

Myles is simply standing behind Draewulf watching. Not moving an inch to save her. He's got his sword raised at Draewulf's back though.

Suddenly the large guard is there on the plank. He's grabbed Rasha's wrist just below where her fingers were able to clamp around the ship's railing, thanks to the airship tilting for her. His men's swords are flashing at the wraiths in my periphery.

I don't stop to question their help—just exhale and flip around to thrust my blade out, but Draewulf's hand is faster than mine. He twists my arm before I can connect with his rib cage, flicking my wrist and sending the blade scampering across the deck as he leans in to settle a disgusted gaze on me.

I blink straight up into those eyes even as the question emerges: *Why is Myles just standing there? Why doesn't he stab the beast?*

Shaking, I put my hand against the monster's chest. "You'll live eternity without your wife. You'll spend the entirety of it knowing she abandoned you because you became what she couldn't stand."

I thrust with all my strength, shoving the power against him, over him, feeling it draw strength from him. He convulses and the energy it brings is intoxicating on a level beyond anything I'm prepared for.

I press harder and allow the vortex to expand beyond my chest to my veins, my nerves, my entire being.

Abruptly Myles's hand slips out and clamps down over my owner-circled arm. He grips tight and even without his abilities, I can feel the response from my Uathúil blood reacting to his as the roar and clash of the wraiths and Terrenes circle the air around us.

Draewulf shudders and his eyes go wide, flashing black and glassy before dimming. Then he's trying to pull away, but it's like the three of us are lashed together by the vortex's hunger for his power.

His body is rippling violently, and suddenly I think he's going to rip apart at Eogan's seams just like Breck. I wince and wait for him to burst out of Eogan's skin.

Instead black wisps emerge as if erupting from the very deck beneath his feet. Swirling up, dipping down to cover him. With another mutter, he shoves them toward me, toward the large Bron soldier who's just pulled Rasha to safety, and toward Myles. The wisps blind me, but not enough that I can't feel Draewulf shuddering harder now, as if using them is draining the life from him in the same way I am.

His chest and arms heave, then they're convulsing, and the black mists swirl back to wind up around his feet, his legs, and slip across my arm. Until they're snaking around my hand, whispering words I can't quite make out.

They circle up and swirl overhead, blackening the sky above us, and the uncomfortable thought flashes—this is how my chest looks inside. A gaping hole of darkness. Then the vortex opens around my soul and spine, and it's like there's not enough air, not enough world around me to absorb. I surrender to it.

From somewhere in the distance I hear Rasha's voice, but it's muddied and too dim to make out.

"Finish it, Nym," Myles hisses. "Take what is oursss."

Draewulf slices a hand back at Myles, but the lord protectorate is no longer there. He's ducked down beside me still holding on to my arm, looking at me with the same expression the Faelen people had last week—as if I am some kind of talisman.

Draewulf tilts his head back as if disoriented. He mutters something and Myles yelps and his grip flinches as the monster curses him. But I swear in that split second I can almost read the doubt, the question. The fear in Draewulf's eyes.

A fear suggesting that when this thing in me takes over, it will be merciless in its absorption. A fear suggesting what I could become with his kind of power. I could use it to save this world. I could be powerful like him.

A heartpulse later he pulls back with a roar, but I keep taking as he recoils. I don't even have to touch him now because the energy's owning my head and thoughts and will. It's consuming me to use me, and the numbing it brings to all the grief and weariness is the most beautiful feeling.

Draewulf drops to his knees just as the black spirits return and collect around him in the same way the roars of wraiths and soldiers collect in the air around us. His Draewulf body flickers in my vision, flashing between wolf and Eogan.

Only abruptly . . . there's a third man.

A different man.

One who looks very much like Lady Isobel.

It's his face that stalls me in the midst of the noise-plagued atmosphere. As if it could shock the very hunger from me because this man is old and frail, yet beautiful in his perfection. A man whose eyes are the blackest onyx and grossly aged by the atrocities they've seen and caused. Aged by the hundreds of lives the monstrous spirit he traded his soul to has devoured.

From out of nowhere the dawning comes and squelches within my chest. *He is as much a slave to the animal he's become as Eogan's body was.*

I drop my hand. The vortex in my blood writhes even while I force it down. Because for whatever reason, I cannot kill this man.

"Nym, what are you doing?" Myles yells beside me. "Keep going—you've almost got him. Take him down! I command you to take him down now!"

I try to shake Myles's hand off and step back, but the next thing I know, Draewulf's eyes flinch and turn repulsed. As if he knows what I'm thinking and cannot bear it. Cannot bear the mercy, the pity for him that is welling up inside me. And I have no idea where it's coming from—this grief for a man who has taken lives simply because he forgot how to live his own.

I'm shaking so hard, trying to clamp down this vortex in me as I lift a finger toward Draewulf. But this time it's in empathy.

And Myles is still gripping my arm and screaming.

"You have power but you can choose differently how to use it," I whisper, with a glance up to where I know Kel is sitting in the captains' quarters.

And this time I mean it. We both know I mean it. "There's always a choice."

317

Draewulf's lips curl up and his eyes narrow.

"Please choose differently," I say, and for the slightest second my voice cracks.

Before he can react further, his head jerks back and twists and suddenly there's a ghoulish cry coming from it that sounds like the very pit of hulls. Myles's hand slips free of me.

Draewulf's yell is followed by a ripping sound, and I swear the fabric of reality, of who we are, rips apart as simultaneously Eogan's body becomes transparent, like a ghost, and Draewulf's wolfish form seems to solidify inside of it.

I back up.

He roars and throws himself at me.

I lunge away just as his body hits mine, and there's a loud crack as if the sky just shattered.

What in—?

I grab out to him, but he slips away and stands. And I'm left blinking, shaking my head because I'm suddenly aware Eogan's physical body is beside me, half covering me, bloody and dead. And Draewulf is alive and uncurling in front of me to his full height.

I gasp.

The sounds of war and death fade from my hearing. Everything fades but the sneer plastered across his countenance as he looks strange. Ethereal. A wisp of a spirit with a man's legs and body, but a wolf's face and claws. And the gloating expression promising that he will never choose differently. Because he made his choice long before I was ever born.

I swallow and pick up the blade from where it fell when Myles dropped it. But just as I push Eogan's body off me and lunge forward to stab the spirit, Draewulf wavers and floats out of reach. He's materializing. His voice, his bones, his skin, his fur. And I can hear him muttering, as if calling himself into full existence, from the wisp that was wrapped inside Eogan's body to the full, solid wolf I've seen once before. In a battle much like this.

A sob breaks out. It takes me a second to realize it's from my own throat. I brush away the tears suddenly streaming from my eyes and attempt to reject the fact that Eogan's body is lying next to me.

I can't look at him. At whatever pieces of skin and bone are left from Draewulf shredding through his body. Just like he shredded through Breck's. Just like he's shredded a final time through my soul.

Focus on the enemy, Nym. Before the last remnants of what I am become utterly undone.

CHAPTER 39

ANOTHER CRACK RUPTURES ACROSS THE SKY.
It's followed by a crack inside me. I can feel it. Hear it. As if someone's poured heat over my muscles and bones, and that icy metal Draewulf sealed them over with when he cut out my Elemental powers a week ago in my room at Faelen's Castle has just warped.

It curls me in half.

I hit my knees as another shudder rocks through me and suddenly that heat is flowing, and the metal and ice are melting to mix in with a fluttering in my veins. *What in—?*

The fluttering reaches my chest and forces me to drop the knife just as Lady Isobel's voice screams, "We have the king!" over the noise of the Bron soldiers fighting wraiths near me. "Take him to my father!"

Draewulf whips his wolfish head toward her at the same moment his fur-covered body becomes solid. The same moment a sensation as familiar as the breath in my lungs surges through my own bones and arms, and all the way to my fingertips. Like a song weaving beneath my skin.

It's a melody I never thought I'd hear again.

I can't help the cry that falls from my lips. Of joy. Relief. Nor the smile that tugs across my face. I stand, wobbling a second before finding my feet and balance. When I do, I look up.

Draewulf is narrowing his gaze at me. His grin of victory falters and something tells me he can sense it. His eyes widen and he staggers back, but not before I see it: *alarm*.

I firm my hands into fists.

Black clouds roll in on the horizon like waves before a cyclone. *My* clouds.

They fill the sky the same way the song is filling my bones even as, from somewhere nearby, I hear Lady Isobel again. I can't move as Draewulf turns to her because everything in me is simultaneously breathing with the elements. I don't even have to twitch my hand to snap a shred of lightning across the heavens. It's so loud it nearly bursts my eardrums as even the airship we're standing on jolts beneath the fury.

"Use it on him!" Myles yells from somewhere. "Aim for his heart!" But when I flick my gaze over, the lord protectorate is inching away from me. I try to lift my arm but my body feels stuck in place while the blood mixes and reacts in my veins.

One.

Two.

Three more seconds and the rain begins to fall.

I close my eyes because it is glorious.

"Nym," Rasha murmurs nearby. I glance over and she points to the sky.

My smile grows again as I nod. "It's back. All of it." I flick my gaze over the landscape and a roll of clouds condenses closer in and unfolds in a black chasm, waiting to consume whomever I inflict it on.

"Nym." Rasha's voice is odd, cautioning. "With both of those powers in you and Eogan not here to help soothe—"

"With both powers in me I can end this." I open my mouth and absorb the air from a thousand sets of lungs. The sound of their cries only feeds the energy in me. Draewulf has his teeth bared toward the red-haired, freckle-faced man whom I presume is the Tullan king. He looks weak and small as he squirms against Lady Isobel's clutches.

Move, I command my body and force my hand up. I twist it to pull four ice picks from the air and hurl them at Draewulf. He swipes three aside but the fourth slams into his shoulder and lands him flat on his back, impaling him to the deck.

Lady Isobel tosses the Tullan king down and lunges for me. I shove a hand toward her and immediately feel her energy flow with mine. Her face hardens as she throws her arm up to press her palm against my heart, but I dig in stronger.

She utters a cry and tries to yank away, but it's locked on now. My vortex is attached to her power and drawing, taking it in the same way she's taken the lives of others. For a second I swear I can feel their lives, their voices and heartbeats pulsing through her energy. She leans over.

Then there's a glint and a flash as she slides a blade from her boot and shoves it up at me.

I'm too slow. I can't duck away in time, and the blade rips into my arm. I brace for the pain when the vortex reacts in my chest. It lashes out and rises up through my veins, and with a single twitch of my hand, Lady Isobel's body goes flying against the dining room wall. Her head lolls and she slumps over.

I look down at my fist.

A loud hiss is the only warning I have to move before a bol-crane claw slices down inches from my side. I jerk backward and two wraiths jump forward, followed by more clamoring over the railing straight for me.

Litches.

The next second, Rasha's beside me, sword in hand, as is the large Bron soldier.

"You were right back at the banquet," he mutters. "About mercy being a more honorable strength." His gaze flashes up to where the airship's boy captains' quarters are. Then he's focused back on gutting the wraith lunging for him.

And how I didn't see it before I don't know, because the resemblance is suddenly uncanny. *Kel. Kel is his son. I'd bet my life on it.*

The next moment the entire world blurs. A mirage like an invisible wave rolls through the very atmosphere around us. It slides past my body and over the ship and air and hits the whole area. Rippling through the other airships just as fast as it tears across the cliffs and Castle.

My vision wavers and suddenly half the wraiths I see, on the nearest airships and on the ground, are changed to look exactly like Draewulf.

I flip around to see Myles standing there, his hands crunched into fists at his sides, his eyes clamped shut. His powers were released too, and he's magnified them enough to confuse the Dark Army and communicate the truth about Draewulf to the Bron airship captains and soldiers.

The wraiths pause midlurch.

The fighting slows.

I stall. In awe. In shock. In absolute admiration for the power he possesses. Why did Myles never show me this? What else could he do with such ability? He opens his eyes and looks at me, and catches me staring at him. What he has, what he is, is beyond anything I could've imagined.

There's a loud cry and in my periphery I see the Bron guards on the two closest airships respond. As if they've only now understood who they've truly been aiding and are lashing back.

Myles's mirage ripples again and then starts to recede and fade. Slipping back from every object it's touching to collect in the visible space around his body.

I turn back to Draewulf just as the wraith closest to me blinks. The thing peers at me with glossy black eyes inside a skeletal face. It lurches its decaying body toward me. I hurl an ice blade and slice its arm clean off, but it keeps coming.

There's something odd about it. I peer closer as it rambles forward. It's not just a wraith with a skeletal face—it's the visage of one of Rasha's Cashlin guards. The one who'd been lying dead beside her maid back in Bron.

Rasha lets out a cry.

"Look to Draewulf!" the large guard yells.

I nod, but before I turn, I send a shard of ice through the wraithguard's head, knocking it to the deck.

When I do glance at Draewulf, he's sliding a giant wolf claw down the back of King Mael's neck. I thrust both hands toward the beast, but the black ice spears I create go through his already-ghosting body. He's dissolving into a wisp again, becoming a spirit and slipping into the king's body through the bleeding, sliced-open skin.

I draw in a gust of wind and lightning to lash against the king and Draewulf's ethereal form.

Only, something's wrong.

My head jerks back, and my mouth opens wide as my gaze is forced toward the sky, which is dark and glistening like spider eyes. The spider within me slashes out against the melody, the harmony of earth and sky surging through my veins. My muscles are screaming, tearing apart, wrenching me toward the ground, as if the very blood in my body is at war. And the spidery fluid is attacking the Elemental song.

Oh please no.

The sky overhead erupts in a mass of darkening clouds and lightning that is chaotic and hostile. It begins exploding from the sky and shredding apart the air and earth around us. Taking down chunks of cliff and the airships as it expands.

The vortex in me responds, swirling in dark fog coils, tugging destruction toward us, as if it could drain all life and energy into itself because it cannot consume enough. It's taking, but not with magic and melody like before at the Keep. This is different. This drawing of life is deadly. A darkness grabbing hold from within and simultaneously trying to feed and own my soul as it steals from everything.

Suddenly I am a gaping abyss pulling from this world. A heart-pulse of power outside of me that was never meant to be a part of me.

And it's exhilarating on a level I never knew possible.

This is what Draewulf is after.

My lightning lashes at the cliffs and Castle. Two more airships go down and two others are sucked up along with a hail of rocks into a spiral of wind and cloud. They're dropped half a terrameter away onto a group of homes and wraiths.

The lightning slices down again and this time it's joined by ice, flattening more of the Dark Army and crumbling towers and archways.

I look to Rasha. To show her I'm doing it. I'm saving the world again.

Except all I see is her face etched in horror.

CHAPTER 40

I FROWN AND LOOK DOWN FOR ONE, TWO, THREE seconds. It's as if a veil peels back and the destruction in front of me narrows into focus.

And for one horrifying moment I can see their faces.

The men running from the hurricane. The wraiths being torn apart. The women screaming as they cover their children to protect their flailing bodies.

It's the cry of those mothers . . .

So familiar to my own mother's wail as she and my father were burned alive in our home.

What is happening? I pull my hand back but the lightning doesn't stop. I look down at the people, their faces staring up at me, blaming me as the fire and black ice slash down around them.

"Nym," Rasha yells. "You have to make it stop!"

I pull my other fist back and open both hands, pressing them against my stomach, willing this vortex to die down and the storm to subside. It doesn't. I press harder against my rib cage, as if digging into my own bones will evict it from my body.

A wisp of black cloud shoots down in a funnel and rips through one of the Castle's rock spires. Stone and debris go flying, taking out wraiths, Terrenes, and Bron soldiers alike.

Please, I beg it. *Oh hulls—*

"Nym!" Rasha screams.

"I don't know how!" I yell, my voice shaking with hate for the fact that I can't control it.

Tears start falling. At least I think they're tears. They're hot on my cheeks compared to the freezing rain, and they won't stop as another funnel cloud hurls down, but this time as it does it sends a breeze wafting over me. And for a moment I swear it smells of sun and heat and pine trees. From somewhere . . . a thought flits through me, like the soft flutter of a bird's wings.

"Maybe that's the point," it whispers.

I frown.

"Maybe the issue isn't trying harder to stop it. Maybe it's simply about surrendering. *Because you are not your abilities.*"

I shiver at the familiar scent of Eogan blended with those last words—the same words of Rasha's from a week ago. Maybe it's not the power or ability or anything else I might believe that makes me who I am. Maybe it's surrendering to *who* I really am.

Remembering who I was made to be.

An image of the Valley of Origin flashes through my head. Of Eogan and me standing on the ledge listening to that melody weave through my soul—calling to the origin of me. To the girl called Nym, born on purpose through a magic that predates any curse or power in my veins. What had Eogan told me there? *Perhaps I was born to shield others.*

To bring mercy.

I swear there's a chirp inside my rib cage and something snaps in there, so hard that I hear myself cry out. I tip my head back and let it come.

Suddenly my blood is aligning, like water trickling through my veins that's quickly turning to a rush, then a roar. As if the Elemental inside is trilling her voice, *her* song, because I have always been her song. And the harmony is now coming in strong, forcing out the fear and dark and expectation.

I feel it pumping from the bottom of my feet, pushing all the way up to my chest, and suddenly I'm coughing and hacking and struggling to breathe.

This thing is cutting off my air and senses, and the world falls dim as my hearing fades along with my sight.

I lash a hand out to grab the deck floor in front of me as my body pitches and fumbles. From somewhere I sense a vibration in the atmosphere. Someone's yelling.

"Nym!" I can feel the voice in the weather. It's forceful. What is he yelling at?

Then I'm gagging because the spider is there. She's digging in her talons, fighting to stay. Her coarse hairs and claws grip my flesh. "Leave," I try to tell her, but my blood just boils and shakes and I swear it's because she's laughing at me.

Except then I'm screaming as she's ripped from my lungs and tearing the very flesh from my bones as she's coming up.

I vomit her all over the metal planks.

My vision clears to see the black mass in front of me, wet and glistening.

I shuffle backward on my knees and the world returns into focus as does the noise of more wraiths climbing over the ship's railing to engage the Bron guards.

I look over to see Draewulf frozen in place, trying to catch his breath, wearing his new weakened body that is the Tullan king.

"Take him down!" Myles is yelling.

Suddenly the black mass at my feet is moving, rising ten feet off the deck to swirl up like a mist in front of me.

I stand.

"Kill it! Stab it!" Rasha cries, and from the corner of my eye I see she's grabbed a sword to do just that.

But my muscles are seizing and my lungs gasping for air—trying to fill the hole left in my chest from the vortex. Before I can move, Rasha spins the sword round with an expert strike at the mass. Her blade bounces off. She lunges for it, stabbing this time, but the sword springs back at the mass's resistance and she's thrown with it. Her head smacks the railing eight paces away.

I gag and pull in air until my body stops shaking enough to notice Draewulf staring at the swirling mist, his expression full of greed and victory.

"Like hulls." I yank down a lightning bolt onto the wisp.

Instead of dissolving, the swirling mass absorbs it, becoming bigger.

"Don't!" Myles yells.

"Fool!" Draewulf says. "You can't kill it with your ability."

I grab a blade from the ground at the same moment the large Bron soldier raises his sword.

We thrust at it and the mass curls and squeals and writhes up in the air. We hack at it again, but our sharp edges have no effect other than to knock us both flat on our backs.

I draw down another lightning strike, aiming to hit the mass, but this time I notice that using the Elemental energy takes the breath from me, weakening me. *Oh litches . . . My body's going into shock. Or exhaustion.*

The only effect my strike has on the thing is to empower it again until it's expanding. It's growing.

My hair is in my face and my clothes are rippling around me as I'm being pulled toward it. A few loose items from the ship's deck fly up into the maelstrom.

From the side I see the frail-looking Tullan-king-who-is-Draewulf. He steps forward and tilts back his head. His expression is giddy. His black eyes alight as he moves for the mass and opens his gaping maw.

Litches.

He's going to absorb it.

I flick my hand and send two wobbly ice spears at him. The first misses, but the other catches his arm. He barks and jerks backward.

Suddenly Myles is there, his mouth opening wide. His face looking ecstatic.

In one swoosh, he steps into the black cyclone and inhales. I can hear his breath, hear his hunger. Suddenly the mass diminishes in a spiral until it's disappeared down Myles's throat. And he has absorbed the dark power.

Draewulf's roar shakes the rocks and stone towers around us. He lashes out at Myles, but the force of energy from the dark entity has already tossed Myles back across the ship's deck and against the door, knocking him unconscious.

Draewulf stalks toward him, but my blade takes him in the thigh.

He turns and pounces for me and grabs my arm. I send a shock of ice toward his face, making him release me and jump back. But not before I catch his look of rage contort into surprise.

He stalls and, slowly, looks from me to Myles, then to Rasha who's getting up from where she had fallen. She blinks at us. At the Tullan-king-who-is-Draewulf. And picks up her sword.

I raise my fist. "Let's end this now."

There's a writhing beneath the surface of his skin that ripples into place and takes over his face. He winces and hunches for the slightest second as if in pain.

Then he raises a brow as his shoulders begin shaking. His breath comes out in an agonized huff. "Another time perhaps, pet."

What? I stalk toward him. The fact that he doesn't move makes me hesitate. *What is he waiting for? Why is he doing this?*

I let it loose just as his shaking becomes violent and knocks him out of the way so my explosion only hits his side. The body of the Tullan king he's wearing crackles with a brittle sound. Then the body's ripping apart, tearing open just like Breck's did so many weeks ago. It dissolves into wisps, melting into the atmosphere except for a small bit of clothing and skin and blood. The blood of a king.

The blood Draewulf absorbed all too quickly.

The wolfish beast stands in front of me and stretches his shoulders and neck before centering his gaze on mine.

He smirks as if I'm a foolish girl but it doesn't hide the weakness he's experiencing. He steps backward and grabs Rasha, feebly knocking her sword aside. She punches him in the jaw just as he leaps with her over the railing. They land on another airship that has appeared out of nowhere to bank beside ours. I rush forward with knives of ice pulled from the sky and land two in Draewulf's chest at the same moment he glances up at my ship's balloon and mutters a foreign curse at it. The words fly up and puncture a hole in it before he sags and stumbles.

And before the next feeble ice blade I've hurled has landed, the airship he's on pulls away. I bring down three more blades anyway but they fly with little force and clatter harmlessly against the ship's hull.

The moment slows.

My heart pulses as the cavernous sensation in my chest steadies and my head clears enough to hear the last of the fighting around me. But all I can see is what's left of the Tullan king's skin and blood and clothing fragments lying four paces in front of me. Already invaded, absorbed, and discarded in one bout of violence.

I bend my fingers into a fist and shove them toward the sky. But the blood in me is suddenly failing. Too feeble. As if the power spent on nearly destroying this place is almost emptied out and in need of refueling.

I glance up and find Rasha's face. Her gaze is on mine.

She is on the swiftly departing airship with Draewulf.

CHAPTER 41

A HORN BLASTS AND, AS IF ON CUE, THE AIRSHIP I'm standing on pulls back from the Castle and cliffs and the host of other ships. It soars up into the sky even as air's flapping out the balloon's small gaping hole, taking Myles and me and Eogan's body and the Bron soldiers with it.

Within seconds, four other airships follow suit—while the rest have either crashed or appear to be overrun with wraiths. Like the one Draewulf's skimming away on.

"Go back! He has Rasha!" I try to summon a storm to stop his ship, but my winds are too weak to retrieve it.

"Take us higher," the large Bron guard yells.

I flip around to face him. *Who does he think he is?* "Your king is dead and the Cashlin princess is about to get slaughtered. And that horde of wraiths down there will destroy what's left of those people," I snarl. "Take us back so we can finish it."

"I'm sorry, miss, but there's not enough of us. We need to regroup and make contact with the captains who are left."

I can sense the wildness invade my gaze. I stride toward him, ready to throw myself and my blade at his face. "If you don't want to go, fine. But you take *me* back."

His expression turns doubtful as he drops his gaze to my chest.

I snort and look down to see what he's staring at.

What in hulls? My red dress is sliced in shreds, as is my bloody skin underneath it. Clawed not by bolcrane claws, but by my own fingers and blade in my attempts to get the vortex out. To get free.

I sag, as if the loss of blood is only affecting me now that I've noticed the obscene amount soaked into my clothes and booties. "I don't care. Take me back." I hurl myself at him, yelling it, telling him to return us to save the only friend I have left in the world and destroy the monster I should've been able to kill numerous times over the course of today. "Please. I have to try. He has Rasha."

A voice slips through the gray fog filling the air around us, unleashing with it a calm that slides through my skin, my head, my spine. "Nym," it says behind me.

I turn but no one's there beyond the dead.

I'm about to glance back at the guard, to demand he obey me, when I see the flutter of an eye and a flash of green peering through the mist.

The rush of days, of hours, of seconds slows down . . .

Until time is standing still and the only thing I know in this moment is that the man who is dead, who was absorbed and destroyed, is running a hand through his black hair and hauling his tall, broad-shouldered self up to gaze at me with those beautiful eyes. They are blinking as if newly awakened, and that unfair tweak of a smile is starting to surface above a confused one. The thought emerges that the rest of the world can go to hulls in the silence that falls.

How long I stand there I've no idea. The moments are lost and forgotten as daft tears find my face and his gaze flickers and firms around mine. I go to move forward, then stop because he's not real—he can't be real—and this is a sick trick of Myles's.

"Once again, I distinctly recall ordering you to run from Draewulf." Eogan rubs a hand over the back of his neck. "Not rush into the center of a blasted war."

Oh litches . . . It's really him.

The sob I try to hold back escapes my lips anyway, and then I'm in his arms and in his eyes and breathing in his scent. His heart is *beat beat beating* into mine because there's nothing between us but the two inches of space where my lips don't quite meet his.

"Gently," he mumbles and it's only then I'm aware he's flinching at how tightly I'm holding him.

"Sorry." I ease my grip but his face is bending to brush his mouth over mine. Warm and firm. His fingers slide down my chin to my jaw, to the memorial scars on my arm. Tugging me closer. Obliterating every thought until I jerk back to search his face. To slip my hands against his chest and make sure he's real and solid and made up of skin and bone and a scar on his neck.

He winces. "Easy on the body. My block still doesn't work against you."

I frown. Because while he should look sallow and weak, everything about his fierce gaze and the determined set of his chin is stronger than I've ever seen it. And his strength is filling me too. I search his eyes. "How are you alive?"

A throat clears nearby. "Your Majesty, I'm pleased you're—"

"Go fix the bleeding ship, Kenan," Eogan says without looking up.

"Sir, as I was saying. I'm pleased you're alive," the large soldier says again. "But I think you need to see this."

Eogan's brow narrows. "What is it?"

"Your Majesty, we have Isobel onboard."

Eogan releases me, and I spin around to see Lady Isobel being held by two guards near where I hurled her against the dining area wall.

I walk over and stop in front of her. And crush my fingers into my palms.

She smiles and spits in my face before slipping a hand free long enough to jut it up against my heart. Eogan steps forward but I stop him.

Because there's nothing in her palm as it touches my heart.

No sensation. No chill.

She pushes harder before the guard yanks her arm down and jerks her backward. But she's not paying any attention to him. She's looking at me and frowning, her expression altering into panic.

Her ability's gone. Ripped out by the same vortex that slammed her into the wall.

"What will your father do to Princess Rasha?"

She sneers at me and clamps her mouth shut just as Eogan leans in.

He studies her, but his answer is for me. "Her father took what he needed from King Mael. Now he'll regroup and head for Cashlin to take Rasha's mother. He'll keep Rasha in case her mother is killed— at which time the power would fall to the princess and Draewulf will consume her. Thus, in order to preserve Princess Rasha and Cashlin, we have to reach the queen first."

"I thought Draewulf needed your block in order to take—"

"He took it," he says quietly. "Not all of it, but he absorbed enough of my blood that he'll make it work."

I peer up at him. "He took part of you?" My voice sounds as appalled as I feel.

He nods and continues staring at Lady Isobel. "Where did you plan to rendezvous?"

She purses her lips and snorts. As if he'd actually think she'd answer.

He shrugs, then nods to the guard to take her below. "Myles too," he mutters, before dropping his rich tone to a growl. "You'll let me know as soon as he wakes. I have some . . . *business* to take care of with him."

"Very good, Your Highness. Although I might mention Lord Myles ingested the power released by Nym. There is a chance he'll be a danger to this whole ship."

"The power will take time to meld with his blood." Eogan looks at me as if to get my thought on it.

"A day at least."

The guard nods and begins to move off with Lady Isobel but pauses when Eogan adds, "But Kenan, feel free to bind his mouth as well as his body."

"Yes, sire."

Eogan drops his gaze to survey me as the guard strides away. His frown returns to that half smile. "Now where were we?"

"We need to go back for Rasha and the Terrenes. Draewulf's been weakened but—"

"So have you." He eyes me.

I glance down at my bloody, torn dress and my ripped skin beneath. He slides an arm around my waist and presses his hand to my side, and I swear he gifts a bit of his calm into me. So much so that my injured chest tingles and turns almost numb as his face turns slightly sallow.

"Yes, but my ability is recharging. I can feel it. And I've—"

"We can't go back. There aren't enough of us and these ships have taken about all they can handle." He peers up at the soldiers working on the balloon overhead, then out to the other four airships flying nearby in formation.

"But the people . . . The power I took on." I hesitate before whispering, "Eogan, it helped Draewulf. It helped the wraiths. And combined with my storms, it . . ."

I can't even bring myself to confess it.

How many innocent people I must have destroyed in that battle. Because my powers were too much, too big, and I didn't listen to him or Rasha about the danger.

Suddenly I can't breathe. I can't believe what I've done. What I started to become.

What I've lent a hand to.

"We have to go back. We have to try and undo—"

"The Terrenes are stronger than you think they are." His tone is sober. Just like his gaze that says he knows well enough. "They survived you and they will survive Draewulf for the time being—especially now that he's taken their king's blood, he'll have little interest in them. The Tullan people will bore underground to mount a far better defense than either you or I can provide in the state we're in."

"But I *killed* some of them."

"And you also saved more by damaging Draewulf and the wraiths. You can't do anything further now unless you want to sacrifice the men on these airships. The only way we're going to help anyone is by getting to Cashlin before Draewulf to aid Queen Laiha."

I look away. But after a moment I nod again.

"Good. Because aside from the Cashlin queen, my priority is this ship, my men, and you."

He tilts his head and catches my eye. And tries to hide a smirk. "Because . . . no offense, have you seen you?" He runs his gaze down my soiled clothes and unkempt white hair and raises a perfect single brow.

I snort and look away. "You're such a bolcrane."

He chuckles weakly and lifts his hand to run his thumb along my jawline and down my neck to that little divot between my collarbones. "A bolcrane who's standing beside the strongest woman he's ever met and thus wouldn't argue with her unless he truly believed we *will* save Rasha and the rest of the bleeding world she's so intent on rescuing." His fingers move up to wind through my hair. "Just like she saved me."

I look into those brilliant green eyes that are full of confidence. *Just like she saved me.*

His words hang in the air.

"How did you separate from him?"

"Draewulf let go."

"No, really."

He gives that unfair lopsided grin, and the familiarity of it brings a solemn smile to my face as his fingers slip down my arm again. Pulling me in. "It's the truth. Apparently he'd assessed for every scenario but the thing that makes you Nym and not a monster."

"Which is . . . ?"

"He didn't count on your compassion."

It's my turn to raise a brow.

"When my block was warped by Isobel all those years ago,

she'd eliminated the ability for me to feel. Draewulf assumed that aspect was still in place, but the more you were moved toward compassion for him, he began to experience that through me. He didn't know what to do with it, and he couldn't help but pull away from the source of that emotion. *Me.* Every time you did the one thing you do so well, his grip lessened."

He slips his bangs out of his eyes and then rubs his neck again, then stumbles.

"Eogan." I reach for him but he just shakes his head.

"I'm fine, just . . . weaker than I'd wish." He sounds annoyed at himself. "When I discovered his reaction to you, I quit expending my energy trying to surface through him and kept my head down. He believed I was weakening, when in fact it was him."

Compassion? That's what separated Draewulf from Eogan's body?

I swallow and look out over the mist-covered rock hills we're dipping toward as the soldiers around us shout out orders and seal up the hole in the airship's balloon. Until my gaze drifts behind us to the dust and soot spirals floating up from the battle we're running from. And the people still there.

Rasha's and my conversation from a week ago on this same ship slips through my head again. *"Strength doesn't lie in power. It lies in your ability for compassion."*

I peer back at Eogan. His handsome face crinkles with tenderness as I grapple with the dawning awareness that I could've just as easily saved him if I'd never taken on that power.

My hand clenches into a fist, but when I glance down, the fingers are curled in again along the knuckles. I frown.

It's reverted to its gimpy state.

I let out a dry chuckle—because isn't that the truth of it all right there. That who we are is not our abilities. Not really. It's more who we are *in spite* of them. Like Kel said, "Maybe it's more the choice in how we use them. Not everything that seems weaker is."

If anything, perhaps who we are *fuels* them, in which case maybe it's compassion that fuels mine. I glance around for the large guard, Kenan. Because apparently, compassion changes things after all. Simply because it changes *people*.

Again I search out the mist and smoke behind us—covering the people we're moving so swiftly away from in an effort to save—before glancing over at Eogan who is so alive and real and standing here as proof that every act, every touch, ripples out like the ocean tides, fueled by the single hunger even Draewulf was at one time desperate for . . .

Love.

Maybe *that* is the true power.

But could it be powerful enough to change an entire world?

I reach up and push my fingers into Eogan's hair to pull his head closer again as he studies me. And my heart breaks in two for that world, but it also soars with hope for what goodness that same world can produce.

It takes less than two seconds for his mouth to become present against mine.

He presses in fiercer, deeper, as he nudges me against the dining wall. His lips searing, burning my bones, setting my soul to crash into his earthen heart like sea storms in winter. Promising that love can fix a multitude of worlds and souls and wounds.

"Hello! Anyone there who can cut me down?"

What? I blush and try to pull away, peering around in embarrassment for whoever may have seen us.

"Helloooo!"

Oh litches. Lord Wellimton.

Eogan keeps his arm around my waist and raises a questioning brow at the bow of the ship.

"Lord Wellimton," I say, smirking into his shoulder.

"Think we should cut him down?" Eogan murmurs so close to my ear it sends goose bumps down my skin.

"Probably. Just be prepared—he wants to kill you."

He laughs and tips his head to one of the Bron guards. Then pulls me to the forward railing where we're aiming straight over the mountains for Cashlin.

I resist turning back again to survey the sky and the land we're leaving.

"We'll save them," Eogan whispers.

I shudder. "What happens if Draewulf reaches her before us?"

"He'll take over her and the Luminescent ability."

"And then what? He'll come for Faelen's King Sedric?" *Will his Dark Army?*

"Then he'll come for me—to kill me in order to completely own my Medien power."

Wait. What? "Your power has a name?"

"It does. And right now he has enough of me to use, but not enough to own Bron and rule."

I narrow my brow. "But he couldn't kill you. He tried and it didn't work."

"He'll be stronger next time. If we fail, he'll not only have Terrene blood but Luminescent as well."

"I don't understand. You mean he's going to try to absorb you again?" The thought makes my stomach curl. The image of King Mael's skin being torn through . . .

Eogan nods.

I know it's selfish of me. Probably wrong to even think it, but I can't help it. "Why didn't he just take Odion when he had the chance?"

"Because as with Queen Laiha, I was the eldest Uathúil of my people, and thus the rightful heir. The blood is bound to our position just as our bodies are bound to our land. The higher the lineage, the more powerful the ability."

My hand flutters to find his. "I won't let him," I whisper. "We'll hide you."

His smile is soft as he shakes his head. "I've hidden for the past four years. The only way to defeat him now is to fight."

"And if he kills you next time?"

He falls silent. Enough so that I look up at him. He nods. "He'll come to Faelen," he says quietly. "But not for King Sedric."

I wait.

"The right to rule was given to five Uathúils—five monarchs. And the line of Faelen's royal blood was always the strongest."

I continue to wait.

"Sedric's ancestors weren't Uathúils, nor were they the original kings. The Elementals were. But even then . . ." He pauses and softens his gaze, reaching his words deep into my soul. "Even Elementals weren't powerful enough to sustain the abilities contained in all five original Uathúil rulers. That's why Draewulf needed you to absorb the vortex—so it'll hold the powers and blood of all five without aging the host."

He's not making a lick of sense. "So why didn't Draewulf just absorb the ability himself then?"

He studies me. "Because the woman who gave it to you was his wife."

I stare.

Until it's clear he's not jesting.

"Draewulf's wife was that witch?"

He nods.

Is he jesting? "Why didn't you *tell* me?"

"I confess to not being the most clear-minded with Draewulf in my head."

"But she offered them to me. She gave me them." My gut heaves in disgust. "Why didn't Draewulf just get them from her himself then? And how could she even have those abilities if she is Isobel's Mortisfaire mum?"

"Just as Draewulf enhanced himself, the witch found ways to enhance her ability too. The Mortisfaire are known for dabbling in magic. However, she stopped before it went as far as Draewulf's, which is ultimately what destroyed their union. Those powers all lead to something, and while consuming them will eventually turn the host like Draewulf, not all of them are the same. The ability the witch offered you is one she kept from him and he couldn't create on his own. Instead, she gave it to you."

"But why? How does that help anything?"

"Because an Elemental will be his downfall, and you are Elemental. As were your ancestors."

I shake my head. "My ancestors weren't Elementals and neither were my parents. I was an anomaly."

"An anomaly in that you were born female, yes. But not an anomaly in your genetic lineage." His voice drops. "A lineage that belonged to the original rulers of Faelen." He watches me as if willing me to grasp what he's getting at.

The airship shudders and the sensation is answered by a matching shiver beneath my skin. In my veins. I blink and frown at him. And swallow as the witch's voice rattles in my chest. *"And whatever you do, don't let him take the final one."*

When I look down, my left hand is twisting even tighter into the crippled stump owner number fourteen made it. And as it squeezes, a tiny black line emerges through the vein beneath its skin. For a fleeting second the feeling of dark hunger edges my lungs.

Like the distinct imitation of a spider testing my sinew before beginning to reweave her web.

Eogan's voice finally emerges again through the wind and sea salt and snowcapped air. "When he comes to Faelen, it'll be for you. Because you're last in line, Nym."

NYM AND DRAEWULF PREPARE TO
FACE OFF IN A FINAL BATTLE DESTINED
TO DESTROY MORE LIVES THAN IT
SAVES. ONLY ONE WILL SURVIVE.

To get the latest details as they release, visit
www.mchristineweber.com

MY POCKETFUL OF
THANK-YOUS

I F I'M HONEST WITH YOU ABOUT THIS TRILOGY, I'D tell you that writing book one was like this scary-wild celebration of friends, and fellowship, and love . . . whereas book two has been more a scraping of the soul. Ultimately a good thing, yes, but also rather terrifying. Ha! In fact, I may have spent much of this story feeling like I was wandering in the dark, suspecting the creation of book one was a fluke because good grief what in hulls was I thinking trying to write another?

Yet in that dark there were people slipping their hands out to hold mine, reminding me that this is a journey and some of the best parts come from the hardest parts (so quit whining and get back to work, and also, have some *Doctor Who* episodes). So here's to you, my dear fellowship of hand-holders. For being the people I want to be like when I grow up.

Especially my husband, Peter, who more than anyone has walked beside me, forging his own awesome path amidst steadying mine. You are the very best person I know and I rabidly love you.

Same with my three muses, Rilian, Avalon, and Korbin, who remind me daily that the key to believing is to pause, breathe, and look for the magic. (Also, shopping.)

My parents and sister, to whom this story is dedicated—for the hours of your time and the honor of your love. And to my siblings, their spouses, and the Weber clan. For believing, and for showing up to every *Storm Siren* bookish event ever just in case no one else did.

Lori Barrow, Jeanette Morris, Danielle Smith—WHERE would I be without you ladies? The Barrows, Morrells, Sara Steffey, and so many other precious friends—for the laughter and sanity and feasting. To Robert Perez, without whom so much would fall apart. And to my Father's House family, my incredible RISE teens and tweens, and my team. As always, you guys have my heart. Thank you for being my home.

To my Thomas Nelson publishing family, who spoil me beyond coherent reason. Thank you for being so much of the heartbeat that moves my world. Daisy Hutton (hugs you), Amanda Bostic (hands you tea), Katie Bond (raves about your style), Keri Potts (laughs wickedly), Jodi Hughes (fangirls), Kristen Ingebretson (those book covers!), Ansley Boatman (mind reader), Becky Philpott (superstar!), Karli Jackson (that smile!), Elizabeth Hudson (fooood), and my editor Becky Monds (aka The PRECIOUS), and everyone else. Y'all are the best pub team + friends a girl could have, and I could not adore you more.

Allen Arnold, whose chats always bring life to my spirit at the right times and remind me to look up for manna. Thank you for this journey, dear friend.

Jay Asher, for your brilliant humor, friendship, advice, and amazing support. And for being normal.

Julee Schwarzburg, for editing me into coherency. Lee Hough—I know you're grinning! Sarah Kathleen and Garth Janzten, for creating awesome with your souls. And to so many author friends who've extended time and kindness—I still can't fathom why you do it, but YOU ARE THE NICEST: Marissa Meyer, Nancy Rue, Chuck Sambuchino, CJ Redwine, Josie Angelini, Shannon Messenger, Lindsay Cummings, Tonya Kuper, Heather Marie, Ronie Kendig, Colleen Coble, Katherine Reay, Kristy Cambron, Sara Ella, and Mary Pearson.

To my local Barnes & Noble family who work so hard to make your authors and readers feel *so very* loved. I treasure you all.

A fanatical fangirl mention to my early reviewers Lauren @Love Is Not a Triangle, Anya @On Starships & Dragonwings, the FFBC, Laura @Crafty Booksheeps, Nick @Nick's Book Blog, Mandy @ Forever YA, Maci & Zoe (ALA!), Jill @Radiant Lit, The Book Bratz, Rissi @Dreaming under the Same Moon, Jen @Jenuine Cupcakes, Alyssa Faith, Sarah @Smitten over Books, Rel @Relz Reviews, Ashley @Wandering the Pages, and sooo many others. Just THANK YOU.

And to all of *you*, sweet readers!!! You rocked my world by picking up *Storm Siren* and talking about it, recommending it, and writing to me regarding it. Thank you for reading this silly girl's writing. You burst my heart at the seams. *squishes*

Jesus. Because you are all this heart exists for.

READING GROUP GUIDE

1. In chapter 9, Rasha tells Nym her strength doesn't lie in her powers but in her ability to be compassionate. Nym responds (internally) that compassion without the power to effect change is useless. However, later on Nym decides that compassion will always change things because it changes *people*. Do you think that's true in our real world? Can compassion alone *always* make a difference? What about power, money, or influence? Are there times when compassion and the means to effect change go hand in hand?

2. For the most part, Myles is quite honest with Nym about what he wants from her in their relationship—and about the fact that he is using her to accomplish his own plans. Nym is just as blunt about how she's using Myles to get what she wants as well. In the end, however, their self-serving relationship not only breaks down but also hurts them both. But was that okay? How might they have done things differently? Have you ever had a friend who

wanted to use you for his or her own gain? What advice would *you* give to Nym or Myles in this situation?

3. Early on in *Siren's Fury*, Nym's friend Kel suggests, "Maybe power comes in different forms, and maybe we get a choice how we use it. Maybe not everything that seems weaker is." What do you think prompted him to hold such a different view than his father (Kenan) and grandfather (Sir Gowon)? What do you think ultimately changed *Kenan's* mind so that he agreed with his son?

4. In chapter 20, Rasha becomes angry with Nym for taking on the dark power after she'd warned her about Myles. However, Nym believes Rasha should've been more honest about Myles's offer in the first place. Should Nym have gone to Rasha once Myles made his offer? Should Rasha have trusted Nym more with her information? Either way, do you think it would have made a difference?

5. Nym is tempted by the same power (and the positive changes it could bring) that Draewulf has. However, she also sees what it's done to him and what it could do to her. Do you think if she kept the power, Nym would've eventually become like Draewulf? Do you think the evil existed solely in the power, or in the one who ingested it? And what makes the Elemental power Nym was born with good and the unnatural one she consumed evil?

6. Eogan and Kel are part of a society that values physical power and unity over emotional strength and

individuality. What are the benefits (and drawbacks) of both systems? Imagine what reasoning or circumstance in their history might have led the Bron people to value physical power above emotional strength.

7. In the final battle, as Nym is fighting Draewulf, she sees a third man—Draewulf's "real" self—inside his body. It occurs to her that Draewulf is "as much a slave to the animal he's become as Eogan's body was." She's struck with pity for him and repeats Kel's belief to Draewulf— that he has a choice as to how he will use his power. Do you think Draewulf truly could've chosen differently? Do we all have a choice about what actions we take and what future we embrace?

8. Rasha and Myles have a somewhat volatile relationship— partly because Myles can be despicable, but also because Rasha's offense toward him goes deeper than simply an annoyance at who he is and the choices he's made. As a citizen of a pacifist nation, why do you think she struggles with him so much? Do you think her past has influenced her attitude and biases?

9. Toward the end of *Storm Siren* (book 1), Nym gained a measure of freedom and healing from self-loathing and self-harm. Even though she's a stronger person in *Siren's Fury* (book 2), those early struggles arise again when she feels alone and bereft of everything. Have you ever struggled with similar feelings or perhaps even with self-harm? Do you know anyone who has? What advice

would you give to Nym? What help offered to you would make a difference for her? If you or someone you know is struggling with depression or self-harm, please talk to a safe person about it. Support, resources, and hope are available to you, including through To Write Love on Her Arms (http://www.TWLOHA.com). Just please reach out. I promise you are not alone. ♥

ABOUT THE AUTHOR

MARY WEBER IS A RIDICULOUSLY uncoordinated girl plotting to take over make-believe worlds through books, handstands, and imaginary throwing knives. In her spare time, she feeds unicorns, sings '80s hairband songs to her three muggle children, and ogles her husband who looks strikingly like Wolverine. They live in California, which is perfect for stalking LA bands, Joss Whedon, and the ocean.

Visit her website at maryweber.com
Facebook: marychristineweber
Twitter: @mchristineweber